Holding

Christmas

A Novella

By

Den Slattery

ISBN # 1-59872-229-8

Other Books by Den Slattery:

Life Goes On
Changed by War
Essential Truths
Essential Practices
Transformed by Christ
From the Point to the Cross

To contact the author:
den98@juno.com
www.denslattery.com

1

The Christmas of 1972 came and went the same way it does every year for most folks, but it wasn't that way for the people of Pentwater, Michigan. Things were very different that year. Some would say their Christmas celebration lasted a few extra months. Yet the rumor was that it never really even started until February of 1973.

Thanksgiving 1972

The snow was lightly falling as Joe Stone closed his front door and began his stroll into town. His heart was heavy and he just needed to get out of the house to clear his head. It was a perfect night for a walk. With very little wind, the large snow flakes were gently floating to the ground.

As Joe walked he thought of the famous words of Charles Dickens, "*It was the best of times; it was the worst of times.*" Those words were more than just the opening line of a Dicken's novel. To Joe they described exactly how he felt.

Joe was still feeling stuffed after a huge dinner of turkey leftovers with all the fixings. Thanksgiving in America was supposed to be a day of giving thanks to God for all of the blessing He has bestowed upon us, but it was becoming a day when there is little mention of God. Instead people gather with their families, eat turkey, and watch football. Each year there also seems to be less of an emphasis on giving thanks and very little mention of the Pilgrims. But Joe wasn't thinking just about the secularization of the holidays, Joe had more important things to focus on.

It was the day after Thanksgiving and he had a lot of things to be thankful for—good health, good family, and a good job. But if the truth were told, Joe was worried.

He looked at the houses and thought of the people who occupied this small part of planet earth. Most of the folks in town were just down to earth people trying to live their lives to the best of their ability. They weren't trying to change the world; they just wanted to enjoy their time here.

As Joe walked he noticed Fred Jones draping Christmas lights over some bushes. When he was only 10 feet away he called out to him.

"Hello, Fred. Looks like you're getting an early start on Christmas decorations."

"Oh. Hi, Joe. No, this isn't early. We always decorate right after Thanksgiving."

"Well, I can't wait to see what it looks like when you're done."

"Hey, just stick around. I should be done here pretty soon."

"Maybe I'll catch you on the way back. I'm on my way into town."

"Okay."

As Joe walked away he thought about Christmas in Pentwater. Like most towns, Pentwater had developed their own traditions for celebrating the holidays. Christmas seemed to be everyone's favorite. The whole town tried to pull together at Christmas time by decorating not just their homes, but the whole downtown area as well. From the day after Thanksgiving until New Years Day people roamed through the downtown area greeting one another with warm "Hello's" and hugs. All the locals knew each other and most of the details about their families. They didn't get too many visitors during the Christmas season because most folks had no idea how great it was to celebrate Christmas in Pentwater.

But what no one knew at the time was that the Christmas of 1972 would not be a normal traditional Christmas in Pentwater, Michigan. That Christmas would change everything and it would all start with a conversation, a letter, and a prayer.

2

Pentwater was founded in 1853 by two men as a logging town because of its location right on Lake Michigan. But by the 1950's tourists had discovered Pentwater. There were only 877 residents who actually called it home, but in the summer that number grew to over 4,000 as visitors filled the beaches and the Inns. Pentwater has often been described as "quaint" by many of the tourists.

Hancock is the main street where all the stores and restaurants are located. There isn't much traffic, so people often stop to chat right in the middle of the road. It's the kind of town that draws people from the big cities. They come to relax and unwind from all the stress they're under *in the business world. It's amazing to watch the tension leave their faces once they arrive in Pentwater and begin to enjoy a slower pace of life. The local residents enjoy the summer months with all the paying guests, but there was always a certain relief they felt when the visitors were gone and their quaint little village was once again their own.

When Joe arrived in the small downtown area he just wandered around looking in the store windows like everyone else. Then he grabbed some hot chocolate, found a snow covered bench, brushed off the snow, and then sat down. He took a sip of the steaming brew in his hand and it burned his upper lip. The hot chocolate was just that—hot! He decided to wait till it cooled down before making another attempt.

Hancock Street was bustling with activity, but he was content to just sit there and watch others going in and out of the local stores. Yet Joe found his attention drawn to the large Christmas tree in the center of town. That tree brought back a lot of memories involving Joe's two sons.

Mike and Johnny Stone were not only brothers, they were best friends.

Separated by just four years, Mike watched out for his little brother. He taught him how to ride a bike, how to make spit balls, and lots of other cool things. Mike was Johnny's hero.

One day when Johnny was just five years old, Mike got on his bike for the very last time. He was going to the store to get his mom some sugar so she could make an apple pie. Her pies were the best in the county. Mike couldn't wait to taste it.

The store was only four blocks away, but Mike had to ride on the road because there were no sidewalks. He had made the journey dozens of times with no problem. But on that fatal day a drunk driver didn't stop at Hancock Street. He didn't even slow down. The police report indicated the driver was way over the legal limit of alcohol consumption, and this was his third accident while under the influence. But by the time everyone knew those details, Mike was dead.

Johnny took it real hard. At times he acted like it was his fault. He loved his big brother, and life was never quite the same after that accident. Johnny always wanted to be just like Mike.

Joe looked at the tree and realized that it was a symbol of that love between his sons, especially at Christmas time.

"Hey, Joe," a male voice called out.

Joe looked in the direction of the voice calling his name and immediately recognized Mayor George Gibbons walking toward him.

"Hello, George. How are you doing tonight?"

"Well, I could be better, Joe, if Evelyn would let me."

"Sounds like there are problems in Paradise."

He looked thoughtful for a moment before responding, as if he was considering the political ramifications of saying too much.

"Oh, it's just the same old stuff, Joe. Her agenda is usually just the opposite of mine, and I always seem to be the one who has to change. Why is that?"

Joe looked down at his cup wondering how to respond. "Well, I would guess that it's been that way for some time."

The Mayor brushed off the snow from the park bench and sat down. "You just hit the nail on the head, my friend. That is the way it's been for most of our marriage. And I haven't liked it one bit, not one bit."

The sound of women laughing drew their attention away for a moment. George didn't want to talk about his wife with other women nearby. So they just watched the women in silence until they entered a store and the coast was clear. Two boys were having a snow ball fight only 30 yards away, and it reminded Joe of his own childhood. He had a strong urge to go join them, but that would have seemed impolite. So he just sat there and watched them play.

"Joe, how is your family doing?"

"Well, everyone is fine I guess. Of course, Christmas isn't going to be the same without Ben and Johnny."

Ben Fritz and Johnny Stone had been best of friends ever since Mike died. They grew up in Pentwater, living right next door to each other. They did everything together—riding bikes, fishing, hunting, and exploring. They went to the same school, and even took a lot of the same classes. That's why it didn't surprise anyone when they decided to join the Army together on January 15th, 1972, as part of the "Buddy System." That meant they would be guaranteed to stay together during their training and their first duty assignment.

The war in Vietnam was winding down so it seemed like a safe time to join. Yet after Basic Training, and their specialized training in infantry, they were sent to Vietnam anyway. As it turned out they were some of the last troops to be sent in. The majority of American troops were being sent home as part of a gradual drawdown. By the time Ben and Johnny arrived in Vietnam there were only about 150,000 American military personnel left. That was down from the 1969 high of over 500,000.

Joe was still looking down at his cup as he talked. "This will be their first Christmas away from home. Although I think it's probably just as tough on us as it is on them."

"I know what you mean. I had to spend a Christmas in Korea back in 1951 during the war, and it was one of the worst experiences of my life. Yet I'm sure it was hard on my family, too."

Just by looking at George, Joe could tell he was right back in Korea in his mind fighting that war all over again.

"George, I guess you realize that you will have to find someone else to throw the switch on the big Christmas tree in the center of town on December 12th this year because my son Johnny won't be here to do it."

"You know I hadn't even thought of that. How many years has Johnny been lighting our tree?"

"He's been doing it ever since his brother died in that terrible auto accident. Mike was supposed to light the tree that year, but after his death they asked Johnny to do it in his memory. Johnny was only five at the time, and he's been lightening it every year since. So I guess that means he's been lighting the tree for . . . I'd say about 15 years now. It was always one of his favorite parts of Christmas. For him Christmas didn't really begin until he threw the switch, saw those lights, sang *Joy to the World*, and drank some of Mrs. Brown's hot chocolate."

"I think my favorite part is just getting everybody together to sing," the Mayor replied. "Of course, lighting our big Christmas tree is what usually brings us together, and it marks the beginning of our twelve days of Christmas, and all of the festivities that are associated with it."

"I think our tree has grown some this past year."

"Do you really think so? It was about 22 feet last year. I wonder how high it is now? I better get someone to check on that." George pulled out a scrap piece of paper and jotted himself a note. Then looking up at his friend he asked, "Say Joe, you don't think there is any chance that they'll be home in time for Christmas do you?"

"I don't know, George. The peace talks are going on right now in Paris, but I'm not sure if they're making much progress. However, we keep pulling more troops out, so it sounds like the war is winding down. Who knows? Maybe they'll all be home in time for Christmas."

"Tell you what. You keep me in the loop and let me know if you hear anything. I won't ask anyone to take Johnny's job until the day of the big event. Let's just hope and pray that he makes it home in time."

"Thanks, George. That would be great. He sure would be surprised to come home and find out that you were waiting for him to light the tree, just like old times."

"Well, I have to go, Joe. Say 'Hi' to the family for me."

"Okay, I will. Say 'Hi' to Evelyn for me."

The mayor waved as he walked away, greeting other people on his way to the office. Joe sat there on the snow covered bench and thought about his son on the other side of the world. He wondered what Christmas would be like in Vietnam. That thought led him to a personal debate on whether or not it was right to hope that the longest war America had ever been engaged in might end in time for Christmas, just so his son could come home.

Joe looked up at the stars and tried to imagine what it was like in Vietnam. With the war winding down his son was probably getting kind of bored over there. Joe prayed, "God, please protect my son, and help him to make it home in time for Christmas."

3

"INCOMING!"

Everyone scrambled for cover. The rocket could be heard pushing the air out of its path as it soared in the general direction of the American soldiers. When it hit the ground the explosion was deafening. Shrapnel flew in every direction. The soldiers were as close to the ground as they could get as they waited for the next explosion, but it didn't come. Slowly they got to their feet and began to search the area for damage. This time no one was hurt. The rocket was fired by a Viet Cong soldier over a thousand meters away. It landed in an open field missing all the buildings of the Phu Bai Army Base in the northern most region of South Vietnam.

Ben looked over at his friend still on the ground. "Are you okay, Johnny?"

"Yeah, I'm fine, Ben. How about you?"

"I'm okay. The VC are getting braver by the moment. They usually save their rockets for the middle of the night, so they can really catch us with our guard down."

"I think they know our numbers are dwindling. With so few Americans still here they know our resistance is weakening."

"Man, I just wish they'd pull all of us out of here."

"I think they will pretty soon. I've heard that the Paris Peace Talks are making progress. We might even be home in time for Christmas."

"Hey, let's go grab some chow so we can get ready for guard duty."

"I'm right behind you."

After dinner the two friends headed for their hootch, grabbed their gear, and then went to the guard shack. After reporting in, they were briefed by the Sergeant of the Guard.

"Okay, you guys know what to look for tonight. Be on the lookout

out for Charley trying to slip through our lines. We have received intelligence reports that they might be planning a ground assault. But before they come at us they will send in some saboteurs to try to destroy our key assets. Corporal Stone, you're in charge out there. Keep your eyes and ears open."

"Yes, Sergeant."

The sergeant left as Ben and John got into their positions in the bunker.

They arranged their weapons and pop-up flares where they could easily get to them.

"Ben, how about if I take the first watch? Then I'll wake you up at midnight."

"Okay. We'll each do three hours at a time. If you get too tired, wake me up."

"Sure thing."

Ben tried to get comfortable, but the mosquitoes had something else in mind. He tossed and turned for ten minutes before finally sitting up. "How am I supposed to sleep with all this buzzing in my ears?"

"Try to cover your head with something. At least then you can't hear them."

John looked back at the tree line about 500 meters to his front. It was hard to see the enemy at night. Shadows were everywhere. The minutes slowly ticked by. But the silence gave him time to think.

"Hey, Ben, you still awake?"

"Yeah. What's up? Did you see something?"

"No, I was just thinking about home. Tomorrow is December 1st and everyone is probably busy getting ready for Christmas."

"Yep. It's hard to tell its Christmas over here."

"What will you miss the most this year?"

"I think I'll miss my family the most."

"Yeah, me too. But I'm also gonna miss Mary."

"That's one advantage you have over me, Johnny. You have someone to come home to. I don't."

"Ben, if we make it home from here, Mary and I want to get married and I want you to be my best man."

"You can count on me. I wouldn't miss it for anything."

Ben rolled over trying to get comfortable.

"Hey, Ben. Can I tell you something else I'm gonna miss this Christmas?"

"Do I have a choice?"

"Not really. I'm gonna miss not lighting the Christmas tree in Pentwater this year. That's how we always kick off the twelve days of Christmas."

"Yeah, I remember. How long have you been doing that?"

"Ever since my brother died. I was five at the time. It was something my brother always wanted to do. So some of the people in town convinced the authorities that I should do it for my brother, and I've been doing it every year since."

"Maybe you should write a letter to the Mayor and tell him that you can't do it this year, but that you'd love to do it next year."

"Why? The whole town knows we're over here. I'm sure he isn't expecting me to show up on December the twelfth."

"You might be right, but it would be a nice gesture."

"I'll think about it. Now you need to get some rest so you can be alert when it's my turn to sleep."

"It's always so hard to sleep during the first watch."

"I know. That's why I like to take the first watch. You'll be hearing from me at midnight."

Ben tried to get to sleep while Johnny watched the horizon and thought about Christmas back home, and the girl he loved.

4

It was snowing in Pentwater as Mary looked out her window, and watched the large flakes drifting slowly to the ground. There was something almost magical about the first few times it snows every year. It covers the ground in such a pure white that it changes the way everything looks. The whole world seems transformed into a winter wonderland. But it also reminded Mary of Johnny. Everything reminded her of Johnny. They had been childhood sweethearts for so long that it was hard to remember what life was like without him.

Mary first met Johnny back in the days when she almost always wore her blonde hair up in pig tails. Johnny was ten and Mary was seven. His first words to her seemed almost like a cut down, "Hi, freckles." Yet the tone of his voice was kind and playful. Mary blushed and looked down. "I didn't mean that in bad way," Johnny added. "I think your freckles are cute."

When Mary looked into Johnny's eyes that day there was a spark that both of them felt. From that moment on they were together. Some people said it was "puppy love" that would fade away, but it never did. Instead, it grew into a deep love and respect as the years went by.

Mary became the most attractive young lady in Pentwater, and even won several beauty contests. Therefore it was natural for people to ask if she was a model. But modeling was not something she was interested in. When asked what she wanted to do after she graduated from high school her answer was always the same, "I want to marry Johnny and have lots of kids."

The young couple had so many plans for the future. They even had a home already picked out. Johnny knew the foreman at Dow Chemical in Ludington, so it seemed like he could easily get a job there.

The future looked so bright until the day that Johnny announced he was going into the Army. It was like a dark cloud had suddenly blocked the light of the sun. Johnny could be sent off to war, and then what? It all seemed so vivid in Mary's mind, especially their final day together.

They were sitting in Johnny's car in front of Mary's house. Mary was trying unsuccessfully to hold back the tears as she thought of being separated from Johnny for a whole year while he went off to Vietnam.

"Mary, we have talked so many times about spending our lives together, but I've never officially asked you the big question. So I'm asking now. Mary, will you marry me, and make me the happiest man alive?"

Without a moment's hesitation Mary looked at him and said, "YES! YES! YES!" She threw her arms around him and they just held each other for the longest time. They wanted to treasure that moment forever.

Johnny was the first to pull back, and as he did he brought out a small velvet covered box. "Then I want you to wear this engagement ring, so everyone will know that you're my girl."

Mary opened the box and peered down at a beautiful diamond ring. She pulled it out of the box and placed it on her finger. It fit perfectly. "I love it, Johnny." She held her hand out in front of her to get a better look. It sparkled in the light. "Oh, Johnny. You have just made me the happiest girl alive. I can't wait to be your wife."

They embraced again and just sat there holding each other without saying anything. It was Johnny who finally broke the silence. "We should tell someone. Who should we tell first?"

"Could we tell my mom?" she asked.

"Sure, we can tell your mom, and then we can tell the whole world."

Mary's mom was excited with the news, but a bit concerned about the timing. "You aren't planning on getting married right away are you? I mean Johnny is just getting ready to ship out to Vietnam."

"No, Mrs. Taylor," Johnny replied. "We will wait till I get back from Vietnam. That is if we have your permission."

"Of course you have our permission. Johnny, you have been a part of this family for the past 10 years. Why would you even need to ask?"

"Well, maam, I just think it is the right thing to do."

"Then you have our permission."

Two hours later, Mary walked Johnny to his car. Neither of them wanted the night to end. They walked slowly hand in hand in the moonlight, listening to the crickets. Johnny's flight was leaving out of Grand Rapids at 5:30 in the morning, so he would have to wake up at 3:30 in order to make it. But at that moment the only thing that mattered to him was being with Mary.

Johnny leaned against his car and then pulled Mary close. Their kisses were long and passionate. When they came up for air, Johnny looked into Mary's eyes. "I want to spend the rest of my life with you. Will you wait for me?"

"You know I will."

"I love you, Mary."

"I love you too, Johnny."

They kissed again long and hard. When Johnny pulled away he simply turned and climbed into his car. With tears in his eyes he waved to Mary, and then drove away.

As Mary watched his car disappear she said, "I'll wait for you forever, Johnny Stone." Then she wiped the tears away and went into her house.

5

On December 7th a letter arrived at the Mayor's house.

Dear Sir,

Ben and I were talking on guard duty the other night about Christmas in Pentwater and how we probably wouldn't make it home in time. We hear rumors that the peace talks are going well and that the war might end any day now. We sure would like to be home in time to be with all of you, but there just isn't any guarantee. One of the things that I'm really going to miss is not being able to light the Pentwater Christmas tree. I've been doing it since my brother died about 15 years ago. This Christmas just won't be the same. But maybe you could keep me in mind to light the tree next Christmas. It sure would mean a lot to me. Thanks for your time.

Merry Christmas.
Johnny Stone

The Mayor put down the letter and remembered what it was like when he was in the Army and couldn't get home in time for Christmas. The more he thought about it the sadder he became.

"Evelyn, could you come in here for a minute?"

"What is it, dear?" Evelyn said as she came into the living room.

"I want you to read this letter from Johnny Stone." He handed her the letter and she stood there silently reading it.

"Oh, George, that is so sad. Those poor boys over there are missing Christmas, and all the festivities. I'll bet a lot of people have forgotten all about our boys over there in that awful place."

Suddenly, George jumped up from his seat. "That's it! People have forgotten. They don't care like they used to. Let's remind them."

"Just what are you suggesting, George?"

"I'm going to call some of the area newspapers and ask them to run Johnny's letter in their papers with a note from me. Let's get people thinking again."

"Do you think they will actually print it?"

"Hey, we'll never know till we try."

As George thought about it he came up with an idea that was sure to get people talking. So he got on the phone and called the Ludington Daily News, the Muskegon Chronicle, the Grand Rapids Press, and the Oceana Herald. All of them agreed to run the article in the next few days. When it hit the news stands the headline read—"MAYOR OF PENTWATER DECIDES TO HOLD CHRISTMAS FOR VETS."

Reporters from all over the state wanted to know what was going on, so did the people of Pentwater. The Mayor had neglected to talk with anyone before going public with the news, and the people who had elected him as their Mayor were more than a little upset. A town meeting was called for the following Tuesday evening at the Middle School.

When the Mayor arrived he saw vans for several of the local TV stations in the parking lot. When he entered the gym the place was packed. One reporter approached him and asked for a comment. The Mayor quickly said, "Let me talk to my people first."

The reporter turned to his camera man and told him to go live.

"This is Sam Sneed with Channel 8 News. We are here in Pentwater, Michigan for a live report coming from the middle school gym. The crowd of angry citizens are here to protest Mayor George Gibbons proclamation to the world that all of Pentwater is going to hold off on celebrating Christmas until two of the young men from Pentwater, both now serving in the Army, come home from Vietnam. The two young men are Johnny Stone and Ben Fritz. The Mayor apparently went out on a limb and made his decision before talking to anyone about his plan, and it sounds like the people are furious. It looks like the Mayor is making his way to the podium now. Let's see what he has to say."

The noise level was high until the Mayor walked to the microphone.

"Folks, can I have your attention? Please." People became quiet as all eyes focused on this man they wanted to expel from his official position. "I know some of you are upset about the story you read in the paper regarding my decision to hold Christmas until our boys get home from Vietnam. I take full responsibility for that. It was my idea and I neglected to confer with any of you good folks here tonight. I'm sorry. But . . . even if it is the last thing I do as your Mayor, I'd like to stick to my promise. Our boys are fighting a war over there that they can't win, and according to all reports the peace talks could end it for them any day now. My proposal is that we hold off on our joint Christmas activities, like lighting the Pentwater Christmas tree, until they get home."

At that moment Jacob Hall stood to his feet and shouted "And just when do you think that will be Mayor? This war has been going on over there for almost 10 years now. Are you just gonna suspend Christmas indefinitely?"

One woman yelled out, "What about the children?"

Then several people began to shout in unison—"Grinch, Grinch, Grinch!"

Others joined in and booed the Mayor. Yet he kept his composure and motioned with his hands for the people to settle down.

"Folks, I'm not trying to ruin your own Christmas celebrations this year, I'm just asking you to help me do something nice for two of our own young men who are serving our country in a far away land. This would mean a lot to them."

Old man Riley stood to his feet using his cane for support. "Mayor, I served in WWII and we spent four years away from home and no one ever held Christmas for us." Others clapped their approval as Riley sat down.

The mayor just stood back and listened.

Jane Landry jumped to her feet and asked, "Are you trying to change the date when we celebrate Christmas? I mean . . . is this gonna become a regular thing every year from here on out? Because if that is what you are suggesting I don't think you're gonna find much support for that idea in this town or anywhere else in America."

Other protesters stood and made their comments, but the Mayor remained silent. As he stood there he was trying to imagine what it might be like if the whole town would just unite on this issue. They could have the biggest welcome home celebration ever. It might even grab the attention of the whole nation and start a movement. But when George looked out at the crowd he saw so many angry faces that he knew it would take a miracle to convince these people. In that moment he looked up toward heaven and silently prayed, *"God, I could sure use some help here. I need a miracle."*

Just then, when it seemed like all was lost, Don Lamb, the Chief of Police, stood, and the crowd settled down. Don was a local hero from the Korean War. He had a real heart for veterans, and was highly respected by everyone in town.

"Folks, I've been listening to all of you complain, and I know this is an emotional issue. However, I want you to think about what our Mayor is suggesting. He isn't asking you to change all of your Christmas traditions, just our corporate ones. All of you know Ben and Johnny, and you were proud when they came home on leave in their uniforms, and strutted around town. They were some of the last troops to be sent to Vietnam, and soon they will be coming home. You all know how controversial this war has been, and how it has divided our country. None of the veterans of the Vietnam War have received much of a welcome home. As a war vet myself, I think that is wrong. So I just want to go on record that I like George's idea, and I think we should show the rest of the country just how to welcome our young men home from the war zone. And if the Mayor's idea of holding Christmas is one way we as a community can show our support, then I think we ought to do it. If you need any help Mayor, I'll be glad to help. That's all I got to say."

As Don sat down people started whispering to each other. It soon became obvious that the tide had changed. What had started out dividing the whole town was now bringing it together. Before the meeting was over people were apologizing, and some were even volunteering to help. George stood back in amazement. Then looking up toward heaven, "Thanks, God. You did what I never could have done. Thanks for this miracle tonight."

6

"Goooood Mornnning, Vietnam! If you can hear my voice out there in radio land then that means you made it through another night, and you are one day closer to going home. Congratulations!" There was the sound of people clapping and cheering in the background.

"Here's a News Flash just in! The Paris Peace Talks are going strong and there is hope of a break through any day now. All of you old timers out there know exactly what that means—absolutely nothing. So just keep on counting your days. And to help you get in the Christmas mood, here's one there playing back home as the shoppers go from store to store in the beautiful snow."

It's beginning to look a lot like Christmas, everywhere I go.

Look at the Five & Ten;
look at it once again. . .

As the music played Ben and Johnny were just getting up. The sun was rising in a beautiful array of colors on the horizon. As Ben looked out at the beauty of the morning he wondered, *how can each sunrise and sunset be so different?* He didn't have a clue. But one thing he did know—it sure didn't look much like Christmas in Vietnam. When the song ended the DJ came back on.

"This just in from someone very high up in our chain of command. I wasn't given a name, but I am told this information is very reliable. Word is trickling down from the top that there are only...seven shopping days left until Christmas. That's right folks. It is December the 18th today. So just a reminder to all of you out there in the jungle, you only have seven days left to get in to your nearest Post Exchange and buy that perfect gift and send it home before you change your mind. As some wise person once said, 'It's the thought that counts.' What was he thinking?"

"Here is another Christmas favorite—*White Christmas* by Mr. Bing Crosby."

I'm dreaming of a White Christmas,
With every Christmas card I write.
Where the tree tops glisten,
And the children listen
To hear sleigh bells in the snow.

The music was suddenly interrupted by the DJ. "Hey, is it looking like a White Christmas where you are? It sure isn't where I am. Maybe what we need is a ticket for an airplane to someplace where it does look like the Christmas we're all dreaming about." The music changed and a familiar song blasted over the air waves.

Give me a ticket for an airplane,
Ain't got time to take a fast train.
Lonely days are gone,
I'm going home.
My baby, she wrote me a letter.

Ben and Johnny put on their uniforms and made their way to the Mess Hall. It was just another day. No one seemed to be in much of a Christmas mood. Back home it might be just seven days until Christmas, but in Vietnam every day was pretty much like all the rest. However, there was one thing that made some day's better—mail call. On December 18, 1972 Johnny received a letter from the Mayor of Pentwater.

Dear Johnny,

I want to thank you for that nice letter you sent to me. I have to tell you that I let a few other people see it and, well, it ended up getting published in some newspapers. That caused quite a stir.

We held a meeting in Pentwater and decided to hold Christmas until you and Ben are here to celebrate it with us. We won't be lighting the town Christmas tree until you arrive to carry on the tradition. As far as we're concerned, the twelve days of Christmas may not even begin until January or February—whenever you all get back here to help us celebrate it.

So be careful and know that we're all praying for you. Hope to see you soon.

Sincerely,
Mayor Gibbons

Johnny was shocked at what he had just read. He jumped up and went over to Ben. "Listen to this, Ben."

After he read the letter to Ben he looked at his friend and noticed a tear trickling down his face. "I can't believe they're going to do that. How did they ever get everyone to agree to it?"

"I don't know, but it happened."

"Let's pray about this."

"Okay."

"God, this is so amazing. Our whole town decided to hold Christmas until we get home. So we ask You, Lord, to please help us to get home soon. And one more thing,

Lord. Would you bless those kind people back home who are setting this whole thing up? Make it obvious to everyone that Your hand of blessing is in this thing. In Jesus Name. Amen."

7

The Americans and the Vietnamese were still negotiating at the Paris Peace Talks. Yet in spite of some progress being made, no agreements had been reached. So the war dragged on.

However, on Christmas they called a 48 hour cease fire. That year Ben and Johnny were allowed to go to a USO Show featuring Bob Hope. Bob Hope was known for his entertaining of the troops, especially on Christmas. Since WWII he had dedicated himself to putting together shows that would encourage the men and women in the military far from home at Christmas time. His shows included humorous skits with celebrities and beautiful women. But he always ended those Christmas shows with the singing of *Silent Night*.

Ben and Johnny sat there with thousands of men and women in Saigon, South Vietnam singing *Silent Night* as the tears rolled down their cheeks. Almost everyone in that crowd wanted the peace of Christmas to come to Vietnam. They thought of their homes, their families, and their girlfriends. Johnny thought of Mary and wished he could be there with her to celebrate Christmas.

Pentwater, Michigan

By the time the Christmas Eve worship services were over, the people back in Pentwater had given up hope that Ben and Johnny would make it home in time for Christmas.

Mary was getting nervous. Johnny left for Vietnam at the end of April in 1972, which meant that his one year tour of duty was almost over. If the Paris Peace Talks came to some kind of agreement, and ended the war in the next month or so, then Johnny would be coming home before his tour was over. But either way, Mary knew that at the latest, four months from now, Johnny would be coming home. She had been hoping and praying for that day to come, yet the closer it got the more worried she became. Would the war change him? Would he still be the same wonderful guy? Would they still get married? She just wanted him home in one piece. Mary had heard how many men got careless at the end of their tour, and died before their rotation date.

"Oh, God. Please keep my Johnny safe and bring him back to me. If You never answer another prayer I pray, please Lord, answer this one."

One Week Later

Christmas was over and the decorations had been put away for most Americans. But for the people in Pentwater, Michigan things were different. They were holding Christmas until further notice. That night the local news carried a new update.

"This is Sam Sneed of Channel 8 News. We are back in Pentwater, Michigan for an update on an earlier report. Several weeks ago, we reported that this little coastal town in Western Michigan had decided to "Hold Christmas" until the Vietnam War is over, and their two soldiers come marching home. Well, it's the second of January now and still no one knows when or if the Vietnam War is going to end. So while all of America is putting away their Christmas decorations for another year, the people in Pentwater are still in a holding pattern. How long will they wait? Your guess is as good as mine, but the people say they will wait till theirs boys are home. This is Sam Sneed with Channel 8 News in Pentwater, Michigan."

The Mayor watched the report on his own TV at home. He was still dealing with some opposition, so he decided to call for back-up. The next day he had a special meeting with all the Pastors in Pentwater.

The mayor had invited all of the pastors in the area to his house for lunch. They weren't sure what this was all about since the mayor never seemed like a very religious man. "Gentlemen, I have a problem. I made a commitment to the people of this town that we would hold off on our community's celebration of Christmas until Ben and Johnny get home from Vietnam." He paused for effect.

"Well, Christmas has come and gone and we're still waiting. That's where you come in. Pastors, I need your help. I want to ask all of you to get your congregations praying for our boys to get back here real soon. Heck, we all know the war is going to be over any day now, so all I want you to do is to petition the Almighty to intervene and have it end this month."

The pastor from the Methodist Church spoke first. "Mayor, this is the longest war our country has ever been involved in, and we all want it to end. But only God knows when that will be. Don't you think it's a little presumptuous of us to ask for it to end this month?"

The Catholic priest was next. "I agree with Ralph. I know you went out on a limb, but you got yourself into this political quagmire, and you're going to have to get yourself out."

The mayor felt a need to defend his position, so he responded. "Gentlemen, I was hoping for a little more support from the clergy. All I'm asking is for you to pray."

Jack Coleman was the newest member of this elite group. As a Charismatic Pastor he had a little different perspective on the issue of prayer. "I'll pray for you Mayor Gibbons, but you have to understand that I can't guarantee that the war will end this month. However, I do believe that God can do anything, and that nothing is impossible with God."

"Gentlemen," the mayor continued, "that's all I can ask. How about the rest of you? Will you pray with me?"

The men around the table looked at each other for confirmation. Finally, the Methodist pastor consented. "I guess it wouldn't hurt to ask. Jack, why don't you lead us?"

"It would be my pleasure." He paused for a moment and then bowing his head and closing his eyes, he prayed.

"Lord, You are in charge of the entire world. You know about those Peace Talks going on in Paris, and You know what's happening in Vietnam. The war has already been going on for nine years, and we would like to see it end so our boys could come back home. So we ask You, our Heaven Father, to help this war to come to an end this month of January in 1973. Whatever is holding up the Peace Talks, whatever obstacle is in the way, work it out so our boys can come home. We pray especially for Johnny and Ben. Please keep them safe and let them come home soon, so they can enjoy this Christmas homecoming we are putting together. In Jesus Name, Amen."

8

Anticipation was building in Vietnam as the Paris Peace Talks continued. Rumors were spreading like crazy. One day the rumor mill would say the treaty had already been signed secretly, and the next day the men would hear that it might never be signed. However, units were still in the process of slowly reducing their numbers. So it seemed logical for the men to assume that someone up above them in the chain of command knew something that they didn't, but no one was talking.

On January 29th as Ben and Johnny were waking up to another day they heard gunfire and flares going off. It seemed odd to do that when the sun was shining. They crawled out of their bunks, and walked over to the door. As they looked outside they saw men in their unit jumping up and down, and shooting their weapons into the air.

"What's going on?" Ben asked.

One of their friends saw them and shouted, "IT'S OVER! THE WAR IS OVER!"

Ben turned to his best friend and grabbed him into a bear hug. "YAHOO!"

"That means we get to go home."

The Paris Peace Talks had reached an agreement, and a Peace Treaty had been signed. Word trickled down that all units would be standing down, and going home within the month. It was a great time of celebration. Helicopters were flying low and doing stunts. The men on the ground were shooting star clusters in the air because they resembled fireworks.

While the soldiers packed, the Vietnamese workers on base watched in frustration, wondering what their fate might be once the Americans were gone.

Many of the Americans pulled out so suddenly that they just left their office equipment, food, tools, and extra gear. Some units even left tanks, helicopters, and artillery. Other units dumped all of their excess equipment into the ocean. They were all in a hurry to leave before some politicians changed their minds about the war really being over.

Before that week was over Ben and Johnny were on trucks headed for Saigon. They were going home just in time for Christmas.

9

"IT'S ALL OVER!"

The headlines of almost every newspaper in the world carried the story of the war in Vietnam finally coming to an end. When the news came to Pentwater, Michigan, the phone in the Mayors office was ringing off the hook. Everyone wanted to help with the homecoming celebration. Even people who had complained about the mayor's idea now called to apologize, and to offer their help. Mayor Gibbons had more help than he knew what to do with. The people of Pentwater were determined to make this the biggest celebration they had ever had. As they worked together, something else happened that they weren't expecting. There was a sense of unity in the community that none of them had ever experienced before.

Joe Stone was just reading the paper when the phone rang. He reached over and lifted it to his ear. "Hello."

"Dad? It's Johnny."

"JOHNNY? Where are you?"

"I'm in Saigon, South Vietnam."

"Just a second let me get your mother. JANE! Johnny's on the phone!"

From the Kitchen he heard her scream, "JOHNNY?" She picked up the phone in the kitchen.

"Johnny, is it really you?"

"Yeah mom, it's really me."

"Where are you calling from? Are you back in the states?"

"Not yet. I'm still in Vietnam, but I'm getting on a jet tomorrow and coming home."

"Is Ben coming with you?"

"Yep! We've been together the whole time, and they're not going to separate us now."

"Johnny, when can we expect you?"

"Probably on Friday. I'll know better when the plane lands in California."

"Oh, Johnny that is such good news. We can't wait to see you."

"I can't wait to see all of you either. Can you call Mary and tell her? They only let us make one phone call."

"Sure, Johnny. We'll tell her."

"Well, I have to go now. I love you both and can't wait to be home."

"Call us when you land in California, Johnny."

"I will dad."

"We love you, son. . . and we are very proud of you."

"Thanks. I'll see you all on Friday."

After they hung up the phone, Joe grabbed his wife and they started dancing right there in the kitchen. After thanking God, they started making phone calls. There were so many people to tell and only two days to get the word out.

10

"This is Sam Sneed with Channel 8 News coming to you live from the Grand Rapids Airport. We are here awaiting the arrival two soldiers just coming back from Vietnam. I am joined here with over a hundred people from Pentwater, Michigan. The two young men, Ben Fritz and Johnny Stone, are both residents of Pentwater. The citizens of that small town in Western Michigan having been holding off their celebration of Christmas until these young men get home.

"Stephanie Quinn is a Librarian in Pentwater and wanted to make a few comments for our viewing audience. Go ahead Stephanie."

"The history of the Twelve Days of Christmas has as the starting date December 25th. It ends on Epiphany with the visit of the three Wiseman recorded in the Bible in Matthew chapter two. The song by the same title dates back to the 16th century when the Catholic Church was fighting persecution. Legend has it that they put secret codes into the song that would remind people of the doctrines of the Church.

"In Pentwater we celebrate the Twelve Days of Christmas as part of our annual celebration. We start on December the twelfth and end on Christmas Eve. I realize it isn't historically accurate, but it has become a custom for us in Pentwater."

"Well, there you have it folks. We just got word that the plane carrying our two young soldiers is landing now."

When the plane landed in Grand Rapids, no one was more excited than Ben Fritz and Johnny Stone. They weren't sure who was going to be at the airport to greet them, besides their immediate family. But when they made their way into the terminal area they were shocked to see a huge crowd of people with signs that said, "WELCOME HOME!" So many people were cheering and clapping that it put the two soldiers into a temporary shock.

Mary ran up to Johnny and gave him the biggest hug she had ever given him. "I love you Johnny Stone, and I am so glad you came home to me."

"I love you too, Mary." Then he kissed her, forgetting all about the crowd watching his every move. When they came up for air they were surrounded by a sea of faces. People were hugging them and slapping them on the back. Cameras were flashing and reporters were shoving microphones in their faces.

"What does it feel like to be home?"

"What are you going to do now that the war is over?"

"Has the military been treating you right?"

"What do you think of all the peace demonstrations?"

It was Ben who finally told them to back off. "OK guys, enough questions already. Just let us catch our breath."

Some of their friends helped with the reporters, while their families began to usher them toward the baggage claim area. After finding their bags they headed for the parking lot and everyone split up, agreeing to meet later in Pentwater.

When Johnny was alone with Mary and his family they began to ask him about his time in Vietnam and what the war had been like. They talked non-stop all the way home.

When they got off the highway at the Pentwater exit luminaries were lining the road all the way into town. Each house they passed was decorated for Christmas with beautiful lights, manger scenes, reindeer, snowmen, and replicas of Santa Clause. Many of the homes had signs in their yards that read "WELCOME HOME." Johnny was overcome with emotion.

Mary leaned into him. "Johnny, it's all for you and Ben."

"But it's February and everyone's house is still decorated for Christmas."

Driving slowly his father looked back at his son and asked, "Johnny, do you remember getting a letter from the mayor about lighting the Christmas tree?"

"Sure, dad. Why do you ask?"

"That's what this is all about. The people in Pentwater all decided to hold off on our joint celebration of Christmas until you guys came home. So for us the twelve days of Christmas begins tonight."

"I don't know what to say."

"Well, you don't need to say anything. It's just our way of saying 'Welcome Home.' So instead of going right home we need to go light that tree in the center of town."

"Tonight?"

"Yes, tonight. Mayor Gibbons promised all the people of Pentwater that he would not turn on the Christmas lights in town until you and Ben were here to see it. So we've been waiting."

"WOW! I can't believe it. After all this time I thought you all had given up on us."

"No way! We've been waiting and now that you're here we thought we should do it tonight."

"Okay. Let's do it!"

When they arrived in the downtown area there were cars everywhere and people lined up on both sides of Hancock Street. They had to park about a football field away from the center of town. When Johnny got out of the car the crowd began to cheer. He looked over to his left and saw Ben starring in bewilderment at the crowd, too.

"Johnny, welcome home, son." It was Mayor Gibbons trying to be heard above the noise of the crowd. "We need you and Ben to go over to where the flags are."

"Why? What's going on?" Johnny inquired.

"We're having a parade, and you and Ben are the guests of honor. You will be marching with several other veterans who served in Vietnam,

Korea, WWII, and even a few from WWI.

You all will be following right behind the color guard."

"Okay."

"Alright then, why don't you two get into position in the formation? Once the band begins to play we'll get things started."

As Ben and Johnny made their way over to the flags, people were shaking their hands, hugging them, slapping them on the back, and even a few of the ladies kissed them. When they got near the flags other veterans hugged them, and said the words all veterans want to hear. "Welcome Home." Then they all lined up and got ready to move out. When everyone was in place the band began to play a very familiar song, and the men started to march. As they marched the people began to sing with the music.

"When Johnny and Ben come
Marching home, hurrah, hurrah.
When Johnny and Ben come
Marching home, hurrah, hurrah.

Oh, the crowds will cheer
And the bands will play
Cameras will flash
And we'll light the tree
And we'll all be glad
When Johnny and Ben are home."

As they marched, the crowd went nuts. They were throwing confetti and streamers into the air. Some were yelling while others were whistling. When they reached the center of town the music stopped. Ben and Johnny were asked to join the Mayor up on the platform.

The crowd quieted down as the mayor walked to the microphone. "Ben and Johnny, welcome home!" The crowd again started cheering and clapping their hands.

Ben put his arm around Johnny as they stood there side by side not knowing how to react to these gestures of kindness and appreciation.

"We want you men to know," the mayor continued, "how proud of you we are. We sent you out as boys, and you have come back to us as men. In appreciation for your service to our country we are going to set up a special memorial for all the veterans from Pentwater who served this great country of ours by fighting our enemies, and defending our freedom. And your names will be on that memorial."

Ben walked up to the mayor to thank him. "Mayor Gibbons and the people of Pentwater. Johnny and I want to thank you for this parade, and for the memorial you are making for all of us who served. We aren't really heroes. We just did what our country asked us to do."

Johnny walked over and joined Ben at the podium. "Ben and I are really overwhelmed by all of this. How can we ever thank you? We're just glad it's over and we got to come home."

The mayor worked his way back to the podium and grabbed the microphone. "Johnny, I told you in a letter that we were going to hold off on lighting our Christmas tree to kick off the twelve days of Christmas until you and Ben were back here with us. Well, we did hold off and I think we have waited long enough. So Johnny, come on over here and light our Christmas tree."

Johnny was so moved by all the emotions he was feeling that he was shaking. Tears were slowly working their way down his cheeks as he thought about all that had happened to make this moment a reality. When the mayor handed him the microphone he just knew he had to say something about his little brother.

"Fifteen years ago, my brother Mike was promised that he could throw the switch to light this very same tree that we are looking at tonight, although I think it was quite a bit smaller back then. Anyway, he never got that opportunity. He was killed in a terrible car accident. So the people of this town asked me to do it on behalf of Mike. Every year since then, I have been asked to throw the switch that lights our Christmas tree, marking the beginning of our Twelve Days of Christmas celebration.

"Last year, Ben and I joined the Army. After our training they sent us to Vietnam. I have to tell you that there were times when I wondered if we would ever see this town again, and now, here we are. I want to thank God for protecting us, and I want to thank all of you for your prayers and support. This hasn't been a popular war, and yet you kind people have stood by us with your prayers, letters, and even sending us boxes of goodies. Your love helped to sustain us on the other side of the world. And now to see how you waited for us to get home before you started the Twelve Days of Christmas is just amazing. This means more to us than you will ever know.

"Some of our friends are being met with hatred and slander. While they are getting spit at, you are throwing a party for us. To all of you who greeted us at the airport, thank you. That was so cool. To all of you here...this parade and celebration is so humbling. I just don't even know what to say except, thanks. We love you all." Then turning to the Christmas tree, Johnny shouted "LET CHRISTMAS BEGIN!"

As soon as he threw the switch the lights came on and everyone cheered. The snow was gently falling to the ground and the lights on the tree seemed to be reflected everywhere. It was a beautiful thing to behold. Among the crowd there was a sense of unity unlike anything they had ever experienced. They were together and united in purpose. No matter what else was going on in the world, on this night in Pentwater, world peace seemed like a real possibility.

The mayor came back to center stage and directed everyone to look to the south. As they turned to look at Hancock Street, Christmas lights began to light up all over their little town. Just then the band took that as their cue and starting playing "Joy to the World" and everyone joined their voices together in song.

"Joy to the world,
The Lord has come.
Let earth receive her king.

Let every heart prepare Him room.
And heaven and nature sing,
And heaven and nature sing
And heaven and heaven
And nature sing."

As they were singing Mrs. Brown brought out two cups of her famous hot chocolate. She handed them to Ben and Johnny. "Welcome home. It's great to have you back with us."

And that's how the Christmas of 1972 began in February of 1973. By the time the twelve days of Christmas were over one thing was clear. Holding Christmas for two extra months made it one of the best Christmas' anyone could ever remember.

A NOTE FROM THE AUTHOR

I did two tours of duty in Vietnam—one with the Marines, and the second tour was with the Army. I was there in 1973 when the war ended and President Nixon brought us all home. He was our hero at that moment in time. However, the story you have just read is not the welcome home most of us received. Instead we were met with apathy, disgust, hatred, slander, and even violence. Things were thrown at us, we were spit upon, and many people called us terrible names, adding to the shame we already felt. It always amazed us how violent the peace demonstrators could be when we showed up. Other people just ignored us or treated us like we were crazy. Most of us dreamed of the kind of reception described in this little book, but few of us got to see that dream become a reality. Perhaps that's why we felt abandoned by the American people and betrayed by our own government.

Many of us struggled with nightmares, depression, and anger. It took years for our government to recognize how wounded all of us felt. They developed a term for our symptoms called Post Traumatic Stress Disorder (PTSD). Most of our problems could have been avoided with counseling, time for debriefing, and a better welcome home plan.

The Vietnam Veterans of America talk a lot about the parade they never received, as well as the shame and guilt they were forced to carry. We all dealt with that in different ways. Some turned to drugs and alcohol to drown it. Others ran away from society and lived in the woods for months at a time. I asked God to help me with mine, and He did. I found forgiveness when I trusted in Jesus Christ. That's what changed my life. Jesus took away my anger and hatred, replacing it with His love. I have the hope of eternal life, so death doesn't seem as scary.

We now have new wars to fight, and new wounded warriors to welcome home. If we learned anything from Vietnam it should be this: all veterans who served in combat environments struggle with memories of war. The buddies we lost, the people we killed, the terrible things we saw. War is not pretty. The modern battlefield is a dangerous and vicious place filled with more blood and gore than you can imagine. You can't expect people who are sent into a war zone to come home unchanged. It does something to them. But we go because our government sends us into harm's way for a reason. Most of us believe that we are sent out to protect the freedoms that we enjoy. So when it's over and we come home, the very least our country can do is to welcome us back to civilization, and make us feel as if we did something noble—something that made a difference. This act of love may not stop all the nightmares, but it will sure help to start the healing process.

As a way of honoring the real men from Pentwater who served in the Vietnam War I have included their names here.

Vietnam Veterans of Pentwater, Michigan

1. Emil Adams
2. John Angel
3. Jim Anthony
4. Don Becke
5. Jim Carlson
6. Brent Cluchey
7. Nick Fekken
8. Richard Gregwer
9. Jerry Gustafson
10. Larry Gustafson
11. Rich Johnson
12. Bruce Maynard
13. Al Pearson
14. Dave Plummer
15. Bob Schultz
16. Mike Sorensen
17. Robert Vandenheuvel

**List provided by veteran Gary Hilbert
Gary is a member of the Pentwater VFW**

I want to thank the readers of the original text who offered suggestions:

Marilyn Cluchey
Chuck & Charlotte Eberbach
Henry & Sue Espinoza
Larry & Loralee Gustafson
Andy & Sue Knudson
Gurden & Lori Paggeot
Stephanie Quinn
Karen Slattery
Ken & Nancy Terryn
Marilyn Warner

DEN'S BOOKS

Transformed By Christ picks up Den's story where *Changed By War* ends. It tells how Den felt a call to the ministry and went on to become an Army Chaplain, and a Methodist Pastor. It is also a book about learning how to pray, how to hear from God, the authority of the Bible and much more.

The cost is $10.00.

Changed By War is the story of Den's experience in Vietnam. The war changed him as it does with everyone. This book has been called :
"Riveting"
"Inspiring "
"Life changing"

See what all the buzz is about by reading Den's bestseller, "Changed By War."

The Cost is $7.00.

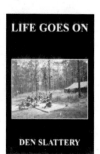

Life Goes On could easily be called *Lessons from Life*. Each chapter tells a lesson the author discovered while living his life. It covers the years from about 1990 through 1998 with stories from Den's life.

The cost is $7.00.

To purchase Den's books, send check + $3.00 shipping to:

4018 Kelsey Hwy   Ionia, MI 48846

endless universe

**MARION
ZIMMER
BRADLEY**

SF

ace books

A Division of Charter Communications Inc.
A GROSSET & DUNLAP COMPANY
360 Park Avenue South
New York, New York 10010

ENDLESS UNIVERSE

Copyright © 1975, 1979 by Marion Zimmer Bradley

*A shorter version of this novel was
originally published as ENDLESS VOYAGE.*

All rights reserved.

An ACE Book

Cover art by Attila Hejja

First Ace edition: May 1975
Second Ace edition: April 1979
Third Ace edition: September 1979

Printed in U.S.A.

" 'Tis not too late to seek a better world."

Tennyson

CONTENTS

—**Baby Stealers**

—**Monsters**

—**Perverts**

—**Immortals**

Those are some of the names the planet-siders have for them. They call themselves

THE EXPLORERS

And the contempt of the earth-grubbers means nothing to them, compared to the lure of the stars. Because they are the last pioneers, the frontiersmen of space. For the Explorers, a metal ship is their one true home, its crew their only family, their lives a constant adventure in an

endless universe

SF

Part One

PLANETS ARE FOR SAYING GOODBYE

I

Planets are for saying goodbye.

That's an old saying in the Explorers. I never believed it before. It never really hit me.

Never again. You never really realize what never means. It's a word you use all the time but it means . . . it means never. NEVER. Not in all the millions of billions of trillions of . . .

Get hold of yourself, dammit!

Everything on this planet had changed, but not the pattern of the Explorer Ship: it was lighted now from inside, and outlined in silver; a chained Titan, shadowed against the dark mass of the mountain that rose behind the new city.

The city was still raw, a mass of beams and scars

in the wounded red clay of the planet's surface.
Gildoran had first seen the great ship outlined
against the mountain two years ago, planetside
time—before the city had risen there, before anything had risen there—and every day since, but
now it felt as if he hadn't ever seen it before. There
were strange sharp edges on everything, as if the
air had dissolved and he saw them hard-edged in
space.

*Never again. I was a fool to think anything
could be different.*
How could Janni have done this to me?
*I thought she was different. Every fool kid
thinks that about the first woman he cares about.*

Gildoran passed through the gates. They were
still guarded, but that was only a formality. On
every planet Gildoran had known—he could remember four in twenty-two years of biological
time—the earthworms kept away from Explorer
ships.

*I took Janni. I thought she'd have to feel the way
I did. Wonder, and awe. But she was bored. I
should have known then, but instead I was flat-
tered, I thought it was just that she'd rather be
alone with me. Maybe she would. Then.*
That seems a long time ago now.

The guard didn't bother checking the offered
ident disk. It was a formality anyhow. Gildoran's
identity was on his face, like all Explorers. He
knew what was whispered about them, but
lifelong training made it beneath Gildoran's dig-
nity to notice it or seem to remember it.

But I remember. Keep away, they say. Keep away from the Explorers. Keep your children away. They'll steal your children, steal your women.

I wouldn't have stolen Janni. But I might have stayed with her.

He walked with the arrogant pride of all the Explorers, conscious, and proud, of the differences that set him off—set him off cruelly, a planetman might have said—from the rest of the swarming humanity around the city, the crews working to load the ships. He stood seven feet seven, although he was tall even for an Explorer, due to a childhood and youth spent at minimal gravity. The white—paper-white—skin and bleached white hair were colorless from years of hard radiation. He knew there were other differences, bone-deep, marrow-deep, cell-deep. Gene-deep. He never thought about them. But he had known from childhood that no one else ever forgot them.

Janni hadn't forgotten them.
Not for a moment.

The crews around the ship parted to let him through, edging faintly back as he passed. But this was at the edge of his consciousness. He would have noticed it only if they hadn't.

Had she only wanted an exotic? Was it only his strangeness that had attracted her? Not romance, but a perverse desire for the bizarre, the alien, the freakish?
Did women like Janni boast of an Explorer

lover, as they might boast the romantic conquest of a gladiator from Vega 16?

Feeling faintly sick, Gildoran moved toward the refuge of the ship.

It's beautiful, more beautiful than anything else they'll ever build here. But it doesn't belong, and neither do I, and now I know it.

Behind him the new city was swarming with life, multiplex human, parahuman and nonhuman life, the life of a Galaxy which had achieved the Transmitter and was no longer limited anywhere by space or time. Life showed all sizes, shapes, colors, and integuments. Isolation and differences had vanished. All through history, from the first stirrings of consciousness in man and nonman, transportation—of people, of goods and services and ideas—had been the one bottleneck jamming mankind to an even rate of growth. But with the advent of the Transmitter, consciousness in the Galaxy had outstripped that limitation, and now there were no such limitations.

Or only one limitation. The speed of the Explorers.
Without us, none of this would be here.
But we're still the freaks. We live in time and distance. They live free of them.
But only because of us.

The hint of a new planet to be opened, a new world to be developed and explored, the creation of new labor markets, new projects and products, new work of every kind from running ditch-digging machines to selling women for use and pleasure, had brought them swarming here from the first minute the Transmitter booths had been hooked into the Galactic network. Right here in the city behind him there were big red men from Antares and small bluish men from Aldebaran, furred men from Corona Borealis Six and scaly men from Vega 14, and there were women to match all of them and more. Every new, just-opened world was like this. A carnival of new life for the young, of second—or third, or twenty-third—chances for the old; for the misfits, the excitement-seekers, the successes wanting new worlds to conquer and the failures who hadn't lost hope that *this* time they'd make it big.

But Gildoran walked through it, indifferent. He didn't bother looking back at the city.

There's nothing there for me now. There never was. Only Janni, and I know now she was never really there. Not for me.

He had no part in this world anymore. Once the Transmitter was set up on any world, the Explorers were finished with it. The Explorer ship which had found the world, explored it, subdued it sufficiently to build a Transmitter there, officially opened it, had nothing left to do. Nothing, that is, except to collect their tremendous fee from Head Center, and lift off to find another one. The *Gypsy Moth* had been here for a year and a half. It was time to move on.

There are other worlds out there, waiting. Plenty of them.
Yes, damn it, and women on all of them.

Someone called Gildoran by name and he looked round, seeing over the heads of the crowd the white bleached hair and starred tiaras of two of his companions from the *Gypsy Moth*. He slackened pace to let them catch up with him.

Raban was twice Gildoran's age, a man in his forties—biological time, of course, although he had probably been born several hundred years before by sidereal or objective reckoning—with the small stars on his sleeve that meant official-dom on the ship. Ramie was a small, fair girl whose great dark eyes showed that she had belonged to one of the pigmented races before the ship radiation got in its work. Now her skin and hair were lucent pale, like Gildoran's own, but the eyes retained a long, curious tilt, and her voice had a light and fluting quality.

"It won't be long now, will it?"

"About midnight," Raban said. "Sorry to leave?"

Sorry, oh God, a wrench like death, never again, never again. . . . Oh, Janni, Janni, Janni . . .

Gildoran made himself grin, although it felt stiff. "You must be kidding. It was a beautiful planet, but look what they've done to it." He gestured toward the noise, and construction scars behind them. "Like a big nasty mushroom growing up overnight."

Ramie waved at the night sky behind her. Beyond the blurring of the first vapor lights, coming on in the growing sunset, a few pale stars were visible behind the mountain.

"There are lots of other worlds out there. One

thing the Universe never runs short of is planets."
She smiled shyly at Gildoran, "Why aren't you at
the Ceremonial Leavetaking?"

"Why aren't *you?*" They all laughed. Raban
said gravely, "I've been thanking all the Gods I
ever heard of, as well as a few I made up for the
occasion, that I'm still important enough to duck
such occasions."

"I almost went," Ramie said. "After all, this
world has been home to me for a couple of years. I
grew up here, really. It ought to mean *something*
to me, even if I'm not sure *what*. And there's
something funny about realizing that we'll never
see it again—or at least anyone we've ever known
on it . . . that even if we spent six months or less
in space, and landed on another world with a
Transmitter, and came back, it would be fifty or
sixty years later planetside, and the girls I played
with would be grandmothers."

Never again. . . .

Gildoran said, low, "I know. It hit me, too."

Raban said "Planets are for leaving. For an
Explorer, anyhow. After a while—" Gildoran
sensed that he meant to comfort them, somehow,
even though his voice was hard and unemotional,
"you get so they all look the same to you."

They fell silent, crossing the great, grassy, un-
developed expanse at the foot of the mountain,
toward the ships, and Gildoran thought about
planets. Before this one, they *had* all been the
same, so maybe they would again. He'd known
four. Not counting, of course, the world where
he'd been born, though he didn't remember that

one. He knew where it was, of course, as everyone seemed to know, although it was bad form to let anyone know that you knew. When you were an Explorer, your home world was your Ship, and the planet where you had actually been birthed, or decanted, or cultured, or hatched, was something you were expected to forget.

He was Gildoran, and his world was the *Gypsy Moth*. And that was all he was. Forever. His official legal ident was G-M Gildoran, just as Raban was G-M Gilraban, and Ramie was G-M Gilramie, and his only compatriots were those bearing the G-M Gil- prefix to their names.

Because you had no other world. You could never go back to any planet, once you left it; the inexorable march of time and slippage outside the sun-systems meant that once you lifted your Ship from any planet you had ever visited, it would be generations further on, unrecognizable, by the time you landed and could visit it again.

While you were living on a planet, of course, you were free of the inexorable drag of time. You could be here today and on Vega 19 tomorrow and three hours later step into a Transmitter booth and be back here again, or on Aldebaran or Antares, and only three hours would have elapsed. (Oh, technically there was a three-quarter of a second lapse inside the booth. It had something to do with Galactic Drag.) But outside the planetary magnetic fields, the freedom from time, the simultaneous transit all over the Galaxy, was gone. You spent six weeks, six months, a year in space, aging only by your biological clock inside. Your cells aged six months, a year. But the Galaxy went on without you; all the network of planets linked by Transmitter went on slipping past, and when you landed on a planet again, by sidereal time it was eighty or a hundred years later.

So when you left, when you said goodbye to a planet it was always forever. And the new worlds might be beautiful, or terrible, but they were always new and strange; and the old worlds, if you faced the shock and went back to them, were new and strange, too. You were immortal, as far as the Galaxy was concerned, but you were always shaken loose from what you had known before. . . .

Gildoran turned to Raban and asked suddenly "Is it always like this? Is every new world spoiled—every time? Are we always just finding new worlds for people to come in and wreck them, and use them up?"

Raban laughed, but the younger two could see how grave his eyes were. He said, "Remember, they don't think of it as spoiling, but developing; civilizing. Most people like their worlds built up a little. Don't judge them."

He shook his feet fastidiously free of the mud at the base of the great ship, and said, laughing, "Maybe civilization isn't so bad. I've often wondered why we don't have them pave the approaches to the ship. After all, we've had to use this walkway for two years now, and I've wrecked my footgear every time!"

He pointed. "Look, the servicemen are clearing away the scaffolding. We'll probably be cleared by midnight. I know everyone was supposed to check in by Tenth Hour. Now they'll probably have a stack of last-minute errands for everybody."

He swung up the steps; Gildoran and Ramie followed more slowly, turning to look down at the workmen loading materials and provisions through the lower hatch ways. Small shacks, recreation units, all were being taken down and rolled away on enormous trundling cranes and machinery. Eventually, the steps themselves would go.

The girl at his side, Gildoran climbed the steps and passed into the familiar, pale-gilded, cool-lighted halls of the lower levels. They were both silent as they went along the lower corridors, stepped into a gravity-shaft and rose upward to the living levels. Raban had dropped off somewhere below, on business of his own; the younger two did not really miss him. He was older and, at least technically, still in authority over them, so that they felt freer when he had gone. But they didn't talk. Gildoran was lost in wrenching regrets and memories, and the girl was silent, too.

I wonder if everyone has something they can't bear to leave, and knows they must.

Ramie had friends here—she spoke of them— she could have had lovers.

Is it always like this? For everybody?

Nobody ever speaks of it. But it must be.

On Level Four, they paused at a desk with a chronometer behind it, and pressed their ident disks against it, watching the patterns—individual as thumbprints—flare on the telltales. A pleasant voice came from the desk:

"Ramie, you're wanted on the Bridge level, please. Gildoran, please report to the Nursery level."

"Duty tonight? We must be closer to Liftoff than I thought," Gildoran commented, and Ramie giggled. "They've reprogrammed that thing. It didn't always say *please* like that. Rushka must have had some new psych briefing." She stepped into an elevator; Gildoran took a slidewalk in the opposite direction. Damn, was he set for a spell of Nursery duty? He quailed faintly at the thought. He was fond enough of children, and the little ones growing up kept the ship from being dull in the long stretches between the stars; but he still liked them better once they were housebroken and articulate!

Still, like everyone else, he supposed he had to take his turn at it. He had a faint atavistic wish they'd leave it to the girls—at least biologically they were supposed to have an instinct for it—but he knew that notion was ridiculous, especially on Ship.

The Nursery was in what would be the maximal gravity level of the ship when they were out in space, and had the optimal conditions of light, air, decoration, and service. Gildoran paused in front of the translucent glass a moment before entering, watching a small group of three children—a nine-year-old and two five-year-olds—sitting on the floor having their supper, raptly listening to a story told by one of the huge, fuzzy brown humanoids who went, for some reason nobody on the Ships knew, by the name of Poohbears. One of the big creatures saw Gildoran through the wall, signalled for the children to go on with their meal, and waddled toward the doorway, puffing in spite of the extra oxygen rations in the Nursery level. Sinuous and free-moving in the low-gravity ship conditions of space, they were clumsy on a planet, dragging themselves along slowly.

The Poohbear said in her sweet, silvery voice "Gildoran, Rae wants you back at the Nursery office. Could you go back there directly and not disturb the children?"

"I will. Thanks, Pooh," he said with an affectionate smile. He supposed it was some sort of hereditary memory or something, but the Poohbears were everyone's perfect mother image. Maybe, he thought, it's just imprinting; after all, they're the first mothers any Explorer ever knows. They were the one race not bleached by space, and their long, dark fleece remained untouched and obstinately dark brown. On every Explorer ship, they were the specialist-experts with the babies.

In the Nursery office, Gilrae—the Biological Officer for this year—was looking through a group of records, and frowning over them. She had already discarded the planet-wear and was wearing the shipboard Explorer custume of a narrow support-band around her breasts and a narrow kilt about her hips, with thin sandals strapped low on her ankles. It was hard to tell her age, she had not changed since Gildoran could remember. She had been his first teacher when he was eight years old, but she looked little older than Ramie. Now her face was drawn and Gildoran fancied, with surprise, that she had been weeping.

Did she find something—or someone—here that she can't bear to leave?

She raised her head and said "Doran, you're back early. I thought you'd be at the Ceremonial Leavetaking."

"I intended to, but at the last moment I didn't."

She tapped the Record scanner before her. She said "We're going to be shorthanded, Doran. I just had word. Gilmarin went by Transmitter to Head Center—they sent us word of new Galactic maps—and he must have made a routing mistake; he hasn't been heard of. And Giltallen is . . ." She stopped and swallowed, hard. "He left a message. He's not coming back."

Gildoran felt an answering catch of breath.

"Tallen. How could he? He's been with us—how old is he? He's *old*——"

"It happens." Now Gildoran understood Rae's tears. In a sudden, intense surge of loyalty, he went and put his arms around the older woman. "Rae, don't cry. Maybe he'll change his mind, there are a couple of hours still——"

"He won't. He's been talking about it for years now . . . and once a planet gets hold of you . . ." Rae sobbed once, then struggled to control herself. She said steadily, "We can't judge him."

But I can. I do. I was tempted, too. But here I am . . .

Rae said, "I thought we were going to lose you, too, Gildoran."

He silently shook his head. Now that he was aboard again, now that he was among the familiar things of his life, Janni seemed a brief madness.

Different, not part of my world. . . .

"Planets are for saying goodbye," he said.

Her smile was faint and weak. "You're sure? Because I have to send you out again, everyone else is needed for last Liftoff check. Have you ever been to the Hatchery on Antares Four?"

"Are we short?"

Rae nodded, looked around to where a little girl of twelve was working at the files and said, "Gillori, I'm parched. Run out and fetch me something to drink, precious." The child ran out of the Section, and Rae said, "We're desperately short, Doran. Remember, only two of the last batch survived, and only one before that. Lori is twelve, which means she can take an apprentice position in a year, but we've had bad luck. Our crew strength is down to forty, and only four children under fifteen. And . . . you know as well as I do that some of the Elders won't be able to handle full duty shifts for a full fifteen years more. We ought to have four or five youngsters ready to take over."

Doran nodded. From his childhood he had been trained to think in terms of five-year, eight-year, ten-year voyages.

"You'll have to make the Hatchery trip."

Gildoran started with surprise. Normally only the older members of the ship's crew were sent on lengthy Transmitter errands. But Gilrae was speaking as if this were a simple one-planet hop to fetch fruits for supper.

"The *Gypsy Moth* has special Extended Credit through Head Center," she told him, "and the Antares Hatchery works with us. We ought to have at least six babies; try to get them at six weeks old and with a full month of biological mothering; and birthed, not hatched."

Gildoran gulped. He said, "How in the sixteen Galaxies do I *carry* six yowling kids through four Transmitter laps?"

Gilrae laughed. "Rent a Baby-Haul, of course. And take Ramie with you." Her face was suddenly very serious. "Doran. Get a Cleared Explorer Route from Head Center. We think Gilmarin tried to plot his own route and strayed onto one of the worlds where they still . . . don't like Explorers. Never forget; one rock thrown, six hours' delay— and you're gone. You could be a hundred years gone."

Her words sobered Gildoran like a faceful of ice-water. All his life he had known this . . . *miss a liftoff and you're gone forever.* But Gilmarin had been his playmate—picked up on the same world as Gildoran, surviving the extensive operations which allowed the Explorers to survive in space with him, his Nurserymate until they were ten, his companion ever since—and now he was gone; irrevocably gone, lost somewhere in the thousands of inhabited worlds in space. . . .

"Rae, can't we put a tracer on him, send someone out after him? Head Center could trace his Transmitter coordinates . . ."

Rae's pale, narrow face went taut. Like all Explorers she was colorless, but her eyes were large and violet, and they seemed now to fill her face. She said almost in a whisper, "We tried, Doran. No luck. We followed the coordinates for three planets and stepped into a riot on Lasselli's World. He must have walked right into the middle of it. All Gilhart and I could do was clear out. Hart applied for Lasselli's World to be blocked to Explorers, but that's like putting up a shield when the meteor shower's over." She reached for his hand. Her fingers were narrow and hard, and seemed to shake slightly. She said "You stay off

Lasselli's World, Doran. And go straight to the Hatchery and straight back. We can't lose you, too."

Gildoran felt faint and sick as he went up to the Bridge level to summon Ramie for help on this mission.

And he had actually thought of deserting his people, when they were so shorthanded?

When Gilmarin was gone, and Giltallen deserted?

Dismay struggled with anger in him.

They hate us on some worlds, just because we used to take their unwanted—their surplus children. We can't have children of our own. We're sterile from space; we'd breed monsters. Without replacements from the planets we open, we'd have to stop traveling between the stars. . . .

And then no more worlds opened. Not ever.

And mankind needs a frontier. Without it, even if the known worlds span a Galaxy, mankind psychologically stagnates and goes mad. It was that knowledge that pushed man into space from Old Earth, thousands of years ago. It was that knowledge that lifted him from the swarming, dying, starving, crowded worlds of the First System, pushed him into interstellar space in the days of the old Generation Ships before the Einstein Drives, kept him expanding, going outward. It was what drove mankind to invent the transmitter; that desperate need for a frontier, to know that they were still able to move onward.

But no one could go to a new world by Transmitter until the Transmitter was first set up there. There was no way to Transmit a Transmitter. Once the *first* Transmitter was established on a planet, anything could be brought through: people, supplies, building materials, anything from any other world which already had a Transmitter on it.

But new worlds still had to be found.

And the Explorers found them. Only the Explorers still traveled between the stars, at the Einstein-Drive speeds which telescoped time for them, and set up new Transmitters for the endless outward expansion of the human race.

And because we used to have to steal children, they hate us.

We have to steal them, beg them, or buy them.

And when they go with us, they're gone forever.

FOREVER.

He stepped off the elevator at the Bridge level. On the Bridge, half a dozen crew members were working around the computers; Gildoran gave his message and the Year-Captain, Gilharrad (who was so old that even Gildoran could not imagine how many years it would be in planetary time) dismissed Ramie to accompany him. His eyes, almost lost in crinkles, reached into unguessable gulfs of memory.

"I was nearly killed once on a child-stealing expedition when I was your age," he said, holding out a withered hand that trembled faintly, "Look, I lost this finger from a knife-thrust, and that was so long ago, planet-time, that they didn't even have regeneration to regrow one for me. We took nineteen babies on that raid, hit three worlds. Of course, that was back when eight out of ten died in the first liftoff and one out of thirty lived more than a month, we didn't even name them until we were sure they'd make it. People haven't changed much, though. They'd still like to kill us, most worlds, if we ask for their children. Even the extra children, the ones they don't want. We're only a legend, on most worlds. But a legend they hate." He fell silent, his old eyes sliding away into the remoteness again. Gildoran, feeling an obscure urge to comfort the ancient, said, "We're dealing with licensed Hatcheries this time. We can simply buy what we need, from people who have a right to sell."

Harrad said, with dim bitterness, "Slavery too. Wait and see. On that one world they may be going through a period of enlightenment—or cynicism. Go back there next time we land—sixty, eighty years planet-time—and I'll bet you a planet-sized fee that they've got it written in their license: *No selling to Explorers.*" He made a feeble movement toward the door. "Better get going, you two. You probably have to take the long way round, and we lift at midnight."

II

Gildoran and Gilramie emerged at the top of the steps, now wrapped in the all-purpose Travel Cloaks. Standards of decency in clothing varied from world to world, so that every psychological type could find a world where they felt comfortable. On some planets nakedness was the norm and clothing considered vaguely insulting, as if you wanted to hide yourself; on others, it was believed that too much bodily exposure blunted sexual drives, destroyed pleasure, so that concealment while you went about your day's work sharpened the impact of exposure in intimate conditions. But the Travel Cloaks were accepted everywhere as the sign that people were in transit and not deliberately flouting local custom.

As they made their way toward the tall, dark pylons of the Transmitter Station, Gildoran glanced at the rawbeamed city. Was Janni still there? It did not matter to him now; their parting had been too final for him to cherish any hopes of a reunion. Anyhow, by now she could be fourteen planets away, or at the other end of the Galaxy. With infinite transit, available to all, only desire could keep lovers together; and for Janni this had failed. Gildoran relentlessly turned his back on the city and his attention back to Ramie, small and smiling at his side.

"Did Rae say whether we should get males or females, Doran?"

"What difference does it make?" Gildoran smiled down at her. "It's chance anyhow." Aboard the Explorer ships, both sexes took their turns at all tasks, from Navigation to Nursery, and besides, you could never tell how many would survive. Gildoran and Gilmarin had been part of a lot of seven, four girls and three boys; two boys survived. They would probably take three boys and three girls. If they were fortunate, two of each would survive the first month in space; statistically, survival rates were now at two out of three. But statistics didn't always work. Twelve years from now, the survivors would be apprentices in every field aboard the Ships. Whatever they were, boy or girl, they would be Explorers.

The two Explorers, tall and pale, shrouded in their Travel Cloaks, passed under the archways of the Transmitter Station. This late in the evening, the crowds had lessened somewhat; at the edge of each booth the lines were shorter than usual. A few merry couples with the look of dissipation, on their way to—or from—an evening of pleasure somewhere. A solitary Drifter or two, emerging for a look at the planet, with the usual look of bewilderment—Drifters took the dangerous route of punching coordinates at random for the thrill of reaching unknown worlds. A group of youngsters, looking sleepy, arriving for a guided tour under the chaperonage of two tall green-skinned governesses; probably a group of young adventurers bound for a survival-skills course on this new world.

Gildoran stopped at an information booth and laid his ident disk against the routing plate, punching a request for Routing Services. After the expected three-quarter-second lag, a disembodied voice demanded in Universal: "Nature of routing request, please."

"A cleared route for Explorers to Antares Four, please."

Again the lag. Then the computer began to chatter out the required information, sets of Transmitter coordinates. Gildoran put a small coin in the slot—information was free, but a printout of the information cost a small fee—he didn't care to take the chance of forgetting a vital factor in the coordinates and arriving on a planet six hundred light-years from his destination!

They stepped inside the glassed-in and green-lighted Transmitter booth, seeing without much attention the rules printed in the two official languages of the Galactic civilization:

STAND FIRMLY ON PLATE

REMEMBER TO RECLAIM YOUR IDENT DISK WHEN LEAVING

BABIES UNDER ONE YEAR OF AGE AND UN-TRAINED ANIMALS MUST BE TRANS-MITTED INSIDE APPROVED SKINNER BOXES

ELDERLY OR FEEBLE PERSONS SHOULD HAVE A LIFE/SUPPORT HANDY FOR BOOSTING UNFAMILIAR OXYGEN LEVELS

NO MORE THAN THREE ADULT BEINGS MAY BE TRANSMITTED IN ANY ONE BOOTH

THIS BOOTH FOR PASSENGER TRAVEL ONLY. FOR TRANSPORT OF FREIGHT CARGO, OR HOUSEHOLD POSSESSIONS WEIGHING OVER APPROVED ALLOT-MENT OF EIGHTY UNIVERSAL KILOS, USE BOOTHS AT FAR END OF STATION

ATOMIC DEVICES MAY BE TRANSPORTED ONLY WITH SPECIAL PERMIT FROM PLANET OF DESTINATION

He touched the buttons carefully for the first set of Coordinates. A warning light glowed, and the booth went dark for an instant.

Every time he used the Transmitter, Gildoran was briefly conscious of extended space. He had wondered, now and then, if it had anything to do with the mental disciplines of the Explorers or his familiarity with the sensation of time-dilation inside the Ships; or if it were hallucination, imagination, or a freak stimulation of brain cells from the Transmitter. After all, the Transmitters fed on energy drawn from the very fabric of space itself, the drifting matter free between Solar systems. He did not know what caused it; he did not know if other Explorers felt it, or if indeed it was common to everyone who used the Transmitter. He only knew that always, in that moment when the booth went dark, that instant of lag which prevented exact simultaneity. . . .

The booth went dark. A sharp dizziness stung the roots of his nose, a tracery of colors flared in his brain, a retinal swirl of brilliance behind his eyes not too unlike the side-effect of drugs which kept them all sane during time-dilation; and again the strange sense of standing among swirling atoms—or galaxies. . . .

A sharp snap like a brief, not unpleasant electric shock; then he came to rest (had he moved at all?) knowing that three-quarters of a second had passed and he stood in another Transmitter booth with the identical admonitions facing him, this time in electric-blue neon lights, and now the walls were glassy-green rather than glassy-blue, and he was four light-years away from the planet he had just left. He shook his head slightly, glanced at Gilramie—did she look a little dizzy, too?—and consulted the printout for the next set of coordinates on their route. Strictly speaking, the Transmitter had no limit; but it was more pleasant for most people not to jump more than four light-years in one Transmission, and the power-consumption, for some unknown reason, went up exponentially beyond that level; so that jumps much longer than that were not recommended except for the highest-priority personnel. Too long a jump seemed, for some psychological reason no one had ever figured out, to have an effect not unlike that of too-fast jet travel. Therefore, long trips were routed into short steps of four light-years at a time, where possible. Possibly, Gildoran thought, the human mind can't really absorb the idea of jumping much more than four light-years at a time.

Four more jumps, with brief swirls of darkness between them, and they reached the planet of Antares Four where the Hatchery was located. A map of the planet, and a jump by short-range Transmitter, brought them within a few streets of it.

It was a large glass-and-metal building, with streaming advertisers floating on the air around it, and solidographs of what seemed like hundreds of chubby smiling babies of every size, color and human phenotype. Ramie smiled at the insubstantial infants and said, "I wonder if they're all as cute as this. Don't they have any homely or cranky or bawling ones?"

Gildoran chuckled. "Certainly not on the advertising posters."

A featureless servomech beckoned them in and said in a gentle, cultured voice, "Welcome, gentlebeings and prospective parents. Will you please wait in this area, and one of our salesbeings will be with you in a brief time. Meanwhile, we invite you to look at the literature describing our newest service." The servo's flexible metal arms thrust some leaflets at them, and it glided away. Gildoran glanced at one:

NOW, your favorite HATCHERY offers a NEW SERVICE! Are you tired of waiting six months for a baby to your order? Women, you now can escape nine months of missed pleasures, troublesome births, suicidal and dangerous postpartum depressions! You've decided you'd rather not adopt, so what to do? NOW, you can stop by for a simple painless visit, leave your one- to four-week fertilized fetus with us, and for a modest fee, you can be guaranteed absolutely against fetal insult, birth defects or deformities; if, for any reason your baby isn't absolutely perfect, we hatch you another one FREE!

Smaller lettering read:

DNA surgery, guaranteed talents, or sex preference at a small additional fee. Ask us about bargains in unclaimed or rejected hatches.

Ramie was looking through an identical leaflet. "This isn't any good to us. We need them birthed, not hatched, and with a full month of biological mothering."

Gildoran nodded. "Rae gave me the specifications. Ramie, ask about musical talent. If Tallen really has gone. . . ." He didn't finish; he didn't have to. Giltallen had been the best musician aboard *Gypsy Moth*—Rae herself excepted. He looked around the waiting room, also filled with advertising solidos, drifting through the air, of chubby smiling infants.

A thick-set, fussy small man bustled in. "Well, well, prospective parents, what can we do for you today—oh, Explorers. I suppose you'll be wanting a quantity?"

Gildoran put his question about musical talent, and the small man's face lighted up.

"Why, as it happens, I have just the one you want. The mother was a top-grade harpist, who paid for study on Capella Nine with Ligettini himself by having five children for me—one every year. She'd study all year, come here and birth them, give them the full month of biological mothering—these are absolutely top-grade merchandise—get impregnated again with sperm from top-level musical geniuses, each with a pre-potency factor of nine, and go off to study again during her pregnancy. All of them but this one were pre-sold, some of them ordered four years in advance. But the last couple had their hearts set on a girl, and she birthed a boy, and they're from one of those religious-fanatic planets which prohibit sex-change operations. Heartbreaking, really, but I can make you this absolutely splendid offer . . ." He mentioned a sum in stellars which struck Gildoran as not too exorbitant. He glanced at Ramie.

"Let's take that one," she said. "It would please Rae so much."

The little man riffled through a folder, and his face fell. "Sorry, gentlebeings," he said ruefully, "there's a hold on that one. To be sold only to a stable couple—no entertainment-mongers, pleasure worlds or—I'm sorry—Explorer Ships. But look here, you people from the Ships want quantity. I can give you a wonderful buy on ten cloned High-IQ Hatches. Quality absolutely guaranteed—we aren't one of those places which sell off our dud merchandise to you people just because we know you can't come back and complain about them!"

Gildoran felt faintly sickened. *Merchandise!* And did they want cloned identicals, even High-IQ? He didn't think so. The interpersonal relationships aboard ship were loosely polarized, often shifting; identicals—ten of them, horrors!—might form a clique of their own, or worse, be so much alike in personality that they would be too uninteresting. Imagine having ten of the same person, making up one-fifth of the crew? Suppose they grew up with some unlikable personality trait!

"No, thanks," he said, groped for an excuse, and hit quickly upon a true one. "We need them birthed, not hatched. And individuals, not clones."

"Oh, come now," said the little man deprecatingly, "don't tell me you people, with your scientific disciplines, have that old superstition that birthed babies are better than hatched ones?"

"For our purpose they *are* better," Gilramie said in her soft voice. "Somehow the experience of full-pregnancy closeness and the month of biological mothering gives them a better ability for imprinting and forming interpersonal relations. And this also adds to their will to live; hatched babies tend to die quickly in space because they don't immediately form an attachment with a mother figure and have less desire to survive."

"Well, you know your own business best, I suppose," the little man said. "Why don't you stroll through the warehouse and look around while I wait on someone else? This one will be quick—I've waited on her before—and maybe you'll see something that takes your fancy."

He opened the door to an enormous room, stretching into the distance, filled with boxes of one-way glass; the modern version of the "Skinner Box" which kept an infant dry, fed, and entertained without human intervention for up to twenty hours at a time. The room was filled with the soft thumping heartbeat-sound which was known to keep infants content. Behind the glass walls babies gurgled, kicked, crawled, howled, or suckled. They seemed happy, although Gildoran wondered if they could really be happy as the babies aboard *Gypsy Moth* were happy, continually mothered and tended by the Poohbears.

"Specifications on the front of each box," the salesman said. "I'll be with you in a minute or two—this will be quick."

He went off to an enormously tall, sallow, but somehow enticing woman, wrapped in a Travel Cloak but with lovely streaming hair and a walk Gildoran could not take his eyes off.

"Yes, Gentlebeing?"

The woman's voice, very sweet and exquisitely trained, reached them from a distance.

"I need six prime females with empath potential and musical talent, high sexuality potential. These are to be trained as top-level pleasure-girls, so make certain they are pretty ones."

The salesman scurried around, making up an order form, while Gildoran struggled against his initial revulsion, *Slavery!* And yet . . . these "prime females" would be pampered all their lives, beautiful and happy. . . .

The salesman was trying to push up the sale:

"Throw in a fine bargain on some distress

merchandise—unclaimed hatches, wonderful
condition but they're already six months old, so
they're past imprinting. But they'll make fine
manual workers or servants—all healthy and
guaranteed good-natured—no genetic defects!
Take 'em off my hands at a flat two thousand
stellars for the three!''

When the salesperson came back, Gildoran and
Ramie had chosen six from the specifications on
the boxes; all were guaranteed high-IQ, with
mathematical and mechanical ability, two were
from families of surgeons on either side, and two
were of hereditary lines with musical talent.
Phenotype or skin color didn't matter of course;
after two years, they'd be Explorers anyway. Hard
radiation at faster-than-light speed would take
care of that.

He watched the servos piling the infants bound
for the pleasure-world into a tall, wheeled structure which looked like a stack of small Skinner
Boxes piled on top of one another; a standard
Baby-Haul for taking infants through the Transmitter. He asked abruptly, "How can you have the
heart to sell them into what amounts to a life of
prostitution?''

The little man shrugged. He said, "On some
worlds, robots are banned, just for that—to make
room for people to earn a living by manual labor.
What the hell—some places won't sell to you because you and I know that about one-third of them
will die. Me, I sell them for anything except
food—I do draw the line at that. A few exclusive
places cater to the carriage trade—''

"What's that?''

"Sorry. Old salesbeing term—I think a carriage
was some kind of luxury-class Transmitter in the

early days. It means, sell only to luxury trade, all singletons, all for sale to families only. But me, I sell 'em to anyone who can pay for 'em, and I ask no questions. And it's a good thing, too—after all, where else would *you* people get babies if we were all that discriminating?"

A legend. But a legend they hate.

The little salesman had gotten himself wound up now.

"After all, there are billions too many babies—most of them we pick up cheap on worlds with a population problem and some freak religion that won't let them solve it—freaky worlds where abortion's illegal or worlds with fertility cults. Better than shipping them off wholesale for slave labor."

"I guess so," Gildoran said apologetically. "Here, I think we want these six." He had noted down the numbers of their display box. "And we'll need to rent a Baby-Haul; we can ship it back in less than an hour, after they're loaded."

He stood watching the servos load the babies. There was one, with dark tilted eyes like Ramie's and soft golden skin, that he wished he could pick up and cuddle. Ramie, too, was watching intently. He looked questioningly at her and she murmured, "Oh, nothing. I was just wondering what it would be like to birth my own—"

"Messy, I would think, and it would interfere with ship routine," Gildoran said, deliberately making a joke of it.

Some questions you never asked. Ramie would learn. . . .

While Ramie arranged for rental of the Baby-Haul and servos to tend it for the long and complex route through the Transmitter, back to the world of their departure, Gildoran accompanied the sales being to a public Computer Station, where he arranged for transfer of credits from Head Center to the Hatchery. Briefly he contemplated stopping somewhere for a last planet-side meal before they returned to the ship. No; they had a longish trip by Transmitter before them—at least three-quarters-of-an-hour, with the necessary hunt for booths large enough to handle a six-baby hauling unit—and the sooner the babies were loaded onto the *Gypsy Moth*, the sooner their troubles would be over.

He had already begun congratulating himself on a successful mission. With the aid of the servos, who were rented ready-programmed, it was easy to find freight-size Transmitter booths. He verified a cleared return route at the Information booth and watched the servos wheel the Baby-Haul inside. He and Ramie stood on either side of the tall nest of opaque boxes, which of course had their own air-systems and optimal temperature inside.

He hoped the little golden-skinned girl with the sleek dark hair and slanted dark eyes would live. It would be fun to see her grow up. You didn't dare get attached to them until you were sure they'd live. . . .

The booth darkened; the disorientation and brilliant swirls of retinal circus—atoms? Star-Galaxies?—raced through his brain. *Snap!* They were in the Transmitter booth. His fingers sought out the coordinates of the second jump, but he found himself wondering how the babies experience Transmitter travel. Did they cry or feel shock or fear at the sudden darkening? Was there a sense of telescoped time?

Does a baby experience time at all, I wonder? Or only his own biological rhythms?

He touched the coordinates; again the darkness, the swirling colors, the snap. He thought, I'll have to check, find out if others—Ramie, Harrad, Rae—if they sense this in the Transmitter.

It had never occurred to him to ask Janni.

And yet—we were so close, for a little while. But we had other things to ask each other.

The third jump; the third darkness-swirl-snap gestalt. And it struck him then, with a sense of irrevocable loss, that now he would never be able to ask Gilmarin—his playmate, the lost, the vanished—about this. NEVER. That word again. Gilmarin, his nurserymate-brother-playmate, that he would never be able to find out whether Gilmarin shared this individual disorientation in the Transmitter, suddenly it struck him as greater tragedy than the now-very-small loss of Janni.

Janni and I shared—a planet. Gilmarin and I shared a life, and I've lost them both. When Janni left me, I felt as if I'd lost something wonderful, and I had; my dreams about her.
But with Gilmarin, I lost a piece of myself,

wandering forever, as he is lost and wandering somewhere in a thousand thousand other worlds where I can never go. . . .

"Doran . . ." Ramie's light voice wavered and sounded frightened, "Are you sure the coordinates were right? Something seems to be wrong."

Snapping sharply to full attention, Gildoran checked the coordinates of the booth; an override light was blinking, and the coordinates on the telltale did not match those on the printout in his hand. He touched the proper set of coordinates again, spelling them out firmly with his fingers and verifying them again on the visual telltale before pressing the ACTIVATE button. . . . one of the many fail-safe devices which the Transmitter provided to keep careless travelers from pressing non-existent coordinates to materialize in an unknown destination. The booth did not activate, and the light began to blink and spell out words above them;

FOR REASONS OF EXTRA-HEAVY TRAFFIC PATTERNS, ALL TRAVELERS IN THIS SECTOR ARE BEING REROUTED TO DESTINATIONS ELSEWHERE ON THEIR ULTIMATE ROUTE. PLEASE CHECK WITH THE PUBLIC INFORMATION BOOTH AT THE FAR END OF THE STATION FOR A FREE REROUTING PRINTOUT. WE APOLOGIZE FOR THE INCONVENIENCE AND REASSURE ALL TRAVELERS THAT THOSE ARRIVING UNREQUESTED ON THIS WORLD NEED NOT CHECK FOR CONTRABAND: REPEAT, ALL CONTRABAND REGULATIONS HAVE BEEN TEMPORARILY SUSPENDED FOR THE DU-

RATION OF THE TRAVEL EMERGENCY
PROVIDED THAT TRAVELERS DEPART
WITHIN ONE PLANETARY HOUR OF AR-
RIVAL.

Gildoran muttered an archaic vulgarism.
"That's all we need."

Ramie asked, "What's contraband?"

"This must be one of the freaky planets—the
ones that prohibit importation of servos or slaves
or drugs or fissionables. Contraband means a substance prohibited by law on this special planet.
But relax; it doesn't apply to us anyhow because
we're in transit and we arrived here without in-
tending to. We'll have to go and get the rerouting
printout."

They stepped out of the booth, Gildoran bending down to peer through the window of the
Baby-Haul. The translucent windows showed
only that two were asleep, the others moving
around; the soundproof box made it impossible to
tell whether they were crying or not, but Gildoran
knew that if they were hungry they would be
fed, and that they would be kept amused if awake,
so there was no need to worry about them for a
while, at least. He looked around, orienting himself in the Transmitter station; they were all laid
out to a standard pattern (this was so that the
traveler could find food, clothing, or bathrooms,
information or service with a minimum of trouble.

"What planet are we on?" Gilramie asked.

Gildoran shrugged. "How in time should I
know? Somewhere between Antares Four and the
planet where we left *Gypsy Moth*, obviously,
which cuts it down to a couple of hundred. Stay

here by the booth, Ramie. There's no point in moving the Baby-Haul through the whole station."

She looked uneasily at the crowd. She said "Gildoran, I don't like it here much. Maybe it's just that stuff about contraband, but it evidently isn't a very free place. Can't we jump straight to the *Gypsy Moth*? I know those coordinates by heart, and so do you. Would it really hurt the babies to do it?"

"I don't know. Probably not, but I just don't know," Gildoran said. "The risk is supposed to be psychological, and as far as I know, nobody ever studied the effects of long jumps on babies. Just the same, it's likely to be an awfully unpleasant experience. I made a twenty-light-year-jump once, and it wasn't any fun. I was dizzy for an hour afterward, and I could hardly see. Why give the poor brats traumas before we've had them half an hour? It won't take three minutes to get the rerouting."

"Well, all right . . . " she said uncertainly. He walked away toward the far end of the station, through a half-seen crowd of people.

They edged back. They always did. He would have noticed only if they hadn't. . . . You never looked at the crowds and the stares; you learned early never to take any notice . . .

"Dirty baby-stealer!" somebody yelled, "Hey, look, another one! They got their nerve!"

"LET'S GET THEM!"
Gildoran, jerked out of his habitual arrogant

lack-of-notice, looked round him like a trapped animal. Someone jostled him; someone kicked; he was surrounded by a crowd pushing in, fighting. . . .

He bellowed, in the ship-language of the Explorers no one could understand, "Ramie! Take the kids and jump! Get back to the *Gypsy Moth*— all the way— FAST!" He turned, by instinct leading them away from her . . . they hadn't seen her yet. His arm shot out; he kicked a man on the kneecap and the man howled and fell at his feet. He butted through the crowd; cast one swift look back. Ramie and the Baby-Haul were gone.

Something snapped into awareness in his brain. *Lasselli's World!* Just a set of coordinates on a Transmitter route-map, but he knew enough to stay away from it—that was what had been wrong. Gilmarin would never have gone there knowingly, but the random bad luck of a computer re-routing traffic pattern had sent him there, just as it had sent himself and Ramie. . . .

Well, the babies and Ramie were safely away, vanished into the booth; light-years away by now. He kicked, elbowed, butted through the crowd, fighting his way through a volley of blows and curses, struggling to stay on his feet. If he went down he was done for, he'd be trampled. . . .

"Kill the dirty Explorer! He won't steal any more babies here and kill them on his ships!"

"Get back!" There was the crackle of a heat-gun. Gildoran felt the crowd subside, draw away; leaving him standing in a cleared space before a dark-skinned youth in some kind of uniform with epaulets, and a baldric with an unknown emblem. He held the drawn heat-gun in his hand and the menace was obvious. The mob, thwarted, muttered and pushed; but it let the dark youngster through to Gildoran.

The stranger said in Universal, "Come with me, Explorer. We'll handle this legally." His voice crackled at the crowd like the snap and zip of his weapon, "Get away from him! I'll handle this!"

Gildoran drew himself up and managed to summon some remnants of his habitual arrogance, although he realized that his clothing was ripped and torn, his face bleeding from a blow. He said to the dark young man, "I protest. You have no authority over me. I was rerouted here by computer override, and all contraband regulations are legally suspended. I demand an immediate appeal to Head Center."

"You aren't going to demand anything," the stranger said tonelessly. "Come with me."

"You have no authority——"

"This is my authority," said the youth, making a minute gesture with the heat-gun. "I'd rather not use it here. Come with me." He said in an undertone, between clenched teeth, "Damn it, man, come on, I can't hold them long—do you want to be lynched? They killed one of you here today!"

Gildoran went, hearing the mutter of the crowd rising and knowing what the young stranger said was true. Gilmarin! Had he died here? Gildoran felt a sob strangling in his throat and set his mouth hard. Die like an Explorer. Marin would have done just that. He could, too, if he had to. He held his head high as they walked outside the station.

They stepped into the blinding light of a double bluewhite sun; Gildoran squeezed his eyes shut, looking through squinched lids at his captor. The strange uniformed man was more than a full head shorter than he, narrowly bearded, but looking no older than Gildoran himself; skin and hair were shiny black, but his eyes were a warm, lustrous animal brown. He let the heat gun drop slightly and said "I thought I'd never get you out of there. Why did you try to fight me? You're safer in custody than with a mob. I'm not going to hurt you." His thick lips parted in a grin. "I've got no authority to. My job is shooting escaped snakes from the forest preserve—that's where I got the uniform and the weapon—fortunately that mob hasn't realized it yet. Lucky I was in the station. Did you come here to rescue that poor devil they got today?"

Gildoran shook his head, and his face must have shown something, for the man said compassionately, "Friend of yours?"

"Shipmate. Best friend," Gildoran said briefly.

Anyway, Ramie had gotten away with the babies; even if he was lost, the ship wouldn't be dangerously short handed.

He said, summoning all his authority, speaking as he did from the Navigation post on the bridge of the *Gypsy Moth,* "I'm grateful to you for getting me away from that lynch mob. But now I really must insist that you get me through to Head Center without delay. I must rejoin my ship at once."

Even if they don't kill me . . . delay me four hours, and I'm dead to the only world that matters. . . .

The young man looked concerned. He slipped his weapon into its holster and said, "That's right—you Explorers can never dare miss a ship, can you? I've read everything I can find about you. I. . . I'm interested. Look, we mustn't stay here. If anyone in the mob steps out and finds us chatting like old cronies I'll just be lynched alongside you, and my heat-gun won't really do all that much good—there isn't even a lethal setting for humans on it. Come on—hurry!"

He drew him along quickly, through a winding side street, and Gildoran went for a moment without protesting, but then dug in his heels.

"No! I can't risk losing myself here, losing sight of the Transmitter on a strange world—"

"You've got to trust me," the youngster implored and drew him into the lee of a wall.

"Look here, you evidently don't understand the political situation here on Lasselli's World, and I haven't the time to explain. Let it go at this: if you went in to the formal authorities and asked to be put through to Head Center, you'd never make it. And they'll be expecting you to try and sneak back to that Transmitter station—I'd bet you a hundred stellars, if I had them, that there's someone from that mob watching every door, ready to raise a riot. There's a gang here trying to control Transmitter travel—yes, I know that Head Center has ruled that illegal, but we're a long way from Head Center. The facts of the matter are that with the Transmitter, anyone who doesn't like a given political regime can step into a Transmitter and be at the other end of the Galaxy in a few minutes, so local citizens are subject to spot-checks and searches at the main Transmitter stations, and offworlders tend to be hustled and rousted so they won't talk to our people and make them discontented. And unhappy people need something to hate—right now, you're *it*."

Gildoran said, "So what do I do?"

The man said, "I have an idea. It won't be easy, but we may be able to manage it. My name's Merrik, by the way; what's yours?"

"Gildoran of the *Gypsy Moth*."

"Well, Gildoran, they'll be expecting you to react just as you did—afraid to get far away from the Transmitter station, afraid to risk getting lost, so they'll be waiting, thinking you'll risk anything to try to slip back in, maybe in disguise. The one thing they *won't* expect is that you'll be able to get to another Transmitter station, maybe fifty kilos away. Oh, they may keep a half an eye on public transit, but they won't expect you to have help. Maybe we can fool them. How much time do you actually have? It isn't a matter of minutes, is it?"

Gildoran checked the chronometer on his wrist, which registered time on the *Gypsy Moth's* planet, whatever local time might be. He felt queer to realize that it was, to him, early evening, while here it was obviously only half-way through the morning. "No, I have about three planetary hours, objective time."

Merrik let out a breath of relief. "Oh, well. That's easily managed. Here, come through this back alley, I'll get you to my apartment. We've got to do something about your skin and hair before you try going out on any public street."

Gildoran, stunned and relieved, followed him. Inside a small lift to Merrik's rooms in a rabbit-warren of a building, he said, "Why are you doing this?"

Merrik shrugged, a little sheepishly. He said, "I'm interested in the Explorers. Fascinated by them. Sometimes I think you're the only real adventurers left. The idea of standing wholly free of time as you do. . . ."

Gildoran blinked; that was a strange viewpoint on it, whereas he thought of earthworms, planet-dwellers, as living outside the drag of time as he did, going from star to star in the blink of an eye—literally—while the Explorers crawled between stars by the Einstein Drive. He tried to say something of this; Merrik, opening the lift door with a cautious look down the hall and hurrying Gildoran inside, said "But think of it this way. We live our whole biological lifespan inside absolute, objective time. I was born nineteen years ago, and eighty-some years from now I'll die, having lived the fivescore years man's expected to live. And I have no idea, except from my reading and study, what the Universe was like a hundred years before I was born, and I'll never—never—never know what the Universe will be five hundred years from now. But you were born maybe five hundred years ago; you lived in a time that's only history to me, and your lifespan can go thousands of years into the future, in that same fivescore allotted years of man!"

Gildoran had never thought of it like this. Merrik was rummaging behind panels, pulling out some garments. "You're too tall to wear breeches, but I have a Travel Cloak that I bought on Rigel III, just swap it for yours. Here, this will handle the skin and hair." He sat Gildoran on a low seat and began rubbing him efficiently with a greenish paste which, surprisingly, dried purplish-black on his skin. He sprayed his hair with some stuff from an aerosol globe.

"Now you just look like a slightly oversized Lasselli. Here, rub it into your hands, up to the elbows, and your feet up to the knees. The cloak will cover up the rest. What race are your people originally, what world did the Explorers come from?"

Gildoran looked at him in surprise. He thought everyone knew. "All worlds," he said. "We have men from everywhere, and women, too."

"You're joking, surely? You all have the same coloring, the same physique——"

"Radiation in space does that, and low-grav conditions on the Ships. I might have been as black as you when I was a baby."

Merrik grinned uneasily. He said, "Trying to tell me we're brothers under the skin? Well, we look it now, all right, except that your eyes are blue. So it's radiation, eh? But doesn't it affect your children? Or is it a mutation that breeds true?"

Gildoran said in astonishment, "But we can't have children; the Explorers are all sterile. Man, why do you think we buy them, and used to steal them sometimes?"

Merrik was open-mouthed. "But no one seems to know that—most people think it's for some religious rite——"

"No," Gildoran said impatiently, "they simply become . . . our children. The only children we

have. We were bringing six from a hatchery, my
friend and I. One of them might be our Captain
thirty years from now."

Merrik looked at him in deep sympathy. "Why
don't you tell people?"

"We've told them," Gildoran said wearily,
"told them and told them. But we can't tell a
thousand thousand worlds with a million people
on each, and evidently legends are more durable
than facts."

"We have a saying," Merrik said "Truth crawls
at light-speed; lies travel by Transmitter." He
smiled and stood up. "Let me pour you a drink,
my friend. And then, speaking of speed, we'd
better make some. I have a surface-sled, a small
airfoil; it belongs to my sister, but she's off-planet
on her honeymoon and left it for me to use. I can
get you to the Transmitter station fifty kilos away.
They'll never look for you there—and if they do
look for you, they'll never know you. I doubt if
your own mother would—no, you don't have
mothers, then? Your own shipmates won't know
you. In fact, with you disguised like this, you
could probably walk right back into the Transmitter station we left, but they just *might* be on the
alert there for an extra-tall man."

Gildoran drank down the tingling liquid Merrik
poured; it left him feeling vaguely euphoric and
refreshed. They went down by lift to the garage
where Merrik's surface vehicle was parked. The
garage held a stray dozen men and women, but
none of them gave Gildoran more than an offhand
glance; he clutched his cloak tightly round him
lest it blow aside and reveal undyed skin. Merrik
helped him strap into the seat of the airfoil car and

they were off, skimming low above the surface of the planet.

Surface travel was something almost new to Gildoran. He sat back, feeling the wind blow through his hair and against his face, slitting his eyes against the blinding brilliance of the double sun. The sky was brilliant white, with clouds almost electric-blue.

Such a beautiful world to hold such ugliness.
And such kindness.

To Gildoran, Merrik's voice sounded a little wistful. "This is the closest I'll ever come to space travel. When humanity got the Transmitter, we gained the ability to travel between stars, but we lost the stars themselves. Sometimes I dream about them—about the stars."

"You have the freedom of a thousand thousand planets, Merrik. Each time I leave one, I can never go back."

"But they're all . . . *planets*," Merrik half-whispered, and his eyes were full of longing. "Space is gone. No one but you Explorers have it now."

They brought the airfoil to rest in front of another Transmitter station. This one was almost unoccupied; they walked in with no one taking the slightest notice of Gildoran with his darkened skin and long cloak. Gildoran went toward a booth. He said "I'll jump straight through to the *Gypsy Moth*. Merrik—how can I ever thank you?" He took the young man's hands in his own.

On this world he had lost a friend. On this

world he had found a friend, and now would lose him, too. . . .

Merrik said "Let me go with you. I'd like to see one of your ships. Up close."

Gildoran put a hand on his shoulder. "Come along then."

Inside the booth he punched the familiar coordinates and braced himself for the long jump.

Darkness. A swirl of dizzying lights, like the drift of stars in space . . . strange pain at the root of his nose and in his ears . . . spinning galaxies, disoriented, whirling . . .

Snap!

With relief, he saw that they were back on the familiar world of the *Gypsy Moth*. Merrik was standing beside him, still looking dazed. He said, "That's the longest jump I ever made, in one leap."

Gildoran's head hurt. He said, "I'm sorry, really. But I don't have a lot of time to spare, and my . . . my shipmates will be worrying about me."

Rae. She must be in a real panic, Marin gone, Tallen deserted. Gods grant Ramie's back safely with the children.

He drew Merrik along, saying, "I've time to let you have a look at the Ship, though. It's the least I can do."

The guard at the gate, a middle-aged Explorer with a kind, lined face, stopped them as they came toward it, saying "Sorry. Too near takeoff time.

Only Ship's personnel now, boys; no more tourists."

"Gilroth, don't you know me?" Gildoran laughed, held up his ident disk, pulled off the Travel Cloak.

Roth clutched Gildoran into a smothering bear hug.

"Doran," he gulped, "Doran, you made it, Harrad and Rae are frantic, it was all we could do to keep them from going out after you, and it's getting so late, so late. . . ."

"I ran into a spot of trouble," Gildoran said, carefully casual. "Ramie made it back all right with the kids?"

"Oh, yes; poor child, she hasn't stopped crying since, but the babies are all on board, probably already tucked into the Poohbears' pockets for Liftoff." The pouches of the huge marsupial humanoids had been found to be safer during takeoff than any artificial-womb or life-support system for infants under three months old. Roth added "Better get aboard—tell Rae and the rest that you're all right. And don't forget to check in at the Nursery, either!"

"Just a minute. Merrik helped me escape—I'd never be here without him. I promised him a quick look inside."

"All right, but be quick, and do check with the Bridge right away," Roth said. "And have your friend out again in ten minutes—the steps are going to be cleared away."

Gildoran escorted Merrik up the steps. He shook his still-aching head, and Merrik, watching his face, said, "You too?" After a minute, he said, "Sometimes, when I make a long jump, it seems that what I see—behind my eyes—must be like what I would see from space. Could it be that we really *do*, somehow, go through all that space, without being aware of it?"

"I don't know. I'm not sure about the meaning of space and time anymore," Gildoran said honestly. He laid his ident disk against the telltale. The pleasant computer voice said, "You are late in reporting, Gildoran, please check at once with Rae at the Nursery level. I have been asked to inform you that Gilramie has already gone to her post on the Bridge. I am also requested to remind the stranger present with you that exactly nine minutes and eighteen seconds remain before ship-sealing."

Gildoran said "I'll give you a quick look at the Bridge." He stood quiet while the lift carried them up, slid open; quiet while Merrik looked, with longing eyes, at the bewildering controls and instruments, the busy figures of the Explorers crew going about their unknown, and to him unknowable, duties. Finally Gildoran touched his shoulder, drew him away, and silently conducted him to the steps again.

One more goodbye. Forever.

He laid both his hands on Merrik's shoulders, feeling torn and lost and desperate.

"Gildoran," Merrik said suddenly, "take me with you. As crew. I'll do anything."

Deeply moved, Gildoran shook his head. Above them the sky was dark and the raw new city showed a thousand searing lights; but beyond them were a thousand searing stars. "I wish I

could. But you'd die in space, Merrik. You have to
be taken on when you're a baby. A year or less.
The kind of ships we use now, you have to grow
up on them. You wouldn't live a month, and it's a
terrible death."

Merrik's dark face worked, but he didn't say
anything. He only put a foot on the top step, turning back for an instant to say, "Gildoran. When
you reach your next world . . . come back again.
You know my world. I know it will be a long time,
but I won't forget. I swear I won't forget."

Hoarsely, Gildoran said, "No, Merrik. No, my
friend. You might not forget. But you'd hate me.
You'd be an old man, and I'd still be young, still
the age we are now. Goodbye, Merrik." He
blinked back tears as Merrik wrung his hands;
then helplessly let him go. He didn't watch him
stumble blindly away over the red mud at the foot
of the steps. He turned away inside and went
dazedly toward the Bridge.

It's the effects of the long jump, he thought,
clutching his aching head, but he knew it was
more.

The tempo of the *Gypsy Moth* was picking up
now; alarms rang, crew members—his brothers
and friends, his only world—scurried to their stations, the computer's soft voice routed orders here
and there. Gildoran turned toward the Nursery
level, dreading the way Rae would clutch at him
and cry over him with anguished gladness at his
return, but yet in some way longing for the comfort of it, too. Someday he would tell her the
whole story, but not now, not for a long, long
time. . . .

The ship was sealed; Gilroth, the last inside,

caught up to Gildoran in the corridor. "Well, it's up stakes and out again, lad. Sorry to leave?"

His love. His oldest friend. His newest friend, the only one who had ever understood. . . .
The last of his youth.

"Sorry to leave? Hell, no," Gildoran said. "Planets are for saying goodbye."

* * *

Something hidden; go and find it
Something lost beyond the ranges. . . .
Lost and waiting for you. Go!
                                    Kipling

Part Two

A TIME TO MOURN

I met a traveller from an antique land
Who said: Two vast and trunkless legs of stone
Stand in the desert; near them on the sand
Half sunk, a shattered visage lies, whose frown
And wrinkled lip, and sneer of cold command
Tell that its sculptor well those passions read
Which yet survive, stamped on these lifeless
   things
The hand that mocked them, and the heart that
   fed.

And on the pedestal these words appear;
"My name is Ozymandias, King of Kings;
Look on my works, ye mighty, and despair."
Nothing beside remains; round the decay
Of that colossal wreck, boundless and bare
The lone and level sands stretch far away.

Shelley

I

"Every year that goes by seems to go by faster," a voice said behind Gildoran. "I simply can't believe it's Rotation Day already."

"What do you mean, *already*?" Gildoran did not raise his head from glumly laying out a small assortment of bowls and spoons on a brightly colored cloth. "This has been the longest year I can remember! I've been counting the days—no, the hours!"

Behind him, Gilrae chuckled. "You don't like Nursery duty much, do you, Gildoran?"

He started to say "No, not at all," then hesitated, looking at the four small hammocks against the wall and the two empty hooks; he had stopped feeling a lump in his throat whenever he looked at the place where they had been, but he still felt a generalized sadness. He was glad that the two babies who had died in the aftermath of the DNA surgery had never yet been named; those names would always have been, to him, like *Gilmarin*; never spoken without grief. He looked at the toddlers crawling on the Nursery floor, crowding around one of the Poohbears; at the three four-year-olds drawing busily in the corner, grouped around their low table.

"I wouldn't say that," he demurred, "but it's lonely down here. I'll be glad to get back to Ship routine and important work."

Gilrae shook her head. "This is the most important work there is, Doran. For the rest of their lives, those kids—the babies—are going to have you in the back of their minds as the perfect person, the one they want to be like."

"Poor kids," he said and laughed.

"No, I'm serious, Doran. That's one reason we always have a special Nursery assignment and why people spend so much time helping down here. But the one on Nursery duty when there's a new batch of babies, he's the one—or she, sometimes it's a woman—whom they all internalize as their perfect adult model."

"Oh, come on," he scoffed. "They're certainly too young for that! Only one or two of them are even talking yet, and one thing I *have* learned about baby psychology is that thoughts follow acquisition of language, not the other way round."

Gilrae shook her head. "Not true. They start acquiring language at least six months before they can say a single word. That's why we don't leave them to the Poohbears, or they'd grow up Poohbears with human bodies. The way they grow up human is to have human contacts and close relationships, and they seem to need one-to-one relationships. Leave them too much with each other, and you get peer standards instead of adult-group standards. We have to raise them with adult standards, or they won't be able to take their proper place in crew relations." She glanced at a chronometer and said, "I should be up for the Rotation ceremonies. Between you and me, Doran, I'm glad it's Rotation Day, too. Gilharrad is just too old to be Year-Captain; I thought he'd retire two years ago and take Floater status. If we had found a new planet this year, I don't know how he would have managed."

Gildoran only nodded—it would have been rude for anyone his age to comment on the competence or otherwise of a Year-Captain, especially

one as old and venerable as Gilharrad. Gildoran
wasn't even qualified to be Captain yet, and his
ident disk wasn't yet put into the lot for the yearly
drawing. But he could agree with Gilrae without
being rude.

As often happened, Gilrae seemed to read his
thoughts. "It won't be long until you're on the
Captain list," she said. "I think someday you'll
make a good one, too." She looked at the array of
bowls he was laying out. "In a way, it's too bad
you'll miss the ceremony—"

"I don't care about the ceremony, but I like to
know right away what my assignment's going to
be next year," Gildoran grumbled. He didn't see
why the Poohbears couldn't give the babies their
supper.

"Well, there will be other years," Gilrae said
cheerfully. She was always so cheerful with him,
he thought resentfully, she treated him as if he
were no older than the toddlers! She looked
around the Nursery again. "I'll be sorry to leave. I
like working down here with the kids and the
Medics; I sometimes wish I'd specialized in
Medic work." Rae had spent this year as biological officer, and whenever there were young babies
in the Nursery, the biologists, as well as all medically trained personnel, spent most of their time
nursing the infants and looking after them. She
added, "I've gotten fond of this batch, now that we
know they're going to live. I suppose it's time to
think about naming them, isn't it?"

"Another few weeks; then they'll be a full year
old," Gildoran said. It would soon be a year, shiptime, since they had left the world where he had
spent his adolescence; he thought, without too

much of a pang now, of Janni. He never thought of her now. If they found a planet today and he went back, she would be an old, old woman, or dead.

Far more often than Janni, he thought of Merrik, who had wanted space, and knew he would never have it; he had known Merrik so briefly, and yet he had come closer to him, in that brief time, than to Janni in a year. Was a friend always closer than a lover?

Maybe, he thought, *because I still miss Gilmarin. All the time, every day. I shall never stop missing Gilmarin. Or Giltallen.*

He looked at Rae and thought of her missing Giltallen as he missed his Nurserymate, playmate, first friend, companion, Gilmarin. He said impulsively, "Maybe there ought to be a Giltallen in this batch of children, when we name them, Rae. Or a Giltallena, perhaps."

He saw her flinch, saw the raw pain in her eyes. She swallowed and couldn't answer for a moment. Then she said, "Not yet, I think. It's too soon, Doran. Give me—give us all some time." Her voice was calm, but he had seen the flinching. She said quickly, "I must go up for the ceremony. I'll send someone down right away, as soon as I know, to tell you your new assignment. Cheer up—three more years and you'll be old enough to choose your first specialty."

She went and Gildoran returned to laying out the children's supper. He didn't dislike Nursery duty, no. But he was a little tired of baby breechclouts and rattles and picking up the toys they strewed from one end to the other of the Nursery. The four-year-olds were beginning to learn ship discipline, which included ironclad rules about replacing everything where it belonged, for the next person's hand; but the toddlers weren't ready for that yet. And worse than the clutter was the food. Nursery rations certainly were as wholesome as the food served elsewhere in the Ship, and perhaps more so, but he was really tired of a bland diet—and Nursery personnel shared what the babies ate. He wondered how the Poohbears managed to stand it.

Or maybe their race always ate bland food on whatever strange world they came from. He didn't really know. The Poohbears and the Explorers had shared ships from time out of mind, but he didn't really know that much about where they had originally come from. Neither did anyone else. Except, maybe, a few specialists in the history of the Explorers.

One of them, at the far end of the Nursery, was urging the four-year-olds, in low tones, to replace their colored oilsticks on the shelf, while another tacked the bright-colored splashes of color up on the walls. One youngster had spilled his color box, and the Poohbear was telling him a story while his lagging fingers replaced each color in the proper indentation in the tray.

". . . and the Captain said, 'But how can it be a proper planet without any ice caps?' And the Scientist told him, 'Planets don't have to have ice caps . . .'"

"It's a little dull down here for you, isn't it?" said another Poohbear, reaching out a huge hand and giving Gildoran's hair an affectionate tousle; he remembered her doing this when he was no bigger than the four-year-old sorting the colorsticks. "Well, I can't blame you, Doran. I suppose a big fellow like you wants adventure, and who knows, if you were up on the Bridge, you might discover a new world for us." Her light voice was gently, deprecatingly humorous.

"Adventure?" He chuckled. "Not much chance of that. We haven't found a proper planet in the last six solar systems—why should this one be any different?"

"But it's *time*, isn't it? demanded one of the four-year-olds, tugging at Gildoran's hand. "Every solar system we go through that *doesn't* have a planet—doesn't that mean there's more chance the next one will have one? When Gilmarti came down and talked to us about probability math"— he stumbled and lisped a little over the word— "she said something like that . . ."

"No Giljodek," said Gildoran, squatting down on the floor so he was eye-to-eye with the child, "Probability"—he pronounced it slowly and carefully so the child could imitate his speech— "doesn't work that way. Here, take this—" He took a twenty-sided die from a shelf, "Throw it twenty times. Do you *have* to get a—oh, say a seven—in those twenty tries?"

The child took the die and threw it, while Gildoran counted aloud. "Seventeen, eighteen, nineteen, twenty. See? One of the numbers could come up twice or three times, instead of every number just coming up once. If you threw it *hundreds* of times, over those times, each of the numbers would come up about the same number of times; but every time you throw it, you have the same chance of getting any one of the twenty numbers. Do you understand?"

"I think so," Giljodek said, wrinkling his

forehead. He was already bleached from space, as pale as Gildoran; the toddlers crawling on the floor were still pink and rosy, with hair dark or reddish.

"So you see, smallest, the probability math only works over big, big numbers. We know that in a hundred solar systems, probably fifteen or twenty will have at least one planet where humans can live; but we don't know *which* fifteen or twenty, and some of those fifteen or twenty won't be suitable for some other reason: already settled with intelligent life-forms, too cold for most races, too warm for most races, just a shade too little oxygen and will need extensive terraforming, and so forth. And every time we go into a new solar system, we are like you throwing the die: you can't be absolutely sure a seven will come up, even if you've thrown it nine times already and haven't had a seven; you could get any one of the twenty numbers, any one time. Our next solar system *could* have a good planet, just as any of the last six or seven could have had one; but the fact that we haven't had one for seven solar systems doesn't mean we're any more likely to have one this time. We could get three good planets in a row from three systems, or we could keep on drawing blanks fifteen or twenty or eighty times in a row. Like drawing blanks in your domino game, with one difference; in the domino game, you run out of blanks. The Cosmos will never run out of solar systems with no good planets in them."

Giljodek's eyes were wide. "Then maybe it's lucky we *ever* find any good planets, isn't it, Doran?"

Gildoran grinned. "Maybe it is, at that," he said,

and stretched his long legs upward, hoisting the
child with him. "Here, sit up to the table,
Poohbear has your dinner all ready."

The little boy sorting colorsticks scowled and
said, "I want to hear about the Captain and the
proper planet!"

The Poohbear continued. "The Captain said,
'How can it be a proper planet if it hasn't any rust
stains for iron?' And the Scientist said . . ."

"Supper!" It was a strident yell. "Story *afterward!*" The Poohbear was jerked backward by a
hearty tug on her long, dark hair from one of the
toddlers.

Gildoran was at their side with a swift stride.
"No!" he said sharply, "You don't *do* that, smallest!" But he kept his face straight with an effort. It
was his special favorite among the babies, the tiny
round-faced girl with golden skin and slightly
slanted dark eyes, pug-nosed and aggressive.
"Say, 'Sorry' to Pooh!"

The baby pouted. "Want supper! No story!"

Gildoran held her firmly. "Pooh may tell a story
to anyone if she pleases; you don't have to listen. Say 'Sorry' and go straight to the table,
baby."

She kicked at him crossly. "Won't!"

"Then," said Gildoran, straightening up again,
with the child between his strong hands, "you go
straight into your hammock, Naughty girls may
not have supper."

She fought and kicked him all the way to the
hammock; he held her, laughing, so that she
could not hurt him or herself, extended at arm's
length. He put her into the hammock and began to
fasten the restraining straps over the small wriggling body.

"Supper!" she yelled, but she was laughing, too, "I want supper!"

"Then say 'Sorry' to Pooh for pulling her hair, naughty girl." He and the little dark-haired girl had had this struggle often; she was the largest and most aggressive of the babies, and the most definite personality. Until this stretch of Nursery duty, he had thought all young babies were alike: eating and sleeping, and very much the same. Now he had begun to realize that they developed very individual personalities within a month or two, one quiet and another noisy, one aggressive and another less so. This one was a wild little animal, but very quick and bright; she already talked in sentences, while most of the others said only one word at a time.

She went limp now in his arms, looking up at him with a coy smile. "Say 'Sorry' to you," she suggested, and he laughed again.

"Not a chance; come on, now, get into your straps like a good girl."

"Not a good girl," she yelled, kicking him again, and as he buckled the first hammock-strap, yielded. "Naughty girl say 'Sorry,' " she whispered, fluttering her long eyelashes as if she was about to cry.

He set her down on the floor. She whispered, thumb in her mouth, "Sorry, Pooh," and the Poohbear picked her up and tousled her dark hair. "Sit down to your supper, now," she admonished, and laughed over the child's head at Gildoran.

"That one!"

Gildoran nodded as he was helping the other children into their small chairs. She was the one who kept the Nursery in an uproar. But Gilrushka, from Psych, said that the noisy, assertive, mischievous children were the ones who would grow up to be the most valuable crew members; the ones who were always asking questions, testing limits, exploring the outer parameters of their world. A "good" child, Gilrushka asserted, was simply a stupid or intimidated one, oné who gave his elders no trouble.

Poohbear stretched her lips back over her teeth in what Gildoran knew to be a friendly grin; to an outsider, he imagined, it might seem a grimace of threat or attack. "I hope the word comes down soon to name them; I need some kind of name for that one—she already has a sense of identity. The others can wait." She put a spoon into the child's hand, admonishing, "Don't eat with your fingers, smallest."

"Why not? *Like* eating with my fingers."

"Because," Poohbear said patiently, "if you eat with your fingers, you will get your fingers all greasy, and then your clothes and your hair and your skin will be all greasy."

"*Like* to be greasy," said the child definitely, and went on eating with her fingers.

"Then," Poohbear said calmly, "you will have to have another bath."

"*Like* 'nother bath," said the child, cheerfully smearing her food on her already-buttery face. The Poohbear concealed a smile again as she gave in. "Bath after supper, then. Giljodek, hold your spoon the other way, and the food will not fall out as you eat it."

"Tell me about the Captain and the proper planet *while* I eat," teased the small boy finishing with his color box, and the Poohbear beside him said, "We don't tell stories at table. I will finish the story later and you may eat now, or I will finish the story now and you may eat later."

"But my supper will get cold," said the small boy, and the Poohbear said, "That is simply the decision you must make; will you wait for your supper or wait for the story, Gilvarth?"

The fair little face drew up in a frown. Finally he decided, "The story won't get cold and my supper will," and hurried off to climb into his chair. Now that they were all at table, Gildoran and the Poohbears sat down in their larger chairs, and Gildoran surveyed his bowlful of bland chunks with boredom. Well, it wouldn't be long, anyway.

The bland chunky stuff was succeeded by stewed fruit, and then the work began of bathing the infants, getting them into their sleeping coveralls, and then into their hammocks. The older children, four four-year-olds, were listening to music at the far end of the Nursery; Gildoran came and set out an array of songs for them to listen to. The other toddlers went into their hammocks without hesitation, curling up sleepily; Gildoran's special charge crawled away in her blue sleeper, sitting and listening to the music with fascination, waving her small fists in time.

"She's musical," the Poohbear commented. "Gilrae said she would start to teach her to play the harp as soon as her hands were big enough."

The child heard and cried out, demanding, "Rae play harp!"

"Not tonight, smallest," Gildoran said, "Rae had to go up to the Bridge. She can't play for you tonight. I'll put on a repro of the harp music for you." He started to hunt out the reproduction cube of harp music, but the baby came and grabbed it up before he could sort it out from the others; she had recognized the design on the side. She was so smart, so clever, he thought, carrying her to her hammock and putting the cube into the wall-slot beside her where it would play softly, for her ears alone.

One of the Poohbears, following him, said softly, "And you still think it's dull down here?"

"Not really," Gildoran said, "but I'd like to talk to some grown people, now and then."

"Well," said the Poohbear kindly, "Here's Gilnosta to talk to."

The young woman came into the Nursery. "I came down to say goodbye to my babies, I'm going to be working directly with Gilban," she said. She looked elated; it was a feather in a junior technician's cap, to be placed directly into apprenticeship with the Chief Medic. "But I'm going to miss my babies," she added, going around to hammock after hammock, hugging and fondling the infants one after another. "Oh, I'll come down again, I really *am* going to miss them—"

Watching, Gildoran thought that he, too, would miss the babies. But for Gilnosta it was a professional first, too; they were her first medical assignment, and since Nursery, he knew, Gilnosta—who was barely two years, shiptime, older than he was himself—had wanted to be on the Medic staff. She had had charge of the babies, special nursing care, after the complex surgery of their first month on board; and during that first month she had been closer to them even than Gildoran.

It was more than this; Gildoran knew he was the only one in the whole crew who had seen her cry, the night they knew they were not going to be able to save two of the six babies. To everyone else, Gilnosta had only repeated what Gilban, the Chief Medic, had said; that saving four out of six was a triumph which would have been considered spectacular, on any Explorer ship, even fifty years ago. They had a right to be proud of it. But to Gildoran she had wept, hopelessly, her grief for the two weakest ones who had died after the surgery. Gildoran shared her grief; and that night he had known, gut-deep, what he had known intellectually all his life; why no baby aboard an Explorer ship, was ever given a name, or allowed to become more than a specimen, until it was certain that he or she would survive his first year.

It was hard enough to lose a nameless infant—a potential shipmate—one who might have grown up to be a Captain, or a lover, a friend . . . one of you. But a person, one given a traditional Explorer name, one with personality and individuality—no, that was intolerable. So the babies were kept in the Nursery, and no one but the Poohbears, and the assigned Nursery personnel, and the Medics who were required to learn detachment, ever had anything to do with them until it was certain that they would live to be named and to become part of the ship's people. Lori, the nine-year-old, and the four four-year-olds listening to music on the floor, were cherished by everybody aboard the *Gypsy Moth*. But the four nameless infants were known only to the three Medics, to the Biologist, who was

Gilrae this last year, and Gildoran; and the grief for the two who died was limited to those few.

Nobody else will ever remember them. We don't even have a name to remember, Gildoran thought. Nobody else would ever grieve for the two.

But the other four, as Gilrae had said, would be forever imprinted with Gildoran's personality as an ultimate, interior, internalized image of what an adult of their own kind should be like. *Not just me,* Gildoran thought, watching Gilnosta hug the little almond-eyed one who was his special favorite, *but Gilnosta herself. And Gilrae.* It was the reward, perhaps, that would compensate for the grief that only they had known; they shaped the remaining children in their image.

Gilnosta was about to leave again—he noticed that she had left the straps loosened and the small dark-haired one was wriggling down from her hammock. What a nuisance; she would head right for the music corner again and have to be pried loose, and this time she probably could not be placated with special music of her own. He hardly had time to think of anything else; he was heading off to fetch the child back when Gilnosta chided, "You haven't even asked me about your new assignment, Gildoran! Or who was drawn for Year-Captain?"

"Oh! who is the Captain, then?"

"Gilrae," Gilnosta said. "I think she'll be a good one; everyone likes her. And Gilharrad said he would never be Captain again; within seven years, he's going to take Floater status. Oh, yes, she added, "You're going to work in Transmitter with Gilraban, and he wants to see you as soon as you can make it. But you'd better catch her first," Gilnosta added, pointing. Gildoran groaned. The small girl with the almond eyes had reached the musicians.

Gildoran galloped after her and caught her up. "You're supposed to be in bed, you little monkey," he admonished, lifted her firmly back into the hammock and fastened the straps over her. She answered, "Want to play drums!"

"Tomorrow you can play the drums," he said, and braced himself for another yelling fit, but she surprised him again, snuggling down into her hammock, smiling up at him sunnily and saying, "Kiss."

He hugged her close, kissing the soft cheek. Already it was bleaching, paler than the rosy color he remembered, the long lashes on her cheek no longer the color of the starless void. For the first time consciously he voiced the thought as he rejoined Gilnosta.

"I can't help it—I'm so glad *this* one didn't die."

She nodded, without speaking. That would, he sensed, always be a raw place to her; he wondered if, like himself, she had found herself loving the children, giving them more than the measured doses of gentle handling and cuddling which the babies seemed to need to develop the will to live after the complicated surgery and the long period of convalescence.

If we had loved the others the way I loved this one, would they have lived, too? He wondered if Gilnosta was wondering that, if it would always be, for her, the kind of dulling, but never completely healed memory that Giltallen's defection and Gilmarin's death, were for him. Did everyone have some such buried memory, never to be shared because sharing it could never ease the burden?

Enough, Gildoran thought. He was through with Nursery duty. He'd had the privilege of shaping a new generation of Explorers, and now it was time to go on to something else. He caught a shaft upward to the Transmitter department.

II

Like all Explorers, Gildoran had a working acquaintance with the workings of a Transmitter. He had been given his first lessons in theory and assembly when he was about eight years old, biological time. But mastering the intricate mathematics of computer assembly and Transmitter tie-ins to existing circuits was something else entirely.

"Of course, the *Gypsy Moth*'s computer will handle most of this, most of the time," Gilrabin said on the first day, "but computers do break down, sacrilegious as it is to admit it, and you have to be able to spot it if you get some really freak answer—you can't just accept whatever it gives you. You've got the talent—I did your IQ assessment when you were in Nursery, you know."

Gildoran hadn't known.

"Oh, yes; you were our babies, Gilrae's and mine," Gilraban said. "We were on Nursery duty that year—they used to try and assign a male and a female, but we're too shorthanded for that now, so they assign one person, and make sure the main Medics are of the opposite sex if they can. That's why Gilnosta and Gilrae were the main ones to work with you this time. But Gilrae and I were there with you and Ramie and poor Gilmarin, and the ones who didn't make it. There was one—a boy—the brightest little thing I've ever seen, but he developed a blood idiosyncrasy . . . well, enough," he finished firmly and continued, "You've got the brains for this. But your brain's getting lazy because you've never had to use those abilities; now you've got to relearn all that math. I think you could make a good Transmitter specialist, if you were interested."

Gildoran said he'd do his best. He didn't really think they would have assigned him to a specialty he couldn't handle. Assignments on *Gypsy Moth* came up by computer, but barring emergencies, natural talents and even preferences were taken into account.

But it took him a long time—a month shiptime—of the hardest work and study he'd ever put in, and there were days of discouragement when he wondered if the computer had made one of those mistakes Gilraban said it could. Then another month of building and taking apart Transmitter mockups and Joffrey coils until he could put them together blindfolded or in his sleep (and sometimes, at the end of a long shift when Gilraban had been unusually exacting, he felt as if he *had* done it in his sleep) before he was qualified to work on a Transmitter when downworlding.

"Now all you have to do," Gilmarti, Raban's elderly mentor, said the day he finally did put together a Joffrey coil blindfolded, "is to go up on the Bridge and tell them to find a planet we can let you practice on!"

Gildoran chuckled. "I don't think they're waiting for me to do that. We need a good planet—one to sit down on and get some rocks for fuel, even if we can't make a tie-in on the Transmitter."

"We could use a world to settle, too," Gilraban said. "We need fluorides, though, and silicone, for the Joffrey coils. What you *can* do, though, is to go up to the Bridge and tell the Captain that there is another qualified Transmitter technician. Not expert, yet, but a qualified tech."

The Captain was Gilrae, this year. At the back of his mind was what Gilraban had told him, that Gilrae had been assigned to Nursery when he was very small. So was Gilrae, then, the internalized image of the perfect woman to him?

How silly! Of course not! I know Gilrae isn't perfect—nobody is. But she's a splendid human being!

Yet the small disquieting thought remained. When he reported to Gilrae on the Bridge to give his news, feeling somewhat stiff and constrained because now she was his Captain with all the authority of the Year-office, she smiled—the old familiar smile he seemed to have known all his life. "That's wonderful, Gildoran. I can't get over it. I still think of you as a youngster; it doesn't seem so long. How long *has* it been, shiptime? I can't believe it's twenty years!"

And then there was a further disquieting thought. Did she think of him as he thought of the little dark-eyed girl in the Nursery, crawling on the floor, wetting diapers, a demanding, disruptive, brilliant child? His little almond-eyed charge looked very much like Ramie, but he was perfectly sure that Gilramie had been a gentle child, wistful, not loud and demanding. Yet, Gilrushka to the contrary, she had not grown up stupid.

Thinking of Ramie made him remember his other old Nurserymate and companion. Gilmarin was gone—probably dead on Lasselli's World—but he remained and Gilramie, and in the month since he had been freed from Nursery duty, he had hardly seen her.

"What assignment did Gilramie have this year?"

"She's working on the Bridge," Rae said, "Gilhart is Chief Navigator, and she's qualifying under him. There's been some pressure to qualify you two," she added, and he saw the faint lines of strain in her face. "We are shorthanded, and we will be until those four-year-olds in the Nursery grow up, and maybe after. Even if we found a world right away, even with the finder's fee, we'd have trouble getting a line of credit from Head Center for more babies; I was sure we'd find a new planet within six months shiptime, and now we have two generations' credit to pay for. You and Ramie are all we have now," she added, but she did not speak Gilmarin's name.

Gilraban had said it; *you were our babies.* Meaning himself and Ramie. And poor Gilmarin. And others who didn't make it.

One little boy, the brightest I've ever seen, but he developed a blood idiosyncrasy. The thought plucked at Gildoran with pain, that he might have had a brother, a Nurserymate and companion, whom he had never known, from his own mysterious world, or elsewhere. Someone his own age, sharing his own problems and growth, as Gilramie did. He found himself regretting that lost and unknown brother, with a sudden emotional pull that was unlike anything he had ever felt before. Was he losing his mind, getting emotional all the time over nothing? He'd been like this ever since that spell in Nursery. Maybe they shouldn't assign Nursery duty to the people who had serious work to do! He was just getting too damned emotional all the time; he'd better go and see Gilrushka in Psych!

But he never did; because when he woke for his next shift, it was all over the Ship; Gilnosta told him first in the dining hall, and Gilmerritt, when he stopped in for a little exercise in the brilliant ultraviolet of the plant rooms. By the time he reached the Bridge, he was prepared for all the jubilation he found there.

"A planet," Gilrae told him when he came, at her invitation, up to the Officers' area, "A good one. Orange sun, getting old and turning reddish, but millennia yet before it cools or collapses. Look—She switched on a screen to show him a computerized blowup picture, "Polar caps, but not much cloud-cover. Sensors don't show much vegetation, but there's enough. Might need some terraforming."

"The place looks bleak," Gilhart agreed, coming up behind them to take another look, "but there's no reason there shouldn't be cities there, and even farms; the soil is probably arable."

"Not if it's that old," said Gilmerritt. She had crowded on the bridge, too; everyone had, eager to find some real or fancied errand that would give them a glance at the new world where their next work would be done. "Look at that sun; there might be soil exhausted by too many millennia, too many races coming and going—"

"No sign of life," Gilban said. The Chief Medic was a big man, tall as Gildoran—who was tall even for an Explorer—and broader than most; powerful and intimidating. "Most planets this age, if they can support life, develop it; and if a planet this old is still barren, there must be some reason. It could have developed life and lost it because basically it wasn't fit for a full evolutionary process."

"That's still only a theory," Gilmerritt said, "The idea that life could evolve in two separate waves—"

But Gilban refused to be drawn, saying, "Maybe this is the planet that will prove it, one way or the other. How long will it be before we're close enough to send down the first landing party?"

III

The landing party went down two days later, but Gildoran wasn't on it. He was annoyed, knowing this meant they considered him too junior for a post of danger. It seemed to rub it in, his youth and insufficiency, when they came up again, jubilant.

"It looks good," Gilraban said, summoning the whole Transmitter crew for a conference in the main briefing room, "The location in this end of the Galaxy will make it almost ideal for a Transmitter tie-in, no black holes or quasars for awkward routing patterns. We won't even have to go through Head Center, but can make the main tie-ins—" He grew technical about the routes to arrange jumps back to the center of the Galaxy, and Gildoran felt elated, realizing that he could understand everything Gilraban said without having to count on his fingers.

"I'm not too hopeful about it," Gilmerritt, the junior biologist, said. "The place is bleaker than we thought; mostly lichens. I don't think anyone will ever want to settle here; all rust and bare desert. It might make a good Transmitter stop, but that's about all."

Old Gilharrad teased, "You're prejudiced, Gilmerritt, because there aren't enough of your precious plants here! You want everything to be a beautiful garden!"

"I don't deny it," she said, laughing. "I like my planets to have everything. What's that old story they used to tell us in Nursery, about the Captain who asked, 'How can it be a proper planet if it hasn't got any green growing things?' "

"And remember the Scientist's answers," Gilharrad said. "There are all kinds of proper planets—a hundred thousand kinds of planets —and *every single one of them is a proper planet . . .*"

"And like all Nursery stories, that's absolute nonsense," Gilrae said. "If it were true, every planet we find would be a suitable planet. But I don't share your prejudice at all, Merritt; I can do without green garden worlds. I didn't have to be quite so alert—no cannibal vines waiting to gobble us up, no local equivalent of the great saurians hiding in the jungle to snap us all up for a light meal and never know he had lunch."

"Every planet has its own subtle worth," Gilharrad rebuked, "and its own especial place in the visualization of the Cosmic Totality. The fact that we don't know how to use the planet is no reflection on the planet's worth, but only describes the limitations of our pitifully small human view."

Gildoran was impatient with the ancient's philosophy; he thought irritably that Gilharrad ought to retire and take Floater status, out on the rim of the Gypsy Moth where he could devote all his time to intricate philosophies. Wasn't anyone else going to say anything? Were they only going to sit there and defer to the senile old man's doddering nonsense? Well, if no one else did, he would.

"Whatever else the planet is good for, we can get fuel from it, and silicone for Joffrey coils," he remarked. "Is it so old that there are no remaining halogens? We need the fluorides."

Gilrae frowned at him. Did she think they had nothing better to do but sit and listen to the old man's maunderings? She said with gentle reproof, "It's usually wise to remember that planets were not created for human use alone."

Gildoran had started, and he wasn't going to be stopped now. "Whatever the Infinite Purpose, or whatever it is that Gilharrad is talking about, the human use of this planet is what concerns us now. I thought we ought to point out what it is good for instead of dwelling on what it isn't. We need fuel, and fluorides, and Gilraban already pointed out that we can use it as a Transmitter stop."

"And there will be a finder's fee," Gilhart said, and Gilrae nodded.

"There's that, of course. But it's been so long between good planets that a finder's fee will only pay off debts. It won't put us back on a sound financial footing. We're still over our heads."

"Just paying off debts is being back on a sound financial footing, compared with having another year without a good planet," Gilhart reminded her, and as they left the Bridge, he slipped his hand through her arm in a close, possessive way.

Gildoran watched, frowning, and Gilramie came up to him, her almond eyes tilting upward.

"What are you looking so stormy about, Gildoran?"

"I am not looking stormy," he retorted sharply. The girl took his elbow, with the habit of years, saying, "But there's something bothering you—do you think I can't tell, Doran?"

He shrugged. "It's none of my affair. But Gilrae was always with Giltallen—they were coupled before I was born—and now she's always with Gilhart. Already."

Ramie said gently, "What was it they used to say in Nursery? 'For everything there is a season; a time to be born and a time to die, a time to mourn and a time to cease from mourning.' I'm glad to see Rae happy again. This last year has been so terribly hard for her. It was a blessing that there were babies to oversee, that she was working as

Biological Officer; otherwise I honestly think she would have died."

Gildoran retorted, "And I suppose you think it's lucky that two of the babies died, so she'd have another loss to think about besides Giltallen's?"

Ramie's dark eyes flamed for a moment with indignation. "That was a cruel thing to say, Doran—it's not worthy of you!"

"I hate to see Tallen forgotten like this. And Gilmarin. Didn't you care—"

"Doran, how can you? Of course I care; I loved Gilmarin, as much as you did. He was my first—" her voice caught and she looked away. "He wanted to make a—a permanent pairing, and I wouldn't. I've blamed myself, wondering how I could have denied him that happiness when he was going to die so young . . ."

Gildoran looked down at his feet, feeling about two inches tall. He muttered, "I'm sorry, Ramie. I didn't know." He had been so absorbed in his own grief, had plunged so hard into his own work in the Nursery, in the small drama of life and death there, he had had nothing to spare for anyone else's loss. Perhaps he had felt that no one could grieve as he did, that Gilmarin had been *his* friend, *his* playmate. He had not realized that Ramie, too, who had been one of their group, would have her own private griefs and agonies; perhaps all the more so. His own adolescence had been spent suffering over Janni, who had deserted him; but Ramie, whose first lover had been one of their own, would have the greater grief.

"Ramie, I'm a beast, I shouldn't say things like that. What can I say? I didn't think, I didn't know."

She clung to him, her head on his shoulder.

"It's all right. You had to grieve in your own way, just as I did."

"But you shouldn't have had to grieve alone," he said, muffled, his mouth against her soft hair, holding her tight.

When she raised her eyes, they were still wet, but she was calm. "No," she said, "I think it was good for me; I didn't have any way to hide from it, so I had to go into it and get it over. That's why it didn't take me as long. Rae has been so cut off; and now I'm so happy, so happy to know she's finding someone else. You haven't seen what it's done to her."

He hadn't. Absorbed in his own griefs and his work, he had not seen.

"I like Gilhart. He's so solid, somehow. I work under him on the Bridge, you know, and I honestly don't think I have any talent for Navigation; it's terribly dull and routine, and my mind just slips away from what I'm doing. But Hart is patient and kind, and he has managed to make me see that it's exciting in a way, being the one to guide the *Gypsy Moth*. Though I'll still be glad to get back to live things; that's just temperamental, I suppose. Are you enjoying your work with the Transmitter?"

He started to tell her about Gilraban, conscious of the new tone in her voice. For the first time in his life, he was conscious of Ramie as a woman and it was not really pleasant. She was a child, she was . . .

She was exactly his own age. Exactly.

He felt uneasy, wondering if, as Gilrae had managed to transfer her affections and desires to

Gilhart, Ramie had decided to put him into the place of the dead Gilmarin. She couldn't be so foolish. Or could she?

"Anyway, I've qualified, and Gilraban says I can work on the Transmitter crew for this new planet," Gildoran said. "I hope this time I get real responsibility here, not just running errands."

It was time, he felt; the last world had finished his youthful irresponsibility, the disillusion of the end of the affair with Janni had matured him. He was an adult now, a man, ready to take on the responsibilities of a man, and he hoped they understood it.

He was chosen for the second party, which would establish their first camp. The *Gypsy Moth* lay in a close orbit, a few hundred kilometers above the surface; but the little shuttle ship went closer still, drifting to dayside over great barren seas.

"Will there be enough water to support life?" Gildoran asked.

"I should think so," Gilrae said. "One of our first tasks will be to put down some artesians. There is an accessible water table, even though it's arid. Artesians will give us enough water for life support while there's just the ship, and once we get a Transmitter tie-in, we can bring in a terraforming crew, seed the place with algae, and start another chlorophyll cycle, which will give us oxygen, too. There's enough to breathe, but a higher oxygen ratio will be more comfortable for humans."

"Look," Ramie said, pointing. "Sunrise."

Over the edge of the barren desert below them,

the red sun was rising, a huge disk, breaking clear and crimson, reflecting tracks on the desert; the glassy sand caught reflections and cast them back in a dazzling blood-colored light.

"Spectacular views," Gilraban said. "We might consider tourists coming here by Transmitter just for that *view!*"

"It *is* amazing," Gilrae said. "I saw it three times with the first landing party, and the effect doesn't wear off."

"What's that?" Ramie asked, bending over the viewscreen.

"Just an effect of the light," Gilrae answered without looking. But Ramie said, "No. I don't mean that. Look—straight lines. I thought you said this world had no sign of intelligent life, Rae."

"It didn't," Rae said, "and most of the lower forms died off when the sun cooled and it went arid."

"But that looks like the ruins of a city," Ramie said. "Take it down lower, Gilhart, can't you? That's an artifact of intelligent life or I've never seen one."

"Cosmos!" Gilhart exclaimed. "I think the girl's right, Rae! What were we thinking of, not to have seen it?"

"Don't be silly, Hart," she said, but her smile was intimate, and Gildoran still winced a little at seeing it. "We could have orbited a hundred times, and we could still have missed it. Take it down, Hart—we ought to have a closer look at this."

It was certainly a city; low clustered buildings, huddled crimson in the sunrise. Rae looked down at it and quoted, "A rose-red city, half as old as Time."

It looked it. The buildings were low, walls crumbling, made of something like adobe—or if it was something stronger, it must have been unfathomably old, for there were no sharp corners anywhere on the buildings, roofless walls gaping everywhere like blind eyes staring at the sky.

"I take it back," Gilraban said. "This place could be more than a good view and a Transmitter stop. Archaeologists will come here from everywhere to study the ruins. But why did they all die?"

"Maybe they didn't," Rae said. "Maybe there are survivors. Hart," she said, "try an orbit that will take us all over the surface, and use high sensor levels to cover any forms of life. We didn't get a flicker last time, but we could have missed it, too."

Gilhart beckoned Ramie up to the controls.

"You take it," he said, smiling. "You're ready for this, I think. Set up a grid pattern all over the day side, why don't you?"

Ramie glowed with excitement, and Gildoran saw Rae smile at Gilhart. Yes, it had been kind of them to allow the young girl to take the responsibility of this exciting new exploration. Would Gilraban allow him this kind of responsibility on the Transmitter crew?

IV

They quartered the planet on a grid pattern for three days. They found one other area which

looked as if it might be the ruins of some man-
made city (or something created by intelligent
life) but otherwise the planet was deserted; no
sign of life except the small howler beasts in the
desert which covered the world from pole to pole.

"Well," said Gilrae on the fourth day, "it looks
as if it's all ours."

"Maybe so," Gilban said pessimistically, "but it
doesn't happen that way very often—for a world
to develop intelligent life and civilization, and
then die out like this. Maybe what killed them is
waiting down there to kill *us*."

"Not likely," Gilhart said. "We haven't seen
any form of life except the little howlers, and
they're harmless. As for vegetation—there's Gilmerritt's report, and I suppose you're familiar
with that, too."

"I am," Gilrae confirmed. "The usual kind of
arid desert plants—presumably everything which
couldn't handle desert conditions died out. We
did exhaustive air samples, and the atmosphere is
fine, though it could use a little more oxygen. The
first terraforming crew will probably seed some
algae and start a vegetation cycle all over
again—once the water table is back where it ought
to be for a proper planet." She smiled deprecatingly and again Gildoran thought of the Poohbears' story—the story he had heard when he was
still in Nursery himself, the story on which, he
supposed, every Nursery child was brought up.

Gilrae looked around the briefing room. She
said, "We'll go down tomorrow and land, take
samples, and make our first assessments of what
needs to be done. Are you going down for Transmitter, Gilraban?"

The older man shook his head. He said "I don't

think so; I'll send Gildoran down. He can locate a site for the first tie-in to Head Center. Check out the bedrock, Doran; remember the mud in the last place? It wasn't anybody's fault—as I remember, there wasn't anyplace on that planet where we could put a tie-in *without* being buried ankle-deep in mud. But let's try to find someplace—*this* time—where there's a good solid rock foundation, and dig down to it. I don't *like* wading in mud!"

Gildoran felt a swell of pride. Rationally he knew this was not an assignment on which a very junior technician could make any serious mistakes—setting up an area for a first tie-in—but he still was excited. It was his first adult assignment; on the last world he had had no assignments more serious than fetching and carrying, handing and helping. He said seriously, "I'll try to find you a good spot," and wondered irritably why Gilrae was smiling. Couldn't anyone take him seriously?

"I don't want to inject a note of caution when everybody's being so hopeful," Gilmarti said, "but don't take any unnecessary risks. A planet that killed off one intelligent race could give us some unpleasant surprises."

"Not a chance," Gilban said definitely. "I'm convinced that the last sign of intelligent life on this world—and I'm judging from the apparent age of those ruins down there—must have been a couple of *million* years ago. My first guess about what killed them—barring discovery of their remains, which doesn't seem very likely, any organic material would have decayed so many centuries ago that we'll never even know what they looked like—would be a plague which spread planetwide and then, having killed off everything capable of catching it, died off from lack of host."

"Let's hope you're right," Gilmarti said, and Gilmerritt said, "In the air samples and the first soil samples, we found very little organic life, and very little one-celled life; hence no germs or bacteria capable of spreading disease, and nothing to vector any plague. Nothing's ever been spread from vegetable to animal, so we won't catch anything from those lichens and tubers; and they caught a couple of the howlers and found no parasites. A remarkably sterile world."

"I like it better that way," said Gilmarti. "I'm not especially fond of doing it the way the *Tinkerbelle's* crew had to, a few hundred years ago—remember the trouble they had on that world that had reached early-feudal, trying to persuade them to have a Transmitter tie-in? They were convinced it was the work of a particularly nasty set of devils and almost sliced up the crew for sacrifices to their particularly nasty gods. Poor Timharald—he was their Year-Captain at the time—*did* get killed off. At least those lichens and tubers and desert howlers aren't going to decide we're devils and sacrifice us up on some sort of altar!"

"That's true. I always wonder whether we're doing that kind of world any favor at all, bringing them the blessings of a Galactic civilization," Rae said. "Of course, history shows that most of them do integrate and find their own cultural patterns; but my own feeling is that barbarian or feudal worlds ought to be let alone for a few thousand years to grow up a little."

"That's a very provincial view," Gilban said.

"It's an ancient scarcity view, saying you want them to struggle along on the very edge of survival, living with all the dangers of a solitary race. Like those people down there," he said, making an inclusive hand gesture including the planet below their orbit, "At the mercy of whatever killed them off—while a Transmitter tie-in could have saved them and let their civilization go on, growing and modifying with the new circumstance."

Gilharrad smiled gently. He looked, Gildoran thought, as if he was already old enough to spend all his time meditating. How old was he, anyway? He said, "Even the Transmitter can't wholly reshape human destiny, Gilban."

"Maybe not," admitted the Medical Officer deferentially, "but I'm convinced that we have a duty to try."

"I think you're missing Gilharrad's point," Gilrushka from Psych said. "The question is whether we Explorers have any right to make the decisions that will shape every world in the Galaxy into the image of Head Center, depending on the Transmitter. Current thought seems to feel—"

"Let's hold that for meditation sessions—all right, Rushka?" Gilrae interrupted. "This isn't the time for philosophical wrangles." But she smiled at the young woman. "The question is who do we send down tomorrow for specimen work and preliminary exploration of Transmitter sites?"

"Take Gilramie," Gilhart said, "She's getting practice in planetary navigation. And someone who can check terrain for geological conformations. With no seas left, there may be no appreciable tectonic or volcanic activity—considering the state of the core samples we got, and the study of the magnetic fields, there are no active volcanoes left and no internal activity that would cause them to become active—but we ought to know. We don't want to set up on a site that's due for new volcanic outbursts within a couple of thousand years."

"Right," Gilrae agreed. "I'll study crew qualifications and pick a group for tomorrow. Is that all for now?"

When they broke up, Gillori, the nine-year-old who, too junior even for an apprentice assignment, was used as the ship's messenger girl, came up to Gildoran.

"Poohbear says we're going to have a riot in Nursery if you don't come down to visit," she said, "One of the babies—the imp, you know which one I mean—keeps yelling for you. Why not come down and see her?"

Gildoran was struck by a sense of guilt; excited by his new work, he had completely forgotten his own special little charge. *The imp.* They would *have* to name her fairly soon; maybe he ought to speak to Gilrae about a naming ceremony—at least for the ones who were talking.

"It's too bad this one isn't a boy," Gillori said, "We could name her Gilmarin."

Gildoran turned on the child fiercely. "Do you really think anyone could replace Gilmarin?" he demanded, and the little girl flinched.

"That wasn't what I meant. But it would be a way to"—she stammered a little—"a way of remembering. . . ."

Gildoran was suddenly ashamed of himself. "I'm sorry, Lori, I didn't mean to shout at you. But

I don't need anything like that to remember—look, do you mind not talking about it, Lori?"

Rebuked, she fell into silence. Gildoran took the shaft down to Nursery, inwardly seething. Did they think anyone could take Gilmarin's place, that he could endure having anyone else with Gilmarin's name, reminding him, night and day, year after year, of their loss? He loved the little girl, but he felt if he had to speak to her year after year by the name of his loved vanished friend, he would come to hate her.

He stepped into the Nursery and was immediately rushed by a breathless charge: a small girl in a tight pink coverall, swarming over him, trying to climb him like a stairway.

"Doran, Doran, Doran—" she babbled over and over again, and he discovered that she was crying. He sat down, holding and hugging her, trying to soothe her.

"Don't cry, sweet girl, don't cry, smallest. Do you think I wasn't coming back anymore? Did you think I didn't love you anymore?" he soothed, holding her tight. She had a sweet clean baby smell; her silky hair had its own perfume.

"Missed you," she hiccuped over again. "Naughty Doran. Not here to put me to bed."

When she quieted a little, he set her on his knee, facing him, smoothing her hair gently. "You mustn't cry," he admonished. "I love you, but I have other work to do."

She listened, and again he realized that this precocious little one probably understood every word he said. He must be very careful not to lie to her or mislead her. He should have explained to her before he left; but he had thought that she was only a baby, less than a year old, that she would not understand.

"Listen, smallest," he said, gently, bouncing her a little in his lap. "I want to talk to you seriously, baby. I love you. I always will. I'll be with you when I can. I can't play with you all the time anymore because now I have other work to do, and Gilbarni and Gilnosta and the others will be spending their time teaching you and looking after you. But I'll try and come down whenever I can, and when you're bigger, I'll take you all over the ship."

"Take me now," she begged.

"I can't, smallest; there are no places for little girls as little as you, and you could get hurt. When you are older, you will go all over the *Gypsy Moth* and be with me, and Ramie, and Rae, and all the other people on the *Gypsy Moth* who are waiting for you to grow up. But I will try to come down and see you every day or two. All right?"

She snuggled against him. "All right," she said, considering. "Come *lots*. Love you."

He blinked, angry with himself; why did he get so damned emotional all the time now? But he said, "Love you, little girl," and knew it was true. The clutch of her small fingers on his hand seemed to tighten directly around his heart. Until this stretch in Nursery, he had never realized it was possible to love anyone so much. Not Janni, ever. Nor even Gilmarin. No one.

He would have no special duties until the next day, when he would go down to the planet's surface. He agreed to stay for a while, letting all the children cluster around him, and when the Poohbear suggested that he tell the older children—the four-year-olds—about the new planet, he gathered them all around him, letting Giljodek climb on his other knee, the others snuggled on cushions all around, very close. Gilbarni, the new Nursery staff youngster—he was about fourteen, shiptime—raised his eyebrows and said, "Thanks, Gildoran. I still have some trouble talking to kids this small. They don't understand a thing."

"Oh, yes they do," Gildoran retorted. "Talk to Gilrushka in Psych. They understand everything you say to them, even if they can't communicate it very well. So be careful."

Gilbarni gave a skeptical shrug, and Gildoran was outraged, until he remembered how he had felt at the beginning of his own Nursery shift; as if the babies were animals howling, incapable of any human communication. Gilbarni would learn, and after all, that was part of the reason for Nursery shifts; the Nursery attendant learned something, too, not just the babies. Gildoran himself had never thought of that before; he had always thought the Nursery attendant took a year out of his own life to sacrifice it to the infants, stalling his real career. Now he realized that he had learned some very valuable things about humanity and love.

"Tell us about the planet," Gilvarth demanded, tugging at Gildoran, and he began, "Well, it's a big planet, with a nickel-iron core—you know what that is? There are polar caps, but very small ones, and there are no seas—"

"How can it be a proper planet without any seas?" Giljodek demanded, and Gildoran chuckled, recognizing the quote from the old Nursery story, quoting back the response: "A planet can be a proper planet even when it doesn't have seas."

Gilvirga, the third four-year-old, an intense, serious big-eyed child, demanded, "If it doesn't have polar caps and doesn't have seas, what *does* it have?"

"Well, if you'll be quiet for a minute, I'll tell you," Gildoran said indulgently, and spent the next half hour telling the children as much as he knew himself about the new planet. He didn't know how much they understood about the technical details, but he would tell them, and let them take what they could from it. The toddler in his lap drowsed, not yet old enough to be interested in any world outside Nursery. But the four-year-olds were intensely excited and finally demanded that he get a visual-screen picture from the Bridge and show them the planet floating beneath, which he did.

"Will we go down?" Giljodek asked.

"Maybe after we get everything set up down there," Gildoran said, "There's nothing there now but little rodents, and things that howl, out in the desert, like little monkeys."

"Do monkeys howl?"

"These do; they have big air-sacs in their throat that vibrate, so you can hear them for a long way. We'll have visuals of them in a few days, and I'll ask Gilrae to send some pictures down." He looked around. "Your supper is on the table, children."

"Eat with me," the baby girl in his lap begged.

"No, sweet; I will have my supper upstairs. That's where my work is now," Gildoran said gently. "But I'll sit here by you and watch you eat—is that all right?"

After supper she clung to him, demanding that

he give her her bath, and he found that washing and drying the small wriggling pink body gave him distinct pleasure. After he finished, she insisted on showing him her drums and castanets, jingling them for him with a distinct sense of rhythm; and when she grew sleepy, he sat fondling her, feeling, with surprise, that he felt calmed and happy.

"Come tomorrow?"

"Not tomorrow, smallest. Tomorrow I am going down to the big planet you heard me tell about."

"What Doran do down there?"

"I will put up a Transmitter, baby, so we can visit other worlds and bring back pretty things for little girls," he said, thinking that one of his first errands when the Transmitter was set up would be to visit a world with a sophisticated music store and find an array of simple musical instruments for her to play with until her hands were big enough for the harp Rae wanted to teach her.

All the children wanted Gildoran to hug them and tuck them into their hammocks—even the least developed of the toddlers, who still could not say his name plainly and lisped "Doda." While he was putting each child into the hammock, he discovered that he had a special fondness for each of them; but somehow, for some reason, he felt closest to the little almond-eyed one, the "imp." He wondered why.

He remembered a long spell of time in the third and fourth months of her life, shiptime, when she had made a slow recovery from one of the sessions of modifying surgery; it was then that the other two had died, and he had been afraid that this one would die, too; Gilban had not held out much hope. Night after night, when she lay awake whimpering, Gildoran had carried her around, propped up in his arms so that she could breathe more easily, or held her, sleeping, for hours, because she woke and fretted when she could not feel the comfort of his touch. Had this formed the bond between them? Even now, when she was healthy and strong, the largest and cleverest of the babies, that closeness remained.

Well, he would bring her some simple musical instruments. It would be good for all the children to have regular musical training, even if only one of them was highly gifted; he would speak to Gilrae about it. He tucked the child into her hammock with a final kiss, and lowered the light.

On the way to the door, he said, "We should name them, Pooh. She, at least, needs it."

"I'll speak to the Captain," the Poohbear said. "Come down again whenever you can, Doran. They really miss you."

"I will," he promised, and realized that he meant it.

V

The landing craft set down in the middle of the barren desert; and as they descended, Gildoran shivered.

"It's colder than I thought!"

"I don't know why," Ramie said, "but for some reason, one usually thinks of deserts as hot. I do, too."

"Well, they come in all temperatures," Gilrae said, "hot, cold, and everywhere in between. At least this one isn't snow-covered steppe!"

"There's not enough water in the water table for snow," said Gildorric, who had come down to make a geological assessment. "But I think if there were, it *would* be snowing."

"Well, thank goodness for thermal clothing, then," Ramie said, smiling, and Gildoran, looking at her triangular face, the slight tilt of her eyes, thought that twenty years ago she must have looked much like his little imp in the Nursery. She was dear and familiar, and it was good to be working with her again, after his year of exile from most of the adults in the Ship.

Gilrae was examining one of the plants close at hand. "Remember: Gilmerritt wants plant samples," she reminded them, and Gildoran bent to look closely.

"A kind of tuber, aren't they? Though admittedly I don't know that much about biology; I thought tubers all grew underground."

"Most of them do, especially food plants," Gilrae said, "but I suppose as the soil grew more and more barren, the last survivors of these plants developed air-roots and air-tubers. Take a good number of samples, will you, Gildoran, if you have room in your bag? And we should check for other varieties; they might be useful on other planets where there are desert conditions."

"You checked them for edibility, then?"

Gilrae nodded. "Gilmerritt ran a dozen tests. They're very high in proteins, and would be a very good food crop for arid lands, since they get their nutrients from air. I suspect that in a world with more moisture, they'd be tastier," she added, and cut open one of the white air-tubers. She offered sample cubes all round; Gildoran made a wry face.

"They might make good Nursery fare—too bland," he said.

"Not gourmet food, that's certain," Gildorric said, chewing the crisp tasteless stuff, "but nice to know there's something down here we *can* eat, if we have to."

"I'll stick to rations," Gildoran said, "but I suppose we could run it through the synthesizer and get some very tasty food. Boiled and mashed, it might be all right, with plenty of spices and seasoning."

Gilrae looked round, assessing. "Gildorric, I suppose you want core samples—"

"Yes, and to check out bedrock," Gildorric said, "Gilraban and Gilmarti thought the ruins here"—he gestured at the horizon, ridged with low rocky shapes—"might be a good place to set up the first Transmitter tie-in. Give the first tourists a good view, attract archaeologists. Set up a special study through Head Center, to get funding for more studies. We might get a small extra grant over and above the finder's fee, for a find of special interest to science."

"That sounds like a good idea," Gilrae agreed. "And I'll get biological specimens. I'll take Doran along to carry the bags; it's not worth the trouble to get a mechanical servo set up—I don't need that many. Ramie, are you going to do anything special?"

Ramie shook her head. "I'm just transportation," she laughed. "Nothing for me to do until you're ready to take off again; I'll come along and help carry specimens and get a look at the ruins." Then, glancing around at the others, "Unless Dorric and you others need me—"

Gildorric shook his head. He and his assistants were setting up heavy machinery. "We're just going to be drilling, checking out seismological studies, making sure we can set up here."

"Maybe I should stay," Gildoran hesitated, "I'm supposed to check for bedrock on a site—"

Gildorric shook his head firmly. "Nothing you could do here; you aren't trained to handle this equipment, and you couldn't touch anything. We'll get your bedrock level, lad, although I have a fair idea it's not far down. Go along with Rae and explore the ruins, if you want to."

Walking toward the low outline of the ancient city, Gildoran felt as if he had been given an unexpected holiday. The low heaped outline of the ruins had made him think they were farther away than they were, that as they approached the piles would resolve themselves into buildings and separate shapes, but as they came closer, he could see that there were only low walls, piled rubble. Here and there a kind of structure rose a few meters, gaping roofless, filled with fallen rubble. Other structures were only low mounds already covered with the growing lichen and the low, prickly air-tuber plants.

"I wonder if this grows all over the planet," Gilramie asked.

Rae nodded. "It must have been an important food crop once—perhaps their principal one. It's a fairly sophisticated plant; highly complex, only one species spread planetwide; there may be minor variations. I don't know if it would sustain life indefinitely—we haven't made exhaustive tests—but it would make a good staple food, balanced with other things."

"I wonder if they cultivated it within the city limits this way."

"It's not impossible," Gilrae said. "That's one city pattern—buildings organized *around* the central food supply—if there are predators, a fairly common pattern. Another pattern is buildings surrounded by croplands. I'm speaking of early stages of civilization, of course, before highly organized distribution of supplies, wheels, rails, air transit, Transmitter."

The city stretched, seemingly endless, kilometer after kilometer. Gildoran was not accustomed to walking so far, but he was young and resilient, and it was pleasant to walk on hard ground, to feel the tug of gravity exercising his muscles. The ruins were rubble, collapsed and faceless; he marveled at the amount of time it must have taken to wear hard stone away like this, unto dulled formless heaps. Memory nagged at him; on the last planet, he had visited, as part of cultural education, many worlds by Transmitter, including ruins in all stages of decay. But nothing, nothing nearly as old as this. He had seen deserted cities, ancient temples, abandoned worlds and cultures; but some trace remained of whatever had built them. Mysterious they might be, yielding nothing of the central ideas behind the civilization, nothing of the philosophies, the religion and thought which had prompted the makers to build temples or cities or great catafalques; but always before, in every ancient civilization he had seen, there were at least physical traces of the population which had raised it toward the skies of their world, in primitive anticipation of the reunion with the civilization beyond their sun and stars.

Here there was nothing; the builders, faceless and unknown, whoever and whatever they might have been, had come and gone, not waiting for reunion with the Galactic culture far beyond their ken.

"Does anyone know if these people were ever visited while they were still flourishing, Rae?"

Gilrae shook her head. "I've checked the records. But we're in new Explorer territory; no ship has ever been in this sector before, as far as I can tell, and there aren't even any rumors of lost races or worlds out in this direction."

"They couldn't wait for us," Gilramie said. "How sad—we'll never know who or what they were!"

And strangely, Gildoran felt an incomprehensible thickness rising in his throat. Like the children in Nursery who had died before they were named, who would be unmourned because unknown, faceless, without potential—here was a race of people he would never know. Something never to touch his life except as an unguessable loss.

Who were they? What had they been? He would never know, could not even guess how they might have enriched the life and civilization of the Galaxy and the Cosmos . . . .

What's happened to me? I never used to think this way!

"I hope Gilban was right about whatever killed

them off, being gone," Gilramie said with a sudden shudder. "When I think of all the millions of people it must have taken to build a city this size, and something that could kill them *all* off—"

"There's nothing here to vector any disease," Gilrae said. "We checked that out, Ramie." She frowned. "Of course there are questions no one can ever answer completely without trying. We have to take *some* risks. That's why we disinfected the landing party, *before* they took off their space suits; thinking about spores. But any spore which could survive this many million—or *billion*—years, would be impossible to detect by any means at our command."

"Some of these places must have been huge," Ramie commented, turning into a gap in one of the low walls. "It's only four or five meters high now. But considering the length of the place, virtually any aesthetic standard would dictate that it should be at least twenty or twenty-five meters high, maybe more. But—what's *that*?" She stopped, glancing around apprehensively at a sudden sharp rustle, a little skittering rush.

Gildoran said, "Look out—"

A sharp, desolate howling rose on the air and a small colony—nine or ten of the small monkeylike creatures who were the only surviving animals on the planet—erupted, screeching with a piercing, ululating yell, from their concealment within a big clump of the air-tuber plants. They paused, clutching one another and gibbering, turning to howl with menacing gestures, at the intruding humans; then fled.

"I feel guilty," Gilramie said, "It's their world now. And here we are trampling all through it."

She spoke in hushed tones; Gildoran realized that they had all been speaking in hushed voices as they walked through the great, deserted necropolis, which hardly bore the shape of a city anymore, with the low mounds overgrown with vegetation. In another few hundred years it would be only low hills, a few ruined lines where walls had once been.

"I wonder," he said, watching the howler troop depart, "if we left them alone, would those little howlers develop into the next dominant race?"

Gilrae shook her head. "Not a chance. Not enough brain size; they seem to be an evolutionary dead-end. They'll probably be extinct in a few thousand years, unless somebody wants to preserve them in a scientific habitat. Few thousand more years left alone, and this planet would have no signs of life at all."

Gilramie smiled and said, "I feel better. Then we're just giving this planet a new lease on life."

"Gilharrad wouldn't agree with you," Rae said. "He would probably say that even for a planet, there is a time for everything—a time to live and a time to die—and we ought to let this one die in peace."

"Gilharrad," said Gildoran, "seems to spend most of his time philosophizing, without much relation to reality." His voice must have been more acerbic than he realized, for Gilrae frowned.

"When you're his age, perhaps you will have earned the right to philosophize, Doran."

Rebuked, he fell into silence. He was warm in his thermal suit, but the endless wind whistled disconcertingly around the low walls, a howl only less pervasive than the distant, unyielding noise of the faraway beasts out in the desert.

Gilrae said, "We ought to think about getting back to the landing craft. I don't think there is that much more to see out here; professional archaeologists might find something of interest, but this all seems to be very much of a muchness. I doubt if there's anything more worth seeing. We might as well fill up a bag with the air-tubers for Gilmerritt—take some leaves too, Ramie—and we'll start back." She turned to the younger woman, but found her gazing intently at a low stone.

"What is it, Ramie?"

Ramie looked up, her voice hushed, and said in a whisper, "I think—Rae, I think this stone has—or had—carving on it, once. Whoever these people were, they had some form of writing."

Rae came hastily to kneel before the stone and put out a hesitant finger toward the worn surface. It was buried in the blowing sand, so that only a meter rose above the surface; but lines of serrations or ridges, formless curves, rippled the flat stone surface a little. "It is," she said in awe. "I don't know if the sand has left enough so that it can ever be deciphered, but the archaeologists will want to see it. I know they'll come here now!"

Gildoran, too, knelt to examine the carving, though Rae warned him not to touch it. "It will have to be photographed, and they'll want to excavate, carefully, to see how far down it goes," she said. "There may be more, in a better state of preservation, if we can find anything out of this wind and away from the eroding of the sand."

"There might be more carvings," Ramie said excitedly. "Let's look around!" She turned round, moving toward one after another of the low overgrown walls. Gildoran thought, himself, that calling them "carvings" was a little exaggerated, but perhaps, in a sheltered spot—

"Those walls under that hillock might be more protected," he suggested, pointing, and Gilrae said, "Maybe for this thousand years; heaven knows how long that hillock has been there, it's really only a sand dune; there might be anything under it. Oh, archaeologists *will* enjoy this one," she said, and her eyes were glowing. As always, fired by her enthusiasm, he came and began to examine the low walls, while Gilrae moved around; she tugged her hood from her head, then, wincing, pulled it back up.

"The wind cuts like a knife—there are regular needles of sand," she said with a grimace. "Does it blow all the time here, I wonder? It's been blowing like this every time."

"Nothing to block it between here and the poles," Ramie said. "Gildorric said we were on the shores of what had been a sea, once. I wish they'd invent a time machine so that we could go back and see what this place looked like. Rae, do you suppose we'll ever have a time machine that will do for time what the Transmitter did for space?"

Rae's quick eyes smiled. "I don't know," she said, "but it's possible, I suppose. Although, since the Transmitter gives us endless planets and so much space to explore, it's possible that there may not be anyone with leisure to think about other dimensions like time." And Gildoran realized that all his life, ever since he could remember, he and Ramie and Gilmarin—poor Gilmarin!—had been clustering around Rae, asking her questions. *The same way the little kids in the Nursery* asked me questions yesterday. He found the thought intensely unpleasant and turned away. Was Gilrae just an internalized image to him? He looked at the woman; she seemed no older than he was himself. Once matured, Explorers seemed not to age until they started to grow older like Gilmarti and Gilharrad! Rae was a beautiful woman, should he think of her as a sort of—of—of mother-figure like a Poohbear?

Ramie was still circling around the stone with the carvings, disturbing a napping howler who made off with a scream. Suddenly she cried out and fell full length on the sand. Gildoran hurried to her side.

"What's wrong?"

"I put my foot in a hole," she said, rubbing her shin, clinging to his arm for support as she clambered to her feet, "No, I'm not hurt . . . look out!" she cried, as Gildoran, too, lost his footing and the ground crumbled away underneath. They scrambled to safety, sprawled full-length, clawing at the sand caving in treacherously around them. Gilrae came, stretching her hands to haul them away to harder ground.

"We'll have to be careful," she said. "All this is sand dune, not hard ground, and there might be excavations. Look," she added, regarding the place where the ground had caved in, "this could have been a cellar—an underground chamber where the roof came down and the sand drifted over. I don't think it would be very wise to set up anything actually on the site of the old city unless we explore it carefully for solidity." She knelt to examine the girl's leg. "Sure you're not hurt, Ramie? Your suit is torn?"

"I don't think the skin is broken," Gilramie said, "just banged a little. Maybe there will be a bruise." She shivered in the chill wind, and Gilrae said, "We'd better get back to the landing craft. Get them on the radio, Doran, and ask if they need anything else from here: sand samples, loose rock—"

Gildoran tugged out his pocket communicator, but when he tried to use it, it crackled and no sign of voices could be heard. He jiggled it angrily, tried Gilramie and Rae's, finally stowed it away in disgust.

"Static; the storm, I guess. And the sand—"

Gilrae nodded. "The sand is full of metal fragments; note how it cuts. Probably magnetic conditions will make it impossible to use the radio a large part of the time."

"That's going to be a nuisance when we get to setting up the Transmitter," Gildoran said, thinking of the delicate inner mechanism of the Joffrey coils and how hard it would be to stabilize magnetic fields and keep the sand out of the works.

"We'll have to devise some kind of housing— temporary shelter to keep the sand out—before you start work," Gilrae said. "And if the communicators aren't working, we'll have to find some kind of line-of-sight signaling system until we can devise some sort of frequency modulation to work around atmospheric conditions. That shouldn't be hard. I—ouch!" She went down, stumbling, measuring her length; and as she picked herself up, they stared at what faced them on the sand.

It was a great head; rising almost a meter from the sand, set on massive shoulders. The erosion of the unending wind and sand had rounded the corners but could not diminish the power of the pointed forehead, the long and feline eyes, the massive arched nose and mouth. It was a countenance of tremendous strength; the three Explorers stared at it, half-hypnotized; some ancient king or god stared back at them from his place, deep-buried in the sand.

Ramie said in a whisper, "At least now we know they were not human, whatever they were."

"What a pity that we will never know what they were," Gilrae whispered.

"I wouldn't say that," Doran said. "We found this; there might be other traces. Maybe underground, or in canyons sheltered from the wind."

"I wouldn't count on it," Rae said, looking around where the fallen ruins, stone crumbled low, stretched away to the horizon. She shivered, looking at the face. "How cruel he looks, and how powerful, how defiant—"

"And look where he is now," Ramie said.

"And yet how important he must have been once, and how powerful, to stand high over this city—" Rae said, still shivering, and quoted in a low voice, "Look on my works, ye mighty, and despair. . . ."

"And there's nothing else," Gilramie murmured. He felt the shiver strike him, moving up and down the spine, a sense of dread and terror. Nothing then lasted. Someday the *Gypsy Moth*, and all of them, would be only a memory . . . gone. Like Gilmarin. Someday, even the toddlers down in the Nursery would be gone, like all the multitudes who once inhabited this vast and crowding city, and everything humans had ever known or thought, as indecipherable as the worn lines on the stone which might, once, have been carved. He was stricken with terror of his own mortality, that nothing would remain, nothing, ever. . . . How could Gilrae stand so calmly looking at the dead city?

Gilrae said softly, "It's scary, isn't it, kids?" and with a sense of mingled relief and resentment—how dared she read his mind all the time, that way?—he realized that she knew what he was feeling, must have felt it always. He suddenly realized that he and Ramie were huddled close together . . . as the four-year-olds had been huddled around him, yesterday, for counsel or comfort, and it annoyed him. Ramie wasn't hurt, she didn't need his support. He moved a little, away from her.

"They're gone and we're still here," Ramie said softly. "Does that mean that Explorers—or humans in general—are more durable? We land on world after world, and never find one where humans have died out; but this race was gone before we ever came here. Even with the time slippage in deep space. I could go back to—to our last world, or to the world where we visited the Hatchery, and the Hatchery might be gone, and everyone we saw there dead, and the government would have changed, and so forth, but there would still be humans."

"Yes, barring a general plague or pandemic; but we've never found a planet where all humans were exterminated," Rae said. "Maybe this race"—she looked at the enormous feline head—"was before any humans had come into our Galaxy at all. Maybe most of the suns where they lived have collapsed by now into black holes. This is a scientific discovery of the highest order, you realize," she added. "We may be lucky—there will be more than a simple finder's fee in this one."

"I wonder where the rest of the statue is," Ramie said. "Has it fallen? Or is the rest of it buried underground?"

"From the proportions," Gildoran said, musing, "if they are anything like human, I'd say the whole statue would have to be eight or nine meters high. The arms and legs—if it had any— might be buried under the sand dunes here or they might have fallen away. Arms and hands are the most vulnerable parts, I seem to remember."

"If it had any," Gilrae warned him. "We can't assume too many analogies with humans." And he scowled.

"Whatever built this city had hands. Or something like them."

Rae looked around. "Where did Ramie go? It's getting dark. We don't want to lose her, and if the wind builds up at sunset, we might have a full-fledged sandstorm. We ought to get back to the landing craft. Ramie? Gilramie!" she called but there was no answer.

The lowering red sun made dim shadows among the tumbled heaps of rubble. Gildoran called too, in growing apprehension.

"Gilramie! Ramie! What could have happened?"

Gilrae said firmly, trying to take stock without letting the dimness and the general desolation trouble her, "There are no large animals here to harm her; in any case, she's able to call out. And whatever else might have happened, she's safe from anything alive. There hasn't been any intelligent life here for a couple of million years, at a conservative estimate. Ramie! Ramie, where are you?"

Gildoran started to hurry away; Gilrae caught at him. She said, and he could hear the faint quiver in her voice, "No, Doran. Stay with me. If the three of us get separated, we could wander all night in this murk and never find one another again. We're already split up; why make three groups?" In the growing shadow, she pulled out her light and flashed it repeatedly around the low stones and fallen walls.

"This is better than shouting; she'll see it and come back to us. I'm not surprised that she can't hear us, with this wind," she added violently, and Gildoran saw her shiver, in the wind that whistled, endlessly, with nothing to break its long sweep.

It seemed too light to have much use yet for the small gleam of Gilrae's portable flasher, but Gildoran began to be troubled. Suppose it grew too dark to find their way back to the landing craft? Well, then, he reminded himself, the others in the party would simply come back hunting for them. If they didn't, or couldn't, then the worst that faced them was a single night spent in the deserted city, listening to the faraway yelps and howls of the little howlers.

"There's no point in rushing off to hunt at random," Gilrae admonished. "Stay close to me, Doran. Which way did you see her go?"

"I didn't. I was looking at this rock, to see if there were any more carvings nearby; I turned around to speak to her, and she didn't answer."

"Then she can't have gone far," Gilrae said firmly. Gildoran looked apprehensively at the darkening sky. How quickly it grew dark, now that the sun was on the very rim of the horizon! Already there was nothing but dusk around them, dusk and eerie shadows.

"The only way to handle this is to search in a spiral," Gilrae said. "As long as we can see that dark spire of rock"—she pointed—"take that for our center and move out, slowly, in a curve—" she demonstrated. "Circle, a little farther out each time. You call; your voice will carry farther than mine over this wind. And flash the light so she knows it's a signal; I'll need to hold mine steady so we won't fall over something and break our shins—or our necks!"

Gildoran followed her, troubled, flashing his light in a regular signal pattern older than history, and shouting, although as the wind whistled through the old fallen walls, he was sure Ramie could not hear it. Between shouts he paused to listen, and during one of the shouts, he heard a faint sound, carried to them uncertainly on the wind.

"Rae! Did you hear it?"

"I heard something; I thought it was a howler."

Gildoran shouted Ramie's name again, and heard again, this time closer, but invisible in the darkness, a faint answering cry.

"Rae! Gildoran!"

"Ramie! Where are you? Call out to us—flash your light—"

Again the faint cry, this time from almost under their feet. Gilrae moved slowly, steadying her light, but could see nothing; then, with a muffled cry, she missed her footing and slid, and Gildoran, leaping to steady her, heard the cry end in a shriek, then a yelp of pain. Then she shouted urgently, "Keep back! Keep back! It's all caved in—ah!" Again the shout of pain, and Ramie's voice, troubled, calling out.

He edged back slowly from the gaping lip that seemed to have opened—a deeper darkness—at his very feet. There was a muffled thrashing, and another cry.

"Gilrae! Rae! Ramie! Where are you?" Gildoran shouted, again and again, groping his way and shining the light to the very edge of the cave-in; but under his feet the ground seemed to shift uneasily and he stumbled back further.

Then Gilrae's voice came from below, taut and shaken.

"Gildoran. Are you all right?"

"Yes. Where are you?" He tried to focus the light into the dark cave.

"We fell. It's caved in here—a roof fell in or something. No, try not to come any closer—"

"Can you show me your light?"

"I lost it when I fell. And I think Ramie's is broken," she added. "It's dark down here; if we can get into my pack, I have spare batteries, so perhaps we can check Ramie's that way. If I can see to find them."

"Are you all right?"

"No," Rae said calmly, "I think I have broken my ankle. Otherwise, yes, and Ramie seems to be unharmed."

"Can I climb down? You'll need help—"

"It would be better to see if you could find your

way back to the landing craft and get help," she said, and he marveled at the calm in her voice, "I certainly can't climb out in this shape, and until it's light, we won't be able to see whether Ramie can."

Slowly, keeping his light fixed on the treacherous ground under his feet, Gildoran circled, trying to see any glimmer which could be the distant, strong lights of the landing craft. On a planet without any light whatever except the distant stars—for there was no moon—he should have been able to see the slightest artificial gleam for many kilometers, but he didn't. Either some rise in the ground hid the landing-craft from them, or the configuration of walls and rubble in the dead city concealed the distant lights from their eyes.

He said, "I don't see the faintest sign of it. I'll try the communicator," but when he pulled it out he heard nothing but static; no matter how he twisted the dial there was nothing but faint angry crackling, and at last he stowed it away again, impatient. He knew beyond all doubt that they were trying to communicate with him, three members of the party separated from the main body, and there was no way they could hear one another. Damned planet, anyway!

"Stand back," he said, returning to the dark rim where the women had fallen, "I'm coming down."

"You should be here and signal in case they come looking for us—"

"They won't come in the dark, and you know it as well as I do. They'll think we decided to make camp in the dead city. In any case, they couldn't quarter all of it in the dark. And Rae is hurt," he added. Through the calm voice he could hear the tight clenched control; she must be in considerable pain, and he had the only working light so they could even see—far less tend—her injuries.

"Speak to me, Ramie—let me know where you are so I won't fall on top of Rae and hurt her if I fall," he said, carefully tying his flasher at his belt so that he could not lose it in his descent.

"I'm here," she said, "and I'll stand over Rae—no, don't try to move, Rae—so that you can't bump into her in the dark."

He could still see, dimly in the twilight, the crumbling ground below. Now, as his eyes were accustomed to the deeper darkness, he could see very faintly the forms of the women below. He felt apprehensive as he prepared to make his way down; the fall had injured Rae, though Ramie seemed unhurt. He kept his light trained at his feet, so that he could see the slanting pile of caved-in rubble, trying to scramble down it without losing his footing; but just the same he lost his balance and slid, landing in a heap on top of the others; Ramie was shielding the other woman with her own body, so that Rae was not hurt by Gildoran's weight.

"Well, that's that," he said, recovering his breath. "Now let's see what's happened to your ankle, Rae. Ramie, hold the light—"

"No, you hold the light; I took a turn with the Medics and I know what I'm looking for," the girl said tartly. "Are you all right, Gildoran?" He felt her hands touch his briefly in the darkness, as if for reassurance, and cling there; but her voice was steady. "Rae, let me try and get your boot off—no, lie still, dear, don't try to move. Gildoran, try—"

and as Rae's low cry of pain followed the lightest touch on the boot, she said, "No. Don't try to unlace it or pull it off. I have one of the stronger knives; it will cut the boot-plastic. Let me cut it off."

Even that was grim, Rae's face whitening in the light of the flasher, her teeth clamped in her lip; and when the boot and the stocking were cut away, the ankle was revealed as a bloody mess of crushed skin, small fragments of bone thrusting through. Gildoran shuddered and turned his eyes away, feeling ashamed; if Rae could suffer it, how could he not look at it?

"I've got a few emergency Medic Supplies in my pack," Ramie said calmly, though he could see that she was paler than usual. "Including disinfectant powder—that's about all I can do for it now. Turn that light around here, Doran, so I can see what I'm doing."

Gildoran felt helpless, simply holding the light while Ramie's competent hands cleaned the wound with disinfectant, bandaged it, and then, the bandages being thin, tore her undergarment to reinforce it with a strong strapping. Gildoran knelt beside Rae, holding the light; but, seeing the woman's pain, finally braced the light where it was steady in a rocky niche and gathered Rae's trembling body in his arms, holding her close as Ramie's hands went unflinching about their painful work. Rae clung to him, shaking, although she did not cry out again, and as Gildoran held her, it seemed that for this moment she was as small and young as the sick infants in the Nursery that he had held and comforted. Always before Rae had seemed invulnerable, indomitable, the strongest person ke knew, a rock of strength in his youthful world; now she was broken and vulnerable, turning to him for comfort, as if he and Ramie were stronger.

"That's the best I can do for now," Ramie said at last and handed Rae a couple of tablets from her pack. "Swallow these, Rae. Here, take a sip from my canteen—that ought to help in a little while. Lie back and rest; when they get you back on board and can look after that ankle properly, there won't even be a scar."

Rae said, with a shaky laugh, "I'm supposed to be looking after you young people. Captain, for goodness' sake! And here I am—" she smiled up at Gildoran, who was still holding her gently. He did not know what to say; he tightened his arms around her shoulders. Rae had always been a part of his life; and now he saw her as if for the first time, wholly different, a woman subject to the same stresses and troubles and fears as himself. For the first time in some months, it seemed, he looked at her without inwardly censuring her for faithlessness to the deserted Giltallen; he saw her as alone, vulnerable, needing help and comfort as much as any other person; not a rock of strength leading them all forward.

Rae had lost her pack in the fall which had cost her her light; but Ramie and Gildoran still had theirs, and they wrapped Rae's shivering, shocked body in the thin foil blankets which could be compressed into one hand, yet perfectly insulated body heat. When they had made her as comfortable as they could, with Gildoran's pack beneath her head, Gildoran flashed his light around where they had fallen.

"Look at that!" Ramie exclaimed, "It's a whole—a whole underground city! And carvings, pictographs—Rae, this is a treasure! It's priceless!"

"And we could have wandered around on the surface for days and never seen anything," Gildoran added. "Maybe that fall was lucky after all—if Rae hadn't been hurt!"

Rae sat up against the wall, blankets huddled around her. She said, "But I'm not badly hurt. And the *Gypsy Moth* will get a bigger finder's fee for a world so rich in archaeological treasures than for a bare desert with carvings too worn to see what they are. Gildoran! Do you realize this means that we'll do more than get out of debt? Archaeologists don't pay as much as miners or some others, but it will really help!"

Gilramie was taut with excitement; duty kept her close to the injured Rae, but Gildoran could see that she was bursting with excitement. "Rae, do you mind if we go and look around?"

"You don't need to ask my permission," Rae said gently, sensing what she meant. "It's Ship's business, child, but if you mean, will I be all right alone, yes, certainly. But—" Suddenly her voice was shaking again. "Don't go too far. There might be—other dangers. Maybe more cave-ins. Rockslides."

Gildoran shook his head. "No tectonic activity; what caved this end in was weight on the underground roof which had simply crumbled with time. The loose sand slid underfoot and carried you down with it."

They walked carefully through the great underground chamber, looking at the carved walls.

Here, where the air had not entered for centuries, and perhaps for millennia, the carvings were undamaged by the erosion of sand, wind and weather. They were bas-reliefs, Ramie found out when she ran her fingers lightly over the rock.

Gildoran turned the small, powerful light on the reliefs. "There's our friend up there," he commented. The face staring at him from the stone was the same as the statue they had seen, the powerful pointed forehead, wide-set feline eyes, massive neck.

"Ozymandias," Ramie said, and at his blank look, elaborated. "The poem Rae was quoting. King of kings in ancient history or legend somewhere; a world he built and thought it would last forever . . ."

"That's what I'm going to name this world," Rae said, behind them, "Captain's privilege . . . what else is there? Oh, *damn* this ankle—"

"Through that arch," Gildoran said, directing the narrow beam of light into a further chamber. "Rae, I hate to leave you in the dark—"

"I'll be all right, go and see," Rae said, and Ramie cried out in surprise.

"Look, rising up there—oh, I know what it is; it's the base of the statue we saw above—and those frescoes on the walls. Tomorrow we can bring lights down here and really see them."

Moving slowly in the dimness outside the circle of light, Gilramie stumbled into another object rising waist-high.

"Look, a stone chest—"

"We shouldn't open it," Gildoran objected, "Whatever's inside it, might crumble away to dust when the air gets in."

"It's already partly opened," Ramie protested, "When the ceiling caved in above, it dislodged the cover—"

Thus admonished, Gildoran handed the light to Ramie and shoved. Inside lay a body, desiccated and small as a child's. Flashing his light, he saw other stone chests and coffins, very small.

"A burial chamber. But what killed them?"

"Who knows? We'll never know," Ramie said. "Plague. Famine. Hunger. War. Look at the frescoes."

The carvings had once been painted, but not even stray flakes of pigment clung, after so long, to the carven walls. Only the stone remained. Following the walls, moving along into further chambers, the two young Explorers saw, fascinated, the feline creatures offering sacrifice to huge stone creatures, rowing strange boats, (confirming the guess that they were beside the shores of what had once been a sea) casting fishnets and cutting up strange sea-creatures, harvesting fields of the air-tubers they had seen, ranged at long banqueting tables.

Which reminded Gildoran that, in addition to being cold with the dankness of the underground chamber, he was hungry. There were rations in his pack—though not enough for three—and the earlier midday meal they had eaten had reduced them. But there were the air-tubers which they had harvested; they could get more tomorrow—there were enough of them, certainly!

Ramie protested. "Look, there are more rooms through there—"

"If more of the roof caved in, we'd be cut off from Rae," Gildoran admonished. "I think we should stay together; we can explore tomorrow."

"Just one more room," Ramie protested, then looked, startled.

"Look, Gildoran, in this room all the stone coffins—they're bigger, all of them, and the carvings reach higher on the wall! How strange, as if the people had almost doubled in size. Or shrank. What would do that?"

"God knows," Gildoran said, turning his light on the carvings. "But come, let's get back to Rae."

Slowly, weaving to avoid the omnipresent coffins arranged in patterns on the floor of the chambers, they returned to the first room where Rae still huddled in the blankets. Gildoran and Ramie divided the meager rations remaining in their packs, while Gildoran with his knife, cut up two or three of the bland air-tubers. He thought, as he chewed the bland whitish stuff, that he would not want to eat it every day.

"Just think, they lived on it, and we're the first living creatures—except the monkeys and those tiny rodents we saw—to taste it in who-knows-how-many thousands of years!"

"But that's just exactly what they did," Ramie said. "No other plant survived. They lived on this, and on the fish we saw them catching. And then the seas dried up and they starved, probably. Maybe it tasted better then; as the sun cooled and the seas dried up, there could have been enough cosmic-ray leakage to create mutations of all kinds."

Rae chewed her portion thoughtfully. "Actually, it isn't bad. Bland, but you want that with a staple food, and this is desert country; there might have been all kinds of cultivated plants. It may originally have been an underground tuber, and as the soil was exhausted, it got more and more of its nutrients from the air; as the ground became desert, less rainfall to leach out soil nutrients and carry them through to roots and tubers. So the only ones that survived may have been the ones which could live on air, like this one. We'll never know." She shivered and Ramie said, "She's still chilled, but the food will help."

Gildoran handed Rae the last of his portion of the ration. "Eat that. No, don't argue; you need the concentrated protein. Rae and I are younger than you are, and we're not hurt. We can manage on the tubers."

Rae started to protest, but Ramie shoved another block of the stuff into her hand. "Doran's right and you know it, Rae," she said, and Gildoran felt her arms around him in the darkness. He hugged her tight, comforted by the touch. There in the darkness, feeling her close to him, he became aware again, as he had been when they spoke of Gilmarin, that his playmate Ramie, his Nurserymate and companion, was a grown woman, not the girl he had always thought her. He kissed her cheek as he had done dozens of times, a gesture of affection and kindness without meaning, and felt, in surprise and some dismay, how she moved closer into his arms; reluctantly felt his body quickening at the touch.

No, damn it, that's not what I want! Is she trying to put me in Gilmarin's place? Firmly—perhaps with more firmness than he intended—he freed himself from her clinging hands; in the faint light of his torch he saw that she was shocked at the rejection, but he wanted to make himself clear.

"Rae's cold," he said, trying to soften it a little. "Here, we'll lie down one on each side of her, and keep her warm. The blankets will cover all of us, if we're close together."

They arranged themselves one on each side of Gilrae, snuggled close together, wrapped in all their clothes and covered with the insulating blankets; and slowly, from the shared body warmth, Gildoran began to warm through and feel the chill dankness of underground less.

"All right to put out the light? The batteries won't last too much longer, the way we've been using them," Rae said, and he assented. In the dark they were very close.

"Like the inside of a Poohbear's pocket," Ramie said with an uneasy laugh. "Back to the womb."

"Anyhow, we're all together," Rae said in the darkness, and Gildoran felt her touch his cheek. "I'd hate to be alone down here. And when morning comes, they won't rest till they find us."

Gildoran shifted his weight, trying to find a comfortable position on the rock floor without knocking against Gilrae's injured ankle. She felt soft and warm in his arms; he could smell her familiar fragrance, not scent or even soap, just the clean woman smell of her that it seemed he had always known. She sighed and he knew that she was still in pain.

"Didn't those pills Ramie gave you do any good?"

"Oh, yes, certainly they did; it doesn't hurt nearly as much now—just aches a little," she said, her breath warm against his neck. He clasped his hand over hers in the dark, and closed his arms around her; even through the layers of heavy clothing, she felt warm and comforting.

"Not cold now?"

"Oh, no, not at all. You're so warm," she said, and after a minute, he heard her breathing quiet, slide into sleep. He sensed that Ramie, too, slept beyond her; the three of them snuggled together in the dark, an animal heap, like small furry animals . . . quiet, warm, drowsy. Yet Gildoran felt troubled.

It was troubling enough to realize that Ramie, his own agemate and playmate, was a woman. He had been so absorbed with the memory of Janni that he had not thought of another woman, and in any case Ramie was too close to him; and now that he knew she had belonged, though briefly, to his lost friend, Ramie was forbidden to him. Yet now he was troubled with awareness of Rae's closeness. Always before she had seemed distant, older, someone to look after him and care for him and command him as a Captain or senior officer commands a youngster; but now he had become aware of her vulnerability, her human need, her womanliness. And suddenly the thought he had been keeping at bay for some time surfaced. He wanted her—he wanted her as a man wants a woman; he needed her in a way he had never needed or wanted even Janni, whom he thought he had loved so much.

And why not? he thought rebelliously. If she could go from Giltallen to Gilhart, why can I not woo her, make her love me? Will she always think of me only as a child? Can't I make her see me as a man, make her care for me?

He knew that her arms around him were for warmth, for comforting in her pain and loneliness. Yet he felt more than that; felt tenderness, yes, and desire. Rae didn't know; and in any

case, in pain from her broken ankle and worried
about their separation from the other party, she
would not be aware of anything more than he had
always shown her, the deference of a junior to a
senior crew member, the close affection of a
shipmate. And this was certainly not the time to
force it on her. But that time would come; oh, yes,
it would come.

VI

Comforted by thinking of that time that would
come, soothed by the quiet breathing of the wom-
en wrapped in his blankets, Gildoran slipped
over the edge into sleep. But the ground beneath him was hard, and he was not accustomed
to this much gravity; his sleep was restless and his
dreams strange. At first he saw the giant stone
statue they had found above, king or god, standing, looming, surrounded by living, breathing
peoples of his own kind, as if all the rock carvings
had come alive, and all the desiccated bodies in
the stone coffins had risen, with their feline eyes
and pointed mask-faces, an alien Day of Judgment. Then he saw the kings on the walls, surrounded by their subjects; casting nets and fishing, cutting up the fish and serving it at great
banquets, golden and jeweled plates heaped high
with the air-tubers they had gathered so many
thousands of years later. Then he saw the king
holding court, and behind him a great procession

of his descendants or ancestors, dwindling away
into the distance, smaller and smaller in the
perspective, vanishing and growing tiny over the
edge of the horizon. Long-dead kings and
longer-dead kings, dying away into smallness
and silence . . .

"No," he said aloud in his dream, half-waking,
"the perspective is wrong." And suddenly, as if
he were looking through the wrong end of a tele-
scope, he saw the nearby feline kings very small,
with the others farther and farther away, growing
larger and more imposing, looming until the
farthest, most distant, longest dead, were giants
like the great statue he had seen. . . .

"That's it!" he said with a great cry, and woke,
to find the dim sunlight of the fading sun flooding
in on them, and the air faintly damp with the light
of dawn. Gilramie made a muffled sound of protest, hiding her eyes from the light. Rae stirred in
Gildoran's arms and said, "What is it, Gildoran.
What's wrong? Why did you cry out like that?"

He sat up and rubbed his eyes, grasping at the
fading memories of the dream. The light, breaking
for the first time in centuries through the broken
roof of the cave-in, was pale on the stone coffins
and the dried body in the one Ramie and Gildoran
had opened. *Small* coffins. The most recent. And
those before were larger . . .

"It stunted their growth," he said. "As the seas
dried up, they had no more fish and no more of the
minerals that came out of the sea. And then the
lack of rainfall meant they had nothing to eat—for
centuries—except this plant." He pointed to the
remnants of the air-tubers on the floor, and then to
the paintings on the wall. "No soil nutrients—just

what they could get from the air. Over the centuries they grew smaller and smaller—"

Ramie pointed to the small corpse in the coffin. "But what happened to the rest of them? The last man alive couldn't bury himself like that, could he?"

"Of course not; we'll never know what happened to the last of them. Without the iodine and minerals of the seas, they probably lessened in brain function until they weren't much brighter than the howlers out there, and the last few generations probably struggled along as savages, not even knowing where they came from." He thought, with a shudder, of naked savages, the last survivors of the great race that had built this city, huddling together in the ruins, not even knowing that their race would die.

We will all die someday. Someday even the Cosmos will wind down and the Explorers will be gone, all of us, even my little one in the Nursery, and not even their names will live. Gone, like Gilmarin. Like Giltallen, who stayed on the world we left, and now he is dead, long dead. We will never know how long dead or where or how he died.

What else could Rae do but mourn when it was the time to mourn, and then find someone else to love, someone who is still there to love? Because Giltallen, even if he lives, is dead to her, dead to all of us, dead as all these forgotten kings carved on the walls there.

"You are probably right," Rae said, and he had gone so far into his thoughts that for a moment he could not remember the train of his thought.

"Once, before the Transmitter, when there were no Explorer ships, but colonies moving between stars at lightspeed, there was an abandoned colony, and when they were discovered again, thousands of years later, they had mutated beyond recognition and, because of a lack of some essential nutrient—I don't remember the details—they had been stunted as a race; they were so small that the tallest of them were no more than a meter high."

"And while you speculate about the causes of death among the dead races," Ramie said, shivering as she crawled out of the blankets, "I might point out that if we starve here, we will not need generations to die out. Have you given any thought, Gildoran, to how we are going to get out of here?"

He went and looked at the rockslide. "I think I could climb up out of that cave-in," he said, and put his foot on it, but the loose rubble rolled and brought stones showering down.

"That's no good," Ramie said, and went into the adjacent room, flashing Gildoran's workable light in the dimness. "Look, here where the roots of the statue are; there's a gleam of light—see?—where the rocks have come away around the statue. I can climb up there, and through—"

"But Rae can't," Gildoran said, "You and I will have to climb out and bring help."

"Rae shouldn't be left here alone," Ramie said.

"You're right. Stay with her and I'll climb up," Gildoran said, putting his foot on the foot of the statue and grasping at the great knee.

She faced him in sudden anger. "Why do you take it for granted that you can climb better than I? I'll go; I'm lighter and can squeeze through that opening more easily. You stay with Rae—"

"Children, children," Rae said in amusement from her place in the first chamber, "there is no sense in fighting over it."

Gildoran chuckled. "Settle it Nursery style. Flip a coin—well, my ident disk. You call it; number or plain."

Yet it was not just the Nursery style; everything on the *Gypsy Moth,* including Rae's election as Year-Captain, was chosen by lot unless it could be rationally handled by computer. Ramie said, "Plain."

He flipped, and the disk rolled along the floor; they scrambled after it, shone the light.

"Plain," Ramie said, picking it up and handing it to Gildoran, "You stay."

"All right," he said, resigning himself, "Here, let me boost you up partway—"

He shone the light after her as Ramie struggled up the great worn statue, forcing her way through the chink of light near the roof of the chamber. She disappeared, was only kicking legs below; struggled upward, shouted back.

"I'll get back to the ship, bring them as soon as I can . . ."

When she had gone, Gildoran went back to Rae. She looked white, worn with pain; but he had no more of the painkillers to give her. He knelt beside her, tenderly tucked her into all the blankets.

"They'll come soon, Rae, and they'll get you back aboard, and before midday your ankle will be all fixed up—"

"Oh, certainly," she said, with a wan smile that only stretched her mouth. "That's not what I'm worrying about. As soon as I get back aboard

Gypsy Moth, they'll have it in a cast. I'll even be able to walk on it. It's just—I'm Captain, I hate abrogating my duties this way."

"They'll understand. You aren't to blame for a cave-in, for goodness' sake!"

She tightened her fingers on his hand and said, "The Captain's to blame for everything. You'll find that out someday."

"If they think it could have been prevented—if they think it's your fault, if they try to blame you, I'll—I'll—" Gildoran began, surging with anger that anyone might try to blame Rae. But she laughed. "You'll do what? You'll tell them otherwise? That's sweet of you, Doran," she said and patted his fair hair as if he were a Nursery child and she an indulgent Poohbear. "But you'll find out someday what it means to be a Captain, and you don't make excuses for what happens when it's your Ship."

Gildoran felt impotent rage; did she think he was only a child? But she looked so exhausted, so worn with pain, that he could not show his anger. He could only try to take her mind off it as much as possible.

"You should see the carvings in the other room. A whole life-style for a nonhuman race," he began. "Kings or Gods, sacrifices, harvests. . . ."

"Yes," said Rae with relief, understanding what he was trying to do, "Tell me all about them, Gildoran. I can't go and see them for myself."

VII

The sun was high, coming down vertically from the direction of the cave-in, when they heard shouts and noises outside. Three crew members came to the rockslide and carefully worked their way down, carrying shovels and a stretcher. Gilban, the Medic, quickly made his way across the rubble on the floor toward Rae; but Gilhart brushed him aside in his rush to scoop Rae up in his arms.

"Rae, oh, Rae, I was so frightened!" He laughed, with relief, holding her to him. "I gave them all a bad time because they wouldn't agree to go out and look for you in the dark, I knew it was senseless but I couldn't bear to think of you alone out here with only these wretched youngsters—"

"They took good care of me, Hart," she said, putting out her hand to stop him. "As well as anyone on the crew could possibly have done—"

"But they probably caused the trouble in the first place," Gilhart grumbled, scowling at Ramie and Gildoran. "You should have taken someone more experienced with you! Oh, my love, I was so frightened—"

"It's all right. I'm all right, dearest," she soothed, and the gesture became a caress, her hand moving across his cheek tenderly. "Look what we have found; there'll me more than a finder's fee this time, and it's worth a broken bone or two."

"Not if it's yours," Gilhart grumbled, barely looking around the carvings.

"That will do." Gilban said sharply, "Put her down, Hart. I have to look at that ankle, and then get her up to the landing craft and then up to *Gypsy Moth*—that leg might need surgery. You two can do your billing and cooing later on."

While Gilban bent over Rae, Gildorric came behind Gildoran to look at the inner chambers. He said, "This is fabulous, tremendous, Gildoran." He listened with flattering attention while Gildoran showed him, with the powerful lights they had brought, the carvings and explained their theory about why the race had first dwindled and then died.

"Could be, very likely was," he confirmed. "Any archaeological crew can tell us. And when we get to the *Gypsy Moth* we can analyze those air-tubers."

"We ate most of them," Gildoran confessed.

"There's billions more," Gildorric laughed, "and I have a pretty fair idea what you'll find; because we gave them preliminary testing. They contain only partial proteins; probably without the basis of fish for their diet, the people couldn't survive. They look feline; probably they have digestions that can't completely metabolize vegetable proteins, and they'd need large amounts of meat or fish, and with the oceans drying up—" He shrugged. "At a guess, lack of iodine and thyroid deterioration. No iodine in the spectrum—no halogens generally, no fluoride for Joffrey coils."

Gildoran thought about the Transmitter, bringing people here—but for what? "No one could live here, then, if the planet is devoid of essential elements—"

"A terraforming crew can take care of that, after we get a Transmitter tie-in," Gildorric said, "Plant plenty of algae and drill down to the water table; use nuclear fusion to get all the water we need for cloud cover and the seas could even come back someday. Oh, this is going to be a good world, but we'll leave it desert a while to preserve what we can of these ruins."

Aboard the *Gypsy Moth* it was quickly confirmed that Gilrae's injuries were minor, though painful; soon, in a walking cast, she was going about her duties as if there had been no interruption. Before Gildoran was sent down to the Transmitter crew working on the surface, he went to the Nursery again, hunting for his special small charge, who dropped the colorsticks she was scrawling with, and charged him, grabbing at his hair as he bent over.

"Want ride," she demanded, and as he hoisted her to his shoulder and obediently galloped around the Nursery, he felt an enormous inner twinge. He might never have seen her again; he might have been killed in the rockslide, be as dead to her as Gilmarin or the centuries of dead and stunted kings lying in their stone coffins in the necropolis down there.

"No, no more rides, sweet. Don't tease," he said firmly as he lowered her to the Nursery floor, "Gildoran has to go down and build a Transmitter, and little girls have to stay here and learn things to be big girls, so *they* can come and build Transmitters some day."

She considered this a minute, pouting, then snatched up some blocks and said, "Build Transmitter!"

It was time—more than time—that this one had a name. She was already capable of abstract thought; now she needed a solid sense of identity. And time would not delay or hold back, but moved relentlessly, bringing to everyone an appointed time. A time to mourn. And a time to forget mourning and to remember the needs of love.

He bent down and kissed the rosy cheek. "Goodbye, Gilmarina," he said, "Build your Transmitter, and I'll go down and build mine."

And he went out of the Nursery, prepared to argue them all down for the right to give this name to the child he loved, in memory of the playmate he and Ramie had loved, but whose time was gone.

Part Three

HELLWORLD

I

It lay a thousand miles beneath them, blue and beautiful in their viewscreens, wrapped in a fluffy blanket of pale clouds, drifting endlessly across its face. There were continents and oceans and polar caps.

"Looks like it's got everything a planet ought to have," Raban said, twisting the dials that kept the world below them in focus. "What does it say to you, Doran?"

Gildoran read out the computer data, summarizing as he went. "Plenty of heavy metals. Nickel-iron core. Low radiation background, no Van Allen-type belts worth mentioning. I think this one is going to be it, Raban."

The older man nodded. "We need it," he said. "We're running a little bit low on iron. Pooh

Three said some of the babies had a low hemoglobin reading—not low enough to be dangerous, but low enough that we shouldn't pass up a planet with an iron-based chemical structure. Final decision's up to Rae and the Captain, of course, but I think we go in." He got up and stretched. "Let's go break the news."

Gildoran spoke formally to the fifteen-year-old girl at the Communications switchboard; "You have the Bridge, Lori." It still felt funny leaving her there alone. He'd spent the last year teaching her the work of her first post, and it had gone so deep in him—you never left a Class C apprentice on the job alone, not even for twenty seconds, not in *any* sector, without a Class A on the job—that he still felt he ought to call someone else to relieve him. He started to ask her if she thought she'd be okay, but fortunately he remembered in time how he'd felt on his first post. So he waited for her formal confirmation "I have the Bridge," and, without another word, made himself turn away and leave the Bridge at Raban's side without a backward glance.

Raban said, as they went down in the lift, "It's about time we found a good one. Many more like the last couple of systems, and we'd be getting into the center of the Nebula. Nothing but frozen giants and dark stars in system after system—and when Rae did find a likely-looking star, its companion picks just *that* time to go nova. Lucky we were still outside Barricini's Limit, or we'd have been drawn in." He looked grave. "I've always believed that's what happened to the *Golden Hind*. It was eighty years ago, shiptime and we never heard anything except that it hasn't been reported on any known world for two thousand years of their time. But when I last talked to a friend from that ship, he said they were heading in the direction of the Greater Magellanic Cloud and there were half a dozen stars going nova in that direction, about then."

Gildoran was too young, shiptime, to remember the *Golden Hind*. It was only a name he'd heard, sometime, somewhere, knowing it was one of the old roster of the Explorer ships.

Once there were a hundred of them. How many are left now, I wonder?

But that was another of the questions you learned never to ask.

Raban said "It's your planet, Gildoran. You want the privilege of telling the Captain about it?"

This was generous of Raban; he could have claimed credit for himself. "Not necessary. We found it together. But before the official word goes out, can I drop down to the Nursery and tell Ramie? I know she's worrying."

Raban smiled knowingly and said, "Sure, you tell her first." And suddenly Gildoran was angry.

"Damn it! I'm sick of this—look, Ramie's working in Nursery. She's worrying about the babies and the hemoglobin levels. I promised, if I got the word, I'd tell her right away. That's all it is. *All.*"

Raban blinked and stared. "Have you two quarreled, Doran?"

He said stiffly "There's no 'us two' to quarrel. No, Ramie and I have always been good friends. I hope we always will be."

*That's no lie. We will be again, when Ramie gets
over this nonsense . . .*

"Look, Gildoran, I'm sorry," Raban said slowly,
"I had no intention of getting you mad—or of
prying into your business, either. It's only that
everybody thinks of you and Ramie in the same
breath, almost. Everybody on board *Gypsy Moth*
expected that you two would be paired and settled down by now."

"Everyone thought! Everyone expected!" Gildoran burst out. "Maybe that's half the trouble!
People have been mentally putting me and Ramie
to bed together since we were twelve years old!"

*Even Ramie, herself. Dammit, can't she have a
little more independence, a little self-respect?
Can't she do her own thinking instead of just
taking what other people think as gospel?*

Raban said slowly "I'm sorry it bothers you,
Doran. But look at it from our point of view, can't
you? You're almost exactly the same age . . .
you're the only two on Ship who are the same age,
since we lost Gilmarin. If it isn't Ramie you want,
who?"

"That's the kind of thinking I mean," Gildoran
said desperately, "what difference does age
make? It isn't as if we could expect to start a
family!" Raban looked shocked and offended as if
Gildoran had voiced some blasphemy.

I've broken another taboo!

"Everybody pairing us off just because we happen to have been hatched in the same litter! I thought we were all supposed to be equals aboard Ship, once we're out of the Nursery, the only caste being what office we're holding at the time! Is that true? Isn't that Explorer custom? Or is that just some kind of pretty lie you tell us, and the truth is that you keep all the children together in their play-pens?"

Raban blinked and shook his head. "No," he said. "No, it's not that. You are our equals. You, or Ramie, might be the Captain of *Gypsy Moth* next year and every living soul on this ship would be under your orders. No, Doran. It's only that . . . well . . . I don't know why it's hard to say this, but it is. We're . . . well, we're *sentimental* about you and Ramie, Doran. Maybe it's hard on you. Maybe it makes you feel as if we were intruding into your private affairs. But that's all it is, just sentiment. After all . . ." he looked away, in the narrow shaft, from the younger man, "after all . . . you were our babies."

It was Gildoran's turn to be shocked and to keep silent, while they stepped out of the lift shaft and moved down the corridor.

They were high in the ship now, far out on the rim where gravity was low, kept at minimum for the Elders; the few elder statesmen of the *Gypsy Moth*, too old for work, too old to bear the gravity or stress of a planet. Even when they were on the surface of a world, they were kept within the antigravity fields for their own safety. Gilharrad, Year-Captain on the last world, had joined them at his own request only a few weeks ago, shiptime; he would never hold another official post aboard *Gypsy Moth*.

They found the Year-Captain, Gilhart, and Gilrae, who was serving as Coordinator this year, in old Gilharrad's quarters. When Raban came in, it was the Elder, not the Captain, who immediately guessed their mission.

"The new planet's a good one."

"Looks like it," Raban said. "It was young Doran who found it, though, and checked it out, so that credit really belongs to him."

The captain, Gilhart, a man (apparently) in the prime of life, short and thick-set for an Explorer, with broad heavy cheekbones and peculiarly deep-set eyes, smiled in a friendly way, and said "Good work, youngster. It's about time."

"I've always thought Doran had an instinct for planet-finding," Gilrae said with a warm smile. She came and laid her arm lightly around Gildoran's shoulder.

Gilhart scoffed "Is that a woman's intuition, Rae?" It sounded like an old joke between them, and Gildoran went stiff under Rae's arm.

"It's not a joke," old Gilharrad said, "I've often thought planet-finding is an instinct. A survival skill for Explorers, maybe. A psychic talent that some people have, like perfect pitch. Oh, yes, you young people can scoff all you like, but in my time more planets have been found by instinct and hunch than by all your scientific computations, Hart."

"I'll have to take your word for it," Gilhart chuckled, "because if it's a talent, I'm evidently tone-deaf. I trust my instruments."

"And much good they were doing you," Gilrae said affectionately. "Three years since the last good planet—I've been seeing frozen methane planets in my *sleep!*"

Gildoran watched the woman jealously.

She and Giltallen were paired before I was born. Now she's forgotten him and she's with Gilhart all the time.

He looked away from her, confused and angry as if she could read his thoughts.

Gilharrad said "Perhaps the planet simply was not ready to be found."

Gildoran looked at the old man. His wrinkled face was peaceful, his eyes half-closed; his body, fragile and emaciated until the old bones barely seemed enclosed by the flesh, lay supported in a flotation hammock; he was smiling a little. The young man said uncertainly, "You're joking, of course."

"No. Perhaps the planet called to us unconsciously, and we reacted without knowing it. After all, what do we know of worlds? Our own brains are only magnetic fields, and planets have enormous magnetic fields. Why should one magnetic field not tune in to another?"

It makes a strange kind of sense. From where he is now, who knows what he sees?

Gilrae said softly, "Planets have a call. Every now and then someone will feel that call, and leave the Ships for some particular world . . . like Giltallen. . . ."

Gilhart said in a low voice, "There used to be a saying: 'For every Explorer, somewhere there's a world with his name on it!' "

Gilharrad said peacefully, "If that were true, then mine must be somewhere outside Cosmos, for now I will die as I lived, here on the *Gypsy Moth*."

The Captain grimaced. "Well, this one's waiting. Let's hope it doesn't have anyone's name on it; we're short handed."

The Elder smiled, a smile of utter content and peace. He said, "Well, go along, you children, and look at your new world. You young people are always excited about every new planet!"

"Well, it's our job," Gilhart said.

Gilharrad shrugged that off. "Planets! Planets are only holes in space! They are only interruptions in the true Cosmos!"

"They're what the Explorers are all about," Gilhart said, and Gilharrad shook his frail head. "You think so? Never mind, someday the time will come when you can see the truth. Our true purpose is only the quest, the seeking. The planets are only the excuse." His eyes dropped over his lids wearily. "I will meditate on this new world and see what place it has within the completeness of the Cosmos," he sighed, and immediately he slept.

The others quietly left the low-gravity room, and only when they were outside in the shaft did Gilhart say, "I wonder if he means all that stuff, or if he's playing a straight-faced joke on us all? I hate to think his mind's cracking."

Gilrae shrugged. "Who's to say what's true?"

Gilhart said, "Well, it's too mystic for me. I take it you're still excited about landing, Rae?"

The woman smiled. "Not really. I just get caught up in subjective time and meditation, and then I have to come down into gravity routines again. I can never meditate properly when we're downworlding."

Raban said sourly, "Shall I fix you up a place in the Floaters level, Rae? Not this year, please. We're too short-handed."

She shook her head, and her bleached hair went flying in the low gravity. Again it seemed to Gildoran that she had not changed a particle since he was in Nursery; he wondered how old she was, and felt a stab of pain at the thought of her changing, however little.

How old is she, anyway? You never knew, unless the person was younger than you.

"Don't mind me," Gilrae said. "I'm not due for Floater status for another hundred years shiptime. At least. Maybe three hundred. It's just . . . oh, well, life would be perfect if we didn't have to work for a living. I used to think of space as just something we had to get through between planets. Now it's the other way around. So let's go get through with it, and we'll never do that till we start."

Down on the Nursery level, the children were being tucked into hammocks by the great slow-moving Poohbears; when Gildoran came in, one of them broke off and came toward him.

"Is there news, Gildoran?"

"Yes. A planet," he said. "Nickel-iron core, so we're going in tomorrow."

The great brown-furred alien smiled with relief. "I was afraid we'd have to try synthesizing it," she said. "Three of the babies are showing signs of primary anemia. Now, of course, there's no hurry. Do you want to come in and say goodnight, Gildoran?"

He stepped into the great room, where the three-year-olds were being tucked into hammocks, and the seven-year-olds were finishing supper. They were already bleached like Explorers, skin translucently pale, hair silvery white; but the four small heads on the pillows of their hammocks were still faintly brown, rusty, blond. One of them wriggled loose and came running to Gildoran naked, squealing his name. He bent and lifted the tiny girl up, hugging her close. In her hand was a pair of castanets which she jingled with rhythmic insistence. He chuckled. This one was never without some kind of musical instrument in her hand.

"Put the castanets away, Gilmarina, and go to sleep."

"But I want to show you my big harp," she protested. "Rae let me play today on the big harp, not my little one!"

"But it's bedtime, smallest," he said indulgently. "Tomorrow I'll come down and you can play the harp."

"Then you tuck me in bed. No, go away, naughty Pooh," said the child, frowning and kicking out at the Poohbear who came to take her, "No love you. Love Gildoran."

Ramie looked up from her place at table between the older children. "I see you still have a fatal charm for her, Gildoran." The Poohbear said staidly, "You needn't bother with her unless you wish, Gildoran. Gilmarina has to learn that she can't have everything she wants."

"No, I'll put her to bed," he said, lifting Gilmarina in his arms and tucking her into her hammock. He bent and kissed the small, rosy, charming face, thinking with a little sadness that in

another year she would lose the last of that pretty
color and be as pale as he was himself, as they all
were. Well, it was only that she would, then, be a
true Explorer, one of them, without even the last
trace of any tie to whatever homeworld she might
have claimed. Really theirs. But she had been that
from the day they brought her aboard *Gypsy
Moth*.

He said, as severely as he could manage, "Go to
sleep now, Marina, and don't make trouble all the
time. You're a big girl now, not a baby." But,
accepting her damp kiss, he knew that for him she
would always be a baby, *his* baby. Was this how
Gilraban felt about Ramie, about him? Did Rae
feel that way, too?

Secretly, for no one would ever say it aloud, he
thought that he knew, just a little, what it must be
like to be a father.

*I wonder if that's why every one of us—from the
Captain to the twelve-years-olds—has to take a
turn, every year, at Nursery duty? Just so we won't
forget?*

Ramie was finishing with the seven-year-olds.
She called to him lightly "Just a minute, Gildoran.
I'm off-shift and we can go up together." Her
smile told Gildoran how pleased she was at the
prospect. He squirmed. But what could he do?
They had to live together on the *Gypsy Moth*,
maybe for hundreds of years. He wasn't in love
with her. He loved her, but only as he loved all of
them, all people who had always been there. But
he couldn't rebuff her, make trouble, cause misery. He waited.

Watching the Poohbears, he felt—for the hundredth time—curious about these aliens who lived among the Explorers without being of them. They had always been there. But why? What did they derive from their contact with the Explorers?

It's necessary, of course. Every one of us—we live so long—is a potential sexual mate for every other Explorer. With the Poohbears for our mothers, we avoid any maternal relationship. Therefore there's never a hint of incest.

But where did the Poohbears come from? Did anyone even know?

He stared at the enigmatic, furred, beloved face of the Poohbear who had come to adjust Gilmarina's covers around her small bare shoulders, with a wave of old, habitual love and affection. But he realized that he did not even know the Poohbear's personal name, or even if she had one. Or even, he thought with sudden shock, if she were a *she!* Somehow the speculation felt wrong, and he supposed one didn't speculate about one's mother's sexuality.

But Poohbear isn't even my own species! Yet she's my mother. Crazy!

Ramie came up to him, jauntily slipping her arm through his. "I'm finished. Let's go up to the Bridge, Gildoran, I want to look at the new planet. I expect I'll be baby-sitting most of the time we're here, but I can *look* at it, and hope there's enough sun to give the babies sunbaths."

"Are you disappointed that you're on Nursery duty while we're downworlding this time?"

"I don't know," she said. "Maybe I'd hoped to be on Transmitter detail. It's exciting to hook it up the first time and feel that you're tying a new world into a network of a hundred thousand worlds. But there'll be other planets, and I'm sure to hit Transmitter detail on one of them sooner or later. There's plenty of time."

"I wish I could be that contented about things."

Damn. There are so many good things about Ramie. I hate feeling at odds with her this way.

She glanced at him sidelong out of her strangely tilted dark eyes, and said quietly, "I'm not always that contented, Gildoran. I just don't like to get hysterical about things I can't change. That doesn't mean I'm just . . . accepting them. I don't suppose you've changed your mind?"

"No," he said, "I haven't changed my mind, Ramie."

Her voice sounded a little bitter. She said "Well, I suppose there's time for that, too."

He made his voice hard. "Don't count on it."

She tightened her hand briefly on his wrist. She said "Gildoran, I swear I won't be angry or . . . or make jealous scenes, but . . . is it Lori you want?"

He flared in real anger. "That's not worthy of you! Lori's just a baby. What do you think I am?"

"As I remember, she made Class B a few weeks ago shiptime. I seem to remember you and poor Gilmarin being very indignant when someone spoke of our group as children, during that time. And you've spent all your time with her for the last year."

Gildoran pointed out with restraint that he had been teaching Gillori to operate the Communications Desk during hours, and was not given to spending his recreation time with little children unless he was on Nursery duty. "You might as well be jealous of Gilmarina—I spend more time with her than I do with Lori, off duty."

Gilramie sighed. She said "It isn't jealousy, exactly, Doran. It's just"—she made a helpless gesture— "oh, call it habit, I'm used to you, maybe I simply haven't the . . . oh, the inner strength to take up with someone else. Maybe I'm just following the line of least resistance. If I knew, positively, that you cared for someone else maybe it would be easier."

Gildoran felt intensely sorry for her, but even through his pity there was enough resentment to turn away without answering. Ramie sighed and said, "Oh, all right, forget I said anything. Pure self-indulgence on my part. Let's go along and have a look at the new planet."

II

There were twelve in the small shuttle ship which always went down first; that was the minimum number to do the basic preliminary work without leaving the ship short-handed. This was always the one real point of danger, the first penetration of a completely unknown planet. As they dropped through the thick cloud-cover, Gildoran felt his muscles tensing with a curious, cold, strangely bracing fear. It was the first time he'd drawn landing-party duty, but he'd heard plenty about what you could find on a really strange planet. When he was still in the Nursery, four members of a landing party had gone into an innocent-looking, deserted swamp; within two minutes, all four had been swooped on, and literally chewed up by swift-flying carnivorous birds. There had not even been enough left of them to bury.

Tradition required the Year-Captain to lead every landing party. It was the only way to divide this dangerous duty with absolute fairness; the Year Captains were chosen by lot, and everyone on shipboard over twenty-one was eligible, unless he or she had been Year-Captain within the past seven years. Gilhart was up front next to old Gildorric, who was navigating; the other members of the landing party had been chosen either because there was a need for the specialty they were filling this year—or because they were junior enough to be expendable. Gildoran knew he still came into that category, and so did Gillori, who was wedged into the seat beside him, chattering from sheer nervousness. One of the Poohbears was among the crew to check the suitability of the climate for the children; if it was doubtful they would be kept inside the *Gypsy Moth*; if it was healthful, an outdoor camp would be set up immediately so that the children could get accustomed, again, to gravity and sunlight.

Lori said "What would happen if there was already an Explorer ship down there?"

Gilrae looked back at the girl and said, "It's been known to happen. About thirty years ago we teamed up with the *Tinkerbelle*, opening a big system with three habitable planets. But none of our signals were answered from space this time, so no Explorers. It's all ours." She frowned faintly, and Gilhart, looking over her shoulder at her instruments, said "What's the matter, Rae? Something not looking quite right?"

She shook her head. "Nothing I can put a finger on. Maybe it looks *too* good—maybe I'm wondering why no one's picked this one yet."

"Law of averages," said Gilhart with his winning grin. "We've got to have some luck. Don't go psychic on us, darling. If you do feel psychic, save it for . . . let's say . . . a more personal occasion." He laid a hand on the nape of her neck, and the woman smiled up at him, still bent over her controls, reaching her free hand up to take his.

Gildoran looked away.

The hell of it is, you can't even have the satisfaction of not liking Gilhart. He's such a damn nice fellow. You can even see what Rae sees in him. Everybody likes him.

It was a relief to hear Lori start chattering again. Lori asked, "What happens if we run out of planets some day?"

"We're in trouble," Gildoran said lightly, then more seriously, "But it's not possible. That's a big, big Universe out there, Gillori. Even if only one star in a thousand had planets and only one planet in a thousand was habitable, we still could go on for a million million years without exhausting the Galaxy, and that's just this one Galaxy."

"It's like the old story of the Marching

Chinese." Gilhart said, "and don't ask me what the Chinese were because I never knew, but there used to be an old story that you could never line 'em up and count them because there were so many billions that by the time you came to the end of the line a whole new generation was born, grown up and having more children. Maybe they were some kind of rabbits. Anyway, by the time we came—theoretically—to the end of all the planets which exist *now*, more stars and planets would have evolved and cooled down and more spiral nebulae would have been thrown off and so forth. Of course, none of us would live that long—probably not even the oldest Floater still alive in the fleet—but theoretically, at least, the Explorers could go on for eternity."

"Now who's getting mystical?" Gilrae laughed. "Dorric, do you have the coordinates from meteorology? Where are we going to set down?"

"Off the equator," the navigator replied, "Southern hemisphere, fairly near the seashore but far enough inland to avoid coastal rainfall belts. I don't much like the wind patterns in the northern hemisphere; too much danger of setting down in a hurricane belt, unless we could wait out a full season and observe. I can't guarantee anything, but this area should have as good a climate as we're likely to find."

"Not too cold, I hope for the children's sake," the Poohbear said in her gentle voice.

"I'll put in a special requisition," Gilrae said.

Gradually the small landing craft dropped down toward the cloud cover. There was the unfamiliar sensation of weight growing as they came within the gravitational field and slackened speed, so that they were no longer an object in free orbit, but a vehicle with a described, not an orbital path above the planet. The brilliant sunlight dimmed and became vaporous and translucent as they went into the thick clouds.

"With this much cloud cover, we might get a greenhouse effect," said the second-string botanist, Gilmerritt, "Once we get this planet opened up it might turn out to be a health resort."

"Congratulations," Gilhart said absently. "You have just won the long-distance conclusion-jump award. Planet not even landed on, and you're building a health resort."

"I'm not superstitious," Gilmerritt said with a touch of defensiveness, "We've done enough preliminary checking from space to know it's habitable, and that was an educated guess based on my experience in my own specialty."

Gilhart swung around to look at her. His face was very grave. "There's only so much checking we can do from space. Even if the last fifteen planets have been perfect—or the last hundred—never forget; there is no single planet in the Universe that's like any other. Maybe ninety-nine in a hundred that look good enough to land on could be playgrounds, health resorts, whathave-you. But sooner or later you're going to land on one that bites back."

"You really are accentuating negative thinking, aren't you, Captain?" Merritt said, a little startled.

He shook his head. "Always hope for the best, but don't expect it. Because that's when Explorers get taken off guard. And, sometimes, when they get killed. Okay, everybody, end of lecture. There are twelve of us landing. I'd like twelve of us to go home again tonight, if you're all agreeable, so pay attention. . . . Dorric—ready to land?"

"Ready, Captain."

"Cut in the atmospherics, and take us down."

The atmospheric drives came in with a roar, and conversation became impossible in the landing-craft cabin. Gildoran, yawning to ease the buildup of pressure inside his ears, felt the tension, briefly dispelled by the good-natured banter, build up again.

His planet.

He had discovered it. To some extent he would always be identified, in the minds of the crew of the *Gypsy Moth*, with this world. It was just one of those things. Not in the rules, of course. Legally it was the Captain's responsibility, and the Science Officer's, to decide whether or not it was a good world, one they could open and lock into the chain of the Transmitter. In the eyes of the Galaxy, the success or failure of this world belonged not to any one man, but to the Explorers as a whole in general, and to the *Gypsy Moth* in particular.

Legally, and according to Ship's rules, Gildoran would get no credit if the planet turned out well, and no blame if it turned out badly.

But it was one of those things. In the minds of the *Gypsy Moth's* crew, it was Gildoran's world, and if it was a good world it would somehow add to his stature and his reputation. And if it turned out to be a catastrophe—well, legally they couldn't fault him, they couldn't penalize him, it was just bad luck, but they wouldn't forget. Not in thirty years of shiptime, not in a hundred years, they wouldn't forget.

He raised his head, blinking with the strain of

the descent, and stared at the rapidly growing image of the green world below them.

His world.

The whine of the atmospherics grew to a scream; then dimished. Instead of plunging through atmosphere, they were floating quietly, in the landing craft; hovering above what seemed to be a flat and featureless sea of green.

Gildoric asked "Do we burn off a space to set down, Captain?"

Gilhart shook his head. "Not right away. We will if we have to, but do a skim at a few hundred feet. Find an open space, if you can. Seems a shame to burn up any of that nice forest, and then we have to start controlling the fires right away. Not to mention the damage to any animal life. A burnoff should be a last resort. Not to mention that if we set down in the middle of a jungle, it's hardly a good spot for a Transmitter."

Rae chuckled. "I remember once when we had to set a twenty-four-hour guard over our equipment for six weeks while we were building. Turn your back for half a second and the small tools and wire just weren't there. Things like monkeys in the forest would snatch them up and we'd find them in the mud a few hours later—I think the little beasties used them for toys. It was maddening."

Gildorric grinned and said, "I think you were still in the Nursery, Rae, when we landed on a world where there were insects who grabbed our wire and chewed it up—and digested it, too. Did we ever have fun getting the first Transmitter up on *that* place!"

Lori asked, "But you *did* get it set up? Do you *always* get it set up?"

Gilhart shook his head slowly. "No. Like I say, sometimes you hit a world that bites back, and then all you can do is run. If you've got anything left to run *with*."

"Don't frighten the children," Gildorric said genially. "That doesn't happen twice in a lifetime. Come here, Hart, and take a look through the viewer. How does this spot at the edge of the lake strike you? We'd have water supply for the camp, and it's grassy edge—plenty of solid ground."

Gilhart poised over the great flat tablelike screen where a projection of the ground surface was visible. "You mean the spot in the lee of those cliffs?"

"More or less. Out on the grasslands, where there doesn't seem to be too much underbrush," Gildorric said. "Those dark masses are some kind of plant, but not so big we can't get through. We can test for bedrock, and if it's solid enough, set up the Transmitter under the cliff somewhere."

Gilhart nodded slowly. "I suppose so. And if not, we could camp here while we explore for a better site. All right, take us down to the surface. And try not to land us in a swamp."

The landing craft slowly descended; came to rest with a faint jolt. Gilhart and a couple of the older crew members were joking with Gildorric about the landing. "You've been in space too long, you've lost your downworld touch, banging us down like that!" Gildoran slowly unfastened his seat straps.

He was in a tearing impatience to get out, actually to stand on the surface of the new world, but there was still some time to wait, while Gilmerritt checked test samples and sensors.

"The atmosphere looked fine from a few hundred feet up, but we want to be very sure what's at the surface." A few minutes later, she nodded. "Plenty of oxygen, and, as you'd expect with all those clouds and all that green stuff, a lot of water vapor in the air. But the temperature is all right, and nothing troublesome in the atmosphere—just the usual inert gasses. Little high in ozone, but not enough to give trouble."

Gildorric glanced at Gilhart, and the Captain nodded.

"Formal command," he said. "Unlock doors. Establish landing."

Raban stood up and moved toward the door. Gildoran felt like crowding behind him. Gilrae met Gildoran's eyes and smiled. She said, "It's always a thrill. No matter how often you do it. This is it, Gildoran. It's yours. Enjoy it."

He wanted to say, "Oh, Rae, I love you," and kiss her, but he didn't; he simply grinned at her, feeling foolish. She reached out and touched his shoulder affectionately.

She thinks I'm a child.

"It's Gildoran's world. Let him touch down first."

III

The whine of the doors opening, a rush of cool,
sharply-scented air; a swift, overpowering impression of greenness. Greenness everywhere;
even the sky, under its thick layer of cloud,
seemed to reflect pale green light below. Gildoran
moved slowly down the steps and took the first
hard impression of weight and a curious, yielding
texture beneath his feet. It felt strange after years
of low weight and super-smooth metaled and
plastic floors underfoot. Now he stood on spongy
green moss or grass, green in a belt of thick lush
green of every hue. A green world, a greenish sky,
the glimmer of green water in the distance somewhere.

He heard the other coming down the steps behind him. Gilmerritt sniffed audibly and said,
"What did I say about greenhouse effect?"

It did smell strange. Was it the smell of the
unknown vegetation all around, or was it simply
that any air would have smelled strange after the
chemically pure recycled air aboard *Gypsy Moth*?

The small landing craft was backed against a
low cliff of some reddish stone, the only note of
relief for the eyes against the green that otherwise
was everywhere. The cliff stretched for nearly a
mile and sloped downward toward a small green
lake, its surface just ruffled by a light wind. On the
far shore of the lake a tall forest grew. Between
the landing craft and the near shore of the lake

stretched a wide green expanse of grassland, dotted here and there with thick clumps of bushlike growth; the cliff was lined with them, too. The nearer bushes were about five feet tall, with thick grayish branches and broad cup-shaped leaves; at the ends of the branches were cup-shaped flowers with a sunlit glitter.

It was very quiet except for the soft humming and chirping of insects which hopped in the grass, hovered over the flowers, and over the cup-shaped bushes. But so far there was nothing larger than an inch or so, except for one pale butterfly which seemed to like hovering over the cup-shaped blossoms. Gilmerritt walked toward the bushes; a trained biologist, she did not touch them, and would not until she was wearing thick plastic gloves—every Explorer biologist knew about the planets with fluoride-secreting flowers—but looked down at cup-shaped flower and butterfly with a pleased smile.

"Judging by looks, it still looks like a good place for a resort," she said. "Let's get started checking it out. I can hardly wait to see a luxury hotel here and people coming by Transmitter all across the Galaxy."

She laughed to show that she wasn't really jumping to conclusions this time. Gildoran thought nothing they built here could ever be as beautiful as the long expanse of green bush against the red granite and limestone of the cliffs, but he turned to Gilhart for orders.

"First step," Gilhart said, "put somebody on watch. Raban?"

The stocky older man nodded.

"Take somebody particularly able-bodied—

Gilbarni, you care to go along?—draw two hand weapons from supplies, and climb up on the cliffs to keep watch for predators. Standing orders apply; don't shoot unless something obviously unintelligent looks as if it was going to attack anyone working down here. Station one man down by the lake, and between you, you can cover the whole landing party."

"Right." Raban and young Barni stepped back into the landing craft; emerged with hand weapons and gloves, and began to move along the foot of the cliff looking for a good spot to climb.

"Rae, did you say this was glacial moraine?" Gilhart asked.

"That's right," Rae said, shading her eyes against the light, "There should be good solid bedrock underneath; it might serve as a location for the first Transmitter set-up, although it's going to take a couple of weeks study to be sure. The first step is to get some core samples—here and down by the lake."

The Captain nodded. "Gildoran, you and Lori can work the core sampler. Gilmerritt, you take everybody else but Gilrae and start getting soil, water, and life samples. Be sure everybody knows about wearing gloves, too. And Gilrae, you work with Poohbear, hunting for a good place for a Nursery camp. You know the kind of terrain we need."

She nodded. "Yes. And may I say something, Captain?" They were all being formal now; they were on the job. Gilhart nodded to give permission, and Rae said, "All of you. Don't forget we need a good, solid spot to set down *Gypsy Moth*. The last world was desert, and just about perfect—lots of bedrock. We didn't have to move it again until we were ready for Liftoff. But the world before that—I'm sure all of you remember except Lori—we had trouble all the time with mud, so look for a spot where we can put down hard-surfaced walkways without too many extra hours of work. Or better yet, a hard, rocky spot. That's about all, Captain. Anything else?"

"Just that we'll break for a meal in four hours' shiptime. Daylight here lasts eighteen hours, so we may have trouble judging time by sunlight."

They scattered to their various tasks; it took Gildoran and Lori the best part of an hour to unload the core sampling tool, and assemble it with the compact battery generators and the wheeled drive for moving it around.

"Clumsy thing," Lori grumbled, and Gildoran laughed. "Rae told me when she was a kid core-sampling drills had to be moved around on a truck. It was less than two hundred years ago that somebody on Vega 14 developed a hand-wheeled one. We can do as much in three days as it once took Gilharrad six weeks shiptime to do on a new planet, poor old chap. And we don't have to wait and carry all this stuff up to *Gypsy Moth* to test it, now that we have the groundlab facilities in the landing craft. There's a complete biological and geological laboratory—well, not complete, but complete enough for preliminary work—right here in the landing craft."

The girl shaded her eyes with her hand. "Doran, are there any eyeshades or protectors in the landing craft?"

"I don't know. The light isn't that bad, is it? What's the matter, Lori?"

"Glare, or something. I'm getting a wretched headache."

Now that he came to notice it, Gildoran had a headache himself. "Maybe it's just gravity when we're not used to it," he hazarded. "You can ask somebody, I guess."

"No, it's not worth bothering, I'll ask Pooh when we break for lunch." She tightened a screw bolt on the sampling tool, and gave it a shove with her hand. "There, I guess it'll run all right if the grass isn't too thick, or these little hoppers don't get inside and jam the wheels."

"There certainly are a lot of insects around," Gildoran agreed. He picked one carefully off his uniform.

"Now what?"

"Run it down by the lake, I guess, and wait until somebody gets enough water samples to be sure first, that what's in the lake is really water, and second, that it will work in our drilling fluid—not too many chemicals that could dissolve the bit or clog it up."

Lori looked at him quizzically. "And what if it *isn't* water, or it's full of dissolved borax or something?"

"Then," Gildoran said, "you can personally have the fun of going into the groundlab and *distilling* a few thousand gallons for us, sweet. Fortunately it doesn't have to be pure enough to drink in order to keep the drill bit cool. But every so often you run into some lake full of sulfuric acid, or some such thing."

Lori wrinkled up her childish face in disgust. "If that lake's full of sulfuric acid, this is no place for a landing camp . . . I think you're teasing me, Gildoran."

"Well, maybe just a little bit. They did a lot of the preliminary checking in the geodesic studies from Gypsy Moth, in orbit. And most of what's in the atmosphere is just plain water vapor, period, so that's probably what we'll find in the lakes and the oceans and the rivers, too."

"So we go down to the lake?"

"Why bother? Gilmerritt or one of her crew will be up pretty soon with the first crop of samples, and she knows we need water for the drilling fluid. Let's hope we're lucky; if it's water, and even halfway pure, all we need is a good long supply of hose, a mixing pump, and we're all ready to go."

It was not long until Gildorric, bearing the early samples, came up from the lake, and reported that the water was just water, and rather exceptionally pure. "There's a lot of water-weed in it, so it might not be much good as a swimming pool," he reported, "but it'll run your drill bits, and it's good to drink—very good. Trace minerals, but nothing much except limestone, in any quantity, and that's wholesome enough. So you children can rig up your hoses and pumps, and get working on the samples."

The machinery was automatic; once Gildoran and Lori had rigged up their tool and chosen a spot for the first sample, there was nothing to do except check the gauges every few minutes to make certain that the bit remained vertical and the hoses containing the drilling fluid did not clog, and they could sit back and watch the others moving around near the edge of the lake, collecting samples, returning to the landing-craft groundlab to test them. When the first core samples came up from the drill, Gildoran examined them quickly for porosity and obvious rock types, then put them aside—they would be more extensively tested aboard *Gypsy Moth*.

Lori said, "I still don't understand why we can't have a Transmitter inside the landing craft and send samples up that way, after we've landed. The *Gypsy Moth* is up here, and we could bring a Transmitter down——"

"Go back to first grade, Lori. The *Gypsy Moth* is in orbit—not just *hanging* there. We can't Transmit to a moving target."

"But everything in the Universe is moving, isn't it? Yet every planet has nine or ten Transmitters——"

"Yes, But one of the things we do here is plot the regular orbital motion of this planet around its sun, and this sun around its position in the Galaxy, and that's all programmed into the Transmitter, so it knows *exactly* where in the Galaxy we'll be at any given miscrosecond for the next million years. That information goes to Head Center, and the nineteen or twenty backup Centers, in case Head Center goes out of contact or its star goes nova, perish the thought."

They had a sizable group of core samples by the time Gildoran's chronometer told him it was time to assemble for meal break. Field rations had been brought down and they gathered in the shade of the landing craft for their food; the ground was soft and spongy beneath their bodies.

Gilmerritt took off her slippers and wriggled her toes in the grass; Gildoran reached out and touched the soft skin of her foot; it was plump and smooth and pretty. Gilmerritt leaned against him

and murmured, "Was that an invitation, Gildoran?"

"It's whatever you want to make it."

She said teasingly "I thought you had everything all set up with Ramie."

"That's what everyone thinks, and I'm getting
weary of it," Gildoran said. He looked across to
where the Captain and Rae, slightly apart from the
rest of the crew, had their heads close together.

*Rae's out of my reach, and I'm damned if I'll
pair off with Ramie because that's what everybody expects.*

Merritt looked up at him. She was a pretty,
round-faced woman with eyes of lustrous green,
and a faintly cleft chin with deep dimples.
"There's something about a planet," she murmured teasingly. "I can live solitary for months at
a time in deep space but no sooner do we go
downworlding than I start remembering that I'm a
woman, and looking sidewise at all of you."

He caressed the plump toes of her foot, the soft
well-manicured nails. Then, reluctantly, he said,
"I think you probably ought to put your slippers
on again, Merritt. The soil hasn't been tested——"

"And it might be full of submicroscopic hook-
worms and parasites that have an affinity for
human skin. I'm sure you're right," Merritt said
reluctantly, and pulled on her silvery sandals. As
she fastened the straps, she murmured, "Don't
look now, but I'm getting some very nasty glances
from little Gillori. It's your fatal charm, Gildoran."

Gildoran felt a spasm of anger. Lori was getting

entirely too possessive. Knowing that the child's eyes were on him, he leaned over and kissed Merritt, long and slow and very thoroughly.

When they came apart, she sighed. "I've wanted to do that for some time. But on the last planet you were all wrapped up in some earthworm girl. . . ."

"That was strictly a downworld thing," he said lightly, and kissed her again before Gilhart and Rae came strolling over from the lee of the cliff.

"Shall I call Raban down for dinner?" one of the crew asked. "They could come one at a time."

"No, let them stay on watch, but take them some food," Gilhart commanded. He passed a hand over his head, scowling. "Are you sure they tested the air before landing, Rae? No, no, nothing to eat, Gildorric. I feel as if I'd been poisoned."

Gilrae said slowly "The air's fine. A little high in ozone until we get used to it, but nothing we can't adapt to—" she broke off. "Lori! Sweetheart, what's the matter?"

The young girl said in a wavering voice "Sorry, I . . . I think I'm going to be sick—" and promptly was. Gilmerritt scrambled to her feet and hurried to attend her; Lori tried to push her away for a moment, then was content to rest against the older woman's shoulder. Rae went to bend over her. Gildoran said, "She was complaining of headache earlier, said it was the glare."

Rae said "It doesn't seem that bright. How do the rest of you feel?"

"Headache," said Gildoran, and the Captain nodded. "Me too—rotten one."

"It's no wonder," said the Poohbear with sudden violence. "This world is so damned noisy!"

Eleven faces turned to her in startlement; Lori did not raise her head but lay limply against Merritt's breast. Gilhart said "Take her inside the landing craft, Merritt. Can you walk, Lori, or do you want Doran to carry you?"

"I can walk," the child said, struggling to her feet, but she let Gilmerritt support her with an arm round her waist. Gilhart said to Poohbear, "I'm surprised, Pooh. Noisy? It seems quiet to me. I don't hear a thing, except the insects humming. Any of you?"

"I suppose it could be the insects," said the brown-furred alien, with a deprecating smile. Her eyes looked strained. "Buzz, chirp, drone, hum, I just don't like it."

"And some of us have headaches," Gilhart said. "It can't be the air—we sampled all that very carefully and tested for any known disease organism."

Rae said, "The headaches could be from the ozone, of course. They probably are. We'll get used to that, but it could take a couple of days. How are the samples looking?"

"Good so far," said Gildorric. "Merritt's with Lori, so I'll report. The water's good, the soil seems good enough and fertile enough—if it grows all this stuff, it'll certainly grow food plants. There are nuts and berries which might test out as edible vegetable protein—and the plants are certainly hardy. So far none of them test out poisonous, either, and none of the insects are any bigger than a hopper."

"Animal life?" Gilhart asked.

"So far, none. We should check the other continents when we get some surface travel down, but so far, so good. As far as I know we could go ahead with the Transmitter tonight, but of course we need to make some more extensive tests. Just to make sure there are no hidden jokers like viruses.''

So far, so good, Gildoran thought; his world was testing out almost too good to be true. Then why did he feel so flat, so let-down, so miserable? Had his expectations been too high? Was it just reaction from being keyed up over the new world? It was a good world, even a beautiful one.

Gilrae asked "How soon can we get the children down, Pooh? We found a perfect spot for the Nursery camp."

The Poohbear looked strained, almost haggard. "I don't like it," she said slowly. "I know I'm being irrational, but I somehow don't feel right about bringing the children down into a place like this."

"It's up to you, of course," Gilrae said, "You and the other Poohbears are in charge of the children. But after all, it was you, Pooh, who reminded me that some of them were showing iron deficiency and were in a hurry to get them down."

"I know. As I said, I know I'm being irrational," the Poohbear said, "but I still can't see it. Couldn't we give them land-based drinking water—it has a good iron content—for a few days until you finish the tests?"

Gilhart frowned. "I'd be inclined to trust your instinct, Pooh," he said. "Let's leave it at that. Collect some land-based water—the lake water will do—and possibly some iron ore to feed into the ship's supplies of chemicals. Keep the children on board until we're sure."

She smiled at him with relief. "Thank you,

Hart. That would relieve my mind." Gildoran reflected that probably the Poohbear was the only person on board the Explorer ship who called the Captain simply "Hart." Except perhaps Rae, in private.

The Poohbear said "And if that's settled, why not let me go inside the landing craft and look after Lori? My ears can't take the noise, and it will release Merritt to finish her sampling for the day."

A light wind was rising as the Poohbear swung her heavy furry body up the landing craft steps. Gildorric said "I wonder what she's worried about?"

"Who can say?" Gilhart was struggling to keep his loose notes together. "Probably their hearing is in a different range than ours. Human hearing is relatively dull—only from fifteen cycles-per-second up to twenty thousand or so. Sounds have been measured up to two million cps or so."

Gildoran was reminded again how little they knew about the Poohbears. Well, maybe everyone needed a touch of mystery. As if this new planet wasn't mystery enough!

Gilmerritt, returning, commented that Lori was still feeling deathly sick and that the Poohbear was looking after her. Before she went off to her work she looked at Gildoran with a long smile, and he returned it.

The Captain said, "With Lori out of commission, you'll need someone to help you, Doran. Gildorric?"

"Anyone who knows how to run a core sampler."

Gildorric chuckled. "I was running a core sampler while the planet you came from was going through the Stone Age, Doran. Let's go."

Gilhart swore, testily. "Damn this wind! I'm going to move my things over in the lee of the cliff there. Those bushes should break the wind, and I can spread out the geodesic plots for this area. Can you give me a hand with this stuff before we go back to work, somebody? Rae, send up some food for the men on the cliff. And make sure the sun isn't getting to them; there isn't much shade up there."

That's what it is to be a Captain, Gildoran thought. He himself would have forgotten the guards on the cliffs, but Gilhart had remembered. He had to remember everything.

All that afternoon, Gildoran worked with the core sampler, at Gildorric's side. They took samples beneath the cliff, near the lake shore, and finally walked around to the far side of the lake, testing the depth of the soil and the depth of the bedrock. Finally, as the light was beginning to fade, they wound up the hoses and dried the pump, wheeling their sampling tool back near the landing craft.

"Good firm bedrock everywhere near here," Gildorric said. "We can probably set the *Gypsy Moth* down below the cliffs and establish our base here, provided everything else tests out properly. We'll need to start the mining machinery, but back in the hills there should be plenty of metals. It's a good, rich planet. Merritt's a fool; this place is too good to waste on a resort hotel."

"It's natural for her to think in terms of her own specialty," Gildoran defended.

Gildorric laughed. "And she's a pretty woman—I saw you flirting with her."

Gildoran had sense enough to ask amiably, "Not jealous, are you?" instead of flaring up.

"Jealous? Act your age, boy," Gildorric said. "I've known Merritt most of my life and we've worked together so many years you wouldn't believe it. But I guess we know each other too well. Let's face it: when you're my age, you know all the women aboard the Gypsy Moth too well. Which is why . . ." He chuckled again, "I'm really getting excited about having the Transmitter set up again, and being in contact with the Galaxy. Just the fact of seeing a few new faces. Don't mistake me," he cautioned. "I'm not saying I don't love Merritt. I'd die for her—as I would for any of you," he added in a moment of complete seriousness. "But she just doesn't excite me anymore. It's been a long cruise. You're probably too young to know what I mean, but when you've been paired at least three times with every woman on the crew, and even made a few offbeat trips with the men, you'll know why most of us save our romance—and our sex—for downworlding."

Is that why Ramie doesn't excite me–I know her too well?

They were near the landing craft now, and other members of the landing party were bringing back their equipment and their samples, getting ready to board. It was Gilmerritt who noticed that the Captain had not yet returned. She went to Rae, as second in command, to ask "Have the guards been called in yet? There's no need to keep Gilraban and Barni up there in the broiling sun now that we're all in."

"That's for Gilhart to say," Rae returned, "but I see no harm in sending for them to come down.

You attend to it, Merritt. Gildoran, have you seen the Captain?"

It was Gildorric who answered, "No, neither of us have seen him since lunchtime, but he moved his plots and papers over in the lee of the cliff where the wind wouldn't be getting at them. Want me to go give him a hand with them?"

"You've got the atmospherics to handle," Rae said, "Let Gildoran go, Doran—and tell him I ordered the guards in, will you?"

Gildoran went off in the direction he had last seen Gilhart moving, toward the cliff lined with tall bushes andtheir green cup-shaped blossoms. The sun was lowering now, and the clouds thickening so that the light had diminished somewhat, but the cup-flowers still seemed to glimmer by some inner light. There was no sign of Gilhart, and Gildoran, puzzled, began to walk along the lower edge of the cliff, his eyes alert, his head turning from side to side for any trace of the Captain. He felt a strange unease that was almost tangible, like a nasty taste in his mouth. After he had walked a few hundred feet along the cliff, and seen nothing but the green-gray branches and translucent cup-flowers, he began to be really worried. If it had been anyone on *Gypsy Moth* except the Captain, he would have shouted his name. And not too gently, either. His distress and worry were quickly mingled with anger; he could imagine what Gilhart would have to say if any of the crew had gone off like that.

In spite of shipboard etiquette, he began to call.

"Gilhart! Gilhart! Captain!"

There was no answer; no sound at all, except for the constant humming of insects in the underbrush—how he was beginning to hate that sound!—and the soft rustle of the wind in the cups of the bushes.

Gildoran shouted, this time at the top of his considerable lungs;

"Captain! Captain!"

Still the silence, broken only by the soft wind-rustle. Then Gildoran saw something which drew his glance quickly; a square of bluish-white, too regular, too bright to be any natural object in all this green, lying amid the cup-flowers. He pushed the branches aside. Thorns on the underbrush stung and lacerated his hands and snagged at his uniform; he put his hand in his mouth and sucked the bleeding fingers, but he thrust on, his heart pounding in sudden violent fear.

He found Gilhart lying in a small hollow between the plants and the red limestone of the cliff base, crumbled in a heap. Gildoran bent over him, angry and apprehensive. Lori had been sick, and the Captain should have known he could get sick too, he shouldn't have gone off alone. How could anyone have heard him if he'd called for help? But against this angry interior monologue Gildoran was kneeling beside the fallen man, unfastening his tunic and thrusting his hand inside, helplessly hunting for a pulse. But he already knew that the Captain was dead.

IV

". . . So we can't go down again until we know what killed him," Gildoran finished, and Ramie's soft almond eyes looked gentle and miserable. "Oh, poor, poor Gilrae! They were so close, Gildoran, they've always been so close to each other. Is she all right?"

"As much as she can be, I suppose," Gildoran said somberly. He was haunted by the memory of Rae's drawn, haggard face, bloodless and wretched as she struggled to pull herself together. As second officer, she was in command of *Gypsy Moth* until a new Captain could be chosen; and though the laws of the Explorers stipulated that this should be done within three days shiptime, there were still those three days to get through.

He was silent, remembering the last stressful half hour of their stay on the green world; the harrowing task of carrying Gilhart aboard, made harder by the gruesome task of stripping him to search his clothes for some possible cause—poisonous insect or animal which might have bitten him and be concealed in them. It had fallen to Gildoran to help roll the Captain in a blanket and carry one end of the heavy lump of clay that had been Gilhart, aboard the landing craft. It had been a silent, sad journey upward through the cloud cover to the *Gypsy Moth*. Gilrae had insisted on kneeling beside the blanket-wrapped body, trying to keep it from rolling about grotesquely; they had let her have her way. They had all been paralyzed by her grief, and all of them had shared it. Lori sobbed with her head in the Poohbear's lap; Gilmerritt clung to Gildoran's hand, subdued, her merry green eyes downcast, and Gildoran knew that the woman was thinking of how Gilhart had good-naturedly teased and reproved her on the trip down. How light-hearted they had been then, and how different this trip back was!

Damn this world! Damn it!

Gildoran spared Ramie all this except the briefest account, knowing she, too, was saddened. "I did my first Class B duty on the bridge when he was Navigator," she said, "and he was so good-natured and so kind, always teasing me, and ready with a joke. And last year I worked in Medic with him. I simply can't believe that he's dead. But he was pretty old, Doran—couldn't it be natural causes?"

"Of course it could have been. It probably was. But we have to know for certain."

While they waited for the news, they went up to the Floaters quarters, to break the news to old Gilharrad. The ancient Explorer heard of Gilhart's death with a touch of sadness, but he did not weep. He sighed deeply and said, "Well, it cannot be helped. The planet simply held the appointed end of his destiny; that is all. I know he would have preferred to die in space, but after all, space and downworld are all part of the same great Cosmos."

Before his ethereal calm, Gildoran was reluctant to broach his errand.

"We are desperately shorthanded, Harrad. Rae has asked if you can return to duty for a little while."

The old man sighed. "Must I?" he asked plaintively. "I've earned a rest, haven't I? I like it up here, with nothing to do but meditate on the Ultimate Cosmos."

Gildoran said gently, "You have certainly deserved a rest, Harrad, but we need you. And after all—" he added, with a certain amount of guile, "Gilhart never had a chance at *his* rest."

Gilharrad sighed again, deeply. "Well, well, I suppose I must," he said, "but just until the little ones grow up to Class B, mind you. And I refuse to go on the Ship's Officer list, I absolutely refuse. I'll advise, I'll work, I'll administer, but I won't hold Major Office, never again."

"I'm sure they'll agree to that," Ramie said, and held the thin old hand in hers for a moment. Gilharrad's flesh looked almost translucent, so bleached and thin that the pink color of the pulsing blood inside the cells was clearly visible, and Gildoran was struck with compassion. But they were desperately short-handed. To lose Gilhart! And so soon after Giltallen and Gilmarin had been lost to them! A scant three years, even before the little ones grew old enough to take their places!

"Poor Hart," Gilharrad mused, easing himself out of his gravity-free hammock. Reluctantly he stood up, sighing as he resigned himself to the drag of gravity again. "I suppose we'd better go down and find out what killed him."

It was only on such occasions as this that the entire crew of *Gypsy Moth*—everyone, except for the babies in the Nursery and the very oldest Floaters up in the gravity-free levels—gathered together in one place. Gildoran took his seat and realized that the huge Assembly Lounge was almost half-empty. What was the normal complement of an Explorer Ship? The ideal number was supposed to be a hundred. Surreptitiously, Gildoran counted. And three seven-year-olds and four four-year-olds in the Nursery. And seven Poohbears.

I wonder what's the fewest we could work the

ship with. What happens if we drop under that number?

Gildoran saw others looking around and guessed that they were secretly counting too.

Gilrae came slowly through the crowd to the front of the lounge. She looked pale, and as if she hadn't slept since Gilhart's death. Gildoran fervently hoped they hadn't made her perform the autopsy. Then she turned to the second-string Medic, Gilnosta, and took a memorandum from her, and Gildoran knew with relief that at least Rae had been spared *that*. It was about all she'd been spared, but she'd been spared that. It would have been hard enough for anyone. But worst for Rae.

Rae, Rae, what can I do to help you? What can I do to let you know how much I love you, how much I care for you, want to help you?

They didn't wait for Gilrae to call them to order. At her first breath there was complete quiet in the room. Her voice was low and strained.

"The autopsy reports on Gilhart show that he died of natural causes."

Of course, thought Gildoran. It had to be. He wasn't attacked by anything. There were no poisonous insects or reptiles near. Ozone isn't poisonous enough to kill.

Gilrae went on. "The circumstances are, we admit, a little confusing. There seem no visible signs of heart disease or arteriosclerosis. The respiratory and vascular systems were apparently in good shape. Yet there is absolutely no reason to believe his death was not natural. He had not ingested or inhaled any poisonous substance—and believe me, we checked that out very thoroughly. There were no signs in any vital organ of attack by any parasite, disease organism or virus—another thing we had to check carefully. Gilhart was apparently in excellent physical condition."

"What did he die of, then?" old Gilharrad sounded querulous. "Certainly not of a surplus of good health!"

Gilrae said patiently, "As nearly as we can tell, he must have suffered a cerebral accident—in other words, a stroke, a blood vessel which burst deep inside his brain. Such a thing could easily elude even a careful autopsy, but having eliminated all other possibilities, that seems the only remaining one."

Natural causes. Gildoran knew he should feel relieved; but there was still a strange heaviness resting on his mind.

Maybe it's because it's my world—and it's turning sour so fast.

Gilban, the Chief Medical Officer—one of the few posts not rotated by lot every couple of years—stood up and said, "I take it this means that we can again go down to the surface? I want to get the children down there as soon as possible. They need gravity experience."

"Yes, Poohbear spoke about that," Gilrae said. "We can go back down any time after we choose a new Captain." She looked and sounded inexpressibly weary. Doran wondered if she had eaten, or slept, since Gilhart's death. "And that's the next order of business—to choose a Captain. Who's on Nursery duty? Gilramie? Go down to Nursery, darling, and bring us up one of the babies for the choosing. And let's be thinking about Exemptions. You all know the rules. Year-Captains for the last seven years are automatically Exempt. Lori and Gilbarni haven't yet held three Class A positions; you're not qualified. Any Exemption Requests?"

Gilban said shortly "I can't handle full Medic status and Captain, too. Exemption?"

Gilrae looked around. "Any objections? All right, Ban, you're Exempt. Anyone else?"

Gilharrad said without rising, "I'm too old, Rae. Can I be exempted, too?"

"I wish you wouldn't ask," the woman said. "We need your experience, Harrad. Can't you take a one-in-fifty chance?"

"I didn't even *have* to come back to Active Status," the old man pointed out, and Gilrae sighed and said, "Just the same——"

They were both distraught, Gildoran thought, or they would have remembered, and he tactfully broke the deadlock. "Gilharrad was Year-Captain less than seven years ago, Rae."

The woman shook her head, confusedly. "Of course he was. Anyone else?"

Gilraban stood up and said "I'm going to have my hands full with Transmitter work. Exemption?"

"Any objections?"

"I object," said Gilmarti, a tall thin elderly woman, "There are eight of us in Transmitter, and we can manage if we have to. Raban can take his chance with the others."

"Exemption refused," said Gilrae, sighing. "Anyone else? All right then, the rest of you put your ident disks into the box, and we'll draw as soon as Ramie brings up one of the children."

They rose and filed past the tumbling cylinder, each dropping his or her small metal disk inside. Raban was still grumbling. Gildoran paused beside Rae, wanting somehow to show his feelings, but she did not look up, and he sensed somehow that any stray word of kindness, a moment of sentiment, and the woman would break down. He put his disk into the box and found Gilmerritt at his side. She went back with him to the seat Ramie had vacated. She looked sad and strained. "Whoever the new Captain is, it's going to be hard, on us, and on him—or her. Everybody liked Gilhart. And if we get someone who actively doesn't *want* to be Captain, it's rough. I think anyone who asks should be Exempt."

"But most of us would rather stick with our own specialties," Doran reminded her. "There are only about eight of us on board who'd be willing to take the job, and they're not always the best qualified. This is the best way, to make everyone take a turn sooner or later."

"I suppose so," she said, but she didn't sound convinced. Gildoran laughed. "Well, maybe you'll get it. Then you can build that resort you were talking about."

She shook her head and said seriously, "Heaven help the ship if I'm Captain. I don't think I have any talent at all for leadership."

Gildoran thought, "Me, too." This was only the second year he had been on the Qualified list. He looked around, and wondered how many of the *Gypsy Moth* crew were feeling just the same way.

Maybe we ought to Qualify people for Captaincy just as we do for Medic duty, or Nursery duty, or Engineering—talent, experience, interest, ability for leadership—if someone's tonedeaf, we don't make him lead music!

Gilramie came in, holding Gilmarina in her arms; everyone began to smile at the sight of the chubby child in her pink-and-white coveralls, her dark hair and rosy cheeks still marking her out from the others.

She's going to be dreadfully spoiled—she's everybody's pet. The Poohbears kept the prettiest clothes for her, or is it just that they look prettier on her?

It crossed his mind suddenly, looking at Ramie's dark, long almond eyes, that before she was bleached by space, Ramie must have looked very much like Gilmarina. He couldn't remember back that far, but after all he and Ramie had been Nurserymates—he ought to have some memory of a charming dark-haired pink-cheeked Ramie before she was six.

Ramie put Marina into Gilrae's arms, and the woman cuddled her close for a moment while Ramie dropped her ident disk into the tumbling box. Gilrae let it spin a moment; Ramie went to where she had been sitting, saw Gilmerritt there, and shrugged slightly, sliding into the nearest vacant place. Her look was neutral, but somehow Gildoran felt guilty.

Gilrae put out her hand and halted the spinning of the box. The small jangle of disks from the inside quietened slowly. She held Gilmarina down close to the box.

"Hand me one of the disks, Marina." The child plunged her chubby fist into the box. "Just one, that's right. Here, someone, take her . . ." with a small squeeze, Rae put Gilmarina into the arms of the nearest crewman. She turned over the disk, and a strange look crossed her face.

If she's Captain it would be good for the Ship, but it might wreck her. No. She was Captain six years ago. She's Exempt.

Gilrae, still with that strange expression, brought up the disk to her face and held it out.

"Gildoran," she said.

Gildoran blurted out, not believing, "Oh, no!"

She nodded slowly and came and put the disk into his hand. She added "Congratulations."

Gildoran was appalled at the irony of it.

His world. His responsibility.

And now his headache.

Gilrae touched his hand; clasped it within her own. She said "Don't look so stricken, Gildoran. Sooner or later it happens to everyone." But he fancied she was thinking that he was no substitute for Gilhart.

Suddenly the woman's face worked, as if she were going to cry, and Gildoran, acting on sheer impulse, reached out and caught her in his arms. He was so much taller that she hardly reached his shoulder, and she seemed helpless and vulnerable as he held her, trembling, against him. He felt that he would break himself with the strength of

his own love, and yet . . . and yet to force awareness of himself, of his own problems and troubles,
on Gilrae at this moment, would be the cruelest
thing he could possibly do.

And then, with the first almost-pleasant
thought he had had since Gilhart died, he realized
that there was one thing he now *could* do; that
was, in fact, his responsibility to do and no one
else would do it if he did not.

He held his beloved gently, a little away from
him, and looking down tenderly at her, gave his
first command as Captain of *Gypsy Moth*.

"You're worn right out, Rae, and no wonder. It's
time you got some rest. Gilban, take her down to
the Infirmary, and give her a sedative. I want you
to sleep the clock around, Rae. We're all going to
need you, and we can't let you make yourself sick
with overwork and strain."

She looked up at him in surprise and gratitude,
and almost visibly, the strain in her face relaxed.

"All right . . . Captain," she said softly, and
went with the Medic.

V

Four days later, and the clearing under the red
cliffs was transformed. Four portable groundlabs
dotted the area between cliffside and lakeside,
and working from the landing craft in flight, they
had burned off an area of vegetation near the
cliffs. This had meant the sacrifice of about half a
mile of thick underbrush, mostly the thick bushes

with the cup-shaped glimmering flowers, but it was that or the forest. Bushes were easier to burn, quicker to grow again if they had a stable place in the planet's ecology, and with the area cleared, there would be less chance of accidental fires near the camp when the *Gypsy Moth* set down.

Gildoran had established a temporary ground camp for the landing party plus the dozen-or-so experts who went out now, each day, making geodesic studies for the Transmitter Site. While theoretically it could be set down almost anywhere on dry land, there were a few practical considerations. It should not be on a serious fracture line or geological fault; Transmitters were better off without the possibility of earthquake damage, and so were the cities that inevitably grew up around them.

Everyone aboard had been—as the etiquette, and the tradition of *Gypsy Moth* demanded—ready to cooperate with the new Captain. Although Gildoran knew that at least half the crew was dismayed when he, the youngest of the qualified members, had been chosen by the relentless process of the lot, manners and longstanding decencies prevented anyone from letting Gildoran see it. Just the same, he had heard Gilnadir, from the Transmitter crew, say in disgust when he thought Gildoran out of earshot, "That boy—for Gilhart?" Gildoran had felt as embarrassed as if he had trespassed in hearing, rather than Gilnadir in saying, such a thing. He felt like yelling at Nadir, "Don't you think *I* feel that way, too? Do you think I *want* to fit into Gilhart's shoes?" Instead he had stealthily slipped out of the corridor, hoping Nadir wouldn't see him.

Just the same, he had not escaped an early confrontation.

The day after Gilhart had been ceremoniously committed to space for burial, Gilban of the Medic staff had approached him. Gildoran had asked, "Is Gilrae all right?"

"She'll do. You did right to order her to rest, though; she was pretty near collapse. However, Captain, I'd like to know how soon you plan to go down again. We have to get the children downworld. They need to live in an iron-rich environment, they need sunlight, they need gravity. Can I order them down with the landing craft today?"

He looked and sounded belligerent; a surly man, he was one of the few crew members taller than Gildoran, who had always been a little in awe of him. He had been Medic Chief since Doran's own childhood.

Gildoran temporized. "Have you talked to the Poohbears about it?"

Gilban brushed that aside. "I know how they feel about it, but they're not Medical experts. I think this is more important than someone's vague feelings." He pressed. "Can I order the Nursery camp set down today?"

There was no help for it. Gildoran said, "I'd rather go along with the Poohbears feelings on the matter—at least for a couple of days, Gilban. They are, after all, the specialists on the well-being of the children." He fished for an acceptable excuse. "It might be more diplomatic not to antagonize them right away."

Gilban fixed the young Captain with a cold stare from long, yellow eyes; a stare which said more plainly than words that Gildoran could choose between antagonizing the Poohbears and antagonizing *him*. He said briefly, "I've given you my opinion as Medical expert. Are you going to take it, or not?"

Gildoran said, "Gilhart agreed to postpone it for further study, and we are giving them land-based drinking water, which should remedy the iron problem right away. As for gravity and sunlight, according to the Poohbears, that isn't nearly so urgent. I think we should take a few more days on the planet to see what made Poohbear so uneasy about it."

Gilban said, teeth clenched, "Gildoran, you're the Captain, but I'd like to remind you that I was Chief Medical officer on this ship before you were out of the Nursery. Are you questioning my competence?"

This is bad. This is very bad. I'm going to need all the help I can get from the specialists, and I've already made Gilban furious. Does he think the power's gone to my head?

Desperately trying to placate the older man, Gildoran said, "I would never question that, Gilban. But this isn't my own decision, it's Gilhart's. I don't want to question *his* competence, either. I don't feel free to set it aside until I have advice from everybody, including those who have actually been on the planet." He very carefully did not mention that Gilban hadn't.

Gilban said stiffly, "Then I can't persuade you to trust my judgment."

Damn it, he was asking for it right between the

eyes, and there was no way Gildoran could avoid it. "I'll always be ready to hear your advice, Gilban, after you've been down to the surface and made a study from there."

Gilban clenched his hands at his sides. His very tufts of hair seemed to bristle with wrath. He said, "It's your decision to make, of course," and went away. And Gildoran knew that for the first time in his life, he had an enemy on the *Gypsy Moth*. Within hours of assuming his first command he had alienated one of the officials whose support would be most important to him.

Gildoran had posted no guards—extensive exploration in the landing craft had shown no land animals of any sort, and no birds; in fact, no lifeform larger than the gleaming seven-inch butterflies which fluttered around the small dymaxion domes the crew had constructed for portable shelters. Ramie, walking at Gildoran's side across the burned area, smiled with pleasure at the iridescent shimmer of the creatures and said, "I wonder if they're looking for the bushes we burned down? I hate to think of killing off such lovely creatures by destroying their food supplies."

"There are miles and miles of these bushes all along the range of hills," Gildoran said, "and if they're like most butterflies, these individuals would live only a few days anyway. A burnoff this size won't damage anything, and it will keep the insects away until we're sure if there are any poisonous ones among them. Once we know, we can initiate control processes."

"These aren't poisonous, are they?"

Gildoran said "I'm no biologist, but Gilmerritt thinks not."

"What's the glitter on their wings? They look like jewels."

"According to our biological report, they almost are," Gildoran said. "A lot of life is based on hydrocarbons, and jewels are just crystallized carbon. In essence, their wing surfaces are covered with diamond dust—crystallized scales of microscopic carbon material. Diamond-plated butterflies!"

Gilramie smiled. "I can see them becoming a fashion among some women. Remember how the glow-lizards on little gold chains became a fashion? Wear a live diamond-plated butterfly jewel. We should get a nice finder's fee for this world—it's beautiful!"

Gildoran smiled at the whimsy, and thought, again, how comfortable it was to be with her, when she could accept him simply as a companion. She must know by now that when he had moved into the Captain's quarters he had assigned the adjoining cabin to Gilmerritt and that they were together, but she had not spoken of it, and he was grateful.

He said "I take it you're down here as Nursery representative? I'm not keeping you from your work?"

"No, Gilban asked me to scout around and locate a good place for the children; drinking water, shade, reasonably away from the noise of the groundlab and equipment. I was tentatively thinking of the top of that little hill; the lake would be pleasant, but we're not sure yet about what forms of life the water might hold."

"Ramie, do you think I did wrong to refuse having the children down?"

"How do I know, Gildoran? I think you were wise to take the most careful course. Somebody's going to criticize you whatever you do," she reminded him. "Gilban thinks you're too careful, somebody else would grouse because you're too reckless. You're going to get the blame either way, so you may as well make whatever decision you think you can live with."

But she still looked troubled, and he asked "What's bothering you, Ramie?"

Her eyes sought out the edge of the clearing where the geodesic crew was running survey lines. "Gilharrad," she said slowly. "I think I would have forbidden him to come down to the surface. There's work enough for him aboard the *Gypsy Moth*. Are you sure he can handle the gravity?"

"He wanted to come, and Gilrae asked for him," Gildoran said. "That's the hard part of it, Ramie. I don't feel comfortable giving orders to people who were commanding the *Gypsy Moth* before I learned how to hold a slide rule—or, for that matter, a spoon. For the children, I had Gilhart's decision to rest on."

"But you can't deny Gilrae anything," said Ramie shrewdly.

"Damn it, Ramie—"

"Oh, Doran—don't! I can't, either—how could I? But I'm worried about Gilharrad. Can't you send him up next time we break? He doesn't look right to me."

When they gathered for lunch in the clearing, Gildoran made a point of observing the old man, but although he was slow-moving and fragile, Gilharrad had good color. When Gildoran asked him, he declared testily that he'd never felt better, that the air was doing him good, and that unless this planet had his name on it, nothing down here could hurt him anyway. "You don't look too great yourself, young man," he finished, and Gildoran gave up. It was true; he had a headache. They all had headaches, and Gildoran suspected that if it wasn't the ozone, his at least was a purely psychosomatic headache; the result of having the weight, if not of the planet, at least of the *Gypsy Moth*, resting on his solitary shoulders.

I don't like this world. It's foolish, but I keep having this sense of impending disaster, and I don't like it.

Later that day Gilmeritt brought him a big sample box. "Did you ever see an insect who looked like a frog?" she asked, "Look at this fellow—an amphibious insect. But look at the big air-bladders in his chest!"

Gildoran looked at the huge red-striped creature. It did, indeed, resemble a monster frog; it was almost eight inches long. "But it's really an insect?"

"No doubt about it."

The huge chest was puffed like a bellows. "He ought to have a monstrous croak," Gildoran commented.

"But that's the charming bit about it," Gilmerritt said, dimpling. "Listen. You don't hear a thing, do you?"

"No. But I've got such a headache I can't see

straight, so I'm just as pleased he doesn't make a racket in proportion to his size."

"That's it," Gilmerritt said quietly. "That's why the Poohbear found this place noisy, and why Lori got sick, and why we all have headaches. The Poohbears evidently hear better than we do. Human ears only respond to sounds between, about, fifteen cycles per second, and twenty thousand cycles. This big fellow sends out subsonics—pulses at about nine per second. And everybody knows that subsonics will make people sick, give them headaches, feelings of fear and general malaise. We were reacting to soundless noise from the croakings of a giant frog."

Gildoran felt a sudden overwhelming relief. So that was the reason behind his vague unease, behind Lori's sudden sickness, behind the headaches and strange nameless fears. Pure, physical reaction to sound waves! "Can we get rid of the frogs in the area of the Nursery camp?" he asked, and Gilmerritt nodded. "It will take a few days to round them all up, but I can bring down a subsonic detector to locate them. I ought to have thought of subsonics before—we have to damp them out for a mile or so around the Transmitter. So there's one of your problems on the way out, Doran." She touched the sleeve of his uniform, a curiously intimate gesture, and he smiled with relief.

"The subsonics won't do any physical damage?"

Gilmerritt shook her head. "Not unless they were of much, much greater volume than anything this size could give off. If this frog thing were the size of an elephant, now, he might be dangerous; as it is, he's just a pest. I thought you'd like to know."

Gildoran nodded, suggested she tell Gilban about it, and watched her go, thinking that, at least, one of their problems was ended. Once they knew that their malaise and headaches were due to a simple, physical and correctable cause, and once the frog bugs were rounded up and released out of earshot, the camp would become quite livable, and this beautiful world could begin living up to its promise.

At that moment he became aware of a clamor of voices in the distance. At first they were only wordless cries, from the general area of the geodesic crew; then he realized that someone was calling his name. He began to run along the burned edge of the cliffs, apprehension surging up again almost to the panic point.

What now? What now, damn it?

It wasn't far enough to use the landing craft, but too far for hearing.

Got to organize some surface transit down here.

Halfway he met them, a tight knot of crewmen and women, clustered together, carrying something that was pale and terrifyingly limp, and with a hideous sense of replay, he knew that not *all* of his apprehension could be written off blithely to the subsonics.

Gilrae, looking even more white and shocked than at Gilhart's funeral, spoke the bad news in a daze.

"It's Gilharrad," she said, softly, "I saw him fall. There was nothing near him. He was tracing a fault line with the portable sonar gear. He didn't even cry out. He just clutched his hand at his head and fell down. I wasn't three steps from him, and he was dead before I could reach his pulse. It was so sudden. So sudden!"

Over her bent head, Gildoran met Ramie's dark, accusing look. And Gildoran had no defense against those eyes.

"Call Gilban and have them take him up for an autopsy," he said wearily.

Poor old man, he wanted to die in space. He had earned it. I couldn't let him rest.

He asked the usual questions, hating what he knew it was doing to Gilrae. No, there had been nothing near him, nothing touching him. Was there anything about it that was like Gilhart's death? Only that it must have been very sudden, as he was passing below the cliffs. "Right there, behind that clump of bushes, next to the big gray-and-red-striped rock under the clump of cup-plants." Young Gilbarni pointed out the spot.

Both deaths took place near the cup-plants. But that was ridiculous, Gilmerritt had tested every plant for organic poisons and in any case there was no trace of poisoning.

When he asked for an autopsy, Gilban audibly snorted, but agreed, with the quite obvious attitude that he was humoring a power-mad dictator. That night, when they consigned Gilharrad's body to space for burial, Gilban gave him the results with weary patience.

"Immediate cause of death, obviously, a cerebral hemorrhage."

"Just like Gilhart?"

"No," said the big man testily, "not just like Gilhart. Gilhart was a vigorous man in the prime of life, and though he was subject to sudden cerebral accidents, like anyone else, it was evidently some sudden strain or attack. It could happen tomorrow to you or me. Gilharrad's real proximate cause of death was simply extreme old age. He was five hundred and seven years old, shiptime. In planetary time—God alone knows . . . centuries . . . Millennia—Several thousand years, at least. He could have died of the same thing anytime during the last thirty or forty years; the blood cells in his brain must have been as fragile as spiderwebs, and one of them simply gave way. You or I should live so long!"

Gildoran knew this was reasonable, but couldn't hold back a further question.

"Then you don't think there's any serious coincidence in the fact of two accidental deaths, from the same immediate cause, within a few days?"

Gilban looked disgusted. "I told you they were not, in effect, the same cause at all," he said. "You, or I, or one of the children of the Nursery, could die tomorrow of a cerebral hemorrhage. Anyone could. Don't try to work up a big sinister tragedy out of nothing, Gildoran, just to justify your own fears about this planet. And by the way, I'm ordering the children down tomorrow. Gilmerritt assured me she'll have the subsonic frogbugs cleared out of that area by then."

Gildoran said "What do the Poohbears say?"

"I didn't ask them." Gilban's voice was cold. "I

don't like having to remind you of this within a few days of your first command, Gildoran, but in emergency I have the authority to override even the Captain's orders on any strictly medical matter. I want those babies down in gravity and sunshine, Poohbears or no Poohbears—if they can't tolerate the noise, you can detail some crewmen for Nursery duty. The babies won't hear the subsonics even if a stray frogbug gets into the camp. I'm not eager to throw my weight around, Gildoran, but the facts of the matter are, you've left me no choice."

Having no choice himself, Gildoran gave in as graciously as he could. That night in his quarters, he gave way to his secret doubts and miseries.

"What could I say, Merritt? I've no claim to be psychic. I think it's simply too much to believe, that they both died of the same thing, at nearly the same spot, within a few days of each other, but what can I prove? Am I supposed to wait for another death to convince him? Have you analyzed the cup-plants?"

"Only superficially," she said. "They seem to have some strange internal organs, I can't figure them out—I suspect they're for reproduction. I can tell you the cups have that glitter, because, like the frogbugs, they're covered with carbon crystals—tiny fragments of diamond. There are other crystals inside and I suspect they digest live insects by grinding them up inside the cup-roots. I found a half-dissolved butterfly inside one of the internal organs, so that the cups operate something like a Venus's-flytrap. But there's no chemical poison involved—I doubt if anyone could eat one of the cups without one hideous tummyache, but no poison, no gas—it was the first thing I checked." She hesitated and added, "Anyway, the cup-plants are all burned off near the camp, just in case; shall I have them burn them off near the Nursery too?"

It was a temptation. Gildoran had a definite dislike for the cup-plants, ever since he had seen Gilhart lying dead under a cluster of them. But he was a scientist, not a child. "No," he said slowly, "certainly not, if they're harmless. There's no sense in disturbing the ecology any more than we have to; we'll have to do enough clearing when we set down the *Gypsy Moth* and get started on a Transmitter." He remembered that first thing tomorrow—in orbit around a planet, the *Gypsy Moth* observed day and night cycles—he would have to consult with Raban and Marti about a Transmitter location.

"I'd counted so on Gilharrad for advice," he said. "I forced him to come back. And it killed him."

Gilmerritt reached up and drew him down to her. She said softly, against his lips, "Hush, Doran. You know what he would have said to that: Planets and Space are all one Cosmos. And you know what he believed: for everyone, somewhere, there's a planet with your name on it. All we can do is the best we can, until the right one comes along. I won't tell you not to grieve, Doran. I loved him, too. We all did. But there's nothing we can do for him, and we have to live."

Her mouth found his gently, trying to give comfort and strength to his search. "All we can do is to live, Gildoran. And I'm here with you."

Why at this moment, drawing Merritt into his

arms in a surge of sudden desire, did he think of
Ramie's dark, accusing eyes?

*I ought to be with her. She and Gilharrad were
so fond of each other. She felt the way Gilmarina
would feel if I died . . .*

He had enough problems aboard *Gypsy Moth.*
He wasn't going to add Ramie to them.

VI

"If the Test Transmitter works tomorrow, we
can set the *Gypsy Moth* down and get started on
the main Transmitter," Gilmarti said, and laid a
group of printouts on Gildoran's improvised desk
in the small dome. He handed them back to her
without more than a glance.

"I'm leaving the Transmitter to you and Raban, Marti. I have to," he said. The old woman's
face took on a quizzical look and he stiffened
against it. Far too many of the crew, he knew,
resented his youth. For the hundredth time he felt
like reminding them that he didn't ask to be Captain. But they all knew that.

Unexpectedly, Gilmarti smiled. "Well, there's
two kinds of knowledge," she said, "knowing
what to do yourself, and knowing how to find
someone else to do it for you. We're doing our
part, Gildoran. We'll have the Test Transmitter
ready in a few hours."

He followed her to the door of the dome and stood in the cloudy sunlight, looking across at the lake. He asked "Where are you going to set up?"

"Back against the cliffs. I've got a crew in there burning off underbrush to make walkways, and the Transmit receiver booth will be down by the lake. If the Test works out all right, we've got hardpan, with granite under it, and no fracture lines or faults as far as we can see. So we can set up the big one. Test Transmitters are intended for only a few ounces Transmission, of course—mouse-sized animals and small weights—so we can make the preliminary gravity and drift allowances. But once we have them calibrated properly, we can use the same calculations for the first big one to tie us in to Head Center."

He saw that the old woman was still excited about it, said so, and she smiled at him. "It's always an exciting thing," she confessed. "Even after all these centuries. A new world tied into the Galaxy. And a chance to see what's been going on while we were tied in shiptime."

"How many years has it been?" Gildoran asked.

His friend on Lasselli's World—could he still be alive?

Marti frowned slightly. "I couldn't tell you without a computer tie-in and a sliderule," she said, "but probably about ninety-seven years, downworld time. Does it matter?"

He shook his head. "Just thinking that the children in the hatchery where we got Marina and Taro and the others would be old people by now, and they're just out of diapers," he said. He saw that she was fidgeting, and remembered suddenly that, though she was four or five times his age, it was up to him to dismiss her. "I'm sorry, Marti, I'm keeping you from your work. Let me know right away when you're set up and I'll come and see the test Transmission."

He stood for a moment in front of the dome, trying to organize his thoughts. He had initiated a practice of making the rounds of the camp every morning. One or two of the older officials acted as if he was trying to keep an interfering finger on their work, but most of the groups appreciated it. When Gildoran had been working, whether on the bridge, in the Medic labs or in the Nursery, he'd liked knowing that the Captain knew what they were doing and that they'd get a sight of him now and then to ask any necessary questions. The Poohbears always welcomed him to the Nursery camp; Gilrae was always glad to see him at the coordinating data dome, and Gilmerritt was always eager to show him what they were doing in the ecological studies. He had to walk warily with Gilban, but so far there had been no Medic emergencies except one of the Nursery seven-year-olds who had skinned his knee in sliding down the rocks, a sore throat from a crewman who'd gotten wet collecting specimens from the lake, and a couple of sprained ankles and wrists from people unaccustomed to walking in gravity after all this time. The usual daily things.

Finally he decided that he would visit the biology groundlab first. In the ten days since Gilharrad's death, they had learned some fascinating things about this world. Their first impression that there was no large animal life was correct—in fact, so far there was no warm-blooded life at all, only the complex interstructure of plant and insect. Gilmerritt spent much of her time in the field taking samples, but she admitted it would take years to work out the complexities of the symbioses and interdependencies between plants and insects. Her main work was to discover any dangerous plants or insects which should be avoided by the teams who would flood in from all over the Galaxy to finish opening up the planet.

She was in the field with her team when he stopped by the groundlab, so he went on. Gilrae was busy with weather charts, but greeted him with an affectionate grin.

"Doesn't it ever rain here, I wonder?" she asked.

"Is there any reason it should? I should think with this much overcast and cloud, there'd be plenty of water vapor in the air," Gildoran said but she pointed to a small furled electroscope and said, "There's enough static electricity in the air that I'd expect some really monumental thunderstorms. Or else, where's it coming from, and where does it go?"

"I'm sure you'll find out, sooner or later," he said, and she nodded. "Someday. Or else the teams coming in afterward will. I try never to get attached to a planet, Gildoran, or to care anything about it. Planets are for leaving."

I'm the Captain now, not a youngster. She can take me seriously. . . .

But he knew that she still shied away from emotion. Gilhart was too recently dead. He could love her, he could comfort her, but as for anything serious—no, it just wasn't in the records for now. Perhaps not for years, for years. . . .

Still, grasping at this moment of closeness and wanting to prolong it, he asked, "Do you still find it hard *not* to get attached to planets, Rae? From what you said to Gilharrad that day . . ."

She said slowly, evidently trying to frame thoughts she had trouble putting into words, "Maybe it's natural for *Homo sapiens*—to long for a particular horizon, a sky and sea of your own. Even Explorers were born in gravity, we're a downworld species, even if we try to be *Homo cosmos*. We've built up our own taboos, but they're customs, not instincts. You know I'm a musician; I think that way. There's an old, old folksong, some of us used to believe it was pre-space, pre-Explorer. I'm sure you sang it in the Nursery. I know I did and I heard Ramie singing it to Gilrita and Gilmarina the other day." In her soft, husky voice, she hummed the melody. . . .

She broke off quickly. "They say there's a special island for everybody. A world you can't resist, a planet with your name on it that calls to you . . . that's why I never could hate Giltallen when he found his, and left us. . . ."

"I thought I'd found mine once," Gildoran said slowly. His throat was tight with a surge of strange nostalgia, almost of homesickness, but for something he had never known. "I thought it was my world, but it was only a girl, and it was the wrong girl. But you've never found yours, Rae?"

Her lips moved in a small smile. "Ah, that's a question you should never ask, Gildoran. But I'll tell you this much—this isn't the one that'll tempt me to stay. Not nearly."

She bent briefly over her electroscope again, and Gildoran said, with a start, "I ought to finish my rounds. I get to talking to you, Rae, and the time just disappears."

She raised a slender hand to touch his cheek; almost a gesture of love. He noticed for the first time in his life that her beautiful hands were lined and seamed. She said gently, "Rank still has its privileges, Doran. Relax. You can stand and talk a few minutes without anyone having the right to criticize you." Her smile turned impish. "But Gilmerritt will scratch my eyes out if you spend too much time making deep soulful conversation with me, so run along, Captain."

Gildoran laughed, slightly embarrassed, lifted a hand to her in farewell, and went on.

This isn't the world that'll tempt me to stay.

Me neither, Rae. I don't know why, but me neither.

Oh hell, there must be a frogbug around—I feel so damned apprehensive.

On the other hand, as he approached the Medic headquarters, he realized he didn't need a frogbug to feel wretched. Gilban didn't make a secret of his feelings, so he made his visit brief.

"Everything going all right?"

Gilban demanded briefly, "Why not?" and Gildoran didn't press the point.

"Just making the rounds, Gilban. Let me know if you need anything or have anything to report. Carry on." And he took himself off again.

After that, I need a lift for my morale. How he hates me!

There was no sense in visiting the Transmitter site; Gilmarti had already reported, and they'd send him word when the test was ready. He would like to see Raban, whom he liked, but there was no need for it. Gilnadir, in charge of the geodesic crew, quite obviously regarded him as too young for the Captain's job and just going through the motions. Gildoran suspected that Gilnadir thought it was part of his work to teach the Captain his job. He tended to overexplain, but he was polite about it. So he listened politely to Gilnadir talking about fracture lines to be avoided, sites of possible soil slippage and rockslides, good building sites for cities, water supply.

"You realize, Captain, this planet hasn't a name yet. We've logged it by number, but it ought to have a name."

"Any suggestions?" Gildoran asked.

Come to think of it, I never found out who names planets. I guess I thought they came already named.

Gilnadir said with careful patience, "It's the Captain's privilege to name the world discovered under his command. Gilhart hadn't gotten around to it. There's no hurry, though. Not until we register it with Head Center."

"I see. I'll check the ship's library, then; I wouldn't want to duplicate anything we already have."

Not that this is a world I especially want to bear my name. It's my world, but it's no prize.

"Make sure Rae gets copies of all these reports,"

Gildoran reminded him, realized a split second too late that this reminder was unnecessary and Nadir was a little offended by it. He amended the offense as best he could, and went off toward the Nursery.

It was the prettiest of the sites they had yet seen on this planet, located on a little hill a quarter of a mile or so beyond the lake, hopefully out of earshot of the frogbugs, and shaded by tall, fronded trees with beautiful jewel-colored cones. The two domes—one for sleeping quarters, one for the Poohbears—were brilliantly colored, their triangular sections in brilliant primary colors. On the grassy slope in front of the domes, a group of seven-year-olds was sitting on the grass having some kind of lesson in elementary mathematics, Ramie demonstrating with the sectioned rods and forms. They all scrambled to their feet to greet the Captain, then broke ranks and came to chatter questions at him. He spent a few minutes talking to the children, apologized to Ramie for breaking up her lesson, and asked where the Poohbears and the babies were.

"Gilrita and Gildando are napping," Ramie said. "I think Poohbear took Marina and Taro for a walk in the woods. They have more fun chasing butterflies. You should have seen Marina this morning, dressing herself up in the jeweled cones and trying to get a butterfly to stay on her shoulder for an ornament, the vain little monkey!"

"Did Gilmerritt give her permission to walk in the woods?" Gildoran asked, frowning. "We're not absolutely sure there are no poisonous plants or insects yet. This world could still have a few nasty surprises like the frogbugs."

"I thought I'd told you; Merritt's *with* them,"

Ramie said, "she was looking for leaf-samples. They only went off toward the edge of the forest."

"I think I'll walk that way," Gildoran said, feeling vaguely uneasy. Ramie gave him a faintly cynical look and said "I'm sure Merritt will be glad to have you—" then, relenting, "and I know Gilmarina will. She's been asking, 'Why doesn't Doran come to see us, doesn't he love me anymore?'"

Gildoran chuckled. "I've been missing her, too. When things settle down, I'll come down to the Nursery and give them some lessons." The seven-year-olds began to clamor again to come with Gildoran, but he said severely, "No, sit down all of you, with Ramie, and finish your lessons."

As he walked away, he thought damn it, now Ramie will think I was making an excuse to be alone with Gilmerrit. Hell, we're living together—we don't need excuses. Anyhow, we'll have one of the Poohbears and two of the babies for chaperones!

The path they had taken was quite clearly marked, a natural separation between fronded bushes and low-growing flowers. He saw a pink ribbon lying on the path and picked it up, thinking that this was proof Marina had come that way, she loved pink and scattered her possessions broadcast. Well, he'd tie it back on her when he found them.

Several hundred feet into the wood, he began to hear voices, and turned in the direction of the sounds. Or was it the insects buzzing in their strange, high-pitched, droning tones? The woods were noisy, and he wondered how the Poohbears with their abnormally acute hearing—how far into the spectrum of sound did they hear?—could stand it. He felt like putting his own hands over his ears. There seemed an unusual amount of noise. . . .

Cosmos! Who was screaming? Gildoran began to run toward the sound, his heart pounding in sudden wild terror. A high-pitched shriek that sounded like Marina . . . a harsh, terrible howl like nothing he had ever heard before . . . screams . . . screams. . . . He crashed through the underbrush and his heart almost stopped.

A scene of disaster lay before him; Gilmerritt lay senseless on the ground. The great brown-furred Poohbear lay thrashing in agony, one of the babies clutched in her arms, a horrible howling moan coming from her lips. Beyond her a screaming, kicking rag of pink coveralls—*Gilmarina!* Gildoran heard himself shouting as he ran, snatching up the shrieking, writhing child in his arms. She kept on screaming in wild agony, and it was a minute or two before he could see that she was clutching at her small pink-sandaled foot. Then, with a final shriek, she went limp in his arms.

She was breathing, but the pink sandal was blackened, and there was a great hole in it. Gildoran felt sick. He straightened, bellowing for help. Marina still cradled in his arms—he wanted to snatch her close, run madly with her for the Medic, but the others were part of his crew too, he couldn't leave them—he bent over the convulsed, moaning Poohbear. Her furry cheeks were contorted in agony, her loose lips drawn back to expose long yellow teeth. Only dimly could he make out what she was moaning. "My head . . . my head. . . ."

Ramie burst into the clearing, stared at them

aghast. Gildoran shouted "Get the children inside
the dome! Then get Gilban up here, and stretchers
and a Medic crew—right away! Hurry!"

Ramie didn't even spend time asking questions
or offering help. She ran. Gildoran gently detached the remaining child, Giltaro, from the
Poohbear's arms. He was limp and lifeless. Gildoran could not tell whether or not he was breathing. He knelt beside Gilmerritt and saw that her
eyelids were fluttering. She stared up at him with
pain-glazed green eyes, moved her head faintly.
"My hand. . . ." she whispered. "Burn. . . ."

The whole hand was blackened like Gilmarina's sandal. She was obviously in shock, but there
was nothing he could do for her. Gilmarina was
breathing but unconscious, and Gildoran was
glad she was spared the pain.

Giltaro was definitely not breathing now, and
Gildoran could not find the faintest pulse in the
little boy's chest. If they had been able to get a
respirator or neurostimulator there within seconds. . . . The face had the same blue, twisted
look he had seen that first day on Gilhart's face.
Cerebral accident. Gildoran was aware that he
was shaking with rage. Damn Gilban. Not even he
could call this coincidence!

The Medic crew was there in minutes, and
minutes later Gilmerritt and Poohbear were on
stretchers and being carried down the hill; Gilban
had pronounced Giltaro dead and offered to take
Gilmarina from Doran's arms, but Doran said, "I
can get her there as fast as you can," and strode
down the hill to the Medic dome.

Gilban bent immediately over the Poohbear
while Gilnosta stripped off Marina's tiny sandal,

looking in dismay at the blistered, blackened foot. "Cosmos," she breathed, "this looks like a laser burn! I haven't seen anything like it since the war on Martexi!" She dressed the hideous burn, gave her a spray-injection of painkiller, and turned to Gilmerritt.

"Will they live?" Gildoran asked.

"Gilmarina will make it," Nosta said. "Cosmos only knows how much good that foot will ever be to her, but she'll live. Merritt—she's in shock. If we can pull her out of it, she'll be able to tell us what happened within the hour." But she shook her head over the Poohbear, and Gilban looked grave.

"There's extensive brain damage. Even if she lives, she's likely to be a vegetable," he said. "I can't seem to stop the convulsions. She keeps going from one to the other. I'm afraid she'll never recover consciousness. What happened to them, Captain?"

It took a moment for Gildoran to realize that he was being addressed. "I don't know," he said, "I heard screams and found them all like that. I think Taro was already dead."

"But what was around them? Had they touched anything?"

Gildoran wanted to shout that he, Gilban, had been responsible for declaring the planet safe, that Gilban alone was responsible for Taro's death and the Poohbear's, for Gilmarina's crippling injury, Gilmerritt's terrible wound. But one look at Gilban's tortured face told him that there was no need to tell the Medic anything. In that moment Gildoran knew the worst of command—in the last analysis, the Captain carries the burden of every-

thing. It wouldn't help the dead and wounded to blame Gilban. He had honestly done the best he could. All he, Gildoran, could do now was to help Gilban, because they needed him.

He said heavily, "I don't know, Gilban. Nobody knows. When Gilmerritt comes round, perhaps she can tell you. Meanwhile, I'll send a biology team, *in space suits*, up there to explore, and find, if they can, what attacked them. There's evidently something there that no one knew about." With a last longing look at Gilmerritt, he went to give the orders.

He did not hesitate an instant to order all the Nursery children up to the *Gypsy Moth* until the truth about this accident was known. The children were their future. They couldn't be risked. And now the *Gypsy Moth* was definitely short-handed, especially since someone would be needed to nurse the casualties night and day. His grief was deep and terrible for Giltaro. This was one of his own babies. He had jumped them across the Galaxy from the Hatchery. He had nursed them after the operations, had watched two of them die before they were even named. Now Taro was dead and little Gilmarina, her life spared, perhaps crippled for a lifetime. He ordered the Poohbears up with them. He had no doubt that whatever had killed Gilhart, and Gilharrad, had struck down the Poohbear too. She was probably dying. He wouldn't risk the others.

He was still waiting for the ordered spacesuits to be sent down—Transmitters from ship-to-ground *would* have been a help here—when Gilraban came to tell him the test Transmitter was set up, and invite him to be present.

"Hold it off a while," he said heavily, "we can't set down until we know what hit them. We can't risk losing anyone else."

Raban grumbled, but he agreed. He also agreed to call in everyone from the woods and keep them inside the burned-over clearing area until they were certain what form of life had attacked the crew.

All that day a sort of stunned, sick silence hung over the clearing. Work was suspended, except for the biology crew in spacesuits exploring the clearing behind the Nursery where the accident had taken place. Gildoran wanted to put on a suit and go out there with them, to tear the place to bits and find out what had gone on there. But he couldn't even have that much satisfaction. He was the Captain. He belonged where people could find him and report to him.

He kept drifting to the Medic tent where Gilmerritt and Marina still lay drugged and the Poohbear twitched and muttered and moaned, then exploded, every few seconds, into another raging convulsion. Gilban looked haggard, his face almost gray.

"You can't stop the convulsions?" Gildoran raised his hand. "Not questioning your competence, Ban, only asking for information."

The man shook his head heavily. "We know so little about the Poohbears, even after all these centuries. They never get sick. They taught us most of what *we* know about medicine, but we don't know that much about *their* biology. When I give her enough sedative to quiet the convulsions, she goes into Cheyne-Stokes breathing—her heart stopped twice, and I had to use a neurostimulator.

All I can do is try the obvious support measures to keep her alive, and they're failing anyway. It won't be long. A few hours at most; possibly a few minutes."

Gildoran said soberly, "Should we get down the other Poohbears? Shouldn't they know she's dying?"

"What good would it do? They ought to stay with the children."

Gildoran said slowly, "I think they have a right to say goodbye. Detail someone from the crew on the *Gypsy Moth* to look after the babies pro tem. And send up a shuttle for the Poohbears, unless you think it would be better to transfer her up in the landing craft."

Gilban shook his head. "The minute we move her, she'll die. No question."

Gildoran went and stood over the great dying creature. Grief and rage tore at him. He looked down into the furry kindly face, distorted now and unrecognizable. A face like this had been the first he had seen emerging from the blur of his baby memories on the *Gypsy Moth*.

Our mothers. My mother is dying, and I can't do anything for her. Damn this world!

He looked at Gilban's bent shoulders, and thought with a pang that it was his mother, too. On a deep impulse of pain, pity and the memories of a lifetime, he laid his arm around the older man's shoulders, and for a moment they stood together.

He hates me. But we're brothers just now. We

always will be. None of us have any world but this, or any people but each other.

He wanted to go on standing there, to weep like a child, to rage and demand of Cosmos why this had happened to them all. But he had work to do. He sighed heavily and went to do it.

The Poohbear who had been in the clearing died a couple of hours later. Gildoran was not present; he looked into the Medic tent and saw her great brown body surrounded by an impregnable circle of five other great brown furry backs, in a tight circle around the dying one, from which even Gilban was excluded. They were chanting softly in an unknown language.

Part of us for centuries. And we know nothing, nothing about them. They seemed as eternal as Cosmos, as deathless as the very stars.

Gilmarina had been sent up to the ship with the other children, under deep sedation. Gildoran went restlessly back to his own headquarters in one of the groundlabs, and Gilraban found him there.

"We can't do anything for the ones that are hurt, Captain. All right to go ahead with the Transmitter test?"

Gildoran had earlier told them to hold off, but now he shrugged. "Go ahead. Get it over with. One thing less to hold us up when we find out what the snag is. But be careful, Raban, we can't spare anyone else. What do you need?"

"Weights and some test animals. That's all right, we requisitioned them earlier, but the test animals we released on the surface are all behaving strangely."

Gildoran said absently, "Maybe we should have released test animals before coming down ourselves. Go ahead with your Test Transmission, Raban."

Gilraban hesitated. "How is Merritt? Will she be all right?"

"I don't know. I'm going back to see. Gilban says she'll live but her hand is a mess, and she was still in shock when I was last there."

Raban said heavily, "I'd go and see her, but I couldn't do anything—I'd only be in Gilban's way. Give her my love when she comes round, Doran."

"I will." When the thickset man had gone away, Gildoran walked aimlessly back toward the Medic dome. The cloudy sunlight was dimming under the perpetual haze, and it seemed to Gildoran that this day had been endless, and that he had spent all this long afternoon aimlessly shuttling back and forth between his own groundlab and the Medic quarters, not able to do anything in either place.

He wished Gilmerritt would regain consciousness, that she would open her green eyes and look at him and he could be sure he had not sent her, too, to her death on this world. He wished he could go up to *Gypsy Moth* and sit in the infirmary and cuddle Gilmarina in his arms as he had done when she was a tiny baby, trying to ease her pain and sickness with the warmth of his love. He wished he could call Gilrae from her work and keep her beside him and pour out all his own grief and misery into her sympathetic ears. He wished

he could sit and mourn for little Taro, a part of the
future they would never know. And he couldn't
do any of these things. He was the Captain of the
Gypsy Moth, and he was in charge of his own
planet, which had turned out to be a world that bit
back. All he could do was go on helplessly fighting against it.

VII

With a painful, repeated sense of *déjà vu*—how
many times today had he entered the Medic
dome?—Gildoran shoved aside the hanging
panel and stepped inside. Then he recoiled, for a
great darkness blocked off the light and kept him
from entering. With a split-second of shock, almost of fear, he saw that the five living Poohbears
were massed before him, looming over him; barring his entry to the Medic dome.

"May I come in, please?"

"No," said one of them, "you may not. *E-te-
ragh-o-mana,* our sister is gone, she has left us on
this world of hell and darkness, and we are lost,
we are alone and desolate."

He looked up into the inscrutable animal faces.
He was abruptly, shockingly conscious that after
all these years he was among strangers, he had
always called each of them, interchangeably,
Poohbear. Now for the first time he heard the
strange alien name she had borne, and he wondered if they were among the peoples who al-

lowed their true names to be known only after death.

None of them had died in living memory.

He said helplessly, trying to placate, "Pooh-bears, all of you, we too have lost our brothers. Gilhart has left us leaderless. Gilharrad and all his wisdom have gone into Cosmos, Giltaro lies dead with all the promise of his youth never to be known. We share your grief—you know that we all grieve with you—but we are all together in misfortune."

The unreadable brown faces held no visible emotion, but it seemed to Gildoran that there was both fury and contempt in the soft voice that answered him.

"You people are of short life and shorter memory. Every few years you take to yourself children of your people, and you can bear to see half of them die like flowers never opened. Every little turn of the century you know you will lose your brothers and sisters. To you death is only a moment, someone else is taken into the place of the dead, and it is as if he or she had never lived. I have seen a hundred of you come and go, die and be forgotten. Do not presume to compare your grief with ours, which is unending and eternal. We have lost a part of ourselves, and we shall never again be as we were before."

Before the words, like a strange compelling dirge, Gildoran bent his head. What could he say?

Man that is born of woman is of few days and born to sorrow. . . .

How, indeed, could he guess at their grief? Was this why the Explorers were hated by the downworld mankind, because they seemed, in human memory, almost undying? Did the downworlders believe they were immune from grief because no downworlder saw them age and die?

But he lifted his head and faced the Poohbears steadily.

"Grief is not less because we must meet it more often and we must learn to live every day of our lives with it," he said quietly. "In your sorrow, perhaps you do not know this, Poohbears. Grieve as you must. As we all must grieve. Perhaps in your grieving you will learn to know us better, and we you. What now can we do for you? Will you have us bury her here? Or shall we consign her to Cosmos as we do our own?"

Silence for a long moment, and the looming Poohbears seemed to close round him. And Gildoran thought, they were about to kill him then, but they opened a path for him. A third said, still in that cold, contemptuous, furious tone, "Our lost one told your people that we should not be here, nor your children. The loss of your little ones is the price you have paid for your foolishness in refusing to hear our wisdom. We shall care for her as it is fitting that we do. Let us carry her forth."

Gildoran said flatly, "None of you are going anywhere on this planet, unless you all want to follow her and die. I'm sorry. I'll make what concessions I can to your rites for the dead, but I can't let you go out there where you can all be killed. I can clear one of the domes or groundlabs and let you have it to yourselves. Or I can arrange to send you all up to the *Gypsy Moth*. Whatever you say. But no one from *Gypsy Moth* goes out of sight on this world until we know just why the deaths happened and what we can do to keep any more of them from happening."

Again their huge forms seemed to close in around him, dwarfing him, looming over him, and Gildoran felt engulfed, terrified. Then the great furred bodies drew back, opening a way for him, and one of them said, "Be it as you will, but we must be alone. We will go up to the ship, and there we will learn to live with our unending grief."

As one, they turned their backs on him and, taking up the body of their dead, carried her out of the dome. Gildoran got in touch with Communications from the nearest groundlab for a landing craft to take them up, and while he was at it, detailed four or five of the skeleton crew still aboard *Gypsy Moth* to take over in the Nursery. Somehow he knew, knew for a fact and without being told, that the Nursery would see nothing of the Poohbears for a long, long time.

When he finally put the communicator aside, he leaned his aching head in his hands. What next? He raised his head to see Gilmarti standing before him. He said wearily "What now?"

"First Test Transmission results," she said formally.

He shrugged. "Not now. I suppose it went off about as usual, didn't it?"

"No," she said grimly. "Oh, it operated. But the final results were all out of whack. The weights lost a few micrograms. And the test animals all died."

Gildoran pressed his fingers to his aching head. Of course. Murphy's Law, the law older than space—anything that can possibly go wrong will go wrong.

A Transmitter failure. He had never known a Transmitter setup to fail. He had used them, without thinking since he was old enough to walk, whenever he was on a planet tied into the world-net. He knew that if one failed, his atoms would be scattered all over the Cosmos, but they never failed. But then, Poohbears never died, either. Nothing was the way it should be on this world and he might as well stop expecting it.

"Do you have any idea why, Gilmarti?"

"Probably our instruments aren't working right. We need to check out the magnetic field of the planet again—double-check it. It's not radiation—we studied that; enough radiation to throw off a Transmitter would have us all dead already. After all, they operate in full Cosmic-ray fields."

But Gildoran was thinking of the singed fur of the Poohbear, the burnt and blackened sandal on Gilmarina's tiny foot, Gilmerritt's ruined hand. Radiation burns? He spoke to Gilmarti about this, but she shook her head.

"Radiation burns don't look or act like that," she said. "I haven't time to educate you about them now, Gildoran, you learned that in Nursery."

"You're right, of course. But if not radiation, what? In Cosmos' name, what *is* it on this planet, Gilmarti?"

The woman said grimly "You tell me and then we'll both know. You're the Captain; that's *your* job. Mine is to get a Transmitter functioning. Yours is to fix things so I can do mine."

She's right, of course. Yet what can I do? I can't say it's somebody else's fault. Ultimately everything that happens on the *Gypsy Moth*—or any world we're on—comes back to me. No wonder we change Captains every year! Who could live with this job any longer than that? No wonder people struggle to get Exemptions.

He said, "Well, all I can do, Gilmarti, is to give you a clear field to requisition any equipment you need to check it out. But not tonight. You look dead. Get some rest, and start again tomorrow. Raban, too. The Transmitter can wait."

"Right, Captain," she said, "although as short-handed as we are, the sooner we tie into the world-net again so we can pick up some more children and supplies, the better."

She was about to leave, but he motioned her back for a minute. He said "Gilmarti. Just hypothetically, what if we had to abandon this world—not tie it in at all? Suppose we never get a Transmitter working at all here. What then?"

She thought that over. "It has happened, of course," she said. "Usually we find out that a world isn't suitable before we set down on it. We'd need more fuel, of course, for the converters, before we leave. Anything will do, of course—rock if there's nothing else. Anything that breaks down into hydrogen atoms, under fusion. But if we're too shorthanded to set up a Transmitter, we could be too shorthanded to work ship."

He didn't tell her the Poohbears were, for all practical purposes, on strike and some of their precious personnel must be used in caring for the children. "Well, keep it in mind, Marti, it could happen. Get what equipment you need to check out the trouble with the Transmitter."

"It would be easier if we could set *Gypsy Moth* downworld, instead of trying to dismantle the equipment and bring it down in the landing crafts."

He nodded. "I know, but we can't do that yet. As long as some of us are up there, we can't *all* meet with freak accidents. Do the best you can, Marti. Make a computer tie-in if you need to. But I can't order *Gypsy Moth* down till I'm sure. Maybe not at all."

She seemed to see that he'd said his last word on the subject and turned to go. Then she looked back abruptly.

"Captain," she said, "Gildoran, have you eaten anything today?"

He realized he hadn't. It was no wonder he felt woozy.

"I've no right to remind you of this," Gilmarti said, "it's not my job. But part of yours is to keep yourself fit to do it."

"I haven't felt like taking the time——"

She said quietly, "If you don't, it's everybody's business. If you'll forgive me for making a suggestion——"

"Please do." I need all the help I can get, he thought, but he didn't say so. Part of the help *they* needed was something he couldn't give them; confidence in their Captain. Somehow he *had* to give it to them.

"Shorthanded or not, detail somebody to wait on you and arrange to look after your routine needs," Gilmarti said. "No Explorer is servant to another—I know that. But your time belongs to the crew, and you have no right to spend it looking after things like hunting up your own meals and sorting your uniforms. It's not a question of privilege. I know you'd hate that as much as any of us would. But when you take time for that sort of thing, you're neglecting your own work—and stealing time from us. Get someone like Lori or Gilbarni, whose work can be duplicated, and detail them for it."

She went away, having said her piece, and Gildoran got on the communicator again and asked for Rae, who had personnel records at her fingertips, to send him someone with something to eat.

He was learning more about command all the time. Maybe that was why they never gave you any special training for the job. You learned it through experience—fast—or you didn't live through it.

When he had eaten and snatched a brief nap, he went back—he'd lost count by now—to the Medic dome. The body of the Poohbear was gone. Gilban was asleep, dead exhausted, on a folding-cot; Giltaro's body was gone. Only Gilnosta, looking white and weary, sat beside the sleeping Gilmerritt. It was completely dark outside now, and a dim light fell on the woman's face.

"How is she, Nosta? Has she recovered consciousness?"

"Not really, but I'm expecting her to come round any minute. I imagined you'd want to see her." For a moment Gildoran was thinking that Nosta was speaking of the relationship between them, but the young Medic added, "You'll have to ask her what she knows about the accident, she's the only one who may be able to tell you anything."

So he wasn't even allowed to express normal concern, anxiety about his paired-mate; just information about an accident to crewmembers! He went and stood beside the unconscious woman. A few days ago she had been just another crewmember, and everyone on the crew had been expecting him to settle down with Ramie. Then Gilmerritt had suddenly emerged from the crew as part of his close-in world, had come sharply into focus for him, had moved into the center of his life. He looked down at her with a curious mixture of tenderness and concern.

This woman is my mate, my partner, we've committed ourselves to share our lives, our bodies, our loves, and yet . . . and yet . . .

Just now, all she could really be to him was the key to the mystery of what was killing his crewmen. He pressed his hands to his head, wishing somehow he could clarify his confused thoughts.

The ship in confusion and chaos, and I'm worrying about my own personal love life?

Against the pillow Gilmerritt stirred and he leaned forward and clasped her unbandaged hand. She opened her green eyes, dark with pain.

"Gildoran?" she whispered and he saw her look slowly around the Medic dome, trying to orient herself in space and time.

"I'm here, Merritt. How are you feeling now?"

He saw pain move across her face. "My hand. It hurts. It hurts terribly. The children—how are the children? I heard Gilmarina scream——"

"Gilmarina's foot is in the same shape as your hand. Giltaro must have died instantly," he said, and saw her face crumple in anguish. "Poohbear died this evening."

Her free hand clutched convulsively at his, but she did not sob.

"Merritt. Darling, can you tell us what happened?"

Slowly she shook her head. "I'm not sure," she said, and he saw her features twitch again as if in memory. "The children were picking flowers, and one of the flowers . . . burned them? Burned me? There was a sort of light—no, I didn't see anything. But the plant . . . it screamed. It screamed like Gilmarina, and it whipped at me. And then . . . I don't remember anything more, except that Poohbear fell across me, and I smelled something like burning meat." She frowned and added, confusedly, "It must have been my hand burning, and then I thought I heard you a time or two, and then . . . I don't remember any more."

Her eyes slipped shut again.

The plant—it screamed?

So the plants were the danger. Gildoran realized that without being aware of it; he had suspected it all along. Gilhart had died in a group of cup-plants. Gilharrad, too. Had the portable sonar gear somehow frightened them? But plants that could emit burning rays? How? Damn it, *how?*

Gilmerritt's eyes flickered open again.

"Will I have the use of my hand?"

Gildoran looked at Gilnosta. The Medic said honestly "It's too soon to tell. When we can spare you for a year, to get you into a suspended-animation tank and grow you a new one, yes, of course. But until then—no, Merritt. I don't think so. And we're too shorthanded—excuse me, dear—to give you a year off."

The woman's eyes squeezed shut. The fingers of her good hand clutched spasmodically on Gildoran's, but she made no protest. There was nothing he could say. In the shape they were in, Gilmerritt could not be spared. Hands or no, they needed her mind, her intelligence, her directing force in the biology labs. Gildoran faced, grimly, the knowledge that it might be a long time before they could spare Gilmerritt for the year she needed in suspended animation to grow a new hand replacing the one which had been virtually burnt off. With one of the children dead and another crippled—although Gilmarina could go at once into a regrowth tank, as soon as there was someone to tend the tank—it would be years and years before they could spare a single crew-member, even a one-handed one. They weren't able to spare Gilharrad—he had come back to them, and now even his frail help was gone.

Gilmerritt drew her hand away from his, turned her face away and lay in a stubborn, withdrawn isolation. And Gildoran understood that, too. Now he must bear the weight of Merritt's disability as well as everything else. All at once he felt broken, overwhelmed. All day, without knowing it, he had been waiting for Merritt to recover, to regain the lost part of himself. Burdened, over-whelmed with his own losses and griefs, he had still hoped somehow that among so much loss, at least Merritt's love for him would be unchanged, that he could rest for a little while in the certainty that had been theirs as a couple. Now that was gone, too.

Then Gildoran was appalled at his own selfishness. Had he been expecting Merritt, in her pain and loss, to comfort him for *his*? All he could do for her now was to love her and to accept even her anger and withdrawal. Disregarding her turned-away face, he kept hold of her good hand until she relaxed and slipped back into sleep. Perhaps what had been between them had not been deep enough to survive this shock. But it had not been merely a surface adventure either, and he would stand by her and do what he could for her, even if she turned away from him.

This damnable planet! This hellish world! It seemed that ever since they first touched down on it he had been going from one crisis to another, without an instant's pause!

Gildoran's world! Cosmos, what a wretched, ironic joke *that* was!

VIII

Gildoran had slept for a while in his groundlab before the crew working in spacesuits came in with their reports. They had checked the clearing and the plants, one by one, and had been able to find no trace of poisonous plants, plants which moved on attack or plants which secreted chemicals capable of causing such burns as the ones which Gilmerritt and Gilmarina had suffered. "We can analyze the plants section by section and organ by organ," Gildorric offered, "but Gilmerritt did that already."

"Then are you trying to tell me the accidents never happened?"

"No," said Gildorric, "but we still don't know *how* they happened, or what the mechanism is." He smiled, grimly, his bare head sticking out of the spacesuit. "Maybe the plants were on their good behavior. No headaches, even." He added, "Maybe it's just that the helmets screen out sounds too. I couldn't hear those damned frogbugs either."

"Sound. . . ." Gildoran broke off. The Poohbears had abnormally acute hearing. Human hearing went from fifteen cycles a second to about 20,000. The frogbugs put out sound at about nine cycles, subsonics. But there were other sounds which humans couldn't hear. A whole spectrum of them, up above 20,000 cycles. And if the frogbugs were giving off subsonics, maybe other insects, or even plants, were giving off other sounds.

"I can't disturb Gilmerritt again," he said. "Who else is here from the bio groundlab?"

"I know my way around in there," young Gilbarni said.

"You brought down test animals and released them. Are there any bats among them?"

"*Bats?*" Gilbarni stared at him as if he had gone mad. "I think there are some bats in the hibernation sector, in the ecology-niche equipment. If you really want one, sir, I can send up to the *Gypsy Moth* and tell Gilmarlo to thaw a few out and send them down. You mean *bats*, sir? The things that fly——"

"And see in the dark, and find their way around by emitting ultrasonic radar shrieks," Gildoran confirmed. "Yes; send for some. And get down some oscilloscopes and a standard-scale vibration-measuring device with extra short-pulse equipment on it. Meanwhile, everybody get some food, it's going to be a busy day."

Gilraban said "We have the equipment to check the Transmitter, Captain. Shall we go ahead?"

Gildoran shook his head. "Nobody outside the clearing except in spacesuits," he said, "until we check out my theory. Nobody near *any* plant that grows on this world, or any insect either."

Gildorric was frowning, trying to follow what he was saying. "You're thinking about ultrasonics? But . . . Marina and Merritt were burned, Doran. Gilhart and Harrad died of cerebral hemorrhage, and so did Giltaro. Are you trying to tell me——"

"I'm not telling you anything yet," Gildoran said. "Let's check it out first. But I should have guessed when I heard that Gilharrad had been using the portable sonar-gear—that sends out pulses of ultrasonics which bounce off solid layers of rock. My guess right now is that he scared something, and it struck back. If I'm right, it could explain everything. We'll know, now, in a few hours."

It was dusk again when, spacesuited, they walked toward the clearing behind the now-deserted Nursery camp. Other workers in spacesuits were taking down the brightly colored structures and only the skeletonlike dome framework remained, green bushes and trees clearly visible through the empty triangular segments. The spacesuit helmets closed out all sounds, even the eerie squeaks of the bats in their cages. Inside the clearing Gildoran stopped and gestured to the others to release the creatures. One by one they fluttered up into the dark sky and began to circle there, and Gildoran visualized them sending out their high, ultrasonic pulses of sound—

And then, one by one, their fluttering ceased, turned into aimless confused flight. One by one they fell, like small stones, into the clearing at the Explorers' feet; some feebly moving, others already dead. Gildorric, bent over an oscilloscope, nodded grimly.

"I thought so. The minute they started sending out their pulses of sound, the sound waves started coming from all over—zapped them, one by one. Evidently the plants here—mostly the cup-plants, but others too—and some of the insects, send out sound waves between 30,000 and 100,000 cycles per second. Most of them are fairly weak, but those diamondlike crystals in the cup-plants, and probably a few others, act as piezoelectric crystals in ordinary electric equipment."

Gilraban said "Then that's what fouled up the Transmitter test."

"Right. Too much stray energy around which we didn't know about and hadn't compensated for," Gilmarti said. "Then that explains the deaths——"

"Right. And the brain damage. And the burns. Sound waves at various frequences can kill—and these must have been pretty narrowly focused—or they can burn as badly as a laser," Gildoran confirmed.

Gilraban said in deep disgust and despair, "Why did none of us think of it?"

Gildoran said heavily, "Because we weren't looking for it. I suspect it's a unique evolution on this planet—ultrasound is usually associated only with technology. At least that settles it finally. No one to go out without spacesuits again, except in the burned-over areas where there's no plant life left. Get what fuel we need, right away. We'll have to decide what to do."

But he knew, as he took the shuttle up to *Gypsy Moth* that evening, that the "we" who would decide would be ultimately himself. Gildoran. That was what it meant to be Captain.

He had called together the most experienced officers on the *Gypsy Moth*; Gilrae, Gilban, Gilraban for the Transmitter crew, half a dozen of the older ones. He thought, with deep bitterness, of Gilhart and Gilharrad. They were so badly needed. And Gilmerritt, lying drugged and crippled in the infirmary; and of Gilnosta, who had been relieved of all her other duties to nurse her and Gilmarina until they were out of danger.

"The crux of the matter is," he said, after briefing, "that we are desperately shorthanded. We were shorthanded before; now we could almost say that *Gypsy Moth* is crippled. Is there any way to salvage this world? I admit frankly that I don't know; I haven't the experience. Raban, could we set up a Transmitter and get through to Head

Center? With a complete terraforming team, we could probably transform this world into a fairly safe one."

Gilraban said, "I don't know. I don't think so. It would take months to compensate for the ultrasonics all over the planet, unless we wanted to make a major burn of plant life—virtually strip it bare. Meanwhile we'd have to live aboard *Gypsy Moth* and commute down from groundlabs— we couldn't make a setdown. And work in spacesuits. Besides if we stripped the planet . . ." he shrugged. "What would they want a Transmitter here *for*, then?"

Gildoran had been afraid of that, but he put the next question anyway. "Gilmerritt could answer this better, but . . . Marlo, can we possibly kill off enough of the *lethal* plants to work here?"

Gilmarlo, the second biologist, said, "Not without a major ecological study; probably not then. Put it this way: if you kill off the most dangerous plants, their natural enemies—the most lethal insects—thrive, and you'll have an insect plague. After that, the insects overpopulate, and kill off even the harmless plants. Then you've got bare rock. Even if we all worked triple shifts—it would take nine or ten years shiptime to replace everything with a stable ecological cycle of harmless plants and animals. No, Gildoran. I'm afraid I agree with Raban. We've got to write this one off. We don't have the personnel, we don't have the biologicals, we don't have the *time*. And," she added, "we don't have Gilmerritt."

Gilban said harshly "Don't blame the Captain, Marlo. I overrode him. Don't you think I know it's my fault that we've lost so many——"

"No, Ban, that doesn't get us anywhere," Gildoran interrupted. "We could blame ourselves and each other all day and all night, if we wanted to. If I'd been sure of my facts instead of relying on instinct; if any of us had been willing to question the Poohbears and find out what it was they didn't trust . . . You did the best you could on the available information; leave it at that. Your job now is to get the hurt ones back in shape."

He turned to Gilrae. If anyone could manage to pull any kind of victory out of what looked like total defeat, she would be the one. "Rae. You've had a lot of experience with planets that looked hopeless. With Harrad and Hart gone, you're almost our senior working officer. Can you see any way out, short of simply abandoning this planet?"

Gilban muttered "I don't see why we should even think about it."

Rae looked first at the medical officer and said, "I know what Doran's thinking, Ban, and he's absolutely right. We've poured too much into this planet to leave it without trying to recover at least some of our losses. We're desperately short-handed; we're crippled. With the Poohbears on strike, we're *worse* than crippled. It's going to be hard to work the ship; it's going to be even harder to hold out until we find another usable world, or until the children grow up. If we could think of a way to save something out of this disaster, we ought to." But she had said *if we could* instead of *if we can*, and Gildoran knew it was hopeless, even as she went on. "But I'm still remembering what Gilhart said just before we landed—'Now and then you meet a world that bites back, and all you can do is run'—while you still have something to run with. If we hang on here, we'll run the risk of further losses, and there isn't any real hope of gains to make up for them. I agree with Raban, Gildoran. We'll have to let it go."

Gildoran nodded slowly. She was right. There wasn't the slightest chance of anything salvaging the disaster of his first command. He might as well go and make it official.

As he went slowly down the shaft toward the bridge, Rae followed him; touched his shoulder lightly.

"Gildoran——"

"I really made a mess of it, didn't I, Rae? My first planet, and my first command——"

He had halfway expected comfort, but she frowned at him. "That is sheer self-indulgence, and you know it," she said. "Don't flatter yourself by thinking that you *could* have thought of a way out. There simply wasn't any. Sometimes there isn't any happy ending, Gildoran. It's human nature to want one. If it's any comfort to you, I don't think Gilhart could have handled it any better. But we'll never know. We've done the only thing we could; now all we can do is try to put it behind us and go on to the next thing. If you want a shoulder to cry on, try Ramie!"

It was like a bath of icewater. He felt the surge of adrenaline like a metal taste in his mouth; too angry to speak, he jerked on his heel and turned away toward the Bridge.

Behind him he did not see that Gilrae's face softened and there were tears in her eyes. He strode angrily into the Bridge deck without thinking, moved into the spot where he had seen Gilhart sitting last.

Slowly, he pulled the ship-to-ground communicator toward him. Lori looked up expectantly from the scanner, but he paid no attention to the child.

"All hands, ship and groundlabs, this is the Captain," he said heavily. He knew that his voice was going all over *Gypsy Moth*—a rare thing—and only for official statements such as this. "By joint decision it has been decided to abandon the planet. Geodesic crew, abandon all exploration efforts and detail crew working in spacesuits to load fuel and metals for ship reserve and raw material for the converter. Dismantle all groundlabs, dismantle Test Transmitter, and return to *Gypsy Moth*, suspending all operations. We will depart the planet one shiptime day from this moment."

Now it was official. He had given the orders which would make permanent the fiasco of his first command. He replaced the communicator slowly and looked into the big screen. It was a beautiful planet lying below them, wrapped in its veils of blue-green, gleaming faintly like an iridescent jewel in its own sun; but it was as deadly as poison.

He thought of Gilmerritt, who had wanted to build a beautiful resort world there; of Marina with the jeweled butterfly on her shoulder. Leaving the planet behind would not solve their problems. We'll have to spare Gilmerritt some time soon, get her into a tank for a new hand, he thought. But when? With the Poohbears on strike—and three deaths—we'll need everybody. The problems had only begun, and this was only the beginning of his year of command. There were two gravely wounded crewmembers to be healed.

There was Gilban's self-confidence to be restored.
He would have to persuade some of the older
Floaters to come back to modified duty. The
Poohbears must be coaxed back somehow. Ramie
was working single-handed in the Nursery. . . .
He looked down at the great blue-green planet
below.

*You didn't get us, after all. You're just another
planet, and you're for leaving, like all the rest.*

"Captain . . ." Lori said timidly. He sighed,
wrenched his gaze from the bewitching ball of
blue-green cloud beneath them and said, "What is
it, Gillori?"

"How shall I log this? The planet has no name
in records, and it should be transmitted to Head
Center when we can."

With a shock, Gildoran remembered that it was
his privilege to name the planet.

Gilhart, he thought. A permanent memorial to
the world which had, after all—in the phrase of
the Explorers—had his name on it.

Revulsion struck him. He could just imagine
Gilrae's accusing eyes if he gave her lover's name
to this hellish world. Better to take the blame
himself. Gildoran's World? Cosmos, no!

"Log it as Hellworld," he said, and thrust his
seat aside to take a last look at the planet below.
"I'm going down to Nursery, to see how Marina is
getting on, and what the Poohbears are up to."

Others could handle the details of getting the
crew and the groundlabs pulled in, loading fuel
and raw material for converters and reserves,
navigating away from the planet.

His world now was the *Gypsy Moth*, and every soul aboard her was his personal responsibility. Ramie, trying to handle eight children, one seriously injured, would have to be given help, and he should ask her what she needed and wanted. She wouldn't have any questions except the necessary ones, and she would understand that he had done the best he could, as she always understood. Gilrae's taunting phrase, "If you want a shoulder to cry on, try Ramie's," came back to him. He thought he might just do that, sometime.

He said formally, "Lori, the Bridge is yours," and turned his back on the scene of his first command.

Part Four

COLD DEATH

I

"Marginal," said Gilmarlo, who was Year-Captain, "very marginal. I don't think this one is worth the trouble. We can't spare the people to explore it, shorthanded as we are. And if we do get down there, and get a Transmitter tie-in, on that wretched chunk of barren rock down there, then what? A finder's fee—a very small one. You could hardly call it a planet at all; just an asteroid, a hunk of rock that happens somehow to have hung on to an atmosphere."

"It's not that bad," said Gilrae. "There are signs of life. A few signs. It was probably inhabited once. But not for millions of years. Like Ozymandias. Maybe by that same feline race."

"That's the point I'm trying to make," Gilmarlo said. "The time for life on this planet is past—very, very far past. We came too late." She scanned the printout data from the computer again, looking around the briefing room at the staff who had assembled there. "And I just don't think we can afford to take this one; we ought to save our resources for the next good one we find. I don't even think there's insect life down there."

"That," said Gildoran, raising his head abruptly, "might even be in its favor—after Hellworld. Where there's no life left, there's not likely to be any danger. And you yourself pointed out how shorthanded we were. You say we can't afford to do this one, Captain, but can we afford not to? There's no assurance that the next one will be any better, or the one after that. Look at Ozymandias; that was the last good planet we had, and even that one was old. I think we're getting into a part of the Galaxy where life came a long time ago and has simply died out. The oldest part—and we're not colonizing, we're recolonizing."

It lay beyond their blind viewscreen, unseen; the world old Gilmarti had discovered three days ago shiptime, and they had been quarreling about ever since.

"The question isn't whether we can afford to explore it, Gildoran," said Raban, "the question is, can we afford to pass it up? It isn't a particularly attractive world, not by my standards anyway. But we are going to have to set down whether we like it or not; we need fuel, rocks for the converter, if there isn't anything else, and since we have to set down anyway, we ought to assess it for opening. We need a finder's fee, even if that's all we get out of it. And we need Transmitter contact with other worlds. I don't see how we can afford to pass this one up. There might not be another good one for two or three years."

"We can't afford to open it unless it's a good one," Gilrae said. "As shorthanded as we are, we couldn't spare a very large Transmitter crew to make the first tie-in. Five years from now, the older children will be able to take real shifts and we could risk it. The ship is self-supporting, once we have rocks for the converters. We can get them by finding an asteroid belt anywhere. I say we wait till the older children are able to do their part, and *then* look for a world that's worth opening."

"We're shorthanded, all right," Gilban agreed somberly, "but that's all the more reason we need to get back into touch with the rest of the civilized Galaxy. We need children. It was a mistake not to get more when we were on Ozymandias . . ."

"The youngest ones in Nursery were only a year old then," Gilnosta said, looking up, "and we decided they wouldn't be able to adjust to a new batch. And it's a blessing we didn't, because after Hellworld, when the Poohbears went on strike, who would have looked after a group of babies? We'd have had to divert half the ship's company into the Nursery. Even now, if we *did* manage a tie-in—and who would want to come to this place anyhow, unless it's made out of solid anthracite or diamond?—and we picked up six more kids, who, I ask you, is going to look after them? The Poohbears certainly won't."

There was silence in the briefing room, while they thought of the Poohbears, barricaded on an unused deck of living space—a deck that had not been used since the ship's complement of *Gypsy Moth* numbered more than a hundred—drawing rations from the synthesizer, but otherwise making no contact of any sort with the ship's company. Not since Hellworld. Not once.

"You're right," Gildoran said. "The Poohbears left us with two four-year-olds in the Nursery and one in a regrowth tank. And four seven-year-old children. And ever since then, we've had to divert more people than we can spare from the ship, into the Nursery. Just for the sake of argument, suppose we had had half a dozen newborns, or kids too young to crawl? How in Cosmos would we have managed?"

Gilban said "I can't believe the Poohbears would have left us if we'd have really young babies. Babies who needed them. It would have given them a responsibility."

Gilrushka from Psych, a slender ageless woman—but Gildoran knew she was one of the oldest on the staff, older than Rae—said, "You may be right. A responsibility, to take their mind off their loss. They may have felt—"

"I don't think any of us, not even you, is enough of an expert on the psychology of Poohbears to say that for certain," said Gilnosta, a little sharply. "Hellworld was a tragedy for all of us, not just the Poohbears. We needed them then—how we needed them! I spent those first four months afterward tending that regrowth tank full-time—I never slept more than two hours at a time; I woke up normally every forty-five minutes to tend it. Do you think we didn't need the Poohbears then?"

"Still, helpless babies—" Gilrushka began, and Gilnosta retorted angrily, "Gilmarina was more helpless than any newborn, in that tank, and what it did to the other kids in Nursery, what kind of trauma that left, we'll never know! If we couldn't count on the Poohbears then, we can never count on them again. Never. For all I care, we can send them all out the airlock!"

Gilrushka said smoothly, "You're certainly entitled to be bitter, Nosta, but I don't think—"

"That's the trouble; you don't *think!*" Nosta snapped. "What would it have meant to us, then, to have the Poohbears? Even one more functioning pair of hands—" and she looked at Gilmerritt and then, uneasily, away. There was a momentary silence in the briefing room, and Gildoran felt his eyes go, with the old guilt, to Gilmerritt. She sat as she always did—as she had done since Hellworld—against one of the curved bulkheads, concealing her crippled and useless hand between her body and the wall.

We needed her so much, we couldn't afford to take her out of service for a year to grow a new hand; not when it meant pulling someone else out of service to tend the tank full-time. And it had to be my decision; and I was her lover. But I was Captain, too, and I had to think of them all, not just Gilmerritt.

Gildoran's thoughts ran round and round on their old guilty track. He had been too inexperienced as Captain; with the Poohbears on strike, and after losing Gilhart and Gildorric, he had not dared to deprive the ship of yet another experienced officer.

Gilmerritt was aware of the looks; she winced, and it seemed to Gildoran that she shrank away even farther into the wall.

Gilban said, his voice harsh and peremptory, "If there has to be blame for that, I'll share it; but there's no sense in going over and over old mistakes. The question is, what can we do *now?* If we spent a year downworlding, we could assign someone, maybe one of the Floaters—someone who's still competent, but can't handle down-world gravity—to tend a tank while we're in orbit. That would settle one of our problems—"

"There's no way we could spend a year downworlding on *that* planet," Gilmarlo interrupted, drawing their attention back. "There's nothing to develop down there."

"We might be able to do mining, or at least contract it out for mining," said Gilraban, "I remind you, Captain, we can't afford to pass up anything. There's no assurance we'll get another good planet in this area; the suns seem to get older and older, and I am beginning to think they had their wave of evolution millions of years ago. I think we ought to go down and evaluate it anyway."

"But there's nothing—" Gilrae began, then stopped. Gilmarlo said, "How about this? We'll send down a landing party tomorrow. We'd have to find the best rock for the converter anyway. Once they see the surface, they can evaluate it and see whether it is worth exploring and making a Transmitter tie-in."

"And there's this," Gilraban said. "A planet like this one won't demand many resources to open it up. Just a Transmitter crew. Whereas a really good world—we'd be there for a year or more, making multiple tie-ins. Opening it up. With this one, we can make the tie-in, collect our finder's fee, up ship, and go looking for a better one. And maybe land the Poohbears, if they really want to leave us; maybe get into contact with some other Explorer ships and arrange for an exchange. Perhaps they would be happy on another ship, and we could have a different group—one with no personal grudges against any of us. That just might be the answer to the Poohbear problem."

There was still some murmuring; some of the *Gypsy Moth*'s crew felt strongly against wasting even the time and energy of a landing party. "Just send down one or two people with equipment to pick up rocks for converter fuel," they suggested.

"That's what I, personally, feel we ought to do," the Captain said, "but there are so many of you who feel we ought to give this planet a chance. We'll send down one landing party, and come to a final decision tomorrow, after we have some real data. How does that sound?"

There were still some protests, but they did accept it; it was, after all, the Captain's decision, and they knew she would go with the Landing party; so danger, if danger there was, would be hers, too. Most of them, though, remembering the barren world they had seen on the viewscreeen, with a mean temperature somewhere near the freezing point of water, thought more of the waste of time than of the danger. What, after all, could touch them, on a world barren and swept clean of life by recurrent ice ages?

As they left the briefing room, Gildoran joined Merritt; they moved together, silently, in the direction of the quarters they still shared. At first because, Captain or not, he had taken on himself a part of the task of nursing her; there were too few others, and she needed care at all hours, and they shared quarters anyhow. Later, despite her bitterness, he had remained, because he feared she would interpret any withdrawal as a personal rejection; she was hypersensitive about her deformity.

"What do you think?" she asked him. "Could we exchange Poohbears with another ship?"

"I don't know." He looked at the lift shaft, which no longer opened on Living Deck Four; the Poohbears had adapted the lift controls so that no crewmember of the *Gypsy Moth* could come up there at all. "We'd have to communicate with them first, and they've cut off communication. I'm not sure we even have radio access to Deck Four any more. If they could modify elevator controls, they could modify communications too."

She chuckled. "Maybe we ought to have a Transmitter into Deck Four; come in and *make* them talk to us."

He looked into her laughing face. *I love her,* he thought. *I wouldn't blame her if she hated me, and maybe she does. But I love her.*

"Do you suppose that they would agree to go to another ship, in exchange for others who would be willing to work with us? And if they didn't want to—could we make them go, Merritt?"

"I don't know," she said, troubled. "I don't even know if we should. They're our mothers, Doran. You grew up in a Poohbear's pocket just as I did. You don't force your mother out of your home. Not even if she's angry with you, not even if she's useless to you." She gave her deformed hand a single cold, bitter glance, and said with a forced detachment, "After all, when it comes to uselessness—"

"You aren't useless," he protested, but knew

she did not even hear him. She said abruptly, "Isn't it your Nursery shift?"

He glanced at a chronometer. "Right." Since the defection of the Poohbears, every crewmember of *Gypsy Moth* worked a two-hour Nursery shift, every other day; it was the only way the children could have the close individual attention they needed. Intelligence, in children, seemed to be a function of close and constant childhood stimulation, constant one-to-one interaction with adults. But he hesitated, reluctant to leave Gilmerritt. Was she sinking, again, into another of the recurrent depressions when, except for her obligatory hours of ship's duty, she would lie in her hammock for hours on end, not reading, not even meditating, just staring at the wall in black brooding?

"Why not come down to Nursery with me? An extra person there is always welcome," he suggested, and she turned on him.

"Damn it, no! I get enough sweetness and light on the Bridge, with everybody finding work for me to do that won't be physically taxing! And if I have to look at Gilmarina again, I think I'll go out of my mind! Have a little mercy, Doran!"

He protested again. "Merritt, don't stay alone—it isn't good for you—"

"Nothing's good for me," she said, and again the compulsive, bitter, detached glance at the ugly, useless claw, which was how, despite their best efforts, her burned hand had healed.

We should have put her right into a regrowth tank. Gilmarina's foot is as good as new, and she knows perfectly well that her hand could be just

as good as that, too. It was my mistake. I did it to
her. I can't blame her if she really hates me. In her
place I would, too.

"Merritt—darling—" he began, but she cut him
off impatiently. "Cosmos! Gildoran, stop hanging
over me!"

"I only want—"

Her face softened. "Oh, I know. I'm no good to
you, Gildoran. I'm no good to anybody. I'm worse
than the Poohbears! You really hate me, don't
you, Doran?"

"Hate you? How can you ask me that?" he said,
dismayed, putting out his hand to her.

But she pushed him away. "I'm so damned tired
of your guilt and your kindness," she said, her
voice cracking, and ran away down the hall
toward the shaft.

Gildoran started to follow her; then, flinching
from the thought of another scene, turned back
toward Nursery. He couldn't do anything for her,
not now. She would calm down afterward, she
always did; and then she would be guilty and
contrite for having troubled him, and cling to
him, begging for his forgiveness, desperately
afraid he would abandon her. The cycle was
familiar by now, but he loved her in spite of it.

Angrily trying to turn off his churning
thoughts, he headed down toward the Nursery.

II

Inside the Nursery was music; Rae was at one end playing her harp, and Gilmarina, seated beside her at a somewhat smaller harp, was stumbling through an elementary exercise in arpeggios. She looked up and smiled sunnily at Gildoran, but she did not move and returned her eyes quickly to strict attention to the strings.

She's found something she loves, even more than me. One part of Gildoran felt chagrined—this was the first time he had ever come into the Nursery, since Gilmarina had emerged from her regrowth tank, that she did not immediately drop whatever she was doing and rush to him for hugs and reassurance. But another part of him was delighted. Gilmarina was growing up, she had begun to find things which absorbed her, delighted her; she had begun to submerge her energy in what she wanted to do, without the constant need for reassurance. She was, essentially, now a year younger than her Nurserymates; she had spent a year in the tank, in suspended animation.

But she's still the brightest of them all. And fortunately, there had been no lasting emotional damage; for a few months after her emergence she had been sulky and clingy, crying for the Poohbears—her contemporaries had long managed to control their awareness of the loss—demanding constant reassurance and attention.

But the foot had regrown perfectly; she was barefoot, and he could see that the left foot, still pinker than the rest of her body (not yet bleached by hard radiation of intercosmic space) was otherwise a perfect match for the right one.

In a corner of the Nursery, Gilbeth, an apprentice Navigator, had gathered the four eight-year-olds around her, and was giving a lesson in elementary mathematical sets and equations. Measuring rods and devices lay all around them. In another corner, Ramie was supervising the two five-year-olds, Gilmarina's contemporaries, in building elaborate constructions with modular rods and tiles; one had built a model of a solar system and powered it with a tiny electronic battery so that it moved slowly and ponderously. Gilrita tugged at Gildoran.

"Come and see! How do you like my orrery?"

"Interesting," he said, squatting down on his heels to survey it at close range, "but don't you have too many planets with multiple moons? Five is a median number, and look, you have an inner planet with seven moons, which is rare; small moons inside the proper limit tend to fall into the sun. It's outer planets which have larger sets of moons in stable orbits."

Gilrita frowned and said, "I like planets to have lots of moons. You can design more interesting orbits for them. Look, I have a planet which goes in a backward orbit, and another one right out of the ecliptic plane."

"Two anomalies in one system?" Gildoran questioned, with a raised eyebrow.

"It's an anomalous system," she insisted, and Gildoran chuckled. "It's your system. Build it the way you want to. What have you got there, Tallen?" he asked the remaining child, and the small boy said, "A model ship. See, this one has a synthesizer right on the Bridge so the Captain can have a meal right there when he's hungry, and there are *twenty* Poohbears, so they won't all get mad and leave us at once."

Over the child's head Gildoran met Ramie's eyes in despair; were the children still grieving? Gilramie said gently, "You miss the Poohbears, don't you, Tallen?"

His eyes filled with tears. "Why don't they love us anymore? When they went away, did they take Giltaro with them?"

"No," Ramie said, her voice tender. "Giltaro was hurt like Gilmarina, only worse—hurt so bad we couldn't even put him in a growth tank and grow him all new again. So we had to let him go into Cosmos, and we buried the body he was wearing on the planet where he died."

Again Gildoran marveled at the way in which the children needed to hear these simple things again and again. They learned intellectual matters so quickly; but they could not manage grief and loss, and needed repeated reassurance. Would any of them, ever, really get over the trauma of losing Giltaro so young, losing their other Nurserymate Gilmarina for a year and having her emerge a year younger than they were, not having grown in the interval?

Maybe, in a way, losing the Poohbears has been good for them, he thought. *They see more of us; before this, they saw only Nursery staff, and Medic and Psych people, and specially detailed*

Educators. Now we all take turns with them and they get to know us all, more intimately.

Ramie said, "Would you like to have Rushka come down, Giltallen, so you can talk with her some more about how you miss Taro?"

He nodded, sniffling, and she said, "I'll get on the comm with her right away and ask how soon she can come and see you. Or maybe you'd like to go up on the Decks and see her?"

"I'm a big boy," Giltallen said, "I can go up on the Decks."

Ramie went to use an intercom, and came back to tell Giltallen that he could take the shaft up by himself to Rushka's quarters. He left the Nursery, and Ramie said, "You were right, Doran, and I was wrong. I was upset when you named them Gilmarina and Giltallen. I thought it would remind me too much of poor Gilmarin, and hurt Rae too much, hearing "Giltallen" all the time. But now when I think 'Tallen,' I think about the little fellow, and I know Rae does, too. A good memory drives out a bad. I never think about Gilmarin now when I look at Marina."

"She's very much herself," Gildoran agreed, looking at the tall white-haired woman at the harp, guiding Gilmarina's hands. Rae smiled at them both and said something in a low voice to Gilmarina; she replaced her harp, covering it, and came to Gildoran, rising on tiptoe to hug him.

"I played on the big, big harp too," she said. "Rae let me."

"I heard you, smallest," he said, stroking her feathery hair.

"Will you take us up on the Bridge, Doran?

Where we can see the new planet? Is is a good planet?"

"Yes, I'll take you up, and no, I don't think it's a very good planet," Gildoran said. "There's nothing there but old rock. But we need rocks to make the converter work, to drive the ship and to break down atoms into other things."

"Can I go too?" demanded eight-year-old Giljodek, and the other children quickly crowded around, begging to be included in the expedition.

"Let me use the comm to the Bridge," Gildoran said, "and I'll see how many of you they can have up there at a time."

Gilmarlo answered over the mechanical device that all of them could come, if they wished; there was nothing much going on. So Gildoran took the youngsters up the shafts to the Bridge, and Gilmarlo, who was not particularly busy at the moment, let them sit one by one in her chair and look over the viewscreen at the planet below.

"Has it got a name?" Gilmarina asked.

"Not yet, child," the young Captain answered. "We usually try to find out what a planet is like before we give it a name. But I thought we might call it Tempest; preliminary weather study from orbit looks as if there were strong winds and heavy cyclone patterns."

"Tempest," repeated Gilmarina thoughtfully. "Is it a nice planet?"

"I don't know. I hope so," Gilmarlo said, smiling as she lifted Gilmarina out of her chair to give the next child a turn. "Well, Giljodek, do you want to sit in the Captain's chair?"

He clambered up, frowning. "I wish I could be a Captain someday."

"Why, you can," Marlo said. "Every Explorer can be a Captain, as soon as you qualify in three Class A assignments, in three different specialties. Unless you choose to be a Medic, then you need only two specialties. But Medics usually don't want to be Captains, they are too busy taking care of sick people. You'll be a Captain someday."

"Really?" The small boy stared. "I thought only girls could be Captains. Like you. And Gilrae—somebody told me she was a Captain four times."

"But Gildoran was a Captain, too," Marlo reassured him, smiling.

"Gilban never was. He said so."

"Gilban is too busy looking after the sick. If he had to stop and be a Captain, and decide how to open up planets, he wouldn't have time to look after sick people," Marlo told him. "Of course you can be a Captain when you grow up. And so can Gilvarth, and so can Giltallen—where is he, Doran?"

"Up in Psych with Rushka," Gildoran told her. "Look, Giljodek, if you push that button, it will clear the viewscreen, and you can see the planet from the Captain's chair."

"What do these other buttons do?"

"These let me see what is going on in the Ship." Marlo explained, "See, I can look into Medic bay, and into Nursery, and into the Transmitter center."

"Can you see into where I sleep?"

"No, Jodek, people need privacy while they sleep," the Captain said. "If you want me to see you from where you sleep, you must come out into the play area where people are doing things together. Or into one of the public areas . . . see, there is Gilban working in the Medic bays. We have no sick people on the *Gypsy Moth* now, Cosmos be praised. And here is the Rim where there is no gravity and the Floaters live. When you are very old and your bones are brittle you can live out there, but that will not be for hundreds and hundreds of years. There is old Gilrimin in a special hammock—she is five hundred and seventy years old shiptime. Someday you will be that old, too."

Giljodek was pressing the buttons one after another; this time the screen stayed blank. "What is there?" he asked.

Gilmarlo sighed. She said "That is where the Poohbears are. Deck Four. They have broken the screen there so that we cannot see them. Remember, they are angry with us."

Giljodek scowled and said, "I'm angry with them. They shouldn't go away."

"But they did, and there is nothing we can do about it," Gilmarlo said. "And now it is Gilrita's turn to sit in my chair and see the views."

When Gildoran took the children back to Nursery, he lingered for a little while, talking to Ramie.

"I wonder if the Poohbears will ever come back?"

"I don't know," Ramie said. "I've wondered."

"It's doing something bad to the children. The knowledge that somebody they loved betrayed them. Even if they came back now, would the children even trust them again, ever believe they wouldn't be abandoned again?"

"Would any of *us* ever trust them again?" Ramie asked. "It seems to me that's the main question. We thought they were part of us. And then they could do something like that."

Hesitating, he told her of the suggestion that Raban had made; to exchange Poohbears with another Explorer ship if Transmitter contact was made with the populated worlds.

"Provided there's another Explorer ship downworlding at the same time, with a Transmitter tie-in," Ramie said, "and provided *their* Poohbears and *our* Poohbears agreed to the exchange."

"Gilmerritt said it wasn't a good idea. She said, 'You don't put your mother out of your house even when she's angry with you . . .' "

"Gilmerritt is kinder than I," Ramie said, "and more forgiving. I couldn't. I can't. There was a time when I wanted to kill them; when I saw what it did to the children, not to have them here. And when I saw what it did, all over again, when Gilmarina came out of the tank . . ." There were tears in her eyes.

Gilmarina came running up, hearing her name mentioned. "Don't go, Doran," she begged. "Stay here. You can sleep with me in my hammock."

Gildoran chuckled. Ship's crew took it in turns, now, to sleep in the Nursery, one and two at a time; but it was not his turn tonight. "Your hammock wouldn't fit me, smallest."

"Then you can sleep with Ramie in Ramie's hammock," Gilmarina said. Gildoran looked down and colored, and Ramie said, laughing, "You don't do that, Gilmarina. Grown-up people decide for themselves who they want to sleep with them."

"Don't you *want* to sleep with Gildoran?" Gilmarina persisted, and Ramie burst into a helpless laugh.

"You don't ask questions like that, smallest."

"Yes I do," Gilmarina said, "you heard me."

"Then let me put it another way," Gilramie said. "Grown-up people don't *answer* questions like that unless they choose to, and I choose not to. Understand, smallest? Besides, if Gildoran slept down here with you and me out of his proper turn, Gilmerritt would be lonely, because Doran sleeps in *her* room."

"Poor Gilmerritt," said Marina, diverted. "Her hand hurts, doesn't it?"

"Sometimes, maybe. Not much. But she thinks people are looking at it all the time, and it makes her unhappy," Gilramie said.

Gilmarina said, "Poor Merritt. Kiss her for me, Doran, and tell her not to be sad, because I love her."

"So do I, smallest," Gildoran said, catching up the child and kissing her. "So do I."

And yet Gildoran was reluctant to leave; when he said goodbye to Gilmarina, his feet lagged in the hall and into the shaft, fearing another scene; and when he came into the quarters they shared, seeing in the semidark that Gilmerritt slept, he was grateful, and tiptoed, quiet, fearing to waken her.

And then, in the small light from the hallway, he saw the blood; and, rushing to her, turned her over. She had slashed her wrist, deeply, just above the burnt, useless claw; and the bed they shared was soaked with blood.

During his year as Captain, he had learned to make decisions fast; it took him only seconds to determine that, although she was unconscious, she was still alive; and, seconds later, he was on the comm device just outside their quarters, bringing Gilnosta and Gilban to him within seconds. Gilrushka, from Psych, followed only a moment later.

"If she'd had the use of both hands, she would have been dead," Gilnosta said, tightening a tourniquet. "She couldn't cut deeply enough to reach an artery. She's all right, Doran, she hasn't lost enough blood to worry about, but she'll need stitching. Let's get a stretcher down here and get her up in Medic."

Following them, Gildoran thought wryly that if she had had the use of both hands, she wouldn't have come to this at all.

"In a sense, if it's anyone's fault, it's my fault," Gilrushka said, standing with Gildoran while the Medics were sewing up Merritt's arm. "I should have spent more time with her, realized the state she was in; she managed to function so well that I thought she was just talking wildly because she wanted your attention, that she was afraid you would leave her for Gilramie. Even so I should have realized how desperate she was." She looked, despairing herself, at the unconscious woman, saying, "The worst of it is, with a planet about to be opened—we simply cannot spare a single person to tend a tank full time. The best thing for her now would be to put her into a regrowth tank before she even recovers consciousness. During a year under electronic sleep, she'd manage unconsciously to integrate all her emotional problems—not to mention that restoring the use of her hand would eliminate her worst

problem. We're even short of supplies, until we
get the converter restocked; but after the landing
party goes down, we'll have supplies for the tank.
Perhaps we should spare her—we'd have to, if she
were dead." She smiled again wryly and said,
"Maybe that's why she's trying to demonstrate to
us—that if she were dead we *would* be deprived of
her services . . . so that we can get along without
them while she's in a tank." She looked up and
said, "She's awake again. Go and speak to her,
Gildoran."

But Gilmerritt simply began to cry, helplessly,
refusing to speak to Gildoran at all.

I don't blame her, he thought. *I don't blame her.*

"Why did you do this to us, love? Don't you
know how much we need you?"

She cried out, raging, "You don't care about
me! You're only interested in the things I can *do*
for you, in my work here! You don't care *how* I
have to live, with *this*—" She strained to lift her
deformed hand, but it was still strapped to the
metal surgery table. "All you care about is a living, breathing body that can work shifts . . ."

"That's not true, darling. That isn't true," Gildoran soothed, stroking her hair as if she were
Gilmarina's age, and she closed her eyes under his
hand and began to weep.

"You don't love me. You can't, not love something like this . . ."

"She's punishing us," Rushka said later, sighing, when she had fallen asleep. "Punishing us for
making her live this way. And of course she's
right. We are going to have to get her into a tank,
or we'll lose her anyway. Oh, she may not try *this*
again. But the first little infection or accident will

carry her off because she's lost the will to live."
She shook her head. "I was against opening up
that world out there," she said, "I didn't think,
even if we got a Transmitter tie-in, that it would be
worth it. But now I hope—Cosmos, how I hope—
that we can open it up. We've got to get some way
to take Gilmerritt off the duty roster for a year, get
that poor woman's hand restored. She can't go on
indefinitely like this." The smooth agelessness of
the Psych's face was drawn and sorrowful. "If we
cannot give her a year to recuperate, with all she
has given us, she will die. Somehow, somehow, it
must be managed. Gilnosta managed it while
Marina was in the tank; we should have had Merritt in at the same time. With the finder's fee for
that world down there—what does Marlo call it,
Tempest?—perhaps it can be done sooner, rather
than later."

III

The landing party was down. Gildoran had
hoped he would be assigned a place on it, but it
was a smaller landing party than usual, with the
ship shorthanded, and Gilraban, who had spoken
in favor of opening the planet anyway, wanted to
go. Gildoran sat in the Meditation Center, trying
to make his mind calm, to contemplate the im-
mensity of Cosmos; but no matter how he tried to
dismiss all other matters from his mind, he could
not make that center of quiet within himself. Gilmerritt, Ramie, all his other troubles ran a race

inside his mind, and finally he gave up, tiptoeing past the others in the Meditation Center and went out. He saw Rae there, peaceful, absorbed; he knew that even if he spoke her name or made a noise, she would not come back from that peaceful distance within herself which she had achieved; and he envied her.

The landing party came up, jubilant; Gildoran joined about half the crew in the larger briefing room, eager to learn what their next year would be.

"No life," Gilmarlo said, "not a sign of it; it's older than Ozymandias, probably by a couple of million years; but the sun has a few millennia to run, so there's no danger yet to a Transmitter tie-in. Fossils; archaeologists and paleontologists will be interested, because whatever life cycle they had here, it wasn't primate-based. Feline, perhaps. And it's a carbon cycle, or was; there are fossil fuels galore, and plenty of semi-industrialized planets still use them. So they'll be coming here via Transmitter for mining."

"Question," said Gilrae, "Why didn't the civilization which was there and died out, use up the fossil fuels?"

"I've no idea," said Gilraban, "but quite possibly they lived and died without industrialization. Or perhaps there has been time enough for more to form since their civilization died. But there's masses of anthracite, huge amounts of liquid hydrocarbons, and probably diamonds, too, since it's a carbon cycle. The planet may not be a gold mine, but it's a mine nevertheless. But I don't think anyone's ever going to want to live there." He shivered. "I'm not warm yet."

"You can't have caught cold," Gilban said, "Any cold viruses down there would have died out thousands of years ago, and I'll guarantee there are none on *Gypsy Moth*. How about your soil samples? Any signs of life? I haven't had time to check yet; they're in the lab under quarantine conditions, but I'll wager you won't find any sign of bacteria or even viruses."

"No, everything seems sterile," Gilmarlo said, "but I don't envy the Transmitter crews who set the things up; I'm cold, too." She drew a long breath and said, "We can start arranging duty lists tomorrow; I'm going off-shift and try to get myself warm. Does anyone have an extra blanket?"

Gilraban chuckled. "Don't ask me; I'm going to be using mine."

"Me too," said young Gilbeth in a small voice. "I'm going to find someone who wants to warm me up." There was a chorus of laughter and a shower of suggestions, some vulgar enough to make the girl blush. The group broke up on ripples of laughter, and Gildoran went to bed feeling full of hope. Gilmerritt was quiet and subdued, the bandages still around her wrist, and Gilban felt she should stay another night in Medic; Gildoran lay awake, thinking of a Transmitter tie-in, contacts with the rest of the Galaxy, news of other Explorer ships, and the excitement of a new world to be explored.

No doubt he would be on the Transmitter crew to go down today. He went to the Bridge, hoping, and a little ashamed of the hope, that Gilraban would still have his cold and not feel like going down to do the survey for a Transmitter site. He enjoyed that kind of work, and he had had all too little of it.

But Gilmarlo was not on the Bridge, and Gildoran asked the navigator what had happened.

"I think she's sick," Gilmarti said, "She was lying in her bunk shivering this morning, when I stopped by her quarters, and said she couldn't make it up to the Bridge. Maybe she has a touch of fever. I'll call down and see if she feels like coming up, if you want to take the Bridge for a minute." The old woman touched buttons and scowled. "What's wrong with the communicator? I'd better get maintenance on it; all I get is static. Shall I go down and see what's wrong, Doran?"

"Yes. I have the Bridge." He made formal acknowledgment and stood at the viewscreen, frowning down at the blind circle of Tempest below, the scanty icecaps, the barren windswept surface. He was feeling something too formless to be apprehension.

Time went on and Gilmarti did not return. Other members of the *Gypsy Moth* crew came and went on the Bridge, but there was no sign of the Captain, or of Gilraban, nor, Gildoran suddenly realized, of any member of the Landing party. Suddenly there was a buzz, and, through crackling static, came a voice:

"Gilban . . . Medic . . . Bridge . . ."

"We can't hear you, Gilban," Gildoran said, going to the Captain's seat and hitting the main comm button, "Can you clear up your signal?"

Crackling static. "Down here . . . Merritt . . ."

Gildoran looked quickly around. He was the senior officer on the Bridge at the moment. "Lori—"

Gillori said quickly, "I have the Bridge," and Gildoran hurried down to Medic. Gilban, wearing surgical respirators, hurried out to meet him, then warded him away with one hand.

"You've got to get Gilmerritt out of here. Right away. She mustn't catch this thing."

Consternation swept over Gildoran. The one thing every member of the *Gypsy Moth*—every member of every Explorer ship—feared more than anything else: an alien plague. He understood, even before Gilban said, "I was afraid of it when I saw Gilmarlo this morning; she was lying in her bunk shivering and I thought we might have a pneumonia from exposure, so I brought her up here. Then Gilraban stumbled up saying he was freezing and felt as if he was dying. One by one they all came in, and the worst is this: Gilbarni's got it, whatever it is. He shared Gilbeth's bed last night, so somehow it's contagious. Probably not very, or everyone who heard the briefing yesterday would have it, including you and me. The first symptom seems to be intractable sensations of cold. I seem to be all right, but I'm not taking chances until we find out how it's spread." He tapped the respirator. "How do you feel, Doran?"

"I feel all right," Gildoran said, but it was not cold that swept a shudder through him. The big Medic said quietly, "We've got to get Gilmerritt out of here. If she catches this thing, she won't live; her will to live is too low already. Want to take her down to your quarters? Stay with her if you have to, or get Gilrushka, but she probably shouldn't be alone." He touched the communicator button; received nothing but a crackle of static. "Of all the damn times for the comm equipment to go out on us! Doran, when you get Merritt settled, go up to Nursery. Don't go in— you've been exposed. Tell Ramie, and"—he frowned—"everybody who *wasn't* in the briefing room yesterday, to barricade themselves in the Nursery with the kids, and *stay* there. Don't go in yourself, don't let anyone *else* in, don't let them out—until we're sure this thing is under control, or curable."

Gildoran obeyed, his face set. These were standard instructions for plague. It hadn't happened in his lifetime, or the lifetime of anyone still alive on the *Gypsy Moth*, but it had happened, a few thousand years ago shiptime. Barricade the children in the Nursery; when everyone else aboard was dead, the children, the few survivors in the Nursery with them, and the Poohbears, all wearing spacesuits, cleaned out the bodies, put them into the converter, and started all over again from the beginning.

They already knew the incubation period was brief; it had hit the landing party with the first symptoms within two hours of their return from the planet, and within twelve hours they had all been shivering and desperately ill. But there were no further cases; those in the briefing room had not been sufficiently exposed, except for Gilbarni. So it took close and intimate contact to transmit from one to another. That, Gildoran thought bleakly, was something; it meant they could nurse the invalids without danger. Gilrushka remained with Gilmerritt, but since this was the first time there had been more than one in Medic in the last two years, they were overloaded, and Gildoran was sent down to nurse the sick, too.

"But what's *wrong* with them?" he demanded. "They said there was no bacterial life, and probably no viruses."

"I don't know," Gilban said. "I have to check

the soil samples, but superficially there's nothing. No bacteria, even though some bacteria *can* live at subfreezing. It's unlikely that any viruses could live so long in such barren soil. But if we're dealing with subvirals—" He shook his head. "The tests will take a long time. Go in and help Gilnosta, will you? I know you have no Medic training, but you can feed them and fetch blankets." He touched Gildoran on the shoulder. "Wear a respirator. Where is Merritt?"

"In the Nursery with the babies. She wasn't in the briefing room." Gilmerritt had sunk into such apathy that she seemed not to care where she was; she had hardly seemed to understand that the entire crew of the *Gypsy Moth* was in danger of death. He no longer feared that the sight of Gilmarina would affect her too seriously; now he hoped it would affect her—in any way. But he had no time to spare in worry for her. Not now.

"I've got to go and finish the tests, find out what we're dealing with here," Gilban said and hurried off toward the labs. Gildoran went into Medic, to find Gilnosta. The young Medic looked harried, exhausted.

"Gildoran, thanks be to Cosmos!"

"How are they?" he asked, looking at the nine blanket-wrapped forms.

"Gilbeth and the Captain and Gilbandel are unconscious," Gilnosta said. "I think Gilbeth is dying. Whatever this thing is, it's fast." Her mouth tightened. "Even if we go down to get rocks for the converter now, we'll have to go in spacesuits. Nobody else is going to be exposed to this."

"What does it seem to be?"

"I don't know." Gilnosta drew a deep, ragged

sigh. "Usually, with chills, the first thing you
think of is fever, and at first there was intermittent
fever. According to the blood samples we took,
every immune reaction in their bodies had been
stimulated and they were simply burning up,
even though they were shivering themselves to
death. But standard antipyretics didn't work. We
tried ice baths and the temperature went down,
but that caused so much distress that we stopped,
wrapped them in blankets, and tried to warm
them. But the more we packed them in hot blankets and fed them hot drinks, the colder they
seemed to get. And now—" she shook her head—
"they seem to be displaying symptoms—it
sounds foolish—of hypothermia. Gilbeth's body
temperature has gone down to 35° C., and that's
dangerously low. Go and check it. Take it by
armpit or rectum—she's unconscious. And whatever you do, don't chill or uncover her. If her
temperature goes down four more degrees—well,
you know as well as I do what it means."

Gildoran knew. He went and bent over the
young navigator. The girl's lips were blue, and
when he touched her, she felt corpse-cold; although the cardiac monitor attached to her ribs
still showed a faint pulse. Her body temperature
was 34.78°, still dropping.

"I kept giving them hot drinks, while they
could still swallow," Gilnosta said. "Gilbeth can't
swallow, but I think perhaps, hot coffee or milk by
tube . . ." Again she sighed. "Raban's still conscious. We mustn't let him slip away. Go and try
to get him to swallow some more hot drinks, Doran."

The big technician was lying in the bunk, electrothermal blankets piled over him; yet he was shivering. He whispered hoarsely to Gildoran, "I feel as if I'd done a spacewalk without a suit; absolute zero."

"The thermals are turned almost high enough to burn your skin, Raban," Gildoran said, troubled, checking them and drawing back his hand in automatic withdrawal. "In fact, it would be safer to turn them down a little; your skin is already reddening. Doesn't it hurt?"

"Hurt? No, I can't feel them at all, I feel as if I were out in the cold . . ." His teeth were chattering. "I had to crawl up here—I couldn't make my communicator work—"

"Here," Gildoran said, holding a hot sugared drink to his lips. "The sugar will warm you even if the thermals don't."

Raban made a wry face; but so weakly that it frightened Gildoran; the technician was such a vigorous, vital man, and he lay here shivering, helpless as a baby. "I've been swallowing that stuff till my teeth are floating, and I can't even let my bladder go to piss, I'm so damn cold! If I drink any more, I'll burst!"

Gildoran clenched his teeth, trying not to show his distress; this was another symptom, and a very serious one.

"Try not to worry about it. Drink this, Raban— you need the body heat of the calories," he admonished, "and if you're too uncomfortable, you can be catheterized. But you need the heat."

Obediently, still grumbling, Raban managed to swallow the hot drink. "It feels warm going down," he complained, "but it lies in my belly like a lump of ice. I feel queasy, as if I hadn't been digesting anything, as if my metabolism had shut right down. He added, plaintively, "Can't you turn up the thermals a little? Just a little? I'm freezing—I'm *dying* of cold!"

That was the trouble, Gildoran thought, distressed, as he returned the cup to its place. As he reported to Gilnosta, she sighed and shook her head.

"Gilmarlo complained of the same thing before she lost consciousness," she said, looking at the inert form of the Captain. "I did catheterize her. And Doran, you won't believe this, but when we drew urine, *it was cold. Cold, inside her body!*"

"It's as if something inside them were drawing out heat," Gildoran said, and Gilmosta nodded. "It certainly acts that way. Something seems to be withdrawing all the body heat from their very cells."

Gilbeth died an hour later, without moving, her heart, on the monitor, simply ceasing to beat, her brain tracings going flat. Gilnosta decreed sanitary precautions for the body, in case the contagion should increase after death. Before the end of that shiptime day, the Captain died, and Gilraban lapsed into unconsciousness, his temperature steadily creeping down, a tenth of a degree at a time, but mercilessly. He died that night.

IV

"I thought we were crippled after Hellworld," Gilban said, looking around the briefing room with a single quick look, "I didn't know what the word meant. There are sixteen of us here; Gilnosta in Medic and Merritt in the Nursery with the kids; and that is our entire ship's complement at this moment. Plus three babies—"

"Not babies," Gilramie interrupted. "Two five-year-olds and a four-year-old, one biological year younger than the others."

Gilban waved that away impatiently. "Also four preadolescents; what are they, seven or eight? And four Floaters out on the rim, too old to work, three of them senile and the fourth coherent but unable to stand up or endure more than half gravity. Plus five Poohbears barricaded and incommunicado out on Deck Four. And that is the entire ship's complement of the *Gypsy Moth.* Rae, you're the senior officer present, with the Captain dead. . . ."

She shook her head. "Gildorric is senior to me. A few years."

"Are they *all* dead?" Gillori asked, her voice shaking. "*All* of them?"

Gilban drew a heavy breath and sighed. "Everybody who went down to Tempest. Technically, Gilnadir is still alive; but we lost the other seven, and I don't think there's one chance in twenty thousand that he'll live through tonight. He's unconscious and his body temperature is down to 31°."

"But what killed them?" Rae demanded, "Do we even *know?*"

"I can give it a name, if you want it," Gilban said with a twist of his lips, "It's a subviral; can't see it except under an electronic microscope, and then not well. We found it when the culture medium it was supposed to be growing on lost normal heat. Naturally we didn't touch it; we used sensor probes. But when we saw frost condensing on the outside of the culture tubes . . ."

"It likes cold, then?"

"No," Gilban corrected, "on the contrary. It leaches out the heat from any organic substance. It evidently leached all the heat out of Tempest down there—" he made a vague gesture supposed to indicate the invisible surface of the planet below. "Every bit of organic life on the planet, down to bacteria and protozoans, then went dormant until we came along, nice and warm, and waiting, and *alive*. It's a heat-trope; attracted to any kind of organic heat, and draws it out from the cells somehow, but I don't understand the mechanism yet." He added defensively, "It would take a whole college of surgeons working full time, a couple of years to track down something like this, and I'm only one man—and I first saw the damnable thing in action three days ago!"

"Nobody expects you to know more than that, Ban," Gilrae soothed, then looked around helplessly. "I'm not the Captain. I have no authority—and with Gilmarlo dead—"

"I have the authority," Gilban said grimly, "and I intend to use it. By Ship's Charter, in a time of desperate emergency—and I don't think anyone would dispute that's what we've got—the Chief Medical Officer has the authority to override even a Year-Captain, and I warn you, whoever is chosen Captain, I fully intend to override him, or her, whenever I think it's necessary for safety reasons, until we're clear of that cold death-trap down there."

"I take it, then," Rae said, "that none of you have any question about the necessity of abandoning Tempest as inexplorable?"

Gildorric said vehemently, "I wouldn't touch it with a sensor probe half a Galaxy long!"

Rae asked "Gilban, do you want the formal authority as Captain? I don't think anyone will protest if you do, and there is a precedent for choosing a Captain by majority acclaim in time of Emergency. It hasn't been done since I was out of Nursery, but it has been done."

"Cosmos, no!" the Medic snorted. "I don't know the first thing about what a Captain has to do, and I don't want to know. The *last* thing I want is to be stuck on the Bridge for a year, away from my own work! Pick anyone you want for Captain—it's nothing to me—but I warn you, if we get some youngster who doesn't know what the hell he's doing, and wants to go down there again—" He stared malevolently at Gildoran, and the young man quailed, remembering their many confrontations on Hellworld. He had been right that time and Gilban had been wrong, and the older Medic must have remembered it, but somehow it had managed to turn out the other way, as if he had persuaded Gilban against his will into Hellworld.

He said now, speaking up, "Rae, what *is* the situation, right now? Do we—physically—have enough functioning people to work the Ship?"

"After a fashion," Rae said. "With not much reserve. We can manage, when we're out in space. But we can't break orbit until we have fuel for the converter. Somehow we've got to manage that."

"We can't wait until we find an asteroid belt somewhere?"

Rae shook her head. "Too many asteroids are just ice chunks, low-grade fuel. We need some heavy elements for the synthesizer, even to get back to a more inhabited part of the Galaxy. We can go down in space suits, if we have to, and get fuel. But we have to go down one more time. We *have* to, Gilban—or we're stuck here in orbit, and we'll die before we can get to another system to pick up fuel."

Gilban shook his head. "Are we going to have to drift in space, then? We can't go down again. That's out."

"Are you prepared to die here, then?" Rae asked. "That's the choice we have. Four, five people could handle it, and they could do it in spacesuits. Not even filterable viruses can get into our self-contained suit mechanisms."

"This is a subviral," Gilban said, "and I don't know; it may get through—"

"From what Gilmarlo said," Gildorric said quietly, "they were out of spacesuits. They had checked and found no bacteria or even one-celled life, so they worked unhelmeted. Whatever that heat-trope is, it must exist in spore form, because it was still active, and there's been no organic life there for millennia."

"But it isn't able to transmit without contact," Gilban said, "Witness: only Gilbarni caught it, and he spent the night with poor Beth. There can't be anything left on the ship; as virulent as it is, and the incubation period is short, someone else would have sickened. Probably me, or Gilnosta, or Merritt, because she was in the Medic area when we brought them in. And we handled the—the bodies; admitted, we wore masks and gloves, but no one caught it from the bodies, even when that heat-trope, or whatever it is, must have been desperate to leave them. So if it had a chance to form spores, I would imagine that the inside of the converter has finished them off. If anything could survive inside an atomic-nuclear converter, we're all dead anyhow," he added brutally, seeing the looks of sudden dread that swept around the remnant of the crew. "I think we have to assume that absolute-zero cold, or the inside of a nuclear converter, can kill that thing. I don't think we can make any other assumptions. But working in space-suits, it should be safe enough to go down for fuel. I won't overrule it, if you say we have to go down. But spacesuits—*closed* spacesuits. And without a Captain, who's going to order anybody down?"

Everyone looked at Rae. Gildoran noticed, thinking that in this emergency they all turned to her. Then it was not for him only that Rae was central to the Ship, but for everyone. Rae noticed, and she colored a little. She said, "We should draw disks for a Captain—"

"No." Gildorric put everyone's thoughts into words. "We don't dare trust the Ship to anyone without experience, in an emergency like this. Rae, take it over by acclaim. I think everybody wants you to."

She looked around, helplessly. But there was no dissenting voice.

"Does everyone want it, then? I warn you, I will demand exactly the same authority as if I had been properly chosen by lot, for the rest of Gilmarlo's term in office. And after it, the same seven-year Exemption from office. Fair enough?"

"I'll accept that," Gildoran said, and Gilramie and Gilban quickly chimed in. Gilban touched the button, then swore, morosely.

"Is anyone left alive in Maintenance? What in the Cosmos is wrong with the Comm equipment? I think we ought to get Nosta and Merritt to agree—"

Gilredic, long and lean and silent, stood up and said, "I've been over it a dozen times. I can only imagine it's something in the planet down there. Let me see . . . hullo," he said, frowning, "It's working again. Try it—"

But before Gilban reached the button, there was a flash of light from the signal. Gilban said tersely, "Medic. It's probably for me. Gilban here—"

Gilnosta's voice came from the small grilled screen.

"I thought you should know. Gilnadir just died. Death rate now one hundred percent."

"I've got to get back," Gilban said and rose. "Rae, you're in authority. I reserve the right to override on points of medical safety; otherwise you're in charge, Captain."

"Poor Gilnadir," Rae said, shaking her head. "Is there anyone else left qualified for geological survey?"

"I am," Gildoran said.

"I worked geodesic on Hellworld," Gillori said, "but I'm not qualified Class A yet."

"And Transmitter is short, too, with Gilraban dead," Rae said. "Doran, you'd better start teaching the kids in intensives. If we lose any more . . . No. I refuse to think about that. Now, about fuel. I can't order anybody down. Not when it's likely to be a suicide mission." She was shaking her head, slowly, distressed. "I'll take volunteers, but nobody who's alone in his specialty. I can't figure it out . . ."

"No," said Gilrushka. The Psych looked haggard and exhausted. "Don't try to take that responsibility, Rae. You aren't God. Put everybody's fully qualified specialties into the computer and ask who's most expendable."

"I'd say I was," Gilmerritt said, coming in quietly. "I'm not even fully functioning physically. I volunteer here and now."

Gilrae stared at her in consternation, but Gilrushka said flatly, "Rae isn't asking for suicide missions. Not conscious ones; you'd be more interested in getting killed than in getting the fuel to save our ship. Anyway, you are the only completely qualified biologist on board, except for the two remaining Medics. Sit down, Gilmerritt, and leave it to the computer."

Finally Rae nodded. "I'll do it that way. Rushka, you'll have to quantify specialties by priority; which ones are most expendable or could be relearned from our educator tapes, in case we *have* no completely-expendables."

Gildoran shuddered; he did not envy the Captain and the Psych that task. He knew they would be fair about it—they would kill themselves to be strictly fair—but it meant that their decisions were literally condemning someone to go down into the jaws of death, on Tempest, to save the lives of the others. In any case, he knew he would have shrunk from the task of declaring that any person on the *Gypsy Moth*, in their tragically reduced complement, was "Expendable."

Would I go? Would I be willing to go, if the computer came up with my name?

It won't. I'm the only fully-qualified person left on geodesic. And one of the two or three left who's fully qualified on Transmitter. I'm as safe as Gilban, I don't have to worry . . .

But would I? Would I have the courage to accept a death mission?

I'll never know. And maybe I don't want to know . . .

He was off-shift; he went to the Meditation Center and tried to clear his mind, floating free, and after a time he managed to center his thoughts on a point of light, a universal sun within the center of the universe, reflecting the universal point of light within himself, stars, planets, sun, galaxies, nuclei, rotating on that invisible center, flux and reflux, violence and calm, eternally ebbing and flowing; death and life parts of the great continuum. When he left the Meditation Center he was at peace; he spent a couple of hours in the Nursery, building solar-system patterns with Gilrita and Gilmarina, preparing the preadolescents for the knowledge that they might, soon, have to come to the Bridge for an hour at a time and learn to tend screens and take messages. They were excited about the thought of new responsibilities, not yet aware of the tragedy which had brought it on. Someone would have to break that to them, sometime soon. He didn't want the job.

But his peace vanished abruptly when he heard that the computer had drawn his name and he was to go down to Tempest with the fueling party.

Rae's face was drawn, and she could not look into his eyes. "That's the word. Gildoran. Believe me—" She couldn't finish.

"No," Gilmerritt cried, sobbing, clinging to him with both hands, "No, not Gildoran. Take me instead—I'm not as much use to you as he is . . ."

"Don't you think I'd rather?" Gilrae said coldly. "But you're not competent, Merritt; medically disqualified. Suicide attempts disqualify for three years. Leave the Bridge or I'll have you carried back down to Medic."

Gilmerritt drew a deep, shocked breath and quieted with a single glance. "I'll stay, and just you try carrying me away."

Gildorric said hesitantly, "Let me take Gildoran's place, Rae. He's only a boy."

"He's on the Captain's list," Gilrae said inflexibly, then her face broke. "I tried. I ran it through three times. Gildoran, Gilredic, Gilrannock. Gilnosta was the fourth choice, but she's our only remaining Medic, and Gilban is old enough to take Floater status—older than I am. Your knowledge is worth more than Gildoran's youth, Dorric. They added it all up."

Gildoran had wondered how he would feel, facing death. Now he knew; numb, and disbelieving. Was there someone to cry over Gilredic and Gilrannock as Rae and Gilmerritt were crying over him, someone to protest the decision of the computer with wild disbelief and despair? He hoped so, and simultaneously he hoped not. Gilmarina would think he had abandoned her; as the Poohbears had left them, as the others who died had left them. He could not bear that Gilmarina might think he had deserted her.

Would it matter, if I am dead, should I care what she thinks? I will not care then; there will be nothing left that can care.

But he rejected that. He did not believe in personal survival after death, but he believed that some things survived death, and dead or alive, Gilmarina's trust was something he would not see violated; not even after his death. He told Rae quietly, "I'll go. Don't cry—it could have been any of us." He was grateful, as he knew within himself that Rae was grateful, that it had not been she who had to order him down. He was, as he now knew, one of her babies. Knowing his own emotions for Gilmarina—*could he order her down to almost certain death?*—he knew what Rae must be feeling now.

But before he left, he went down to the Nursery again, and finding a quiet corner near the hammock, sat down on a puffy seat and drew Gilmarina on to his lap.

"I have to tell you something, smallest," he said. "You must be a big girl and not cry if you do not see me again. I have to go away. I will come back if I can. I promise you I will try to come back to you. But I have to go down and get fuel for the converter, with Gilredic and Gilrannock, and there is something very dangerous down there that could kill all of us. If I don't come back, you must remember why I had to go away." He touched the corner of her eye. "It's because I love you, Gilmarina. Please don't think I went away because I didn't love you. I am going to do this because if I don't go, the *Gypsy Moth* and everybody on it will die. And I love you and want you all to live."

Her huge brown eyes stared up at his, filling with tears. "Can't somebody else do it, Doran? Why does it have to be you?"

The old question. Why me? He said, "I can't explain it to you, smallest, but the other people on the ship don't want it to be them either. And it has to be somebody. Don't cry," he added, touching the feathery eyelashes again, stroking her hair. "If everything goes well, you may see me again tonight, I will be here to tuck you into your hammock. Only if I don't come, remember it will be because I loved you, not because I didn't want to come. It will be because I loved *all* of you."

Because, if all three of us refused to go, everyone on the Gypsy Moth would die. Everyone in Nursery. The Floaters out on the rim. Gilmerritt, who has to live long enough to know what life is worth. Gilrae, because a Universe without Gilrae is not worth living in. Gilmarina . . .

He knew, suddenly and without a moment's hesitation, that he was glad to die if the alternative was to watch the *Gypsy Moth* die, slowly, starving and freezing, empty of fuel; if the alternative was to watch Gilmarina suffering and dying.

"Kiss me, smallest," he said, bending to lay his lips against the pale cheek. There was not a trace now of pinkness there; she was pale, bleached; an Explorer, she belonged to *Gypsy Moth*, marked out on all worlds where she would go as forever alien. "Kiss me, but don't say goodbye. I'll come back to you if I can."

She swallowed hard, but she did not cry. She said steadily, "Good night, Gildoran," and he wondered if she understood. Well, he had done his best; now she would not suffer from wilful abandonment; perhaps she would remember that he had not violated her trust as the Poohbears had done.

V

"I don't know what's going on," Gilrae said, "The communicators are all working again. And Deck Four is open, too. We can see the Poohbears. I don't know if they can hear us, and they haven't tried to communicate. And their lift shaft still isn't opening on Deck Four. *Something* is going on."

"Maybe if they know what's happening, they'll come back," Gilrushka said. "They left us because they couldn't endure the death of one of their number. If they knew how many of us are dead now—"

"Be damned to them," Gilramie said, her face implacable, "I'll never trust them again; they left us when we needed them most."

Gilrae sighed. "We need them worse now than we did then; how will we ever take on any more children, without Poohbears?" Gildoran, waiting in the bay outside the airlocks, knew that she was just delaying. He said gently, "We'd better go down while we're over dayside, Rae," and she nodded. Her face was calm now and frozen. Suddenly she leaned forward, and, as she had not done since she thought him lost on Lasselli's World, clasped him close and kissed his cheek. "Be careful, Gildoran. Don't throw your life away. Gilban's going to be working all the time you're gone, to find . . ." She couldn't finish the sentence, but he did, mentally: to find a cure in case you three get it.

He got into the landing craft. Peripherally, at the edge of his mind, he thought that he had never landed one of these alone, before, and he might even have enjoyed it, under other circumstances. Fastening his helmet—this time they would take everything they needed, including air; the air of Tempest was breathable, but it was probably contaminated with the spores of the deadly heat-trope—he began the preflight check on the landing craft.

"Helmets fastened before we leave *Gypsy Moth*, Gilredic, Gilrannock," he said, and watched them comply.

They moved away from *Gypsy Moth* and Gildoran, watching the great ship recede in the viewscreens, wondered if he would ever see it again like this. Well, there was no advantage in thinking this way, doing everything he did as if it might be the last time; all he could do was to go quietly about routine, not thinking about whether or not he would ever do it again.

"Prepare for atmospherics," he said and cut in the controls, feeling the vicious surge of gravity against his midsection belts.

Before they landed, he made them recheck all the fastenings, as if they were going to do an outship spacewalk, something only Maintenance ever got a chance to do. "The surface here could be as dangerous to us as interstellar space," he warned tersely. "Don't relax even for a minute. Gilredic, do you have all the machinery ready to go?"

"Right; ramps will unship for unloading," the

skinny technician said, "Check communicators.
Cosmos, it's lucky they're working again! And it
is luck—we didn't do anything at all to them."

They set down on the bleak surface. Bleak, bare,
barren; all those words floated through Gildoran's
mind as he looked out through shatterproof glass
at the surface of Tempest. Reddish-black barren
rock lay everywhere, and over the surface little
dust-clouds whirled up, racing back and forth.
Tempest. Gilmarlo had given it a suitable name,
after all, with the storms raging on the surface;
and they had set down in a quiet spot, with no
cyclones or hurricane-strength winds.

Tempest. A good name. But Deathtrap would
be a better one.

Poor Gilmarlo didn't have any better luck with
her first command than I did with mine. Less. I
walked away from mine. I lost two men, one child
and seven Poohbears. Gilmarlo lost . . .

That's enough of that. No more self-pity.
There's a job to be done.

For Gilmarina. For Rae, and Merritt, and all of
them. Even for the Poohbears; they may not care if
we live or die. But we care about them . . .

Enough!

"Unship the ramps," he ordered crisply, "Get
the machinery down."

It rolled on the surface easily, with no mechanical problems, and after brief checking of soil samples with his space-gloved hands (guarding
against the slightest tear which might admit the
heat-trope) he selected a site and set the machinery to digging up great chunks of the ore-rich

rocks. There were enough heavy elements in them that the converter could synthesize enough for all foreseeable needs in the next few years and they would surely find a solar system before then.

But we must get back toward the civilized part of the Galaxy. We need contacts, we need children. We need a future . . .

He remembered bleakly that he would probably have no part in that future. Well, there were others to decide that. "How's the machinery working?" he started to ask, realized that his own voice in his ears, through the communicator, was only a crackle of static. Damn the communicators—they had gone out again; when they returned, Gilredic, for Maintenance, had better get right down to it and find out what in the Cosmos was wrong with them! There were no energy sources on this planet to create static—it must be a pure mechanical malfunction! And if Maintenance couldn't handle it, who could? He forced away the thought that Gilredic might not live long enough to check out the communicators or anything else.

It took him about an hour, perhaps two—he had lost track of time and they hadn't yet managed to find a way to make a chronometer visible through the spacesuit arm—and the machinery was running hot, little puffs of steam rising from it in the chilly air. Breathing only the stale spacesuit air from *Gypsy Moth*, Gildoran longed for a breath of chill fresh air . . . but even one whiff might be filled with the deadly heat-trope or its spores. Did they take only organic heat from cells? Or were they organic at all? Did they form some strange interface between organic and inorganic life? Had they burrowed down to the very center of Tempest to absorb heat from the volcanic core, cooling though it was? Was that *why* it was cooling? Was there any way to determine how the heat-trope worked? Maybe that should be a riddle for Gilmerritt—she was the biologist. Gilban was so absorbed in the medical implications that he had no time for theoretical knowledge of how the thing worked. As he said, it would take a whole college of research scientists a whole year, and he was one Medic with eight dying crewmen on his hands. Would he have three more to-night?

That line of thought led nowhere. "We might as well take her up," he said, then, realizing they could not hear him through the maddening crackle of static in the communicators, beckoned and indicated, with sign language. They shipped the heavy machinery, made a few final arrangements stowing the fuel; inside the landing craft, hatches sealed and the place flooded with pure air from the *Gypsy Moth*, Gildoran thought about loosening his helmet. No. They were probably doomed anyway—all three of them—but there was no need to take unnecessary chances; and there in the back of the landing craft was the rock from Tempest, perhaps saturated or infiltrated with the deadly heat-trope. Until that stuff was in the converter—all of it—he wasn't going to open his helmet or let either of the other men in his charge open *theirs*.

Slowly, at first, then with gathering speed, the little craft lifted from the surface of Tempest for the last time. Looking back at it, Gildoran hoped nothing else with life would ever touch down there.

We will have to get back in touch with the civilized part of the Galaxy now. We must warn other Explorers about this one. It could cost the life of another ship.

He stifled the thought that it might already have cost the life of this one. A few hours would tell; but he, Gildoran, might not be alive to see.

He wondered, approaching the *Gypsy Moth*, if he would have to execute the tricky maneuver into the landing bay by sign language too, on the viewscreens; but capriciously, the communicators had begun to work again with no more than the normal background trickle of static when they were inside the gravitational field of a planet. Perhaps this planet had anomalous magnetic fields which affected the communicators. It didn't matter; they'd be away from it within the hour, and hopefully no human foot would ever touch it again.

He found himself remembering, as he watched the great hatches lock, old Gilharrad's theory that planets were only holes in space, interruptions in the greatness of Cosmos. Well, this one was certainly a cancer on the face of its Galaxy! Absolute zero must quarantine them, or that heat-trope might have spread from world to world . . .

"Stand by to open landing craft," he ordered, looking out at the spacesuited figure in the docking area. He felt a rush of relief washing through his whole body, realizing that they were safe again inside the *Gypsy Moth*'s bowels. *Safe as a Poohbear's pocket,* he thought, and felt again a painful sting of loss and regret.

"Negative," said a voice from the communicator. "We are taking no chances; we are going to decontaminate everything. Remain inside the landing craft until decontamination process is finished."

From overhead in the docking bay he saw the fine mist of decontaminant spray, and knew they were flooding the landing craft with the powerful corrosive which would destroy any known kind of organic life.

"Eject fuel rocks into hopper," was the next order, and Gildoran knew that the fuel rocks from Tempest, possibly saturated with the deadly heat-trope, were going to be decontaminated even before they went into the converter. He recognized the voice—what was old Gilmarti of the Transmitter crew doing in the landing bay? That was a silly question. Shorthanded as they were, anyone was likely to be doing absolutely anything on *Gypsy Moth* for the next few years, and he might as well get used to it.

If he lived long enough to get used to anything. . . . He cut off the self-pity and followed Gilmarti's orders to descend from the landing craft.

Still spacesuited, they went through the airlock and inside. Another technician was trundling the heavy machinery away. Gilmarti grinned at him self-consciously, but could not meet his eyes.

"Gilban wants all three of you in Medic tonight. In case you start showing any symptoms."

Gilban and Gilnosta welcomed them to Medic, giving them a meticulous checkup. Gilredic asked, "Shouldn't you wear spacesuits for that?"

Gilnosta shook her head. "We nursed the most acute cases. Evidently it's not airborne, but contact-spread; Gilbarni caught it from Gilbeth, but that's closer contact than we're going to have with any of you—until you are pronounced safe, anyhow. Maybe their decontaminants caught the last of it. But we'll play it safe; sleep in here tonight, and if any of you start having chills or that high fever—well, we have a new idea for attack," she explained as Gildoran got out of his clothes and into one of the loose robes they wore in Medic. "Gilnadir lived longest: he was the one they packed in ice. We'll lower your body temperature as if you were going into cryogenic anesthesia for major surgery. That will hold back these heat-beasties, whatever they are; I've theorized that the more heat we gave these things, the more they multiplied and spread and invaded the body; so that in ignorance we did the very worst thing. We packed the victims in thermal blankets turned up high, and the heat-tropes thrived on it. We fed them hot drinks and they withdrew the heat from the very body fluids—I remember we drew off cold urine still inside the bladder. This time anyone who gets it will be packed in ice, then cooled down as far as we dare. That might discourage them."

Gildoran agreed that it was worth a try.

But the day passed, and the night, and none of the three who had gone down to the surface of Tempest showed the slightest symptoms. By that time they were out of orbit and Tempest lay far behind them. Gildoran had begun to wonder if they had bested the heat-trope, if their spacesuit precautions had won, when Gilzand, a technician Gildoran did not know well, came into the Medic bay. His eyes were wide with dread verging on terror.

"I'm cold," he whispered, "I can't get warm, no matter what I do."

Gilnosta whispered aloud, "Oh, no! Cosmos, no!"

But there was no help for it. Shivering and protesting, Gilzand was packed in ice; his distress was so great that Gilban brought electrodes and sent him into deep hypersleep. "He'll mend better that way, and anyhow, fear and emotional distress wouldn't help him any," he declared, looking down at the sleeping technician.

Gilnosta asked "Tube feeding or intravenous glucose?"

"Neither," Gilban said, "the very calories we feed him might feed those things. We're going to starve them out. If it kills him, well, he'll die anyway, we don't know any cure for this thing. But he can afford to lose up to twenty per cent of his body weight before we have to start worrying about that."

"What was Gilzand's last assignment?" Gilnosta asked. "Was he handling anything from Tempest?"

"I don't know," Gilban confessed, "I'll ask the Bridge. Damnation!" He scowled. "That communicator is out again. Doran, get Gilredic on it, and go on up to the Bridge and ask someone what Gilzand was doing when he got sick."

When Gildoran reached the Bridge, Gilrae's eyes widened, and he saw that there were tears in them. Had she cared so much, then? But all she said was "Praise be, you're safe, Gildoran. All of you."

"Not all," Gildoran said reluctantly, "Zand is in Medic, and he's got it, whatever it is. And he didn't go down with us. I hope he was handling something from Tempest." The alternative—that the heat-trope was loose on the ship and they were all doomed—was too terrible to contemplate.

Her eyes widened. "Yes," she said. "he was cleaning and stowing the machinery you used down on Tempest."

Gildoran remembered the machinery at work, digging out the rock; heat rising like steam in the icy air of Tempest. Yes, that would attract the heat-trope. And, like damned fools, they had decontaminated the outside of the landing craft, and the outside of the spacesuits, and even the rocks they had put into the converter; but they had not decontaminated the machinery, which had been carried back to *Gypsy Moth* in the comparatively warm interior of the landing craft.

Gilrae said "We should put that damned machinery right into the converter before anyone else handles it."

"We can't," said Gilmarti, "We don't have it in duplicate; it's a lifeline for the *Gypsy Moth*. Without it, no more fuel—we're dead."

"We're probably dead anyhow," said Gilrae, "but we might try decontaminating it. In spacesuits. Meanwhile—" she glanced at Gildoran— "now that Gilban pronounced you officially free of contamination, you ought to go down to Nursery and put Gilmarina out of her misery. And Gilmerritt."

"I'm on my way," he said, "but first, get Gilredic on the communicators. Gilban is going to need workable communications—"

"Is it out in Medic again?" Rae asked, "Mine, here, is certainly all right. Look, I can even get

Deck Four; it's open, the microphone pickup, and I can hear the Poohbears talking among themselves in their own language, though none of them has tried to communicate with us." She touched his cheek lightly. "I'm glad you're back, Gildoran. Now go up to Marina and tell her you're still alive."

VI

"You're still alive," Gilmarina kept repeating, clinging to him. She would not let him go. "You came back, Doran. You came back!"

"I told you I would," Gildoran said, soothing the sobbing child in his lap, "I told you I would come back if I could, Marina, darling. Don't cry. Be my brave girl and don't cry; it's all right now."

"I didn't cry when you were gone. Not once. Did I, Merritt? I'm crying now because I'm so happy, so glad you're not dead down on that awful planet . . ." she said, burying her face again in his chest.

Gilmerritt was blinking, too, holding him with her good hand. "I was so sure I would never see you again . . ." she said, and he pulled her down close to him and the child in his lap. "We were lucky," he said soberly, "but it's not over yet. Gilzand is dying. He handled the machinery from Tempest, and evidently the heat-trope got him."

"It doesn't need a living vector, then? It can come in the rock and soil?" Gilmerritt asked, frowning. "That means the organic decontaminants aren't working. It has just occurred to me—" She got up quickly and went to the communicator panel.

"Landing bay," she said, urgently, "Who is in the landing bay? Cosmos, it's probably too late. The landing craft is clean, it went through the absolute zero of space on the way up here, but everything inside it—where you people were with the outsides of your spacesuits . . ." She broke off. "Hello. Gilmack? Listen to me; this is urgent, this is the Biological Officer. Seal off the docking bay. No one to go inside it except in spacesuits, and no one to go near the landing craft. Who put away the spacesuits that were worn down to Tempest?" She listened a moment. "Tell me, is he . . . oh, no!" She turned to Doran, shaking her head. "Mack says that Gilrannock tended the spacesuits, and he just went up to Medic complaining of cold. And their communicator keeps going in and out . . ."

"Merritt, what are you trying to say?"

"I'm saying that I don't think that thing is organic at all," she said, "I'm going down to the lab and put Gilban's culture samples into the converter before somebody assumes they're dead and recycles the culture medium. With her usable hand, she pushed aside Gildoran's attempt to stop her. "No. You took your risk. I have to take mine, for the *Gypsy Moth*. My life isn't worth anything, and yours is. Stay here with the children, Gildoran."

"You mean you *know* how that thing works—"

"Yes," Gilmerritt said tersely. "It eats heat energy and it excretes static. Any organism degrades energy; the heat-trope takes in energy waves in the heat wavelengths and excretes radio waves. The communicator problem started in the briefing room when the eight who went down to Tempest were infected with it; it spread all over the ship when the eight were dying of it; it cleared up after they were dead because it had become dormant after consuming all their organic heat. It's lucky we put the bodies into the converter so quickly after they were dead. Tell me, when Gilzand came up there, sick, did the communicator in Medic start acting up again?"

Staring, Gildoran realized that Gilmerritt had solved the riddle. He sat holding Marina on his lap, watching her go. She had insisted on taking the risk herself but she might have saved them all. Was this a clever form of suicide? Would she somehow manage to contaminate herself with the culture samples? He had to assume that she would not bring that danger into the *Gypsy Moth* again; after all, her first action when she knew was to seal off the docking bay, and all the spacesuits worn on Tempest. So it was not reckless suicide which would endanger others; and contaminating herself, her body, could endanger the entire *Gypsy Moth*.

"Look," Gilmarina squealed in wild excitement, looking at the viewscreen which had suddenly flickered into life, "It's a Poohbear! Pooh! Pooh! Where are you?"

The face of the great marsupial filled the viewscreen. The voice, against a background crackle of static, light and clear and beloved, filled Gildoran with an aching nostalgia; but the Poohbear's voice was aggressive.

"Gildoran! What is happening down there. What are you doing? We have been listening, and we do not know. What are you doing?"

All of Gildoran's wrath against the great creatures they had loved, and who had betrayed them in the hour of their greatest need, flooded to the surface.

"We're dying—that's what we're doing," he said bitterly, "Eight of us are dead already, and two more are dying, and the rest of us may follow. Not that it would mean anything to you. One of yours died, and we were told in no uncertain terms that we mustn't dare to compare our grief to yours. But we have too much grief now to worry about yours. Stay up there on Deck Four and indulge yourselves in it for the rest of your lives, until all the rest of us are dead. Then you will have the *Gypsy Moth* for yourselves, and you can make of it a great floating tomb, if you will!" He stopped, in consternation, hearing what he had said; it had come flooding out of him, unbidden, from some inner recess of his being where he had fought his own battle with the fear of death. The Poohbear said nothing, only stared at him. Then the screen went blank again and silent and the Poohbear's face was gone.

That's all we needed. To worry about them, to make them angry when for the first time in two years they showed the slightest interest in what was happening to us.

I should have been polite, maybe begged them to come back . . .

No. We managed without them, and if they had been with us, we would not have been so short-handed, not taken this terrible risk.

We could have ignored Tempest, passed it up for a better planet, risked two or three at most to go down and get fuel.

The Poohbears didn't worry about us; why should we worry about them now?

But he softened, as he looked into the empty screen. Maybe that had been the trouble. *We never really worried about them. We took them for granted.*

The communicator crackled softly with static, and Gildoran shuddered. Would he ever, now, hear static again without fearing the cold death which had swept over them so swiftly?

Gilmerritt's voice came from the small screen. "Doran, will you come up to the Bridge? We may have to try something . . ." And he set Gilmarina down.

Gilrae had called the conference for the smaller briefing room; and looking around, Gildoran knew why. There were so many faces absent. At their last conference they had spoken of how desperately shorthanded they were; now eight of those who had been there to make up the pitifully small complement of *Gypsy Moth* were dead and two more lying in hibernation, all but dead, their body temperature lowered almost to the point of death. None of them spoke of their desperately crippled state.

Swiftly Gilmerritt explained what she thought had happened.

"We decontaminated the *outside* of the landing craft; but the outside was safe—it had traveled through absolute-zero cold and could not carry the heat-trope. The heat-trope clung to the machinery because it was absorbing the heat generated in the rocks, and in the metal parts, during the mining process. So the machinery is contaminated, but cold; it probably cannot transmit the heat-trope unless it is warmed up again, but we will never dare handle it again except with spacesuits or gloves until it has been sterilized in absolute-zero cold. The same is true of the last three spacesuits worn down to Tempest. And" —she paused—"of the *inside* of the landing craft—everything you people might have touched with your contaminated spacesuits."

"What's the answer, then?" Gilmarti wanted to know. "Put machinery, spacesuits and landing craft all into the converter and make others?"

"That's one answer," Gilmerritt said, "but with the skeleton crew we have, it would mean abandoning them until the babies grow up and can build them. I don't think I want to wait until Giljodek and Gilvirga qualify, for landing craft replacement; we might find a good planet and want to open it up."

"We can't open a planet up with our present component," Gilmarti said somberly. "Not till the kids grow up. But we could find a good planet and make a Transmitter tie-in. We *have* to make a Transmitter tie-in, so we can get the word back to the rest of the Explorers. We have to warn them about the heat-trope. That may have been what killed out other races in this end of the Galaxy."

She had voiced Gildoran's own thought. The heat-trope was certainly the most dangerous thing they had found; it was even fortunate that they had been shorthanded when they landed, or the landing party would have been a full complement of twelve or fourteen, not the eight they had actually sent down.

"But we can't go near anyone in the rest of the Galaxy as long as the *Gypsy Moth* is carrying the heat-trope contamination," Gilmerritt said. "And we can't put down a landing craft on any planet where we might still be carrying it; not to mention that if we go into the landing craft without spacesuits we can get it again. For all we know, they may be nestling inside the drive units of the landing craft; the matter-antimatter in the *Gypsy Moth* has no heat, but the landing craft atmospherics run on fossil fuel and produce heat, and those vicious little heat-beasties are probably growing in there right now. They need a dose of absolute-zero cold to kill them."

"We could flush the fuels directly into the converter," suggested Gilmarti. "Whoever did it could wear a spacesuit. The technician who took the rocks to the converter didn't get contaminated; he's free of the cold-death."

"And then we have another spacesuit contaminated," Gilrae reminded them.

"We could put the spacesuits into the converter," Gildorric said. "We have fifty or more spacesuits. With our present component, we don't need so many; recycling them into the converter would give us plenty of heavy metals. And a margin of safety for supplies."

"We could do that," Gilmerritt said, "but whoever handled them would contaminate *his* suit, and so forth *ad infinitum*. It doesn't seem to be so transmissible as all that . . . if it were, every blanket and sheet the sick ones used would have to go into the converter—"

"Gilban already did that," Gilnosta said. "I thought he was crazy. But the sheets and towels and so forth *are* organic compounds. So he was right even if it was for the wrong reasons."

"Did body wastes go into the converter, too?" Gilmerritt asked, and sighed with relief when Gilnosta nodded.

Gilmarti said, "Have all the contaminated spacesuits put into the converter, then the last person take a spacewalk outside *Gypsy Moth* to sterilize the last spacesuit."

"That's roughly what I was going to suggest," Gilmerritt said, "only more thorough. And we can salvage the landing craft, too. I suggest that we put all the contaminated machinery into the landing craft, tying it down. That I, and Gilmarti who might be contaminated, but probably isn't, put on the suits, and one other person, go out in the landing craft—and once we're out in deep space, in orbit around the *Gypsy Moth*, we depressurize . . . and open the doors to deep space. Absolute-zero cold will sterilize everything inside the landing craft . . . and our spacesuits . . . and the machinery. Then we shut the doors again, repressurize, and come back aboard."

Gilrae looked at the younger biologist in consternation. She said, "Gilmerritt, do you know how dangerous that is? If any kind of gravitational storm came up while you were outside *Gypsy Moth*, you'd be blown away and drift forever."

"It's a quicker death than the cold-death," Gilmerritt said. "And I saw the first symptoms of that, in Gilmarlo and poor little Gilbeth. I'd take a nice quick death in space anytime."

"I think it's the only way to be absolutely sure," Gilmarti said soberly. "You *do* know that Gilzand just died?"

Rae nodded slowly, "I wasn't going to mention

it. We have enough to worry about and grieve over," she said. "Gilzand just died. And Gilrannock is dying, unless Gilban's drastic cold therapy works; and I don't believe we can lower his internal temperature enough to kill the heat-trope without killing him first."

Gilmerritt said flatly, "I am going. No, it's not suicidal. But if I do die—and I don't particularly care one way or the other—I can better be spared than anyone with two hands. No—" she held up her hand. "I'm not the only biologist, Gilrushka. Rae is a better one than I will ever be, and if we have more use for a biologist than a Captain, she can appoint the oldest and most useless person on the Ship. Right now I am the most expendable person you have."

Silence fell in the briefing room. What Gilmerritt had said was so tragically true that there was not really any way to question it. Even if it were a suicidal urge that prompted her to recognize her own expendability, that did not lessen the truth; the emotional instability of the suicide wish made her all the more expendable.

And yet Gildoran knew he could not let her go alone into her own cold death; out there, knowing they had accepted her as being the least valuable person aboard *Gypsy Moth*, her own sense of lessened self-worth might prompt another impulse of suicidal despair. What would she do? Open her suit, when she could die without endangering the life of anyone else? He said, "You can go, Gilmerritt; I don't think anyone here will stop you. But I am going, too. To take care of you. I'm under a death sentence, too, unless we stop this thing."

"You? Gildoran, no—" Gilramie protested. But

he faced her, unflinching. "I have to do this for Gilmerritt. And for myself, too."

"Look," said Gilramie, in a hushed voice, "The Poohbears are watching us." Every face in the briefing room turned slowly to the viewscreen, where the massed bodies of the six surviving Poohbears watched them, silent, enigmatic behind their furry masks and great teeth.

"Damn the Poohbears!" Gildoran said harshly. "Let's get on with it."

VII

In the end, they finally and completely refused to take Gilmarti. The chance that she had incurred any contamination was one in a million or less; far less than that Gilban had become contaminated caring for the sick. It seemed that the heat-trope did not start into one host until it had exhausted the first, and the dead bodies had been handled only with surgical gloves, which had gone into the converter with them. She insisted that she was needed to wear the other spacesuit; instead they tied it down, firmly, into one of the bays.

Gildoran sat at the controls of the landing craft; he had justified his coming (though Gilmerritt had tried to get him, too, to stay behind) by stating the truth; that Gilmerritt was not experienced in handling small craft.

He saw the *Gypsy Moth* recede into the distance. If this did not work, at least they were safe from contaminating it further; the others would lose the landing craft, but they could manage until they found some inhabited planet, and ask for rescue. So whatever happened, the others were safe. Gilmarina. Rae. Ramie. Even tough old Gilmarti and the Poohbears. Whatever they decided to do. The crackle of static inside the communicators kept reminding them of the seriousness of this—as if, Gildoran thought wryly, they needed reminding.

Gilmerritt's voice was shaking. "Ready to open the doors?"

"Not quite." Working deftly with the waldos of his suit-fingers, he came and lashed Gilmerritt firmly into her seat.

"You don't need to do that," she said softly, "I won't do anything foolish like walking out into space. I don't feel I have to die, not anymore. If all the rest of you can live with what we've all been living with, I can live until something can be done about my hand. This"— she made a faint clumsy gesture with her suit-arm, which Gildoran correctly interpreted as meaning, *this mission*—has shown me that even—even deformed this way, I'm still worth something to the rest of you. And to myself—"

"And to me, Gilmerritt," Gildoran said, just as softly. "I won't risk losing you, not now. I know you won't do anything reckless—not now—but you could slip. Accidents do happen. And I'm not taking any chances."

He lashed himself into his own seat, then, and thumbed the control that would open the hatches to the sterilizing cold of space, giving the heat-trope which had brought cold death to the *Gypsy Moth* an ice-cold death of its very own.

"Clear away hatches," Gildoran gave the order, knowing this time that it was safe. They surrounded him on the Bridge, with hugs for him and Gilmerritt, crowding around; everyone, it seemed, wanted to touch them, to reassure him or herself that the two were still alive, that there was not another loss for their already decimated crew. Then they moved aside, as the huge dark form of a Poohbear moved through them. Then another.

"This must be said to Gildoran," the Poohbear said, "because it was he who bore the withdrawal. We told him that we could never compare your grief with ours. In the little time that has passed—" and Gildoran realized that, to a deathless race like the Poohbears, the time between Hellworld and now must have sped by in the twinkling of an eye—"we have kept apart from you, but once the first sharpness of our grief had passed, we listened, and we learned. We have learned that you are not, as we thought, immune or indifferent to grief; but, as we never learned to do, you shortlived ones learned to live always with the knowledge of grief and death and loss to sharpen your love. And although we do not yet know how to do it, we have discovered that we must try. Our lives will be forever darkened by the loss of our sister; we can never speak her name more; but perhaps you can teach us how to live with the knowledge of death, as you have done all these years when we loved you, never knowing." The Poohbears gathered in close, holding out their arms in appeal. "Will you accept back the love which, in our grief, we had forgotten how to give?"

It was not a question; in moments the Poohbears

were surrounded by Explorers, hugging them, flinging themselves into the arms of the only mothers any Explorer had ever known.

It was later—much later—when Gildoran remembered to ask. "Gilrannock?" He asked Gilnosta, bracing himself for the news of one more death, but needing to know that it was over, that all precautions had been taken to know that the cold-death would not strike again from the dead.

"Oh, he's alive," Gilnosta said, "and conscious. They don't transfer to another host until they've exhausted the first. So we lowered Gilrannock's body temperature—he was in electronic sleep, of course, and unconscious—until we guessed that those heat-beasties must be getting uncomfortable. Then we gave them a nice warm host to transfer into."

Gildoran stared in shock. "A laboratory animal?"

"Oh, no," Gilnosta said, "A nice, warm culture medium; a gel for growing bacteria, enclosed in a solid permeable membrane. And when *it* started cooling, we assumed that the heat-tropes had all transferred into it; we monitored it with a radio, and it was giving off static constantly as they ate up the heat from the warm gel. Then we took it up in surgical gloves . . . and consigned it to the converter. We were very careful thawing out Gilrannock—for fear there might still be some of them left. But he warmed up normally, and not long ago he asked us for an iced fruit drink; said he was too hot." She drew a long breath of relief. "So the last of the living heat-tropes are in the converter, and to hell with them. In fact," she added, "you could say that's just where I sent them. Inside a nuclear converter is as close to hell as any of us is ever going to get."

"Well, they crave heat," Gildoran said. "and you gave them more than they could ever absorb. So anyway they died happy."

Gilnosta shivered. "That," she said firmly, "was the last thing on my mind."

And the *Gypsy Moth* moved on through Cosmos, turning back toward the inhabited center of the Galaxy.

Part Five

A WORLD WITH YOUR NAME ON IT

I

"Nobody's talking about *blame*," Gilrae said wearily. "It's bad luck, that's all. Two impossible planets in a row. What I'm talking about is *facts*, Gilban. The fact that we're crippled. The fact that we now have no functioning biological officer, with Marlo killed on Tempest, and Merritt only able to direct. The fact that we have literally too few hands to work ship, even with Rita and Gilmarina and the other children working two hours a day on messenger service and such instead of doing lessons."

Gildorric smiled without mirth and said, "I once told you it couldn't happen twice in a lifetime. Now it's happened twice in seven years. If it happens again, we're dead."

Gildoran looked around the small briefing

room. By common consent, they had ceased to use the large one, since Tempest; it was simply too empty. They had managed to work the ship, for the years since Tempest; with the Poohbears—the one good thing that had come of the Tempest tragedy—again taking responsibility for the youngest children, and the older children working shifts doing messenger duty on the Bridge, they managed to function. But it couldn't go on much longer. And now they were back in known territory; they had retraced their path, back into the part of the Galaxy they had left.

"We need to down ship as soon as we can," Rae said, "We need children; if we must, we can finance it through Head Center. We need supplies. And we need—" she glanced at Merritt, who flinched, with the old habit of concealing her crippled hand.

Gildoran thought, *she's right. We've got to set down and give Merritt her chance; if we can't spare her a year in a tank to grow another hand, we have got to give her a chance to go earthworm, if she wants to, get it on a planet.*

I don't want to lose her. But I can't bear to see her like this, either. It had been his mistake on Hellworld which had crippled her, and his further mistake which had not dared withdraw an experienced officer from the ship when he was so inexperienced as a Captain. And after Tempest, they had not been able even to spare Merritt; they were so cruelly shorthanded.

I should have insisted. They would have had to spare her if she had died of the heat-trope—and she was the one who saved us.

But now, in any case, it would not be long until they found a world of some sort; they were back where suns were thick as electrons in an atom of transuranic metal. And they had only enough fuel for a few weeks of cruising, shiptime. The decision could not be avoided much longer.

Rae was saying, "We simply can't take the chance of setting down on another planet which might not be suitable for opening. We need children. We need fuel, and supplies. We need news of the Cosmos and the world-net——"

"Why?" Gildorric asked scornfully. "What are they to the Explorers?"

Gilrae said, "Do you believe that we exist independently of the world-net? That we can go on forever without contact with them?"

"If need be," Gildorric said. "We are Explorers. It is our journey and our quest that makes us Explorers—not the worlds we find."

"He's right," Gilnosta said. "We can't crawl in, crippled, to any world that will have us, going begging to Head Center for supplies and help to keep us going until we find another world! We're Explorers," she repeated proudly, "We go in as conquerors—or not at all!"

"It's an attractive mystique," Gilrae said. "Unfortunately, it's only a mystique. And, like all such mystiques, it's very far from the truth. Among other things, we need contact with the world-net and the world-lines of the Transmitter to let Head Center know we're still alive and still searching. How many Explorer ships have simply vanished, without trace? Do we want to be written off, too?"

Gildoran felt a sense of shock. Explorers never

spoke of that. Suddenly he wondered; had the other ships been destroyed? Or had they simply grown so full of their own lives out in Cosmos, so reluctant to interrupt their endless voyage with occasional touchdowns, that they had taken to the infinite reaches of space, abandoning any purpose in their voyage, remaining forever dissociated from planets and downworlders, spinning on their own axes in endless hubris. . . .

Gilrae said urgently, "No! We need planets, just as the planets need us! We need contact with other Explorers. We need contact with other downworlders, we need children—we need it to keep us human! To keep us from forgetting why we're Explorers!" Her face was grim and decided. "I'm giving the Bridge orders to set a course for the nearest charted, inhabited world. We set down there for overhaul, and to find out where the other Explorer ships are now."

She dismissed them and said no more, but Gildoran could guess what was in her mind. Terribly shorthanded as they were, the only hope now was to find another Explorer ship and combine their crews and forces.

Was this the last voyage of the Gypsy Moth, as herself? Were they simply too shorthanded to go on? And what happened to an Explorer without a ship, when his long, long voyaging was done?

Wouldn't it be better to die in Cosmos, endlessly circling the long stars in an untouched, imperishable tomb, than to end their lives tied to downworld time, earthbound?

Gildoran was off duty for the moment, and had no wish to return to his own cabin, which he still shared with Gilmerritt—he had remained only because he feared, if he attempted to withdraw, that it might plunge her into deep depression. It was not an unwelcome arrangement entirely. Between her moments of depression, Merritt was a pleasant, companionable partner, and the strong sexual compatibility had never really disappeared.

There's no one I want more than Merritt. I suspect it's only the fact that I'm tied to her that makes me rebel against it.

He found that old habit was taking his feet to the farthest end of the living quarters, and into an empty room. There, surrounded by Gilramie's familiar things, he could relax and wait for her to come off-shift. He told himself he wouldn't wait for her, there was no need for that, he'd used her often enough as confidante and crying-towel during the bad year of his captaincy. But as usual, the stressless feel of her quarters relaxed him so much that he fell asleep, stretched out on her couch, and only the soft whirring of the opening door alerted him to Ramie's return.

He sat up, feeling a little dazed.

"I'm sorry, Ramie, I didn't mean . . . I'll go right away."

She laughed. "Why? You're not in my way, and I saw Merritt on the Bridge, so she certainly won't be missing you. What's on your mind, Gildoran?"

Rae's decision to set down," Gildoran said. "You know we may never take off again. What would we do? What would happen to us, Ramie, if the *Gypsy Moth* never got off the ground again?"

She came and sat close to him on the couch. She

still looked like a child—slender, almost breathless, her huge dark eyes serious and steady. She said, "I'd be sad, of course. But it wouldn't be the end of the world. It's a big Galaxy out there. There's sure to be somewhere I could go, something I could do somewhere."

"But . . . to be an earthworm . . . never to be an Explorer again. . . ."

Ramie said "There are other Explorer ships. If I felt that way, it would be Cosmos—not the *Gypsy Moth*—that would be important to me." Her smile trembled a little. "What would hurt would be losing you—all of you," she amended quickly. "But we'll worry about it when it happens. More likely, once we're downworld, we'll be able to modify the ship's computers and technology to operate with fewer personnel. At worst we can wait there until the children grow up a little— Gilmarina and Rita will be Class B in about two years—and everything will be all right."

Gildoran said, a little sourly, "Just a born optimist, aren't you?"

Ramie shrugged. "What did you want me to do? Tell you how hopeless it all was? I should think you'd get enough of that from Gilmerritt."

"You really dislike her, don't you? Or is it still only jealousy?"

"I don't dislike her. I *admire* her, for carrying on, even as well as she has done. It's outrageous, what she's had to go through. If I were crippled like that, I don't think I could carry on at all," Ramie said. "If anyone ever had a right to complain, she's the one. But it's been hard on you, too. As for being jealous . . ." another small shrug.

"I'm used to it by now. Maybe it's just perversity. I want only what I can't have."

It's very strange. Ramie is closer to me than anyone alive. Why don't I love her as she wants me to? Why? Is there something wrong with me? She's certainly just as desirable as Gilmerritt. Maybe more so. And yet . . . and yet . . .

It was several weeks of shiptime before the Bridge crew called them together to tell them that they were in orbit around a great blue-white sun with three habitable planets, at least one of which had been technologically colonized.

"We've gotten Transmitter readings from it," Gilrae said. "We'll make contact and ask permission to set down. From there we can Transmit to Head Center, or to Host, and make plans for the future."

Gildoran was working Communications when the first contact was made.

The voice on the panel sounded excited.

"The Explorer ship *Gypsy Moth?* We have heard nothing of any Explorer ships for twelve planetary years, but you are more than welcome to land here for repairs. It is our pleasure to offer you our hospitality. If you are not in dire emergency and can wait a few hours, a formal invitation will be extended to you from the Councillor. I have heard that the Councillor has a deep personal interest in the Explorer ships. If not, I am empowered to grant you landing permission."

Gildoran replied that no, *Gypsy Moth* was shorthanded but not in desperate straits, and that they would be happy to wait for the Councillor's formal invitation.

"That's a relief," said Gillori. She was working as apprentice Navigator these days. "Suppose we'd set down someplace where they hated the Explorers, like that world where they killed Gilmarin and almost killed you?"

"Lasselli's World? In that case," Gildoran said, "I suppose we'd just go on to the next star-system. But I'm glad we've found a place." He smiled at the girl. She was really a young woman now, he thought; she must be quite nineteen, and competent to hold any Major Office aboard *Gypsy Moth*, with the single exception of Transmitter and Medic Crew. Next time we draw for a Year-Captain, Lori will be on the list. It made Gildoran feel old.

It was less than a shiptime hour before the planet made contact again, this time to read out a formal invitation from the Councillor of Laszlo (that was as near as Gildoran could come, in Universal Phonetics, to the name) that the Explorer Ship *Gypsy Moth* was welcome to set down, giving them a choice of ports which had facilities to handle them, and extending an invitation to a formal reception for up to three dozen of the ship's personnel. Gildoran made the standard courteous reply and signed off, thinking with a faint grin, to get three dozen for an official reception, we'd have to bring along the children in Nursery and a couple of the Poohbears, too!

At least they *had* the Poohbears. Between Hellworld and Tempest, they hadn't had them, and after brutal, killing seven-hour shifts everyone aboard, from the Captain down to the

children, had had to take extra shifts at baby-
tending in Nursery and on the regrowth tank
monitoring Gilmarina. Civilized man couldn't
live at that pace, but they'd managed it somehow, until Tempest, when—without being asked
—the Poohbears had come back to them.

*Maybe on this world we can find some children.
Although it's not certain we have the technicians
for the necessary DNA operations any more.*

It was the first time he'd been on the Bridge for a
shipdown. Last time the *Gypsy Moth* had been set
down on a planet's surface, he'd been a Class-B,
running errands. He'd been down in a landing
craft on Hellworld and Tempest, but it wasn't the
same. As, under Gildorric's direction, he and Lori
piloted the enormous ship down to the port, he
thought that in a few more years, everyone with
any actual experience of landing an Explorer ship
would be dead, or resigned to Floater status.
Explorers could do just so much with computers,
on a strange planet. Downworld computers never
bother to keep data for starship landing. The
Explorer ships are the only ships there are—the
colonized worlds used the Transmitters, they had
no need of programs for a starship landing.

Ramie, who was off-shift, had brought Rita and
Gilmarina to the Bridge to watch the landing,
something they might not see again for years. He
was struck by how much Gilmarina looked like
Ramie, now that her skin and hair were completely white. They had the same dark eyes with
the epicanthic fold that gave them a long, slanting
look, the same round smooth face, the delicate

build and slender hands. Ramie came to Gildoran's side and said, "Remember what dear old Gilharrad said about planets—that the best worlds were found by ESP and hunches? I don't know why, but I feel good about this one. I think we're going to find what we want here."

He smiled at the young woman and said, "I hope you're right. Anyway, they're welcoming us. For the rest, we'll just wait and see."

II

Once they had landed, set up steps and unsealed the doors, they discovered that they had been guided down to a landing-space in a great open, flat, country, surrounded at a distance by low rings of mountains, not high, but rocky-red and flattened at their tops. The sun was dazzlingly blue-white and everywhere, vegetation grew lush and thickly.

"I'd expected a desert," Gildoran said, and Merritt replied, "Not a chance. The tremendous amount of ultraviolet in the blue-white stars makes for lush plant growth."

It reminded Gildoran of something. Someplace strange and very long ago. The last planet he had seen had been Hellworld, and that certainly couldn't be it. The population of Laszlo was, like all worlds in the Transmitter world-net, enormously varied, all types and sizes and colors, but the predominant type, and therefore probably the indigenous or original colonizers, were of a single racial stock, tall, unusually dark-skinned, the majority well over six feet tall, even the women. . . .

Lasselli's World! Laszlo.

Was the name only a coincidence?

Somehow he didn't think so. Surrounded by the royal welcome which the inhabitants of Laszlo gave to *Gypsy Moth* and her crew, it didn't seem important. If Lasselli's World and Laszlo were the same world, at least the political climate had changed and they were safe there. Safe? The Laszlans couldn't do enough for them!

For the first few days none of them did anything much except rest. The long, shorthanded voyage had taken its toll of them all. Gildoran found himself seized by uncanny lassitude and the stress of gravity told more than he remembered. Ship's gravity, just strong enough to give them orientation and prevent vertigo, was something else entirely.

Several days later Gilrae came to his quarters and said, "Someone must take a trip to Host and find out what's become of the rest of the Explorer fleet. I haven't the heart to put it off on anyone else. Will you come with me, Gildoran?"

"You're going by Transmitter?"

Rae said tartly, "Well, I'm certainly not going to take the *Gypsy Moth*."

"All right, I'll come." It had been a long time since Gildoran had made a trip by Transmitter. Not since that strange trip with Ramie—how long ago? How old was Gilmarina now? Twelve, biological time, but she had lost a year in the tank.

Her Nurserymates were thirteen. Thirteen years, then, since he had set foot on a planet, except for those disastrous few days on Hellworld, and the terrifying hours of his mission on Tempest.

As they walked through the huge open land-bowl he felt the luxurious heat of the great sun beating on his back.

Feels good, to be on solid ground. The feel of that sun. I wonder how we survive, so long in space without sun or wind or the feel of gravity under our feet. . . . Man wasn't made to live in space.

He told himself sternly not to be sentimental. For him, gravity wasn't even a childhood imprint. He'd been picked up for an Explorer ship before he was a month old, and the retailoring of the very cellprint of his body, his very innermost cells, had been made, tailormade just for that—to live in space. He wasn't a planetman, an earthworm, the differences were cell-deep, atom-deep. And yet . . . and yet, that sun, the cool sharp wind blowing against his cheek. . . .

He asked Gilrae, "Does it feel good to be on the surface again? Or are planets still just—what was it Gilharrad used to call them, just interruptions, holes in the Cosmos?"

"Dear, dear old Gilharrad," she said with a fond smile. "No, it feels good, but mostly because now I know you're all safe."

"Well, if we had to find a planet to set down on, permanently, we couldn't have found a better one," he said, then wondered exactly why he had said it as she raised a startled face to him. Did he mean that—would he want to stay here indefinitely?

There's a planet somewhere with your name on it. . . .

He had the uncomfortable sensation that Gilrae could follow what he was thinking, but she forebore to say anything, simply asking, as they approached the Transmitter terminal, "Have you ever been on Host? I wish we could have gone directly there. But it's almost fifty light-years from here; I don't think *Gypsy Moth* could have made it."

"If I was ever there, it was when I was too young to remember," Gildoran said.

"It's the home world of the Explorers," Gilrae said, "as much of a home world as they have. All our stored data is there. I have a transcript of *Gypsy Moth*'s log with me, for the Archives-Major store." As they stepped into a Transmitter booth, she said, "It's a good thing we put in. Our Transmitters are obsolete. I'll have to send Gilmarti over for briefing on the new models. It seems the old four-light-years limit has been pushed out. These can handle twelve LYs without damage or disorientation."

She touched a set of coordinates, and there was a brief, sharp sense of whirling darkness, a small electrical snap, and the console before them had changed from blue to green and after repeating the maneuver twice more, they stood on Host.

It was a small planet, so small that it seemed to Gildoran, as he stood under the twilit gray canopy that was Host's sky, that he could see and feel the swift rotation, the rapid motion of the little planetoid about its dim and faraway sun. Or was that simply an illusion based on the swift overhead passing of some heavenly bodies which could have been moons or elaborate artificial satellites? It was cold, even through the thick warm Travel Cloaks with which they had provided themselves on Laszlo.

As they left the Transmitter terminal—it was a small one, Host evidently had little transient travel—a line of assorted humanoids stepped back before the Explorers.

Marked out. Alien. You would have noticed it only if they hadn't.

But then he saw the expressions on their faces. Not fear or hatred, this time—respect, verging on awe. And then the tall quasi-uniformed female at the head of their line said in a clear, carrying, perhaps mechanically amplified voice, "Please form into an orderly line and we will commence our tour with an inspection of the Explorer museum. . . ." and he understood.

Gilrae lifted an eyebrow at him and said, "That's new. Last time I was here, we were fighting to keep our allotment from being disallowed. For centuries—since before I was born—we've had a small subsidy from Head Center for locating new planets. But then I remember Head Center was trying to cut us down—they said that if we couldn't make enough on finder's fees to support our own ship, we should get out of the business. Two or three ships actually *did* go broke and had to decommission." She was smiling, a little tremulously. "I was prepared to find, when we downworlded this time, that we'd been entirely disallowed, and Host had closed up shop. There was some talk then—I don't know how many centuries ago planetary time—that there had been enough planets discovered for the foreseeable future, and that the Explorers were just a luxury the civilized Galaxy couldn't afford—siphoning off money and energy to a frontier. Time we settled down, they said, and learned to live on the worlds we had."

She paused for a moment before a small carven memorial. Two figures carved in some alabaster-white metal, pale and elongated and obviously of Explorer type, stood triumphantly on a small jade-green planet. It was the first time Gildoran had ever seen a public inscription in the language the Explorers used among themselves. There was a translation into Universal ideographs below. Both inscriptions read:

TO THE CREW OF THE SEA WOLF
LOST IN A NOVA IN THE VICINITY
OF THE NEBULA IN ORION
"To strive, to seek, to find, and not to yield."

"That's new, too," Rae said, "or should I say—since my time. I've no idea how long it's been, planet time, since I was last here."

There was a small building whose doorway said—again in the language the Explorers used, *Authorized and Ship's Personnel Only.* Gilrae pressed her ident disk against the sensitive plate on the door and it opened.

Before a computer console, a tall pale Explorer

was seated; he turned as they came in. "Gilrae of Gypsy Moth," he said warmly, turning. "We heard the report of your surfacing. We were afraid you'd been lost in space, my dear."

"Sarndall of Spray," Gilrae said, and embraced the strange man warmly. She introduced Gildoran, who felt strangely ill at ease. It was the first time he had ever met anyone who was so obviously one of them, an Explorer, and yet not one of his own. He didn't know how to act with the stranger who was not a stranger.

Gilrae asked, "Where is Spray now, Dall? Or shouldn't I ask?"

"Downworlded and decommissioned," Sarndall said, "Three successive lots of children all died, and we became too shorthanded to go on; and we lost our Poohbears in an epidemic; seven of them died in one night. We were too disheartened to try to go out again. Fortunately, there was work for most of us here on Host."

"Is the news all bad?"

"Not all, though it's not good. You saw the monument to Sea Wolf? But Tinkerbelle just surfaced—and they have four new planets opened and eight healthy four-year-olds growing up. And how is it with you, Rae?"

"Not good," Gilrae said, and gave the old Explorer the log transcript. "The details are in this." She gave him a brief account of the Hellworld and Tempest disasters.

"Lethal soundwaves from plants, eh? That's a new one," Sarndall said. "I'll file it in the list of dangers.

"We've met that cold-death thing before in that same sector, I think; maybe ships should be warned out of that sector for a few thousand years until it exhausts all possible hosts and dies out. Of course the computer people will make that decision in the long run, but it's worth thinking about. So you're not opening a planet now?"

"No, we had to make a forcedown. We're on Laszlo."

"Good place for Explorers," Sarndall said. "Funny thing about Laszlo. For sixty years planet time, they were on the warn-off list. About a hundred and nineteen years ago we had a report of an Explorer mobbed and killed there, so we put out warnings. Then, about thirty years ago, they chose a new government—President, King, I forget what nonsense they call their leader——"

"Councillor," Gildoran murmured.

"Something like that. Anyway, his first official act was to get in touch with Host and open Laszlo formally to Explorers. They have a few special projects there that would interest you, I suspect."

"I imagine we'll find out about them," Gilrae said. "We're invited to a formal reception there. Up to three dozen of us. We'll have to take everybody down to the Poohbears to make up that number!"

"So bad?" Sarndall answered.

"We're thinking of decommissioning," Rae said frankly. "That bad."

Sarndall's eyes were suddenly greedy. "Don't do that," he begged, "If it's a manpower problem, let us join on. There are twenty-nine of us, all dying to get out into Cosmos again. . . ."

"It's a thought," Gilrae said, "but of course the decision isn't mine. It would be up to the whole crew."

As they were leaving Host again, waiting in line behind the tourists who had completed their tour of the Explorer museum for the single Transmitter booth, Gildoran said, "That could be the solution to the manpower problem, Rae."

"Maybe." But Rae looked grave. "It almost never works," she said. "It's been tried. But it makes for two factions aboard a ship; us and them. We're not a family anymore. Not a single crew all of whom think of Gypsy Moth as our own special single home, but two crews. Each trying to run the ship its own way. As a last resort, it might be better than trying to decommission. But not much better."

Gildoran, too, had felt the strangeness; to be with an Explorer who both was and was not one of his own. All his life, since he was able to speak, every Explorer he had ever known was one of his own crew—his shipmate, his Nurserymate, his own family; to be loved, protected, defended against the entire Cosmos, against every other being in Cosmos. Everyone who was not one of Gypsy Moth's crew was an alien, a stranger, who could never understand. . . . Even those you thought you loved, like Janni, never really knew you, or cared to.

Except for that boy—what was his name? Merrik—on Lasselli's World. He had suddenly become a friend—and then he had had to say goodbye again.

And then, suddenly, he visualized the familiar halls, rooms and decks of Gypsy Moth filled with strangers. Explorers, yes. Part of the crew. But not—oh, no, never brothers, crewmates. Never known, beloved. Of them and yet not of them.

Strangers and not strangers. Alien and not alien. Gildoran shuddered.

Cosmos forbid!

He watched Rae programming the coordinates for Laszlo, and a random memory flickered in his mind, a memory of strange coordinates etched into an override signal . . . one unforgettable day in his youth.

Laszlo. Lasselli's World. Strange and the same, yet different beyond recognition. As they stepped out into the fierce blue-white dayshine, stormy with colorless clouds and the flicker of lightning in the upper atmosphere, he heard himself say, "Home again." He corrected himself quickly, back to *Gypsy Moth*, which was home, but that was not what he meant, and Rae's surprised eyes, raised to his, knew it.

He said "Did you know this was Lasselli's World, Rae?"

"Yes, I knew. I didn't know you did."

"Gilmarin was killed here."

And I'm calling it home!

"I know," Rae said quietly. "And I was born here. No one knew except Gilharrad, and he's dead. He lost his finger when he stole me—and three others—from here. And it was for that, I suspect, for the memory of that raid, that Gilmarin died." She drew her Travel Cloak closely about her. "The place gives me the creeps. Do you mind if we go back on board *Gypsy Moth* right away?"

III

During the next few days Gildoran explored the downworld with Gilmarina, enjoying her first uninhibited taste of sunshine and freedom. Ramie, or occasionally Gilmerritt, sometimes accompanied them on these excursions, and when he saw family groups enjoying themselves in the green parks of Laszlo, he realized that a family was less a biological unit than a functional one. In every way that mattered, he and Ramie were Gilmarina's parents.

Gilmerritt was a little hesitant about showing herself on the surface. In this day and age, a deformity like her crippled hand was truly astonishing, and people stared sometimes. She was appallingly sensitive about it, and Gildoran didn't blame her.

He broached the subject to her, in their shared quarters aboard *Gypsy Moth*, one night. "There's no reason you can't go into a growth tank anytime now, Merritt. There is an excellent regrowth center here. And we will be here at least a year, waiting for the children to grow up. We wouldn't leave you anyway."

"I know," Merritt said, "I visited the growth center the other day."

"Then shall we make the arrangements soon?"

Merritt shook her head. "Not yet," she said, "I have work to do. I want to do some research there."

He looked at her in astonishment. She said seriously, "Do you mind, Gildoran? I . . . first, I don't want to be away from you so long. And besides . . . there's something special I have to do. But do you really mind? Are you . . . are you ashamed to be seen with . . . with this?" She raised the blackened, useless claw.

Gildoran drew her close. "Darling, don't even think of that. I'd love you if you had no hands at all. But . . ." he shook his head, faintly bewildered. "For so long, it's the only thing you've wanted——"

"People tend to lose their sense of perspective, sometimes," Merritt said slowly. "Just now I think there's something more important. Do you mind, Doran?"

He said, holding her tightly in his arms, "You must do what seems best to you, my love." Here on this new world, where everything seemed new and fresh and somehow more real than in their isolated world between the stars, he was becoming freshly aware of how deeply and dearly he cherished her, how he would miss her if she were away from him so long. He found himself almost selfishly glad that they need not be separated. And yet he wondered what it could be that seemed so important to her that she would delay further the regeneration of her crippled hand. She did not offer to tell him, and he did not ask. He saw her poring over technological and medical journals, and she spent a great deal of time at the regrowth center, but he did not know why. She had always spent a great deal of time in reading and studying her chosen specialties—he suspected that in time she would have switched from the biological crew to the Medic crew—but until they landed here, he had somehow felt that her obsessive interest in regrowth techniques was, at least in part, a way to make him feel guilty for the delay in salvaging her hand. Now he knew it was not that—but what could it be?

He accused her once, almost teasingly, "I suspect you want Gilban's job some day. Chief Medic Gilmerritt?" And she laughed and did not deny it, but that was all.

She was at the conference, too, where the Major Officers met to discuss acquiring some more children. The Poohbears, having no little ones left in Nursery, were all in favor of it. Gilmerritt's was the first voice raised against it.

"I think we must wait," she said. "We are going to be here at least a year, perhaps more. We cannot make the DNA modification until shortly after we take off. With the techniques we are using now, the child must be raised in free fall and deep space to develop the full Explorer mutation. If we take newborn or new-hatched infants now, they will be too old for the DNA change by the time we leave here."

Gilrae glanced at the chief Medic. "Gilban?"

"With our present technology, Merritt is right," he said. "I heard on Host that the Spray, being shorthanded, took a group of five-year-olds, hoping to diminish the time before they would be old enough to work ship. Not a single one survived."

Gilrae said quietly, "We needn't wait. I promised to put it to you. The crew of the Spray wants to join us—and there are twenty-nine of them. This would give us a crew of more than sixty. We could be off again next month, if we wished—

with a crew of children for the Nursery—and be fully operational again for the first time in years.

To the murmur of voices—half approving, half in protest—that rose at once, she raised a hand. "We don't have to decide now," she said. "It must be put to vote. Think it over. We'll call another meeting and decide. But remember before you decide that the alternative is probably decommissioning. The Councillor's formal reception is tonight. It's not compulsory, but the Laszlans have been very kind to us, so please don't absent yourselves without some good reason."

Ramie caught up with him in the corridor. "Doran, did you hear this about the *Spray*? You didn't look particularly surprised when Rae brought it up."

"I heard it on Host," Gildoran said.

"It could be the answer," Ramie said. "We could all stay together, that way."

"But strangers—on *Gypsy Moth* . . ."

"They wouldn't be strangers. They're Explorers. Like us."

"It would be better if they *were* strangers," Gildoran said helplessly. "We could learn to adapt to them—and they to us—as we do when we're downworld. But the crew of another Explorer ship—with its own traditions—of us and still not of us—I honestly don't think it would work, Ramie."

"No, not if it split us into warring factions," Ramie said. "I see your point. I've often thought the perfect solution would be to be able to sign on adult volunteers whenever we needed them. Then there wouldn't be so much *difference* between Explorers and downworld people. We wouldn't be freaks to them, and they wouldn't be alien races to us. It wouldn't be any more of a difference than transferring from Nursery to Transmitter crew. We'd all just be people together." She considered a moment, her pretty pale face pensive. "Maybe we could do that with another Explorer crew. But it would be hard, because we'd expect them to be just like us. And they couldn't be." She sighed and shook her head. "Well, maybe the right answer will turn up."

"If we have to join with the Spray," Gildoran said harshly, "I'll go earthworm! Better live here among strangers I know are strangers, than try to pretend they're not."

Ramie looked startled and shocked. "Could you do that to us, Gildoran?"

He turned away, saying harshly "I wouldn't be the first, and I won't be the last."

He thought about that as he was pulling himself, with an ill grace, into dress clothes for the Councillor's formal reception.

Maybe I would be the last. What did they say on Host—that perhaps they were going to cut off the Explorer ships? Well, I'm sure the Cosmos will survive very nicely without them, for the next few million years at least. By then, maybe they'll have something better.

Gilmerritt, in a slim green sheath the color of her eyes, stepped up behind him. "You're going to the Councillor's reception?"

"I don't suppose I could get out of it," Gildoran said. "Rae asked everyone to go. Aren't you?"

"I'd rather not. But I will, if you're going," she said. "Who is the Councillor?"

"How would I know? Some important politician, I suppose, who has a thing about Explorers. I don't know whether he romanticizes us, or whether he just wants to know whether we really do kill and eat the children we steal or buy."

Gilmerritt made an expressive face of disgust. "Are there really people who still believe that?"

"Merritt, there are people who will believe *anything*," Gildoran said.

"Then maybe we'd better take Gilmarina with us. To prove otherwise," Gilmerritt said, and Gildoran shrugged. "If she wants to go, I'm perfectly willing. But it seems a shame. She's really too young to have to be let in for these wretched formal affairs."

Gildoran found Gilmarina with Rae, playing a tall electronic harp in one of the Recreation rooms. Marina had recently been released officially from the Nursery and had a room of her own, which she shared with Gilrita.

The Nursery's empty now. Strange how dead the Ship feels without babies aboard. And the children are the only future we have.

Gildoran stood, silent and unmoving, listening to the woman and the girl playing an elaborate duet. It was Gilrae who saw him first and broke off in the middle of an arpeggio.

"I see you're dressed for the Councillor's reception. Shall we all go together, then?"

Gilmarina looked astonished and delighted. "Can I really go, Rae?"

"Of course, darling, if you want to," Rae said, and Gilmarina smiled. She had deep dimples in each cheek. "I'd better go and dress! I can imagine that it would hardly be protocol to turn up in Ship uniform!"

Gilmerritt laughed. "I doubt if the Laszlands would know the difference," she said, "they surely don't expect us to know, or abide by, their dress codes. Dress codes follow such subliminal cues anyhow. In worlds with the Transmitter, I doubt if anyone pays much attention any more. But it must have been a full-time occupation, to stay appropriately dressed, in the days when that was an important consideration."

"It was," Gilrae said. "I spent my twenties helping open up a world which became a pleasure resort, and it amused me to learn something about the psychology of appropriate dress there, and to compare it with the other worlds I visited. Of course, on a pleasure-world it's a deliberate thing—and quite artificial."

"Isn't it artificial everywhere?" Merritt asked. "Except, that is, on worlds with extremes of climate, where you'd freeze or get sunstroke in the wrong clothing?"

"I don't know," Gilrae said. "It's a matter of subtle cues given and received, and if you give the wrong ones for the society, you may be in trouble."

"I imagine that's why Travel Cloaks were invented," Gildoran said. "Imagine an ordinary woman on one planet going out for a day's shopping, stepping just a few light-years away for something a little different to wear, and discovering she's suddenly subject—in her ordinary house-dress—to being sexually accosted."

Gilmerritt shrugged. "I'm sure it happens," she said, "but unless she's terribly neurotic, surely she wouldn't mind. She could always say no, or pretend not to understand his language."

Gilmarina returned, in close-fitting tights and a brief flared tunic of brilliant crimson, her pale hair tied into a glittered scarf.

She's a woman, and a pretty one. But she's still a baby, to me. She always will be.

The women admired Gilmarina's dress and they all started down toward the Transmitter. Gildoran was wearing ordinary dress uniform, silver and blue—the Councillor, confound him, wanted them not as guests but specifically as Explorers, so why not? Rae, as befitted an Elder, wore pale draperies, with artificial snowflakes in her snowy hair. Gilmerritt, in her green sheath, and Gilmarina in her brilliant tunic, were pretty women who might have come from any world of the millions who surrounded them.

"I suppose any attention to dress will wear off in a few years," Gilrae said, as they set the Transmitter coordinates for the destination of the Councillor's Residence, "No one alive could possibly learn all those subliminal cues for more than one or two planets—four or five, if anyone wanted to make it a lifetime study or specialty."

"And what a waste of time," Gilmerritt laughed, as the brief sparkling darkness surrounded them.

Do we go through the Transmitter all together? Are we somehow intermingled, atoms mixing in the interspace between the Terminals. How do we know that each of us gets our own flesh and blood

back? Am I part of everyone I've ever shared a
Transmitter booth with?

He briefly considered signing up for Transmitter crew on their next voyage. But the possibility
that the *Gypsy Moth* might never take another
voyage caused black depression to settle down on
him like a blanket.

"You don't look very festive, Gildoran." Gilrae
slid her arm through his. "This is a party. Cheer
up."

He didn't feel at all festive. But for Gilrae's sake
he let a smile cover his face like a mask.

"I'll do my best," he said. "I imagine that must
be the Councillor's Residence over there, with all
the lights and floating balloons around it. I'm glad
it's not far—this must be in the Polar regions!"

They crossed the paved square through lightly
falling snow, and went into the brightly lit Official Residence.

IV

What Gilrae had said about clothes could
equally well apply to entertainments, Gildoran
thought as they paused in the outer, marbled hall
of the Residence to be divested of their Travel
Cloaks by noiselessly moving servomechanisms.
Formality in some places was random informality
in another. An official reception on one world
might mean that you stood quietly in line and
listened to speeches by dignitaries; on another it

might mean that you lolled about on cushions and sang drinking songs. It had been years since Gildoran had attended any formal entertainment—or for that matter had mixed in large groups except with his own shipmates.

The most formal thing I've attended in thirteen years is the yearly Captain-choosing.

He murmured something of this to Rae as they went below lines of overhead crystal chandeliers, and she nodded. "Someday—any millennium now," she said, "some group or other will attempt to create guides for intercosmic etiquette. I believe they have something like that already but only in high diplomatic interplanetary political circles. When customs get homogenized all the way down the social scales, decadence starts." She chuckled a little. "But as long as the Explorers keep opening up new worlds, decadence can be indefinitely delayed. Maybe we're the little leaven that leavens the whole Galaxy."

"Citizens of Laszlo and Honored Guests," the abnormally sweet mechanical voice of the servomech proclaimed, "The ship's officers of the Explorer ship *Gypsy Moth*. Gildoran; Gilrae; Gilmarina; Gilmerritt."

A fat little woman close to them murmured audibly "Oh, they're the Explorers! Councillor Marik is simply mad on the subject, you know!" She smiled up sweetly at Gildoran and asked, "Could you tell me why your names are all so much alike?"

Gildoran couldn't see that their names all were that much alike, but he replied courteously, explaining that every Explorer ship had a specific coded identification which was made into a single syllable—*Gil* in the case of *Gypsy Moth*— and given as the first syllable of the name of every person on that ship, so that from the name of the Explorer, any Explorer in the fleet could immediately identify him by the ship he came from.

"And how many ships are there in the Explorer fleet?" the woman asked.

"I really couldn't say. Perhaps Gilrae could tell you," Gildoran said, carefully not looking at the other woman.

Another man in the crowd around them said, "The ships have such strange and romantic names. Where do they come from?"

"The ships? Most of them were built on Host," Gildoran replied.

"No, the names! Where do the names come from?"

"They are names of ships sailed by explorers on mankind's original world," Gildoran replied, "or at least that's what the legends say. Ships were a form of land transit, I believe, and in those days explorers went out to find out all they could about their own world before they went into space. The names of some of those ships have been preserved in legend, or as far as we know that is true. Of course, after so many years, who can tell?"

A servomechanism glided up to him and attracted his attention by a discreet tug at his uniform sleeve.

"Gildoran of the *Gypsy Moth*? Councillor Marik wishes to speak to you personally, if you will be so good," it murmured.

Just about the last thing Gildoran wanted was to

go and chat with some higher-up political biggie who romanticized the Explorers, but he couldn't think of a single polite way to refuse. He followed the servomech to the Councillor's raised throne-like chair.

Councillor Marik was a shrivelled little figure, dark-skinned, but his hair was white as Gildoran's own. He looked up as Gildoran came close, and said:

"You don't remember me, do you, Gildoran? No, how could you, after—how many years has it been? More than a hundred, for me. You said you wouldn't come back, because I'd be sure to hate you. . . ."

Something in the voice touched a string of memory in Gildoran. He said "Merrik!" with a curious sense of warmth.

Was this why I felt this world was home, because I found a friend here I would never forget?

"You don't shoot escaped snakes in the forestry preserve any more, then?"

The old man chuckled. "You *do* remember, then. As for you—it's true, you don't look a day older. No, I take that back," he said, scanning the other man's face. "What's happened? I understand your ship's in trouble. But it's good to have you as a guest here."

It was with a curious sense of things falling into place that Gildoran took a seat beside the Councillor and began to tell him what had befallen the *Gypsy Moth* in the years between.

If I choose to stay here as an earthworm, at least

I shall begin with a friend. Not wholly as a stranger, then. And a friend, after all, in high places. Certainly I shall be able to find something worthwhile here.

Marik listened to Gildoran's tale in silence, seeming fascinated. Finally, when he heard of the choice facing them—to join with another Explorer ship or decommission—he said seriously, "But that is terrible! Not that you wouldn't be welcome here, any or all of you. But every Explorer ship we lose——"

"Even Head Center seems to think we're a luxury the Galaxy can dispense with," Gildoran said.

"Head Center likes playing God," Marik said, "but this thing is too big for politics on this scale. I don't think you realize what the Explorers mean to us, Gildoran. You're too close to the problem—what's the old saying, you can't see the ocean for the surf?"

Gildoran said "I'd be curious to know what you think the Explorers mean. To most of the people of most planets, we're either freaks, or a dangerous strangeness, a legend people hate."

"You're our safety valve," Marik said. "Our permanent frontier, our endless open end. As long as the Explorers are finding and opening new worlds, we can all be different, keep our individuality. Once the discovery of new worlds ends, once everything is known, we begin to stagnate; we begin to die. It's like a race gone sterile; with nothing new beginning, that race, or that world, begins to die. When life is simply repeating the known, when nothing new enters the equation, we find first a loss of new ideas, then of creativity in general, then general decadence. It's happened, historically, to every new planet when it's been entirely explored and mapped; from that moment it begins to die and go decadent. Man can't live, psychologically, without a frontier. And even if we—all of us—can't go exploring, we can survive, psychologically, knowing that new worlds *are* being found, that *someone* can go and find them."

It reminded him, a little, of what Gilrae had been saying—about homogenizing of manners being the beginning of decadence. But he asked bitterly, "Why do so many people ban us from their worlds, then? Why do they deny us children?"

"Because they don't understand," Marik said quietly. "I've spent my life, Gildoran, trying to make sure that Laszlo will understand. I think you'll find you can have all the children you want, here." He smiled a little wistfully and said, "I myself would be happy to know that someone of my blood would be exploring the stars, a thousand years after my old bones were dust. And I'm sure there are millions who feel just as I do. Here and elsewhere."

That would be the answer, perhaps, Gildoran thought as the crew of the *Gypsy Moth* left the Residence much later that night, and walked toward the Transmitter Terminal. A world where the Explorers were not freaks and hated aliens, but an Explorer home world, where they could come each time they opened a new world; where they could return for their children instead of buying or stealing, where every family on this planet had a child on the Explorer ships—and if

Head Center chose to close down Host, and phase out their support of the Explorers, Laszlo could remain as their home base. . . .

But as they entered the Transmitter he turned and said to Gilrae, "Take the girls home, will you? I'm going out for a while——"

"I'll go with you," Gilmerritt said, "unless you really want to be alone."

"I think I do. Thank you, darling, but you go home with Gilmarina. I'll see you tomorrow."

He stepped into a booth and pressed the coordinates for the main Transmitter Terminal on Laszlo. Here, in this terminal, he and Ramie had nearly been killed. Now they were honored guests.

He went outside, into the cool, soft night. Laszlo was at a central location in the Galaxy and the night was brilliant with thousands upon thousands of close-in stars. It seemed to him that from the surface of this world the stars were somehow brighter than ever in space, that the soft winds and clouds touched his body with a warmth he had never known.

I don't want to leave this world again. No matter how many worlds I see, there will never be another world which is mine, in this curious unexplainable sense. If I leave Laszlo, it will be tearing myself out by the roots, never to be whole again.

All that night, and all the following day, Gildoran went from Transmitter to Transmitter, jumping around the planet, from dayside to nightside, walking in the sun and rain, in park and desert, beauty spot and stinking slum, trying to find some part of Laszlo which he could honestly leave.

It was night again when he returned to the *Gypsy Moth*, sleepless, hungry, his eyes aching and his heart heavy. When he boarded and pressed his ident disk against the lock, the computer said "Gildoran, urgent you report to Recreation Area One. Ship's Council is about to convene, and Gilrae has been trying to locate you for hours."

When he came up to the area, he had half-expected to find the whole ship's company assembled and was astonished to find only Gilrae there.

She raised her eyes, with a look of relief so great that he thought for a moment that she would burst into tears.

"Gildoran," said she. "I was afraid you had gone for good——"

"If I went, it would not be for good," Gildoran said.

"For good or ill, then," Rae said wearily. "You are thinking of deserting, aren't you?"

"I wouldn't say that, exactly. But I'm uncertain about what's ahead. And uneasy."

How had she known?

As if she read his thoughts, as Gilrae so often did, she raised her eyes and said, "There's a look they get, when a world takes hold on them. You have it. I can't imagine why—a world like this one, it gives me the creeps. But then, no one except the one it's happened to can ever explain it. I saw it with Giltallen, for months before he left us.

And now you. . . ." Her face twisted as if she were about to cry.

"Don't, Rae. I'm here."

"But for how long?"

He wanted to make a quick promise, but then, meeting Rae's eyes, he knew that with her, at least, he could be only completely honest. He said, "It depends mostly on what happens in Ship's Council, Rae. I can't live with our joining the *Spray*."

"Ramie told me you felt like that," Rae said quietly. "Do you dislike them all so much?"

"It's not that I dislike them. I don't know them," Gildoran said. "Better a strange world than my own world suddenly made strange——"

"Even if the cost is leaving all of us?" Rae said. "I can't imagine what Ramie—or Gilmarina—would do without you. And as for me . . ." she leaned back against him with a sigh. "But I certainly don't have to tell you what you mean to me, Doran, it's the one thing I'm sure you know. And I know you're not doing this just to make trouble. I know how you must feel. I know it all too well. . . ."

He held her in his arms, knowing Rae was dearer to him than anyone alive. But she understood and he knew she wouldn't fight him, whatever he wanted to do. . . .

He loosed her as others of the *Gypsy Moth*'s company began to come into the room, one by one. Ramie cast a bitter look at him, as she came in. She said, "So you've come back again? Did you come to blackmail us into settling things your way? You know we can't lose you and still go on."

Gildoran said quietly, "That's not fair, Ramie.

Every one of us has a right to a free choice. You will choose your way no matter what I do. I could try to talk you into staying with me, you know."

Ramie flared, "And if you did—wouldn't that be a kind of blackmail too? Trying to get me to choose your way, just because you know how long I've loved you? Yes, I do love you. No one else has ever meant anything to me. There's been no one else for me, there never will be."

"Now who's trying blackmail?" Gildoran flared. He did not know whether the wild uprush of emotion he felt was love, or desire, or pure hatred. "You could have anyone you wanted!"

"You don't have to rub it in. I know that you don't care anything for me!" Ramie almost shouted at him.

Gilrae said wearily "Ramie. Doran. This is . . . this is unseemly."

"We're not in Nursery, and we're not quarreling like babies," Ramie said, turning viciously on the older woman. "You've no right, Rae! It's easy enough for you to talk, when you know that every man on *Gypsy Moth* loves you first and never after cares for anyone else——"

"Ramie! Ramie!" Gilrae said, in honest shock. "How can you say such things?"

"Ask Gildoran if it isn't true! Ask him if he's ever really loved anyone else—"

Gildoran rose in anger, swinging around to face both of the women. He said brutally, "Damn all women! I wish I'd never come back, to listen to this! You're like a pack of jackals!"

Ramie stood facing him, angrily, tears pouring down her cheeks. Gilrae buried her head in her hands, and her shoulders were shaking. Gildoran was appalled, but after a minute he realized, and was shocked to see, that she was laughing.

Ramie looked shocked, too, when Gilrae raised her head and she saw the other woman's laughter. Gilrae said, "I must be really getting old. This just seems funny to me. But, both of you . . ." She stretched her hands to them, and Gildoran saw, with shock, that although she was laughing, her thin, lined hands were trembling.

"Doran. Ramie. Whatever happens with either of you, don't go into it like this. Don't settle it in a storm of emotion. It may be the last thing that ever happens to all of us as one. After today it will be too late, and it may affect the Explorers—not just *Gypsy Moth;* all that are left of us. You can't let an—an emotional flareup destroy all of us. Think it over and try to decide. . . ." She broke off. "I won't say, *decide without emotion.* It's an emotional decision. I realize that, perhaps more than any of you. God knows I feel emotional enough about it. But try and decide what you really want—what you'll want, not today, but months from now. Years from now. And decide so it won't be too late."

The other crew members were coming in now, taking seats all over the room. Gildoran slid into a seat and suddenly realized that he was sitting exactly where he had been sitting when seven or eight years ago he had been chosen Captain. It seemed a lifetime ago. It *was* a lifetime ago. Ramie started to slip into a seat beside him; gave him an angry glare and moved to another. Had Rae tried to locate her, too?

Briefly Rae explained the choice that faced them. They were too shorthanded to work *Gypsy*

Moth for another thirteen or fourteen years ship-time until another crew of babies could grow up to help them. Their choices were either to decommission *Gypsy Moth* and disband the crew, or to join forces with the crew of the *Spray*, creating one ship's crew from two.

"Each of you has a vote, from the oldest Floater to the youngest child," Rae explained quietly. "It is your future, too. A majority will decide. I should state also that if a majority votes to decommission, or to join *Spray*, the vote will be binding on the minority. We will vote from eldest to youngest. Gildorric?"

"Join *Spray*," the old man said briefly. "I wouldn't live three planet-years in gravity. I just hope I live long enough for us to get free of the planet again."

"Gilmarti?"

"Decommission," she said. "Better an earthworm than try to mix with another crew."

"Gilban?"

The Chief Medic frowned and said, "Abstain. I'll go with the majority, whatever you decide."

The voting went on. Gildoran tried to keep count but could not. When Gilramie's name was called she said, "Join with *Spray*. The time might come when we could separate again, if there were enough of us, someday. But it means keeping the Explorers alive."

Gildoran knew he was next on the roster. Gilrae's face was haggard, almost desperate, as she said, "Gildoran."

My life is here.
The call of a world, a world I've made my own.

*And yet . . . how could I cut myself off from
Ramie, even if all we do is quarrel? She's part of
my life. From Merritt, who's so much mine, who
has needed me so much—from Marina, whose
very life came from me. . . .*

"Gildoran?"

*To share the Gypsy Moth, day by day, year by
year, world by world and century, with strangers
. . . strangers trying to be part of us. . . .*

He saw Ramie's white face, twisted in anguish,
He opened his mouth to say, "Decommission,"
and the words would not come. He said at last,
fighting the syllables through a dry throat, "Abstain. I'll go with the majority. It's a case of lesser
evil, either way."

Rae's chest heaved, as if she was struggling to
breathe.

He wanted to speak, to burst into a flood of
explanation, but Rae had called the next name.

"Gilbarni?"

"Join with Spray," the boy said, "Explorers are
explorers. No planet's worth staying on."

I felt that way once. . . .

"Gillori?"

Lori's round face was pale and frightened. She
said, "I vote to decommission."

"Gilrita?"

The other of the "babies" said, so faintly that
she could hardly be heard, "I vote to join Spray.
We could use some new friends."

"Gilmarina?"

Gilmarina murmured, "I'll . . ." She looked pleadingly at Gildoran and said faintly, "I'll abstain. I don't really know enough about it to vote. I'll agree to whatever the majority does."

Gilrae bent over the tally of the votes. Gildoran waited, hardly able to breathe. The next few moments would decide the fate of all of them. Some people might have been keeping an accurate count. He envied them. They already knew, without this murderous suspense. . . . He wished he had the courage to get up and walk out, into the sunlight of Laszlo, into the world he had sworn should be his, the world with his name on it, his special island. . . .

Gilmerritt rose and said "Rae, this wasn't necessary. If I may speak——"

Someone shouted, "Give us the results of the vote!"

Gilmerritt said, "I tallied them. There were ten votes to join *Spray;* ten to decommission, and three abstentions. There is no vote, and we need no vote." Her face was pale. She held up her useless clawlike hand. "I have been studying regrowth and DNA techniques," she said. "For obvious reasons. Our techniques are obsolete. With the new medical techniques at the command of the Laszlands there is no reason we cannot sign on adult volunteers. I won't go into the technology involved. No one but Gilban and Gilnosta would understand it. But in general it's a matter of bone-marrow regeneration, with transplants and DNA transfusions. This means that anyone beneath a certain age—actually the age when bone growth is complete and the epiphyses sealed—

can sign on to an Explorer ship. There will be no need for taking children as babies—although we may still wish to, because one of our greatest pleasures is to see them grow up as a part of our world—but the adult volunteer, with a few minor surgical modifications, and a few weeks now and then in a regrowth tank, can perfectly well survive the journey into deep interstellar space. We might still choose to join forces—for a time—with people from the Spray," she added, "but it is no longer a question of two separate factions. We will all be different—and equal. It will take time to teach the newcomers the ways of the Ship. But already, on Laszlo, Councillor Marik has found us three dozen volunteers. We can go whenever we will," she finished, "and we will always have a home base here on Laszlo. Whatever new world we find, we will come back here, for new crew members, for children, for a world which will always be our own home world," she finished, before her words were drowned out in an outburst of wild cheering.

V

"After this year," Gilrae said, "I'm applying for Floater status. But whether I get it or not, I'm finished. This is my last term as Captain."

Ramie laughed and said, "I've heard that before, too."

Rae said, "Wait till you've been Captain a time or two and see how you feel about it."

Gilmerritt said, "I've better things to occupy my time. Speaking of which, I'd better get down to the Medic area and see that the tanks are all ready for null-grav conditions. How are the volunteers making out on the Bridge, Rae?"

The woman looked around. "As well as any other Class-B crew," she said. "After six months of intensives, what did you expect?" She smiled affectionately at Gilmarina, bent over a Communications console, looking tense and a little scared. She said "Give me shipwide hookup, Marina—All hands attention, this is the Captain. *Gypsy Moth* will depart from Laszlo in forty-five minutes Universal Time. Please adjust chronometers. In thirty seconds we will have a Universal Time Signal. . . ."

Gildoran automatically checked his chronometer to the small repeated clicks and beeps of the signal.

When it had finished, Rae continued, "*Gypsy Moth* will depart from Laszlo in exactly thirty-eight minutes and twenty seconds. All shipboard visitors must now depart from the Ship. All crew personnel to Departure Stations, please. Intership hookup, Morgan, please."

Morgan—a Class B Laszlan, said, "You have it, Captain."

Gildoran looked round the Bridge, occupied with four crew from *Gypsy Moth*, three from *Spray*, and six Laszlans. It was strange to see dark hair, pigmented skins on a Bridge within a few minutes of takeoff. Gilrae was taking reports from Nursery, asking about the condition of the twelve Laszlan babies snuggled down there under the care of the Poohbears.

Gilrae put aside her Communicator and said

"You three had better get to Departure Stations."
She stood up and briefly embraced Gilmerritt. She
said, "I won't see you for a while, Merritt; by the
time I come off-shift you'll be in the tank, I suppose."

Merritt nodded. "I offered to stay and supervise
the medics. But five of the Laszland Class B
people are DNA technicians and surgeons, so they
don't need me." She kissed the older woman's
cheek. "See you next year, wherever—and whenever—we are then."

Glancing briefly at Gilrae for permission, Gilmarina left her console and came to fling herself
into Gilmerritt's arms. She said, "Good luck, darling. I know perfectly well if it hadn't been for you
I'd be worse off—Gilban said my foot was worse
than your hand. If I could have taken your place,
I'd have done it, to give you a chance. . . ."

Gildoran asked, "Do you need me on the
Bridge, Rae?"

"No indeed. Cosmos! It's such a relief not to be
shorthanded," Rae said. "Take Merritt down and
tuck her in, if you want to."

On their way down to the Medic deck, Gildoran
said, "It seems strange to see people who don't
look like Explorers on the Bridge."

Merritt smiled faintly. "Give them four years in
deep space, and they'll be as pale as we are. Anyway, it shouldn't bother us to have the babies with
dark hair and skins, and if there's an occasional
volunteer who doesn't bleach all the way, I think
we'll get used to it. It might even be a pleasant
variety. Didn't Rae say that homogeneity was the
beginning of decadence? Even the Explorers
could become decadent, I suppose, if things went
too well for too long."

"That'll be the day!" He said, "What will we do without Rae, if she keeps her threat to turn Floater?"

Gilmerritt smiled again. "That'll be a long time yet," she said, "Rae *is* the spirit of the *Gypsy Moth* for all of us, and I think she knows it. And by the time she really *does* leave us and turn Floater— well, then it will be someone else. Maybe you." She slipped her good hand through his arm, as they entered the Medic quarters.

Gilban was waiting for them, while the Laszland apprentice Medics put things in order. Helping to supervise them, Gildoran saw the familiar slender figure, pale smooth hair, strange tilted eyes.

"Ramie, this is a new assignment for you," Gildoran said.

"I wanted a change," Ramie said. "So I'll be taking care of you, Merritt. Are you all ready?"

"In a few minutes." Without self-consciousness, Gilmerritt began stripping off her clothing, ready for the regrowth tank. Ramie picked up a razor and sheared off Gilmerritt's heavy hair. "Easier to look after you," she said, "and by the time you're ready to come out, it'll have grown again."

Gilmerritt lowered her eyes. She said, "Don't look at me, Gildoran."

Gildoran took the woman into his arms. "Don't be a fool, my love," he said. "Do you think I care what you look like, after all these years? Hurry and get well, darling." He picked up the ugly clawed deformity of her hand, stroked it gently and laid his lips to it.

Cosmos! I'll miss her so. . . .

She clung to him for a moment and said "Don't be lonely. It's not fair. You know I won't know or feel anything. Don't you dare miss me when I can't miss you." She reached for Ramie's hand, looking up at her seriously with her great green eyes, and said with strong emphasis, "Ramie. Don't let Gildoran miss me. Or be lonely. Promise."

Ramie kissed Gilmerritt quickly on the forehead and said "I promise. I'll take good care of him, too."

Merritt lay back on the shelf; Ramie covered her with a sheet and Gildoran held her hand while the first of the needles went into her wrist, the one which would put her into the preliminary sleep while her temperature was lowered to hibernation level. Later the useless hand would be amputated and the wrist placed into the regrowth solution, so that a year from now, she would emerge from the tank with only a sense of long dreams—and a hand identical to the one she had been born with.

The intership hookup announced, in Rae's voice, "Gypsy Moth will depart the planet in exactly four minutes and eighteen seconds. Stand by for thirty-second countdown. Four minutes . . . three minutes and thirty seconds . . ."

A preliminary roar of sound, interspersed with bursts of static, began to shake the Gypsy Moth, and the floors and walls around them began to tremble. Ramie said, "We'd better strap down, Doran."

Everyone else on the Medic deck was already fastened into takeoff seats. The two Explorers went to adjoining seats and fastened the takeoff harnesses around waist and shoulders. Through the growing noise of the takeoff and the drives coming into action, Gildoran kept hearing Merritt's parting words. "Ramie. Don't let Gildoran miss me. Or be lonely. Promise." And Ramie had promised.

Gildoran reached out his hand between the seats and felt Ramie's slender fingers close over his own. Yes, they belonged together. Merritt knew that, too. He didn't know how it would work out. It wouldn't be the same kind of relationship he had with Merritt. It didn't matter. Whatever it was, it would be the right thing for the two of them.

"Thirty seconds . . . twenty . . . ten . . . seven, six, five. . . ."

With a shuddering, a scream and a glorious roar, the *Gypsy Moth* lifted from the surface of her homeworld, on another stretch of her endless voyage into Cosmos.

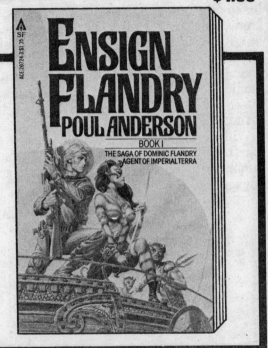

Brilliant New Novel from Award-Winning Author of Alien Embassy!

In **MIRACLE VISITORS**, Ian Watson has created a fascinating novel that explores the UFO phenomenon, a novel that will endlessly intrigue and envelop the reader.

$1.95

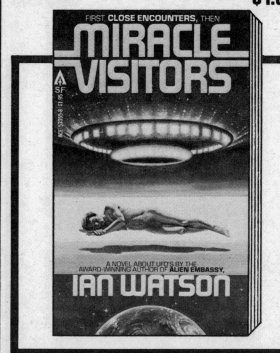

FIRST, **CLOSE ENCOUNTERS,** THEN

MIRACLE VISITORS

A NOVEL ABOUT UFO'S BY THE AWARD-WINNING AUTHOR OF **ALIEN EMBASSY,**

IAN WATSON